The Dread Knight's Redemption

Freedom or the Fire Volume Two

Joshua Calkins-Treworgy

BooksForABuck.com

2008

The Dread Knight's Redemption

Joshua T. Calkins-Treworgy

Published by BooksForABuck.com

June 2008

ISBN: 978-1-60215-075-1

The Story So Far

Soon continues the epic quest of Byron of Sidius and his allies against the machinations of the warlock, Richard Vandross. But first, I would show you briefly what has come before.

Byron of Sidius, once a Paladin and holy man enlisted in Tamalaria's paramilitary organization, the Order of Oun, has been turned into an undead abomination, a Dread Knight. This wicked sorcery fell upon him at the hands of Tanarak of Sidius and his apprentice in the vile Mount Toane. But when Tanarak was felled years later, the soul of the holy man was set free to take full control once more. True it was his soul, freed, but the body was that he had been cursed with.

After years of running and hiding from his former pursuers, the Dread Knight discovers that a new evil is loose in the realms of Tamalaria. That evil is a one-eyed warlock by the name of Richard Vandross. Like Tanarak who came before him, this man seeks the artifacts of ancient evil known as the Orbs of Eden's Serpent. With them, he will hold the power to dominate or destroy the realms as he wishes.

After a brief skirmish with this power-hungry man, Byron believes his duty done—it is not. Chasing down Vandross's back trail, Byron comes upon a ruined Cuyotai village, where Vandross has taken a second of these Orbs. Byron is joined here by Shoryu Tearfang, a nimble young Cuyotai Hunter. With the Ki Fairy Alex already at his side, his party now numbers three.

Following after Richard Vandross, Byron and his companions come upon the ruins of Fort Flag, an Order of Oun outpost. Here they also find Bael, the Lizardman General who, up to the assault on the Fort, had been in command of Vandross's armies. But Vandross, now able to use the Orbs to summon legions of Hell-spawned demons, has no further need of him, and discards him like so much waste. Byron saves Bael from death, and the Lizardman pledges himself now to Byron's cause, but he cannot join him as yet. Byron sends him to the Elven Kingdom to warn and assemble his Lizardman brethren there.

Onward goes the company to Desanadron, the largest metropolis city-state capital in the realms. Vandross's forces besiege Desanadron. The city's defenses are led by a human Pyromancer by the name of Selena Bradford and a human Paladin, James Hayes. After aiding the city in routing Vandross's army, this unlikely pair joins Byron, Alex and Shoryu.

Byron, knowing where Vandross will go next, leads his group south, into the Elven Kingdom. There they gather and ready the capital, Whitewood, for Vandross's inevitable attack. More allies join Byron and his cadre, including Ellen Daires, an Elven Gaiamancer (who is passing fair, and takes an immediate shine to Shoryu) and a Dwarven Boxer, Morek Rockmight. Just before the assault does come, David Spore, a one-armed human martial artist, further joins Byron's party.

Despite their preparation, the company and the city's military forces cannot stop Vandross from seizing yet another of the Orbs of Eden's Serpent. His invasion force is repelled, however, and Vandross forced to retreat to his mountain fortress. When the battle is done and over, Byron leads his group out of the kingdom, to the north. Somewhere in the northwestern mountains, in the Dwarven Territories, lies the final Orb of Eden's Serpent.

Richard Vandross knows that Byron and his company haunt his moves, block his ambitions. He and his new General, the Shadowbeast demon Vilec Roak, lay a trap, taking David Spore from them most permanently.

It is after this trap has been sprung, after David Spore is foully murdered, that we rejoin Byron and his company, heading north into the mountains to try to stop the warlock Richard Vandross from laying his hands on the last Orb of Eden's Serpent.

Even should they stop him at this goal, however, can they stop the madman from his other aims? Read on, friends, and you shall discover the answer to that question.

Chapter One
It Shall Be Done

Once again, Richard Vandross thought, Vilec Roak is going to barge in and apologize for his inadequacies. Vandross knew that his beast had died, but he had been prepared for that eventuality when Roak told him that he intended to use the creature in his plot. Losing him for nothing was unsatisfactory.

Mere injury was enough to please the one-eyed devil—he had told Vilec Roak as much before the Shadowbeast Prime and General of his armies had departed to watch the scenario play itself out.

But now, as Vilec Roak slinked into the room, the Shadowbeast wore a toothy grin that split his face from ear to ear.

Success? Vandross wondered. *That would be a pleasant change of pace.* "Tell me all about it, Vilec. I had low hopes for this little exercise of yours. How well did it go?"

"To begin, my lord, let me first say that I apologize for the use of Brink. It has indeed been lost. However, with the aid of one of our Illusionists, I was able to convince Byron's fools that they struck a heavy blow to a massive detachment of Shadowbeasts. Most of them, however, were mere phantasms. Our practitioner was able to adapt the imagery to react to their attacks. In all, we lost twelve Shadowbeasts."

"And our enemies," Vandross asked, raising his good eyebrow.

"They are one fewer, my lord. The Monk, David Spore, is slain."

Vandross grinned inwardly, pleased beyond words. Monks could be troublesome, he had learned over the years. Potent, competent fighters, and equipped with magic sutras. This David Spore had been a pain while aided by Byron and his friends. Though he didn't seem as vital a component to their success as the others, his death would be a heavy blow to the company's morale. After the loss of their friend, and the betrayal of a seemingly injured man, Byron and his companions would be unsure of everyone and anyone who approached them or asked for aid. They would be effectively rendered incapable of helping anyone for a while.

"Does this news please you, my lord?" Vilec Roak asked, taking a knee.

Vandross bellowed harsh laughter, throwing his head back and guffawing like a madman.

"It is sooth, yes, I am pleased beyond your knowledge. Our losses you kept minimal, through trickery and guile. And as a result of your little plot, one of their number lies eternally lost to them. Vilec Roak, to think that I was losing faith in your abilities to lead this army. Let it be known throughout our numbers that you are worthy and capable." Vandross rose out of his throne, moving to stand just before the Shadowbeast General.

"Stand, Vilec Roak. Tonight, we shall celebrate this first step toward their utter destruction. And on the 'morrow, we shall plan for their next defeat. Come," he said, walking confidently out of the throne chamber, toward the entrance of Mount Toane. "Let us go to one of our new 'protectorates'."

Vandross referred to one of the villages he had sent his armies to occupy near his home lair.

Human and Shadowbeast walked along together, out into the light of early afternoon. Major Tamriel, the huge and dark humored Renka, stood outside of the mountain with his Sergeants Moran and Doran, the other two bear demons that Vandross had summoned to his purposes.

"Tamriel, Vilec Roak and I shall be going to one of my townships for a celebration. One of Byron's company has been slain this day, and we must do this accomplishment proper ceremony. In our absence, I leave Mount Toane under your care and supervision."

"What of Colonel Molis," the hulking, furred demon asked, signaling for his men to stand at attention.

"Ah, right," Vandross said, thinking on his First Colonel, his first creation while still in the thrall of Tanarak of Sidius. Molis was a half-demon man who he had sent with a detachment of men to harass the city of Ja-Wen further. He would crush that city-state as surely as any other territory, and claim it for himself; but Molis's task was one he deemed necessary. He wanted to reduce the number of defenders there before he went in for the kill.

Though Grigory Molis had given him little in the way of interaction beyond silent scorn and low-level disgust, he had done as his master commanded. "No, Major. He is engaged in the slow damaging of Ja-Wen, and I shall not recall him. You are more than capable of this task in his stead. In the off chance that outsiders attack Mount Toane, you have my permission to carry on the defense as you see fit.

"Now, General," he said, smiling widely as he slapped Vilec Roak on the back. "Let us make haste! I intend to drink my fill and plan further woe for the Dread Knight. Ha." There was more contempt than genuine mirth in Richard Vandross's laugh, but he did find hilarity in misfortune of his enemies. Finally, he had struck a blow to Byron and his companions that would leave a permanent mark.

Having gathered the servants under his command, he had amassed a number of useful tools for his conquest over the land and the undead warrior. But now he wanted more. He wanted to slay one of them with his bare hands, or at least be the main hand controlling the figures that would topple more of Byron's damaged company.

Vandross tore a rift in the air before him, the shimmering, blue tinted image of an occupied township visible on the other side of the tear. He stepped through with Vilec Roak in tow, and materialized in the center of the town.

The town's cowed inhabitants gasped in amazement at his sudden appearance, and he could smell and taste their fear: sweet like honey in his nostrils and on his tongue, the aroma of sweat coursing through the air to join the other sensations. He felt exalted in the presence of such terror, feeding on the waves of emotion that emanated from these hopeless folk. He closed his eye, letting the warmth of it flow through him, a babbling brook in the center of his soul's landscape. The Orbs inside of him responded, Power, Vengeance,

Spite and Deceit writhing in ecstasy. Smiling with his eye still closed, he lowered his chin to his chest, letting out a low grunt.

"Foolish, blasted incompetents," he screamed in the twin harmony of his possessed voice. "Know you not your new ruler when you lay eyes upon him? I demand respect, knaves. Bow to me, for I am Richard Vandross. I am your endgame, your omega. Kneel, and you shall suffer little more than humiliation and groveling."

On cue, all those assembled who were not under his army's ranks dropped to their hands and knees, touching their foreheads to the dirt. "Ha ha ha ha haaa! Excellent. Now, who shall offer my General and I their wife or daughter for this evening? We are reasonable curs, but we require the company of females as much as the next fellow. Who among you shall receive my grace with an offering?"

He looked around at the assembled men and women, their eyes filled with horror, panic, and desperation. One of the young Human women present had caught his attention: a woman barely older than a girl, her figure full and voluptuous. But she wore the simple dress of a modest commoner, and her hair glistened with natural oils and grease.

She would need a bath, he thought, but she was perfect. The slight, gentle slope of her cheeks suggested that she took care of herself, and if properly attired and cleaned, perhaps with a touch of makeup, she would be gorgeous. The girl had a long, swan-like neck, and her skin was pale as moonlight where it could be seen. She was unblemished, undamaged, perhaps untouched by carnal knowledge. He would defile her, Vandross decided.

"You there," he shouted, pointing an armored finger directly at her like an accusation. "I will know your name."

The girl remained half slouched. But she looked him in the eye, her lower lip trembling with unconfined fear or anger, he could not tell which.

"I am Kelly Jonas," she said, her voice warbling like a dying bird.

Fear, Vandross decided with satisfaction.

"Why would you ask, villain," she continued, spitting at him.

Hmm, he thought, rubbing his beard with his left hand, his right on his hip in a thoughtful pose.

"You've got spirit, I see." He grinned at Vilec Roak, who had adopted an amused countenance. "What do you think, General? Is this girl worthy of my attention?"

"Oh yes, she is." The Shadowbeast stalked toward Kelly Jonas and wrenching her to her feet by the arm. He tossed her roughly toward Vandross, who caught the girl by the wrist a moment before she punched at him.

"And I can sense that she is untainted, my lord. A prime choice."

"Bastards." An older man behind Roak barreled headlong into the Shadowbeast, heaving him to the ground. The man had the frame of a small bear, all width and disused muscle turned to fat, his shaggy beard hanging an inch from Vilec Roak's face. The man pulled a small smithing hammer from his tool belt, and struck at Vilec Roak's arms over and over in a fury, the General easily blocking the attacks.

With a thrust of his hips and a flick of magical force, Vilec Roak tossed the man aside, hovering over him an instant later.

"And who is this man?" Vandross asked the girl, staring into her eyes from only a few inches away. He felt her body turn cold and rigid, gripped by the power he commanded and the threat that he might take out on her any punishment due to the fallen smithy.

"He is Thomas Jonas, my father, and blacksmith of this village," she whispered. Twin fangs of fear and guilt sank into her, venomous power coursing down through her blood. She had become compliant in a moment's time, and Vandross, while pleased, wasn't entirely certain if this newfound cooperation was yet another side effect of his powers, or simply a young woman's desperation and loss of hope. "If you will spare him, I will lay with you," she whispered into his ear, reaching up on her tiptoes to speak to him alone.

Vandross, his hands still on her shoulders, pushed her out to his arms' reach. Turning toward Thomas Jonas, he gave Vilec Roak a brief sign to back off and keep an eye on his prize. Then Richard Vandross knelt down next to the fallen smith, who had scrambled back from the Shadowbeast.

"Look at me, old fool," he rasped at the smith.

No fear lay in those eyes any more. Instead, there floated only fury, seething and boiling over. The Human would surely do something foolish, but Vandross cared not. "I am going to give your daughter her first taste of true womanhood. I am going to violate her in ways she has surely never even heard of. I am going to spill my seed about her face and hair, for I shall not sire you a grandchild of power such as mine. Yours is blood too lowly and base for such honor."

The smith's face had gone slack, either in defeat, or as a feint. Again, it didn't matter.

"I shall spare your life now, for she has begged it of me. But you shall still receive punishment for your attack on my General, who also is one of your new lords. Do you understand?"

"Just kill me," the smith growled, facing Vandross squarely.

What sort of man was this, that he did not feel despair in the face of the one-eyed warlock and his forces, his powers? Insanity did not hold him, and from what Vandross could tell, aside from his skill with the occasional abrupt assault, no powers availed to help this man.

"Kill me and spare my only daughter your filthy desires, villain. Strip my flesh from my bones, let vultures feast upon me." He ripped his shirt open, exposing it to the air, daring the scavenger birds to descend upon him. "Have me drawn and quartered, but do not dare lay a finger on her innocent head, or surely the great God Oun shall banish you to the Hells." The man had just requested torturous methods of death over the perversion of his daughter's body, and Vandross fumbled with his thoughts for a long moment. How could any man be so determined? What sort of person chose a horrible death over the temporary pain of their child?

A flash of memory played in his mind's eye. His mother and father, running through the streets. They had propelled him into the waiting arms of a neighbor to keep him safe from the bandits. They had tried to save him, but in the process, they had been slain. Vandross felt his control slip. Such tactics only lead to death, and the misery of being orphaned. This act put this smith in the same league as his own lowly, worthless, powerless father. He needed to be punished.

Byron of Sidius had done something similar, a long time ago. He had been ordered to kill his wife and son, under the direct command of Tanarak and himself, Vandross thought. But his soul had somehow gained the strength to refuse him and his master. Now, years later, Vandross faced a much less capable man, willing to sacrifice himself to the imagination of a warlock in order to spare his child.

"My lord," a serpentine voice called to him, sounding as though it came from a hundred miles away.

He recognized it as Vilec Roak's. After he cleared his throat, he stood and faced his General, who appeared worried.

"Are you well, my lord?"

Vandross shook his head to clear his jumbled thoughts. At that moment, Spite spoke in his mind, his voice slithering and slurring like the serpent he took the form of. *There is a great punishment for this man,* it said to him. *Think on it for a moment.*

And think on it he did, smiling broadly as he listened to Spite. Such awesome humiliation, Vandross thought, his blood pumping faster as he thought about it. He had his answer, and it was far worse than any threat of death the smith would dare.

"Thomas Jonas, I shall spare your life, as your daughter has requested. But you shall still receive your punishment for your transgression against myself and my General. Hear you now what I have in store for you both." He swept his gaze over the girl. Gods, he thought, she was beautiful. He let his gaze linger, relishing the thought of what was to come. "I shall ravish your daughter as I have told to you. And you shall watch me do so," he said, reaching a state of near sexual climax as the man flattened himself on the ground and screamed his anger and remorse into the dirt.

Such despair, Vandross thought, his mind reeling with the narcotic effects of feeding on raw emotion. *I shall have such sustenance for all the days of my life.*

Hoisting Kelly Jonas over his shoulder like a rag doll, he motioned to Roak to grab the forlorn smith, who grappled with the Shadowbeast for a moment before going limp in defeat.

Ah, what a marvelous day this shall be, Vandross thought as he waved to his slack-jawed subjects. *They shall all know me for generations to come, and they shall fear me in all times.*

* * * *

The moon hung directly above the seedy inn room where Richard Vandross committed his atrocity. Blood ran down the length of his arms, mixing with the rivulets of sweat he had earned from a hard night's labors. He had ravished the young woman, Vilec Roak cackling in the background as he restrained Thomas Jonas the blacksmith.

Afterwards, Vandross had strangled the girl, and as the smith had finally surged to his feet to assault the one-eyed warlock, he launched a viper of black force at him. The smoke-serpent sank its fangs into Jonas's neck, wresting the life from him.

But the smith was strong and full of fury; he somehow managed to rip the serpent free from his throat, bounding across the floor and striking Vandross hard on the jaw.

As Vandross reeled from the sheer force of the blow, he thought his jaw was broken. Turning back, Vandross lined his fingers up into a wedge, thrusting his hand into the smithy's chest, tearing the heart and lungs right out of his body. Blood sprayed him, caking his front side from forehead to toe, its coppery aroma infecting him like an aphrodisiac. He savored its smell, relishing it the way one might do so if he had returned home after a long time. To baste in the blood of one who threatened him, to tear the life out of another living thing with his own two hands; these things were sweet nectar to his soul.

Using the stained sheets upon which he had ravished the girl to wipe himself down, Vandross dismissed Vilec Roak and walked into the washroom. Without realizing what he was doing, he stood in front of the mirror, staring at his reflection.

His face appeared gaunt, deprived of real nourishment, the thick stubble of his beard unkempt in the fashion of madmen and beggars. His jaw had a severe thrust to it, partially natural and partially from the blow he'd just gotten, giving him the appearance of a natural predator. At this he grinned, noticing the gleam of his teeth in the dim light. But a moment later, his eyes caught his attention. They glowed bright crimson, filling his vision with the promise of destruction. From behind the patch over his injured eye, smoke swirled with the light, a slow pulse developing as he stared at his reflection. A wave of nausea swept through him then, and he fell to the washroom floor, unconscious.

He regained awareness shortly afterward, and struggled to his feet, looking around at the familiar hallway of his soul. Vandross sprinted down the hall, not bothering to take notice of any changes that may have further occurred since his last visit. Not slowing, he thrust aside the twin doors leading into the chamber containing the Orbs' manifestations.

Here, however, he was given reason to pause. The chamber had become enormous, and was filled with small altars and strange relics.

Power flowed through the air, clouds of black smoke floating slowly about, shadows with crimson eyes like his own standing in small circles while chanting a low, rhythmic mantra.

Power, Vengeance, Spite and Deceit stood apart from these smaller groups, up near the altar on which rested the cask of the Glorious Mother of Destruction. They looked up at him as he stalked toward them, bare-chested, bare footed, and seething with violence.

He had been summoned, he knew, and would not have minded so much if it had been while he slept; but this time, they had pulled him from his own reality during his waking hours.

"Power," he growled as he got within earshot. "What is the meaning of this? I do not see any reason for you to have called me here at this time. I was not even asleep for the gods' sake."

The elegant woman who represented the first Orb adjusted her stance only slightly, her head covered in a veiled hood. In spite of this, Vandross could feel her smiling at him like a madwoman.

"We have made a discovery that I did not think you should wait to know of, gracious host. In truth, it was Vengeance who first brought the matter to our attention." She hooked her arm around Vandross's and gently guided him closer to the altar, the cask now only an arm's length from him. He felt power emanating from within the container, power the likes of which he had never imagined possible. The power to bring down entire nations with the snap of his fingers, and it would shortly be all his. Just one more Orb, provided the wretched Dread Knight and his companions didn't get there first.

"There lies the Glorious Mother of Destruction, host. It is only Despair that we await, but we have not been able to locate or sense him anywhere. I have sent copies of you all over the realm of Tamalaria, but have found nothing."

That's right, Vandross thought. He had forgotten about Power's ability to make ethereal copies of his being. Up to this point, he had only used it the once, and then left it forgotten.

"So what is the point of all of this," he barked at her, still annoyed that he had been forcefully summoned just to see that there took place certain activities and rituals inside himself.

"My host, it may be that we can unlock the great power without Despair." Power cooed at him, rubbing his arm.

She's just a spirit, Vandross thought to himself. She isn't real, so don't even start thinking about a second romp. After all, he thought with a half grin, I'd essentially be fucking myself. As he cleared his head, the weight of what Power had said sunk in.

"Wait a minute," he said, trying to clear his head. "You mean that there is a way to access it without the final Orb of Eden's Serpent?"

The female manifestation raised an eyebrow and nodded.

"You mentioned this once before, but you seemed resistant to the idea. What are the risks in trying this?"

"The, risks, are, great," shlurped Vengeance. "If there, is a, mistake, in the ritual, you may find, yourself, damaged. We, require, your consent, to continue. That, is why, you, were summoned, here. Even, if, you are, not damaged, physically, there may be, other, repercussions."

Vandross looked about from creature to creature, trying to weigh the risks against the potential gains. What form would Despair take, he wondered? None of the Orbs appeared like the others, nor did they have similar powers. It might be beneficial to him to have access to the Glorious Mother of Destruction now, but Power and Vengeance had not been specific about the damage he may suffer as the result of a mistake. The consequences could be dire, perhaps life-threatening.

"You can hold off for now. Complete as much of the preparations as you see fit, but do not perform the final ritual. We shall find Despair if possible. I do not think he is beyond our grasp." He thought about Byron's fallen comrade. Monks had strange powers, even by magical standards. They were known for protecting ancient artifacts, even suppressing their powers, in the monasteries they made their homes. If one such brotherhood had the final Orb, they might have secreted it away. And Byron was heading further north, it seemed, into the mountains. "Power, make another copy of me, and send it into the northern range of mountains. Have it search for Monk-run monasteries, nothing more. Get its report and dispose of it afterwards."

"Host," she asked, raising an eyebrow once again, this time in question. Vandross explained his thoughts on the Monks, telling her that there might be a particular order that held onto the artifact of arcane power. "If the copy finds that it is under the care of a single Monk, have the man slain. If there are two or more, recall the copy. I want nothing botched, no half-assed measures in this effort. Do you understand?"

The woman bowed deeply to him, smiling as she did so. "It shall be done, my host," she said in a whisper.

A whirl of energy flowed around Vandross, and he found himself awake in the washroom of his rented chambers. *Hellfire*, he thought. *Hell and blood!* Still seething at the Orbs' apparent power over him, he looked up into the mirror and punched the reflective surface.

Blood ran between his fingers as he held his fist against the shattered glass, the soft tinkle of shards striking the floor. Shadows encroached upon the outskirts of his vision, blurring everything into a vague blob of shades of gray; he was certain he was going to pass out again. But as he turned, he saw that he was more than conscious. The shadows around him had actually begun to wax and wane, taking on vaguely humanoid shapes before returning to their host objects.

They were reacting to him, he realized with a shock. His abrupt violence, the stench in the bedroom of his crimes, the glow of his damaged eye; all these things had caused the shadows to come to life for his command. They were not demons—they didn't appear to possess souls. The shadows didn't move or take shape until he fixed his full attention on them. Lifeless, shapeless extensions of himself, he decided. He would figure out a way to make use of them later. For now, all he wanted to do was finish dressing himself, grab his armor, and teleport himself back to Mount Toane. The bodies of the Jonas family could remain where they lay sprawled. After all, he thought with a chuckle as he tore a rift in the air, they wouldn't be missed.

* * * *

"Report," Vandross said as he came out of Mount Toane and stalked groggily up to Major Tamriel. Vandross had shuffled straight to his chambers after getting back in the middle of the night. Upon awakening, he had bathed himself, donned a new suit of black and blue armor, and decided to continue on with his normal routine. This involved a morning report from whoever had kept watch overnight, which more often than not, meant speaking with the great bear demon.

The Renka snapped off a sharp salute, standing straighter than usual.

Vandross raised his good eyebrow, and folded his arms over his chest. The Renka smelled like old grime and mutton, a rather odd combination, Vandross thought. Then again, Tamriel and his kind didn't exactly eat a standard Human diet—few of Vandross's forces did. The Shadowbeasts ate grasses, weeds, and other sorts of plants not suitable to the normal person's palate, let alone digestive tract. Brink, when the great beast demon had been around, had consumed every living animal it could get its huge hands on. The Khan in his employ hunted in the dark hours of the morning, dragging deer and moose into the mountain by the half dozen, just to feed one of their packs.

Thus, it was fortunate that his forces had spread out to his new territories. The immediate area surrounding Mount Toane had taken a severe blow to its ecosystem as a result of the one-eyed warlock's armies. The more intelligent creatures, such as wild dogs, wolves, and horses, had decided unanimously that the new inhabitants of the region were too dangerous to live with, and had moved on. Aside from dull-witted creatures, the food sources had become scarce. The only clear exception to this were the few bears that lived in the area, but the Renka had made it clear to the first poor bastard who had tried to hunt one that this was unacceptable. A Khan Hunter had returned with a bear corpse, and had been ripped apart violently by the hulking Major. Tamriel hadn't been screwing around. He had buried his claws in the top of the Khan's head, gripped, and ripped in opposite directions, literally ripping the man in half.

"Whilst you were absent from Mount Toane, little occurred, my lord. There were no unexpected assaults, no strange magics, and nobody has gone AWOL. All is in order, my lord. But something did catch my attention, and I am uncertain what to make of it."

Vandross nodded, waving his hand to motion the Renka to continue.

"It was at about the midnight hour, my lord. The entire mountain shook as with terror, and there flashed a dazzling light from the northwest, in the direction of the village to which you went. Did something happen there, my lord?"

Vandross shook his head, waving the question irritably aside.

"Nothing to concern yourself with at any rate, Tamriel. Tell me, who's watching the entrance today?"

"That would be Lieutenant Amon and his pack of Khan," Tamriel rumbled, stretching his massive arms. His eyes had developed bags under them, his body still unaccustomed to being incarnated in mortal flesh. In Hell, the demons needed no rest to carry out their duties. The hellfire and demonic power channeling through the rings of Hell from Pandemonium gave enough energy to all the demons. Now, the Renka had need of food and rest, things he was not accustomed to requiring.

Vandross was surprised that the Shadowbeasts seemed to get by so easily, while in comparison, the more potent demons were tiring out and becoming sluggish. Then again, the Shadowbeasts had little or no pride, and would consume anything and sleep at any time available. Almost like Humans, Vandross thought with a smirk.

"They shall be here promptly, my lord. Requesting permission to knock off for a good sleep," he said with a snappy salute.

"Granted, Major. You are off duty for now. And for your own sake, don't come back on today. Take the day off, unless I personally send for you, Tamriel. Dismissed." He returned the salute and watching the bear demon lumber away. Something in the way that Tamriel had become less intimidating concerned him; too much time in the mortal realm might ultimately render him effectless. Or perhaps if he gave the Major something a bit more aggressive to do, he would return to the state he had been in when first Vandross had summoned him. He wanted the Renkas available as the first line of defense if Byron and his company gathered an army against Mount Toane. Though Moran and Doran struck him as being next to petty Shadowbeasts in power, they would at least serve as sword fodder. Vandross had become increasingly certain that it would come down to that, despite any efforts he made to crush the Dread Knight. But more of his party could be destroyed, and that would make things a bit more difficult on Byron. Vandross's armies could destroy anyone they wanted, but he increasingly wanted Byron to himself. He would destroy the Dread Knight with his own hands.

At this point the growling figure of Lieutenant Amon marched out of Mount Toane, his orange and black striped head thrust forward like a primate. A thickly furred and muscled man, Amon's body possessed more tiger-like features than humanoid, giving him a bestial personality and temper to go along with his general physical appearance. Part of his aggressive tendencies, the one-eyed warlock knew, came from the fact that he had not wished to serve in Vandross's armies. He had only come along to preserve his people, that they might one day return to the Allenians and crush the Simpa Race.

Vandross had appointed him an officer's rank for the simple reason that he was an effective leader of his people. Among Khan, leadership was determined was through a battle-royal, unarmed, until one man stood alone. Amon had ruled his pack for years. Each time a new challenge was made on the post of leadership, he had laid waste to his challengers, upon occasion killing the Khan who had issued the challenge. Few of his kinsmen bothered with the battles anymore: they enjoyed the privilege of breathing. As a result, even here in Vandross's armies, none of the Khan questioned their place.

Amon snapped a sharp salute off at Vandross, who returned it after a moment.

"Lieutenant Amon, sir," the tiger-man growled. "I, along with my personal vanguard, am here to relieve Major Tamriel."

"So noted, Lieutenant." Vandross moved back toward Mount Toane. "I assume you shall send a runner to me in the event of attack?"

"Of course, sir." The Khan looked at a point somewhere in the distance.

Military service seemed to suit the man perfectly, Vandross thought.

"Everything shall be carried out accordingly. Gentlemen," he barked, spinning on his heel to look at his men. "To your posts. Everyone."

The Khan moved to their assigned posts without questions or indication that they objected.

Vandross nodded his satisfaction, and moved into Mount Toane. His mind wandered, and as he stalked through the great rock halls and caverns of the mountain, he found himself thinking back on days long past, days in which he served as the apprentice instead of the master.

His first entrance to Mount Toane had felt like a test of his physical and mental mettle, a rite of passage that he hadn't been up to; yet he had gone into the bottom most caverns and tunnels of Mount Toane with his master, Tanarak of Sidius. There, he had viewed a small glimpse of what was to come for the land of Tamalaria. He had known that Tanarak would fall, despite the warlock's own confidence and power. Something in the images that played on the walls told him of Tanarak's fall, and how fortunate he would be to be in the position of apprentice when the warlock was slain. He would have a way of absorbing Tanarak's powers, and could become even greater than the old freak.

That first night, however, after seeing the Chamber of Fate and its stories shown in magma light, he had been greatly disturbed, even terrified. Tanarak had summoned a platoon of Shadowbeasts, simply to practice his arcane powers on them. One by one the old warlock blasted them back into the Hells, leaving piles of ash and salt where there had stood demons.

The practice itself did not move Vandross in any way, but Tanarak's complete lack of emotion haunted him; the man took no pride, not even any satisfaction, in his exercise. He simply appeared to be going through the motions of slaughter, as though such actions were a common part of his everyday life.

In the years that followed, Vandross would learn that they were indeed thus, and that he himself took great satisfaction in the slaughter of his enemies. But that first night, he had curled up in his bed of stone and straw and rocked himself to sleep. He had agreed to accompany Tanarak to learn the arcane arts of magic, the spells and powers of a warlock. Such mages had no restrictions on the type of magic they practiced, and held great power over those spells they mastered. Since he had been very young, Richard Vandross had wanted to wield such power. And now he did, he thought with a smile. Now he did.

Another item of note had caused Vandross some discomfort that first time in the lower chambers and depths of the mountain. He had detected a great demonic presence, one in another class entirely from the Shadowbeasts that Tanarak had summoned and destroyed. He had felt its power, its hunger, but instinct told him that this essence, this presence, could do nothing without a physical body. He had asked Tanarak about it, and the old warlock had grinned with his mouth, though his eyes had belied no single emotional response.

"I know of what you speak, apprentice," the old warlock rasped, peering around the chamber. "A demon of the sort is too powerful to be allowed access to the Mortal Realm without a host body. Such restrictions were put in place many hundreds of years ago by the Gods in the Heavenly Palace."

"Would the demon be in control of the host," Vandross asked, still wet behind the ears in those days.

"Not total control. It would be like sharing space inside your own body and soul. Unpleasant to say the least. In addition, this sort of demon can only be summoned by one who can control demons. You will learn to do this in time, my apprentice, but not as yet. And if ever you decide to awaken this beast, do not give it space within yourself. Give it a useful mortal who can then be yours to command."

And Vandross had done just that, years later, creating Grigory Molis.

Crimson and pitch rock faces stared back flatly at him in every corridor, their surfaces barely discernable from one another. But Vandross had learned every inch of stone in this mountain, having made it his home twice now, once its second-in-command, and now its master. His armies were not much different from Tanarak's, he thought with a trace of bitterness; he had wanted to be so much different than the old warlock, so much more effective and destructive. In one respect, at least, he had gone a different way. He had not manipulated the political structures of cities or kingdoms, had not used the back door to glean power and standing. He had sent waves of soldiers to crush resistance and occupy that which he wanted, a much more effective way of securing power over his new subjects.

So much alike, he thought, *but so much different.* And one more point separated him from Tanarak, one thing he wanted to have in *common* with the dead warlock: Tanarak had possessed all five of the Orbs of Eden's Serpent. Strangely, though, he had not unlocked the Glorious Mother of Destruction, though he had spoken of it cryptically on occasion, muttering about the power he would have with it. Vandross intended to attain the final Orb, and unleash the final power of the Orbs upon the world, where his master had not. But for the moment, he had no idea where the Orb of Eden's Serpent was, and so would have to be patient while Power's shadow copies went in search of it.

How long would he be forced to wait, he wondered as he passed into a rock stairwell that led downward into the mountain, toward the Chamber of Fate. Would he ever gain possession of the fifth Orb of Eden's Serpent? Or would Byron and his companions secret it away, finding it before he could? If they did, he would be forced to attempt the unleashing of the Glorious Mother of Destruction before it was safe to do so. Then again, it might not even be safe with all five Orbs, so why not take the risk? *No,* he thought, shaking his head roughly. That was the other Orbs speaking. He wanted to take every precaution; he was Richard Vandross, warlock and ruler, not madman and fool.

As he reached the bottom of the stairwell, he stopped, shocked into recognition. *Surely there was good reason for coming here*, he mused, rubbing his beard. He stood ten feet from a granite door, crudely created by stone melding, a Dwarven Racial power that allowed their kin to shape rock and stone at will. On the other side of the door lay the Chamber of Fate, a high vaulted circle of stone that hung over the lava pits of Mount Toane.

When he opened the door, the first thing he would see would be the stone catwalk from the slim walking circle around the outside of the chamber to the central pad of suspended stone. There, on the central pad, could be seen a pair of stone seats, crafted by the same technique as the door. Hundreds of years ago, Mount Toane had belonged to Dwarves, and much of the furnishings had been crafted by the beloved technique of stone melding. Superstitious folks, Dwarves, Vandross thought. But the Chamber of Fate was one superstition that his master, and even he himself, had come to believe in and depend upon.

As he threw open the door with one hand, he gasped once again as he gazed into the lava chamber. *Of course*, his mind screamed. *Of course*. As Richard Vandross took one look into the Chamber of Fate, he screamed in fury and horror as he realized that the Chamber of Fate was the model from which his soul's central chamber had been copied. And there, across from the doorway in which he had stood, cast in shadows, was the image of a hulking Knight of some sort bringing its flaming sword crashing down on the skull of the shadow his own body had cast against the wall.

Seeing this, Richard Vandross fled up through Mount Toane in blind panic and fear; he needed the Orb, and he needed the final powers it would grant him. If he did not attain them, he was doomed.

* * * *

Several hours later, Richard Vandross rolled out of his bed, falling hard onto the compact floor of his bedchambers. "Damn it all," he muttered, rubbing his eye. He couldn't sleep well, his mind still haunted by the image of his skull being split in two by a Knight with a flaming sword. It had been too real for his liking, too life-like, and only had one reasonable conclusion that could be drawn from it: Byron of Sidius would slay him. Regardless of how many ways one looked at it, the message was clear.

For perhaps the first time, he consciously regretted his loss of Locke, the Keeper. But such regrets would have to wait. He had other things to take care of first.

Vandross moved from his bedchamber to his washroom, disrobing and pouring steaming water into a basin from a tube that pulled water from the mountain's fiery base. Using a small container of fine sand, he scrubbed away the outermost layer of grime, feeling as though he tore away the outer layer of skin along with the accumulated dirt. Rinsing off, he arose from the basin and redressed, new tunics and heated armor feeling good on his skin.

He had a meeting with Colonel Molis at noon to discuss the progress made by his armies against the defenders of Ja-Wen. As soon as that meeting ended, he intended to draw Power forth from his body, and ask her for a report on the progress of his shadow copies. After that, he would go hunting with Lieutenant

Amon and his pack.

In the evening, after he had satisfied his hunger with a nice dinner, he would invite Tamriel to play some chess. He had tried to invite Vilec Roak on several occasions, but the Shadowbeast General hadn't shown much interest in the greatest of games.

All in all, he had a full day ahead of him as leader of the new world order. *Well*, he thought, *off to the throne room.*

He was surprised to see Colonel Molis had waited for him at the foot of the grand throne. The half-demon snapped off a salute, his gleaming yellow eyes the only thing visible inside of his full plate mail armor and helmet. He looked not unlike Locke, except that Molis's armor was a shimmering greenish, silver color, and he stood only six feet in height.

"Colonel," Vandross said as he returned the salute and assumed his throne. "What news from Ja-Wen?"

"Sir," rasped the half-demon. His voice sounding similar to Vandross's when the power of the Orbs took hold of him, a twin harmony of human and demon voices speaking at the same time. "We began the siege by concentrating our efforts on the northwestern quadrant of the city, hoping to first strike at their elite defenders.

When we stormed that section of the city, we found only standard soldiers and constables of the law. Thinking that they had simply rearranged their distribution of forces, I sent runners to all parts of the city, disguised as townsfolk. Much to my chagrin, none of the elite troops could be found. It appeared that they had abandoned their posts after our first assault on the city. I became suspicious, of course, when none could be found." The half-demon shifted his weight on his feet uncomfortably, removing his helmet to reveal a handsome man's face, with streamers of shadows flowing off of his head instead of hair. His eyes were the color of old ashes, the distant look of apathy locked in them. Vandross couldn't remember when last he'd seen that Human-like face, but had come to respect the man's prowess and tactical mind. Now, however, he sensed hesitation.

"Is there something wrong, Colonel?"

"My lord, for these last eight days we have harassed their city, destroying their defenders utterly, crushing their pockets of resistance under foot. But yesterday, a small group of men and women, warriors we had not seen before, rushed at our encampment from the outskirts of the city. They were only one score in number, yet they managed to cause severe casualties to our forces. I believe they had been hiding in the outer residential districts all along, waiting for us to drop our defenses."

"Hmm. Describe these warriors for me, Colonel," Vandross said, raising an eyebrow. An effective counter-attack, eh? Twenty people, Molis had said. What sort of casualties had they generated in their brief blitz on Molis's men, he wondered.

"They were an assembled force, organized and well disciplined. They did not appear to be any one Race or Class in particular, my lord. Humans, an Elf, a pair of Dwarves, a Cuyotai, a Werewolf, Jafts, a Minotaur, and even a couple of Gnomes. Their kind are typically cowardly and scientific, but these two had mastered the arts of Aquamancy and Q Magic, respectively. It was a varied arrangement, all working in unison, my lord, much like our hated nemesis," Molis referred to Byron and his rag-tag company.

Vandross agreed with his Colonel on one fundamental point; Byron led a small group rather effectively, considering that they did not have a large assortment of Races or Classes among them. Still, their talent and power more than made up for the lack of numbers.

"Those who attacked took us by surprise, and destroyed two hundred and fifty of my men," the Colonel said.

Vandross gasped; twenty ordinary men and women, regardless of skill, could never have accomplished that much.

"As I have said, my lord, they were well prepared for us. Not so, we for them. However, they all have been dealt with."

"Well, there's a spot of good news," Vandross said with a sigh.

"My lord, there is one thing more I must show you," the half-demon rasped, reaching into one of his satchels, and withdrawing a small patch of cloth. On one of the surfaces of the armband was the symbol of Oun, overlapped by an eyeless skull.

Richard Vandross twitched, setting the cloth ablaze with a thought, and howled with fury up through the highest reaches of Mount Toane.

"Byyyyyyroooooooon!"

* * * *

Vandross ranted and fumed a half-hour before calming himself down and summoning Power. He had reduced the walls in the throne room to scorched rubble with blasts of vitriol and lightning, power coursing through him, flames shooting forth from both eyes. Strangely enough, the heat did not burn away the patch over his ruined eye, and he retained a measure of dignity when at last he forced Power into existence.

The tall, coy woman bowed her deference to him, and he waved a dismissive hand at her gesture. "I want to hear something good, Power," he growled through barred teeth.

"And so you shall, gracious host," she whispered to him, her soft voice echoing eerily around the chamber. "Of the six copies I sent forth, one has reported seeing a group of some three or four Monks carrying a cask. I assume from their location that they are taking the item with them to a safe place in the northwestern most mountains. There are few cities in that region, and most of them belong to the Dwarves."

Hmm, Vandross thought. *Dwarves.* Superstitious folk, that much he knew about the stalwart humanoids. And utterly fierce. He could not hope to successfully lay siege to a Dwarven stronghold as he had Whitewood, especially if Byron and his company arrived first, which seemed inevitable. But Dwarves were superstitious, and untrusting of magic. Dwarves possessed unequaled combat tacticians, brave and deadly warriors, and potent Clerics for the purposes of healing. Aside from Gnomes, they were the greatest scientific minds in all of Tamalaria, insofar as their technology was used for war. They had developed siege engines that used a black powder to cause an explosion much like magic, except for the fact that the fire of science did not die like that of magic. Dwarves used similar designs in smaller form, creating weapons they called 'hand cannons'. No, he would not risk an assault on Dwarven territory.

But he might not have to. No self-respecting Dwarf would let an Orb of Eden's Serpent's into his city. The Monks would be refused, turned aside from safety. They would have to find a cave or another monastery to hide the Orb in, somewhere in the mountains.

Out among the wilder, less inhabited mountains, however, Vandross ran the risk of running into another, even more lethal sort of foe: Dragons.

Vandross could handle a Dragon or two, but they lived in packs in those foothills and valleys. This sort of thing would require stealth and skill, a smaller, more mobile group. One that he would lead himself, he decided before speaking again.

"My host," said Power. "Are you well? There is much on your mind, I sense."

"Then you sense correctly." Vandross clasped his hands behind his back as he paced in a circle around the Orb's manifestation. "There are risks to be weighed, Power. I shall suffer no miscalculations. I don't want to lose more of my minions needlessly. I shall require council with my best officers. Return now to my flesh, Power." Without even thinking about it, he drew her back into his being, her material form winking out of sight with a dark glimmer of shadows.

Going to his specially assigned game chamber, he sat among the many stone seats and mentally summoned his highest officers and advisers to his side.

Within minutes, seven men, Vandross included, occupied the chamber. Directly across from Vandross sat Vilec Roak, the Shadowbeast General. Looming in one tunnel entrance stood Major Tamriel, the great bear demon. On Roak's right, sitting stiffly upright, was Colonel Molis, the half-demon. Skulking in the shadows across the chamber from Vandross was Lieutenant Amon, sharpening his claws with a whetstone. Lounging on one of the pool tables Vandross had erected was Talus Cur, an Illeck Q Mage in command of Vandross's special magic-wielding squads. These Mages and Clerics had not been given military designations, as it seemed ill-suited to their nature. And lastly, the highest ranking Beastmaster, a Sergeant Robin, stood behind Vilec Roak. The Human had come in handy for providing meals and beasts of burden needed to maintain the mountain as a base of operations.

"Gentlemen," Vandross began, adjusting his armor to make himself appear more relaxed.

Though these men held power, they all feared him in some way, and it occurred to him that it might be more effective to get them to be helpful if he did not daunt them. "I have learned where the fifth and final Orb of Eden's Serpent is, and where it is going. Monks from the north have it in their charge, and they move swiftly for the northwest, into Dwarven territory. I intend to claim it, and thus give myself and our army enough power to crush all those who would oppose us. He would feast on fear as long as he had to, and then fall into the Immortal Rest, and let his armies and minions fend for themselves. He cared not what happened to them once he left the picture, only that he wanted them to help him achieve his ends now. "But that is a dangerous region, even for one such as myself. I shall require aid in this, but we cannot have open warfare with the Dwarves, or the Dragons. I need options, gentlemen."

Silence, thick as stew, filled the room.

As he searched the faces of all of the assembled men, Vandross took heart in the fact that they all seemed to be debating in their heads the best course of action. Of course, one or two of them would offer overly simplistic plans, shot through with flaws the size of a boulder, but he would listen to them each in turn before he cast down any suggestions.

As he had suspected he might, Lieutenant Amon was the first to test his mental might in this situation.

"My lord, I do not see the problem with confronting the Dwarves in a military strike. Their numbers are not as vast as ours, and we have resources that they do not. If we properly rationed the men, and marched every last battalion out to the Dwarven cities, we could destroy them one by one. It could work."

"No, it couldn't," Vandross said with a hint of irritation. "Whilst engaged with one city, the army of another city would flank us and harass our forces constantly, killing hundreds of my men. And dividing the forces at our disposal into smaller portions might prove just as fatal, only on a smaller and more time-consuming fashion. The Dwarves cannot be beaten over the heads like Elves, Amon," he said, trying to sound as condescending as possible.

Amon returned to his spot leaning into the shadows, going back to the unsavory task of thinking. Khan tended not to like long, involving thought, Vandross noticed. "Any other suggestions," he asked, spreading his arms wide with a smile on his lips.

"My lord, it is possible that, with the aid of more of my kin, I could lead a small group into the mountains," Tamriel boomed, his voice rebounding off of the walls of the chamber. Lowering his voice to compensate for the acoustics of the room, he continued. "We Renka are hearty demons, and feared among the Dwarven Race. We could intimidate them into giving more men safe passage," he said, folding his arms across his barrel chest.

Vandross thought over the Renka's proposal; it was a nice, clean way to move more forces into the region. But what would they do then? He had already told himself that the Monks with the Orb would probably be turned aside from Dwarven cities. Dwarves were not the only problem here, and neither Amon nor Tamriel had suggested a solution for the Dragon dilemma.

"That can be considered," Molis chimed in before Vandross could voice his concerns. "But Lord Vandross has made a point of the Dragons. Your kind are not so feared or exalted by the great Wyrms, are they bear demon?" the half-demon Colonel asked with a measure of disdain.

Tamriel bared his teeth at Molis, growling deep in his throat.

"What right have you to mock or disdain me, halfbreed," Tamriel growled.

Uh oh, Vandross thought. He couldn't afford in-fighting so far up the chain of command. He stood to put a stop to further squabbling.

"Major, Colonel, please. We are gathered here with the same goal in mind. Tamriel may very well have a valid solution to the Dwarven problem, but the Colonel does have a good point. Lieutenant Amon can lead a moderate sized force into the mountains behind the Renkas, but what do we do at that point? We need to pool together our resources and thoughts, gentlemen. That's why I called all of you here, instead of one or two of you."

Tension remained hanging in the air, a guillotine ready to drop at any moment, but that tension seemed reduced, the executioner's hand stayed for the moment.

"Dragons respect powerful users of magic," offered Talus Cur, a paper-thin smile on his face. "As well as mind games, my lord. Perhaps the General and some of his Shadowbeasts should make ready some tricks and pitfalls, simple enough that they can be placed on the spot, since we shall be traveling."

Vandross tried to think of a flaw in this, but Cur hadn't suggested in his tone that this was the final solution to the Dragons; rather, the Illeck had left plenty of room for addition or editing of his plan. At this moment, the Beastmaster Sergeant Robin stepped forward.

"Mind games, yes," the lanky Human said, his voice a half-whisper. "Convince one or two to have council with you, watch a marvelous display, yes. And when you have it distracted, someone of great physical prowess can lay a few key strikes to it, to weaken its body and keep its mind reeling. That," he said, thrusting a finger to the air in revelation. "That is how I shall gain command of a Dragon, and order it to aid us, to allow us safe passage and perhaps even bodily assistance. I shall have mastery of a great Wyrm," cried the Human, slavering at the corners of his mouth, his eyes gleaming like a zealot who has flung himself into engulfing flames because he believes it is what his god asks of him.

Colonel Molis leaned toward Richard Vandross, whispering to him as softly as he could.

"I think Sergeant Robin is a tad enthusiastic, but he makes a good suggestion, sir. Having control of one or two of the Dragons would be most advantageous for us, and I myself can handle the task of damaging the selected Wyrm."

Vandross nodded his agreement. "Though what you propose is risky, Sergeant, I admire your willingness to assume such a daunting task. Few Beastmasters have ever gained control over a Dragon." Vandross smiled broadly at Robin. "And those who have tried usually wind up maimed or dead. It is a difficult spot to put oneself in, but I will not allow you to do so unless the others here assembled agree with what you suggest. Gentlemen?"

Vandross looked for approval from the rest of his officers. But they all looked to each other and nodded, everyone feeling out the others' reaction to the idea of having a Dragon in their army; every single one of them grinning at the implications.

"I believe, my lord," rasped Vilec Roak, standing to his feet, "that I speak for all of us when I say that although it is a hazardous action, we are willing to accept the risks. If this effort is successful, we shall gain a tool of invaluable worth, a mighty Dragon. But we must gather our separate plans into one cohesive whole, my lord."

"That is what I'm here for. And this is how it shall be done." He went into detail as he wove the individual portions of their schemes together like a fine map of fabric. In the end, it was a plan worthy of his lofty goals and his lust for power. He would thusly gain control of the region, and begin a thorough search for the Monks and the Orb of Eden's Serpent they carried with them. Once attained, he would unleash the power of the Glorious Mother of Destruction, and the whole of Tamalaria would bow to him in terror. His pursuit of eternal fear would be within his grasp, but he would not unleash that power right away. He would return to Mount Toane, and learn the ways of the Orbs when all were together, before he attempted the greatest power he would ever know. Well defended, and well prepared, Mount Toane would withstand any army until Vandross had taken the time he needed. He would succeed where his former master had failed; his plans would not end in defeat and ruin.

Chapter Two
Into the Mountains

Four days later, Byron and his company sat in a small rock circle amid the lower foothills leading into the northwestern mountains, a hard blowing wind sweeping chilled air across their skin and bringing the sounds of mountainous creatures such as goats and wild cats. The smell of ozone promised of rain or snow, and neither would have been unexpected or unwelcome.

The blasting furnace that was the Upper Plains had been slowly cooking the party for days on end, and Shoryu had been forced to strip off his upper tunic shirt, his fur laced with thick streams of sweat. Now, he huddled with Ellen Daires, keeping her frail Elven form from shivering itself apart, while Selena Bradford and the others simply gathered closer to the fire than usual. Even Byron felt the sting of the sharp, icy wind as it slapped at him. The only member of the group that seemed perfectly at home was Morek Rockmight, the Dwarven Boxer.

"It's just a wee bit of wind," he had grumbled, admonishing the others for their discomfort. The taciturn Dwarf had become ever more withdrawn since David Spore's demise at the hands of the Lizardman, Phazion Lurik.

Byron knew that hadn't even been the man's real name, but he knew not what else to call him except a deceiver and bastard. The few times the assassin had come up in conversation had been tense, and Morek had only referred to him as 'the traitor'. But Byron felt himself, even more than the Lizardman, responsible for David's death. He had given his trust to a man who hadn't even proven himself to be an ally of the land, much less Byron and his crew.

"It may be that you are at home in these mountains, friend," said Ellen, her teeth chattering together as she huddled even closer to the young Cuyotai. "But we are not. I apologize for my own weakness," she mumbled half to herself.

Morek gave her a blatant glare that brimmed with anger, not so much at her, as with his present circumstances. The horses, he had informed Byron, would not be able to bear them up into Dwarven territory, or further into the nearer mountains, toward the monastery that was their destination. The paths were too sheer and shelters too small to accommodate them, and Dwarves didn't use horses much, except in stews that included ingredients like 'well that bit's a secret'. He had reasoned that he would be able to guide them to enough shortcuts to make the trip easy on them.

"Sorry about that," Morek said, much to Byron's surprise. He had expected a confrontation, but instead the Boxer had kept his calm for the moment, opting instead to be silently angry. "I'm just anxious to do somethin'," he said, pacing back and forth.

As evening drew to a close and night began in earnest, Byron decided to take the first watch with the taciturn Dwarven Boxer. The two men, such glaring contradictions of one another, began the watch by silently walking in a tight perimeter around the rest of the company and the fire. Before long, Byron felt compelled to ask questions, waiting only until their march took them far enough away from the group that he and Morek would not be heard.

"Morek, my friend, will you not share your grief with me in a more healthy fashion than the one you have been using?" He tried to put a hand on the Dwarf's shoulder. Unfortunately, while Morek was tall for a Dwarf his age, standing nearly five feet in height, his body was still uniquely Dwarven, with bulging musculature, paunch gut, and sloped shoulders.

Byron nearly took a face-dive into the dirt, his armored hand slipping right off. Correcting himself, he adjusted his armor awkwardly. The smell of ozone gathered and thickened as miniscule bits of snow fell from the mountain skies around them, the wind swirling them into vivid visions and patterns.

The air took on a less tense quality, its chilliness now somehow acting as a salve to Morek's emotions, and the stoic Dwarf improved for a minute. Gone were the lines of concern and anger; his eyes closed, his nostrils flaring as he breathed in the mountain air.

"Ahhh, there's no air quite like the stuff you breath when you come here, Byron," he said, opening his eyes.

A deep hurt still lingered there, Byron noted, but it hung back, momentarily forgotten as feelings of comfort flooded into Morek. He was home again, completely in his element. Nobody in the entire company knew this region as well as Morek, and he would serve as their best point man while traversing the northern mountains. "It may be thin, but the air has an untainted quality, purer than those plains we just passed through. It's the sort of place where the men are separated from the boys, in all things. I tell you, Byron, this is where I belong." Morek lowered his voice a notch. "It's where David would have belonged. He was a good chum, he was. Good fighter despite the handicap, too. And he'd be just fine back in Whitewood if'n I hadn't dragged him into this mess."

"Ah, good master Dwarf, you forget yourself." His hand finally found Morek's shoulder without slipping off. "It was I who got everyone here involved with what is essentially not their battle. You had good reasons all to hate Richard Vandross, and his armies of wicked men, but had I opted to walk away instead of personally seeing to each of you, then it would be only myself who traveled into such dangers. The blame is mine, Morek. Mine, and Richard Vandross's."

Byron smiled gently at the stocky little fellow, but Morek clearly did not believe him.

Dwarves, Byron mused for a moment, sure are bull-headed fellows. Most people quickly turned to find an easy scapegoat: not Morek, however. His people were both proud and noble, and so they felt no difficulty in assuming guilt, even when the guilt was not theirs.

"Perhaps it is truest said then that you, me, and Vandross are to blame," Morek said, rather half-heartedly. "It matters little now. Come on, our watch's over."

With nothing more to say, and no more time to coax some positive reaction from Morek, Byron roused Selena Bradford, while the Dwarven Boxer nudged

Shoryu awake. Byron lay down next to the fire as it guttered and spat in the soft breeze, and fell quickly asleep.

* * * *

Everywhere she turned, Shadowbeasts cackled as they danced around her, their yellow gimlet eyes leaving trails of glowing light as they pranced about.

The smell of acrid smoke and blasted stone hung thick and heavy in the air around Selena Bradford, and for perhaps only the second time in her life, she felt true terror at the prospect of flames.

Guttural barks and snarls escaped the strange holes that served for mouths in the twisted faces of the demons, each more threatening and bestial than the last. The ground around her shook and quivered with the stamping of so many eldritch life-forms in one small cavern chamber, and more than once Selena thought she could taste the earth's very blood on her lips.

Amid the jumbled throngs of demons, her friends struggled in vain for their lives. All except Byron, who could not be seen anywhere in the chaos around her.

The Pyromancer tried to conjure magical force to her aid, but no matter how deeply she reached within herself, she found no more resources for her magic.

Still, the Shadowbeasts made no move on her, only attacking her allies as they fell back toward her, battered and bloody. Then a new rumble shook the mountain around her, a deep, primal roar of rampage and destruction.

What manner of beast or man could make such a dreadful sound? she wondered.

Soon, her question was answered. A lumbering, wraith-like figure emerged from the far entrance to the cavern, cloaked all in black with paws covered in dark brown fur and blood.

The creature threw back its hood to reveal a demonic bear's head, all muzzle and flashing teeth. It reared its head back and laughed at her, its mirth filled to brimming with scorn and disgust.

"Pathetic mortal," the creature boomed, glaring at her as a hungry animal might its next meal. "Your power has limitations, fire wielder. You cannot hope to defeat me and my kinsmen. We are unfettered, free of the bondage of mortal needs and constraints. Now you and your fellows shall weep in agony, and beg for death before end of your suffering. Ha ha ha ha haaaaa!" With a heave, the creature entered the chamber, and brought its huge paw down at her.

"Augh," she gasped quietly as she sat up, seeing Byron's glimmering eyes staring at her in what she assumed was concern. "Just a dream," she muttered, looking quickly away from the Dread Knight.

"Are you all right? Perhaps you should rest some more," Byron said quietly, trying to ease her back to the ground.

"I'm fine," she said, watching Byron huddle close to the fire to fall asleep. She felt a pang of regret for being so abrupt with him, but the massive undead warrior didn't seem bothered. *He probably figures it's in my nature*, she thought glumly.

Rolling out of her blankets, Selena pushed herself to her feet, shambling about a bit to get the feeling back in her legs. They had become stiff from being locked straight, as they had been in her nightmare. Reaching into her rucksack, she pulled out the last of her rationed food, a small wedge of cheese and the heel from a loaf of bread. The company would have to forage for food sources as they climbed into the mountains, until they reached the hospitality of the monastery or the dining halls of a Dwarven barracks. Morek had mentioned that there were military quarters even this far east of Traithrock, the easternmost Dwarven territory city, and its nation's capital. The Dwarves didn't claim much land as their own, but what they had, they protected with an army far more fierce and trained than any other in the land of Tamalaria. Yet despite their war-like nature, they were gracious hosts to passers-through, often sending parties in search of those few who became stranded in the upper hills and valleys of snow. Surely they would recognize Morek Rockmight, one of the Head Councilmen of Traithrock. The mighty Boxer might not be well known outside of his country, but surely his reputation preceded him here.

"Are you well, Selena," a boyish voice asked from her shoulder, and she spun in surprise to plant her palm against young Shoryu's chest.

Sighing her relief, she lowered her hand, called back her power.

"My apologies, I didn't mean to startle you," he said, a wry grin on his snout. "But you oughtn't to put your hands so close to my heart, miss. It belongs to another."

"Oh, stuff it, Shoryu," she snapped, smoothing out her robes. "I'm in about as good a mood as the Dwarf."

"Then that is dire," Shoryu said, his face smoothing into a serious countenance. "Good master Morek is downtrodden from the loss of our friend David Spore, and I cannot blame him for this." His face twitched oddly, and he snarled at Selena suddenly, his teeth bared, his claws thrusting out of his fingers.

Selena, confused and a little afraid, took a measured step back, but saw a moment later that Shoryu had returned to himself. What oddity was this, she wondered? "Tell me, friend, what troubles you so?"

Shoryu didn't seem to have realized what he had done, and she let it go for the time being. Selena walked the same perimeter as Byron and Morek had earlier in the night, and repeated her dream to the Cuyotai Hunter as best as she could remember it, leaving out the part about how helpless she felt. She sensed that he would deduce that much from her tone, so she found no need to make a point of it.

"And that's it," she finished. "I have been plagued by this dream for nearly an entire week, even since before the Monk passed. The only difference is that now he isn't in the dream, as he had been at first. But it's just a silly dream," she said, scoffing at herself for being so disturbed by nonsense like dreams and nightmares. "It signifies nothing."

"Perhaps, and perhaps not."

Selena raised an eyebrow at Shoryu, silently asking for him to elaborate.

"Among my people, it has been said that dreams sometimes hold the power of future fact. Upon occasion, they tell the tales of times gone past, history lessons meant to guide the errant back to their rightful path. And other times still, they are mere fluff, images and symbols without meaning or significance. But you do not believe that, do you, Miss Bradford?" His voice grew hushed and filled with hidden meanings, much like her nightmare.

Damn it all, she thought vehemently, *someone throw me a bone here.*

"Look, if you've got any idea what any of it's supposed to mean, just come out and say it. I'm tired of trying to read into things and decipher codes, solve puzzles that are seemingly impossible in design. Tell me what you think it means."

Shoryu looked at her with shock in his features, taken aback by her hostility.

Oh Hells, she thought, hanging her head as she rubbed her brow. The boy doesn't deserve such harsh treatment. With a sigh, she said, "It's my turn to apologize, Shoryu. I didn't mean it like that. It's just, well, I've a bit of a temper on me. Sort of comes with the job, you know?" She tried to force a smile, but she could feel it turn into a grimace, and so she just let her face go slack.

"I understand." Shoryu patted her roughly on the back.

Ye gods, the boy is strong, she thought as she lurched forward.

"What I believe is this. You fear that we shall have a confrontation with Richard Vandross and his armies inside of their lair, in Mount Toane. At least, that much I gather from your description of the caverns. You fear that more of us shall die there, which is not unlikely. As Byron said to me, not all of us shall survive this journey. It may be that it is my fate to join my ancestors in Khalentrab, which in the common tongue translates to 'paradise'. Then again, I may live on after Byron has led us into Mount Toane. It may even be that Byron himself does not fell Richard Vandross, but another among us. We cannot know these things until we make the attempt."

Shoryu put a hand on Selena's shoulder lightly, as much to reassure himself as her. "But I know one thing for certain, Miss Bradford: Mount Toane and Vandross's lair will be where this all comes to a conclusion. We shall survive until that time."

"What about David," Selena muttered as they walked in an ever-widening circle around the camp. "He should have been there with us in the end: instead he was snuffed out by treachery. A mad warlock's machinations took him before our journey's end, and they may well claim more among our small numbers, Shoryu. What then? How are we to live long enough to storm Vandross's lair when we are so few?" She nearly burst into tears, feeling helpless and small in the face of the odds they stood against. Vandross had thousands upon thousands of soldiers and minions at his beck and whim; they numbered less than ten men and women as a company.

"Think not on our disadvantage in numbers, but on our skills and powers. Did not we survive the onslaughts of Desanadron and Whitewood? Did not we survive this most recent battle? Demons of the dream world harassed us, and still we managed to overcome them." A look of battle-lust shined in his eyes, euphoria brought on by memories of victories taken, and perhaps a measure of lycanthrope rage. "No, Selena Bradford, Human and Pyromancer." H shook his head as he brought himself to a stop. He pointed his snout toward the moon high overhead, its nocturnal luminescence reflecting off of his eyes. "We shall fight on. In the end, we shall stop the madness of Richard Vandross."

The rest of their watch went past in utter silence, Selena shamed by Shoryu's courage, and the Cuyotai silenced by his own outburst.

* * * *

Thin shafts of sunlight filtered through clouds thick and gray with threats of snow and rain. As James Hayes and Ellen Daires awakened the sleeping members of the company, a howling wind tore through their small encampment, blankets blew yards away and had to be chased after, the cooking of a meal became nearly impossible. Selena kept raising fire from the pit, only to watch it be snuffed out by a powerful, arctic blast from the mountain paths.

The group unanimously decided that it would be easiest to simply eat the last of their dried provisions and move on. They had a hard trek ahead of them.

Morek Rockmight took the lead, directing the company to a small, almost hidden, footpath that would lead them at last into the mountain region. His footing was sure, his ambling gait slow enough to keep everyone together, but swift enough to ensure progress throughout the day. In this manner, Morek lead them for several hours, ever moving upward and forward, gaining elevation and losing heat as they went. The forks in the paths he led them down carried little wind or precipitation, often with a jutting path of mountain rock over their heads to protect them from the downpour that came after three hours of marching.

It was a mix of rain and snow, soft white crystals of cold floating down between hammering droplets of clear water. A strange sight, Byron thought, entranced by the display of dual downpours. Each member of the company, he saw as he looked around him, was equally fascinated, save Morek, who had probably once seen this sort of thing on a regular basis.

Too bad, Byron thought. *The Boxer sees such wondrous things as this, yet thinks them mundane and ordinary.*

The majesty of such territories might be lost on one who lived among them though, the Dread Knight admitted to himself. Morek would probably think the desert of Mukabia, also known as The Desperation, in the east to be fascinating, since it would be unlike any environment he had seen.

At around noon, Morek guided the company into a small alcove in the side of a cliff face, a small area protected from the wind and elements by the natural gut rock around them.

Shoryu did not join them, informing them that he would return shortly after finding food. The remainder of the company huddled around a fire conjured by Selena, warming themselves with its magical heat and swigs of the strange liquor that Alex produced from his Fairy space.

It had a thick, brackish appearance, Byron noted, declining a sip, but the others seemed to like it well enough.

Shoryu returned only ten minutes later, a goat slung over his shoulder with a single arrow shaft sticking out from between its eyes.

What he left behind was the pack of mountain lions that had surrounded the goat. Gripped by a sudden and uncontrollable urge, Shoryu's field of vision had burned crimson, and he had slavered madly as he tore into the mountain lions with claws and teeth. The first he felled by darting past it, slashing its throat open with his right hand. Using his momentum, he had bowled into the second of the animals, tumbling with it in his arms. When he landed atop the animal, he bit deep into its throat and wrenched his head back, spraying blood onto the hard packed snow of the path.

The third of the lions pounced on his back, but as its paws squeezed his shoulders, Shoryu reached back, grabbing it by the scruff. He yanked it over his head, and held it there, letting it thrash helplessly. Inside of his mind, he'd wailed helplessly. *This is the price*, he thought. The price of the blood I give mighty Byron.

With a heave, he'd lofted the mountain lion over his head, and brought it down hard over one knee, snapping its spine and killing it.

He had turned then to find the mountain goat paralyzed with fear. In control of himself once again, he trained a single arrow on its head, and fired. This he brought back to the company after using fur to wash the blood from his hands and mouth.

"A most excellent shot, my love," Ellen observed with a pang of guilt. A Gaiamancer, Byron recalled, would only eat meat if no other food could be gathered. But Shoryu surprised them all by also throwing down a small satchel filled with a strange red fruit.

"Minda berries," Morek grumbled. "A tad too sweet for my tastes, thanks all the same lad."

"Oh, they are mostly for Ellen." The young Hunter took the goat aside to skin it and remove the most usable sections of meat. The Elven Gaiamancer immediately picked away at the berries, her hunger apparent as she ravished the whole lot of them in a manner of minutes, leaning back with her head in the crook of her arm as she relaxed to digest.

"You oughtn't to have eaten those so swiftly, friend Elf," Morek said, cleaning his nails with a sharp bit of rock.

Ellen sat up and gave him a puzzled look. "Give it a few minutes, you'll understand," the Dwarf said with a half-smile.

Shoryu handed Selena the best chunks of goat he had taken and produced arrows from his mystical quiver. The Pyromancer pierced each cut of meat with an arrow, handing everyone their own cut. They all held their bits of meat over the fire, taking in the bitter smell of cooked goat meat. Only Byron and Ellen declined the meal, neither having a taste for the meat, each for different reasons.

Byron drifted, then came to his senses. Where was Ellen? Byron looked to where she had lain only a few minutes before. He raised an eyebrow bone at Morek, who chuckled under his breath.

"Minda berries give you the raging trots if you've never had them before," he whispered to the Dread Knight. "She's probably gone to make a toilet hole for a few minutes' use."

Byron couldn't help but laugh a little, but he saw the concern on Shoryu's face and stopped.

"Will she be all right?" Shoryu asked in a whisper full of dread.

Morek burst into further laughter, apparently finding hilarity in the company's general ignorance of his country.

"She'll be fine, lad, just fine. But you may have to carry her for a bit after she's done with the lee. Ha ha ha ha haaa."

Shortly after that, Ellen returned, exhausted and walking with a strange gait.

The company pressed on, Shoryu carrying the poor Elven girl on his back. After a few minutes' walk, Byron noted of several slain mountain lions that appeared to have been half buried in a snow bank, as though to cover them from discovery. He could just make out the pattern of claw marks on one's throat, and looked at Shoryu, who strode a little ahead of him. *This is the cost*, he thought. *And it will only grow.*

The afternoon passed swiftly, except for Ellen and Byron the company renewed by a fresh meal.

Upward they climbed, slowly but steadily thanks to Morek's keen knowledge of his homelands, choosing the more discreet and shallow paths.

In six hours, the sun began its slow descent toward the horizon, and the northern winds that they had mostly been protected from by cliff faces and higher mountain ranges blew through the cuts they marched into.

Ten or twenty minutes after the sun set, Morek led the company into another alcove, this one more like a cave.

Selena called fire to her hands, waving it around the cave walls to ensure they were not sharing space with anyone or anything.

After a cursory check in every direction, the company was satisfied that they were alone, and Selena brought her fire into a central blaze in the cavern, giving the party light and heat for the evening.

Shoryu had packed away some of the meat from the earlier meal, enough to satisfy everyone's hunger, and some of the berries that his beloved had eaten too many of during their midday meal. Ellen took only a few, letting the potency of the sweet fruit work for her instead of shoving a handful down her gullet as before.

Conversation was kept to a minimum as they ate, but all eyes focused on Byron and Morek as the meal was finished.

"What will we do when we get to this monastery we are searching for?" Shoryu asked, his voice low and quiet.

Ellen rested with her head in his lap, and the young Cuyotai Hunter stroked her hair as he spoke. "What if they don't have the Orb?"

Byron had been prepared for this question and was able to respond immediately.

"If they don't have it, my young friend, it is likely that they have taken it into one of the Dwarven cities to the west. If that is so, then we will take what hospitality the order can give us. If we are invited to stay the night, we shall, but one night only. Then, we shall depart for Traithrock, the nearest Dwarven city, and capital of the territory owned and governed by the Dwarves."

Byron noticed that all eyes had fixed on Morek, who was shaking his head when Byron looked at him. "What is the matter, master Dwarf?"

"There ain't no way, Monks or no, that such an artifact would be allowed into my city." The Dwarven Boxer folded thick arms across his chest. He kept his eyes shut and his head down as he spoke further. "We are a proud and fierce people, as you have said, mighty Byron. We are among the hardest laborers in all the land, our smithies are renowned for their work, and our armies are vast and potent. But we are also, much to my chagrin, a superstitious people by and large." He finally looked up into the faces of the rest of the company. "As a nation, we have only a handful of citizens who recognize or follow any established religions. Dwarven faith is mostly a gathering of superstitions we've carried with us for generations, and with each new flock of young, the number of those superstitions grows. We have certain established beliefs, but no belief system, like the Order of Oun or the Prekanadan," he said, referring to an old Minotaur tribal religion.

At first, Byron wondered how Morek could know of such a system, but it wasn't too surprising after he reasoned it through. Minotaurs, like Dwarves, were mountainous folk, and seldom strayed from their tribes, which were arranged according to faith rather than family.

"Artifacts like the Orbs of Eden's Serpent or even the ever-touted Staff of Order would not be welcome in our cities. Magical weapons and armor, we've got no issue with: we understand the nature of them. But religion-based artifacts worry us."

"So if the monastery doesn't have the Orb, where might the Monks try to take it?" James Hayes's tone betrayed a hint of despair. He obviously wasn't very comfortable in these mountains, and the prospect of not finding their quarry swiftly sat ill with him.

"Then they'd be forced to take it into the northwestern most range," Morek replied, leaning back and pulling out a simple block of wood from his rucksack. A moment later, he produced a small knife, and began carving away at the block. "And we'd best hope that if they've gone that way, they didn't go far. Dragons live in those caves and valleys, letting their presence be well known. They respect my people for who they are, and the fact that we make no trouble for them. About a century ago, a few settlers from Traithrock decided they'd try to go and establish a village in that area. Needless to say, they came back in quite a hurry."

"What happened," asked Shoryu, eager for a story, his eyes distant and unfocused.

He would play a little image reel in his mind, Byron thought, as he had whenever a member of the company shared a tale. Just like a young man with dreams of adventure. Adventures where the heroes all lived happily ever after. Their own journey had already brought them much more pain and suffering than accomplishment, and Byron longed suddenly for the days when a fairy tale might cheer him up. Such stories, he realized, were rubbish, the stuff of too much imagination and not enough harsh reality. In the fairy tales he remembered, demons were always defeated with relative ease, or by some simple trick the hero kept up his sleeve. And no matter how hurt the heroes of those stories were, they always pulled through, finding cures to curses, and healing from friends and the earth itself. What hope could those fictions have against truths like Shadowbeasts and warlocks, madmen who schemed constantly to bring misery to all the peoples of a land? None.

He stood and moved away from the company as Morek told them how the Red Dragon Caamur had told the Dwarven settlers to flee, while he torched their homes with his breath of fire.

He shook his head in disgust at his despair, and settled at the edge of the cave to take the first watch. The company discussed who would take which watch, and Byron soon found himself sitting across from Shoryu, who grinned at him like a devil.

"Is there something amusing about me, Shoryu," he snapped, a bit too harshly for his own liking. But the young Cuyotai Hunter seemed to have learned a while ago how Byron's moods could be properly gauged, and continued grinning.

"Not exactly, good Byron," Shoryu admitted, looking off into the west, where the cave entrance faced. "Ellen and I have been discussing what we will do when this mess is sorted out. My friend, we are to be wed in her home city of Whitewood. When first I left the ruins of my home with you, those many moons ago, I thought I would become a man without a purpose, without a people, certainly without a family. Now—" he looked at Byron with tears in his eyes.

The Dread Knight was taken aback by the shimmering dampness in the young Cuyotai man's eyes; was he afraid, or saddened by something he didn't speak of? Or were they, perhaps, tears of happiness? Byron had heard of such things, but had never experienced them himself.

"Now, my greatest friend," Shoryu continued, "I will have all of those things and more, with her. And I have you to thank." Shoryu walked over to Byron, offering him his hand.

Ah, a good handshake. Byron offered his hand in return.

With a heave of unexpected strength, Shoryu hauled the Dread Knight to his feet and clasped him in a hug that nearly bent his armor.

Byron clapped the man-boy on the back as he returned the embrace, thankful for contact.

As Shoryu held him at arms' length, he smiled, tears now running down his furry cheeks. "I hope you can be there when it all comes together, good Byron. Either in body, or in spirit, you are always welcome at our side." Shoryu returned to his side of the cave entrance and resumed his watch, as did Byron. The Dread Knight felt at ease, at peace with himself for the first time in days. Shoryu, it seemed, had come to terms with the idea that Byron would not retain his life after the defeat of Richard Vandross. That made things easier on him,

Byron realized with a shock. He had been terrified of leaving the Cuyotai Hunter in a state of loss. Maybe, for once, things would go well for someone.

* * * *

"Byron," the Voice called softly in the darkness of the undead warrior's slumber.

He had been dreaming of his greatest victories as a Human Paladin, a Commander in the ranks of the Order of Oun. As he stood on the field of some unremembered battle, he smelled grave soil, and felt the ground tremble beneath him, the threat of an earthquake imminent. As he looked down, a line ripped through the ground, splitting the earth beneath him and creating a gap through which he plummeted.

He felt the flesh on his skull burn away, but it caused him no great pain. Blackened, curled chunks of his face fell away as he descended ever-further into the abyss.

With a sudden impact, he found himself lying flat on his back in the middle of the cemetery that held Voice. He rolled over onto his stomach, disoriented by the impact with the hard packed dirt, his head tilting.

"Byron."

"You have interrupted a rather enjoyable dream, Voice," he growled as he flexed his fingers, checking to make certain nothing was broken.

He seemed whole and intact, but he didn't want to take any risks; after the incident with the Dreamstalkers, he knew that dreams could be deadly.

There was a soft laughter.

"Ha ha ha. You have kept your sense of humor. That is well, mighty Byron. The Keeper Locke has spoken with me, and given me information. Will you hear it?"

Byron nodded, and walked over to one of the shaggy-looking trees to lean against it, his arms folded across his chest.

"Good. I have already told you that Richard Vandross does not intend to dominate the land as its ruler. He intends to feed off of the land's fear and misery for millennia. But he risks destroying the world utterly, Byron. Once he has the final Orb of Eden's Serpent, he will not be able to sate his thirst for carnage and rampage with just the land of Tamalaria. Far to the south, across the Great Open Blue, lies another continent, which has been mostly a rumor here in Tamalaria. I speak of the land of Tallowmere. He will eventually tire of reigning over this land, and shall seek to feed on the people of that land as well, Byron. His madness shall consume him, for the Glorious Mother of Destruction shall drive him beyond himself."

"So what can we do about it?" Byron waved his hands in a defeated gesture. "We are already in search of the fifth Orb, and there isn't much we can do until we find it. Even then, what can we do to keep it from him? He'll come after it until he has it and everyone in his way is dead or dying."

"The Orb of Eden's Serpent can be destroyed," the Voice declared.

Destroyed? Byron was caught in a moment of surprise. *Can that be done?*

As if reading his thoughts, which likely Voice was doing, it responded.

"Yes, mighty Byron. It can be destroyed. But the magic and force required to do it is vast. Within your group lies the power and potential to do it, but you must all be very careful when making the attempt. If something goes wrong, one of you will end up absorbing the artifact. It needs a host, and shall look for any opening to make one of your number over to its own designs, which won't be good at all. The Orbs are sentient beings within, and seek always to be joined to one another. Do you understand?"

Byron nodded. If a member of the company absorbed the Orb, he or she would be compelled to join Vandross's cause, and the warlock would likely destroy that person in order to gain possession of the final Orb. The Orb itself would likely do nothing to defend its new host, that it might rejoin all of the others within Vandross's soul.

"How exactly do we destroy it? Tell me what must be done." Byron felt a jostling in his shoulders. Someone was trying to wake him up.

"I shall reveal all to you when the Orb is in your possession. Until then, you have much work to do, Byron. Go well." The Voice echoed from the darkness.

"Stay well," Byron responded, rejoining the waking world. As the yellow lights flickered in his empty eye sockets, he saw that Morek Rockmight held a handful of snow over him, ready to press it to his skull.

"That shan't be necessary," he told the Dwarf as he sat up. He looked out of the cave entrance into a world veiled by expanding blankness, snow falling in sheets over the mountainsides. The day's trek would be arduous, and they might not make great progress. Still, movement had to be made.

The company packed up its few belongings and prepared to journey into the wintry landscape, Morek in the lead, Byron bringing up the rear.

Selena stayed in the center of the group, expanding her magical heat to each member of the party, that they might not be subdued by the chill of the air and snow.

As they made their way around the side of the cliff face they had camped in, the blast of a northern wind met them head-on, immediately slowing them to a crawl. Only Morek moved now with any kind of assurance, his footing balanced and calculated, leaving as good a trail as his stout body would allow.

For a while, they proceeded in much the same fashion as they had the day before, changing routes and pathways to continue climbing higher. But at around midday Morek took them through a tunnel in one of the rock walls. On the other side of the narrow, short pathway, they marched down a slope toward what looked like a small village.

The slope ended two or three hundred feet away from the outermost dwelling, but their progress here was unimpeded, as mountains cut the wind off in all directions.

This appeared to be a secret valley, hidden from the rest of the world, and isolated from the worst of the weather by its elevation and natural borders.

"This is the village of Contestia," Morek pronounced, looking back at the company. "We are now east of Traithrock, and not far west of the monastery we seek. An underground series of tunnels leads from this village to the gates of the monastery. Here, the servants and training hopefuls reside, as well as the family members whom the Monks cannot train. Their elderly, their common workers, their children, all reside here." He related these facts with an air of respect. When he stood twenty feet from the village, he brought the company to a stop. "We'll wait here for them to give a sign."

As the company waited, an elderly man dressed head to foot in dark green robes with black roses embroidered on them approached. He leaned heavily on a walking staff, one hand on his bent back, his long white beard nearly touching the snow.

Byron looked at the old man's feet, and was surprised to find that he wore nothing more than wooden sandals. Surely the old man suffered from the cold?

The elder's eyes narrowed as he looked at Morek, who gave him a deep bow. The old man raised a gray, bushy eyebrow, and smiled in turn, bowing in the same fashion to the Dwarven Boxer.

"Greetings, Morek, master of fists," the old man said in a congenial voice. "I am pleased to see you again. Much time has passed since your last visit." The elder put a hand on Morek's shoulder.

"And greetings to you, master Wong." Morek put one hand on the man's opposing shoulder. "Master of grapples."

As Morek said the word *grapples*, the old man flinched and twisted, vaulting high over Morek's head, using his momentum and Morek's body weight to toss the Dwarf at Byron and the rest of the company.

They all moved aside, shocked into silence.

Morek landed on his feet, leaning forward with his left hand on the ground for support, and the old man, master Wong, followed swiftly behind with his staff flailing through the air at him. Morek dodged and weaved, strafing around Wong with his arms up to block any blows the old man delivered. Finally, as Wong swung overhead, Morek rolled to the side and forward, standing up with his knuckles thrusting just underneath the old master's jaw before he stayed his hand.

Neither man moved; Byron saw that Morek had essentially declared a winning blow, but that the dwarf did not see that the wise old master had brought a knife point to his side.

"It appears, good master Morek, that we have a draw," the monk said.

Morek looked down at the knife blade. Byron heard him mutter a curse before withdrawing from the old man.

"It is well, good Morek." Master Wong threw his hands in the air and embraced the Dwarf, then leading him back towards the company, who were looking to one another in confusion.

"What just happened Morek," James Hayes asked as the Dwarf and old Human drew near.

"Oh, we do this every time I come to visit, just to make sure we're each doing all right, keeping up our practice and abilities. Folks, I'd like you all to meet master Fei Chi Wong, the leader of the village. He used to be the headmaster of the monastery," Morek added as the old Monk bowed deeply to the company.

"Greetings. I would like to know your names, so that in the future, I might know who good master Morek's friends were."

"I am James Hayes," said the Paladin as he stepped forward, inclining his head slightly to the Monk. "I am a Paladin, formerly of the Order of Oun. A pleasure to meet you, sir." He extended a hand.

Master Wong shook it a moment, then turned his eyes back to the company. Byron had kept well back and out of plain sight the entire time, keeping his shadows wrapped around his upper body. He would postpone this meeting for as long as he could.

"I am Shoryu Tearfang," said the young Cuyotai Hunter, stepping forward through the group with Ellen holding his hand. "I am a Hunter, and the last survivor of my tribe. I have a great deal of respect for Morek, for his prowess in battle is great." Shoryu bowed, and Ellen stepped closer.

"I am Ellen Daires, Elf and Gaiamancer, sir," she said, her voice small and demure.

"I am Selena Bradford, Pyromancer," said the crimson-clad woman as she stepped forward.

Master Wong fawned for a moment, taking her hand and kissing it.

Selena stood shocked as he held her hand.

"I have heard of you, Sorcerer Supreme Bradford," rasped the old man, his eyes squinting shut as he smiled widely at her. "Your power over fire is well known. Perhaps you could warm my bed tonight, hmm?" The old man grinned like a fool.

Selena took a step back in disgust, her face stuck in a gaping expression of shock.

"Erm, don't mind him," chuckled Morek as he scratched the back of his head, nervous and awkward. "Master Wong's become a bit of a lecher in his golden years." The old Monk leered at Selena, who made a dash to stand behind Byron.

Oh, just great, thought the Dread Knight. Let's call some more attention to the undead creature whom half the land still knows as a tyrant. "See that little fellah, master Wong," Morek said, pointing to the Ki Fairy. "That's Alex."

"Ah, yes, a trickster Fairy," rasped Wong as he tilted his head to get a better look at Alex.

The Ki Fairy had turned himself with his back to the old man and Dwarf, and had proceeded to moon them.

"Oh. That is rude, you little imp." Wong raised his staff and brought it down on Byron's shoulder, where Alex had been a second earlier. A loud metal ting resounded through the air of the valley, and Wong looked straight up at Byron's face.

"And I, am Byron, leader of this company," Byron rumbled, trying to keep his tone neutral. "You might know me as Byron of Sidius."

"Yes, I indeed know this," Wong said with a squinty-eyed smile. "I also know you as the man who, not long ago, saved the cities of Desanadron and

Whitewood. Word travels fast through our network of wandering Monks, Byron formerly of Sidius." The old man turned in the direction of the village.

Byron stood shocked, glued to his place in the snow; how had word of his deeds already come this far? Could it be that he had at last shed the reputation of Tanarak's servant? Anything, it seemed, was possible.

"Come now," the Monk called over his shoulder. "Let us offer you our hospitality and answers to any questions you might have."

As the company followed, Byron felt an aura of magic, increasing in intensity as he drew nearer to the village. No snow touched the rooftops, or the streets of the village, and a moment after he made this observation, he felt himself pass through some sort of barrier, into a mid-spring-like environment, the heat pleasant and unexcessive, the grasses high, and the smell that of outdoor cooking fires.

"This is incredible," commented James Hayes as the elder Monk led them down the main thoroughfare. "You've used magic to keep the entire village protected from the elements. Do you use the same magic to grow your crops and tend your animals?"

"Yes, indeed master Paladin," said Wong a smile permanently glued to his lips. "But it is not magic, as such. We Monks use spiritual energies that come from within ourselves, and within all living things. We manipulate these energies and use them to our gain. As for the protection from the elements, that is taken care of by strategically placed sutras, which must be replaced every few days. I tend to this task as a part of my duties. Come, I would like you all to meet the other elders."

Wong took the company down a couple of side streets to a low, long building made of cherry wood. The sounds of old men arguing in a strange language issued from within, and master Wong slid a thin door to the side to admit the company into the entry room, which also served as the main meeting hall. Several knee-level tables had been pushed together, and six other elderly Monks sat on their knees on either side, gesturing wildly with their hands as they spat words that sounded guttural and fierce. As Wong cleared his throat loudly, intentionally, they ceased whatever argument they were engaged in, and stood to face the company. Each man looked to be in his golden years, even the one Elven elder.

"Greetings, elders of this humble village. May I introduce an old friend whom you know, and some of his companions?" Wong first introduced Morek, who bowed deeply to the elders. They returned the bow as a group, and smiled at the Dwarven Boxer.

"Have you been well, master of fists," one old Human asked.

"Indeed, I have master Pi'shar," Morek replied with a smile. The two made some comment to one another in the Monks' strange tongue, and had a good laugh afterwards. Byron came forward and leaned in close to Morek, as well as James Hayes.

"You can understand what they're saying," asked Hayes before Byron could utter the same question.

"Oh yes. It just takes some time to study the language before you get the hang of it," Morek whispered back.

Wong introduced the rest of the company in the same fashion, and after he was done, approached the tables of elders.

"Now, may I introduce the elders? Myself, you already know. This," he said, indicating the Elven elder. "Is master Lou Ming Wa, a great combat Monk in his prime. He is a master of the art of Jut-kwo, an art of kicks and knees."

The old Elf bowed, and Byron heard a slight pop of joints and bones. How old was this man? Elves lived for thousands of years before they died of age, so this particular Monk must have seen much of the comings and goings of things over the last millennia.

"This is master Pi'shar," Wong continued, moving to the first Human. "He is a master of the art of Kei-rei, an art that focuses on self-defense techniques. This, is master Julong," he indicated the only Jaft among the company of elders. Surprisingly, Byron noticed, the man did not carry the usual funk of his Race: the smell should have been overpowering in such a building, but it wasn't even there. "Master Julong is a general practitioner of martial arts, and one of the few Jafts wise enough to fully master the art of sutras."

The old, blue-skinned humanoid gave a deep bow to the company.

"This, is Master Voodon." Wong waved his hand back to indicate the bowing Lizardman. All of the elder Monks were clad in the same exact garments as Master Wong, with the only difference being the size of their robes, and the color of their collar, which must have meant something, Byron thought. "Master Voodon is a skilled practitioner of the art of Bruk-haja, a Lizardman-developed martial art that focuses on the unarmed breaking of bones and rending of muscles. Our fifth elder, is master Tuk-zwei," he said as an ancient, hunched-over Minotaur stepped away from the table to better be seen. Both horns appeared to have been sharpened with care, and his long, black goatee shone in the lamp light with oil. He had an ear missing, with a burn line where it had been. "He is a master of Panther style, a kung fu which requires great grace."

Great grace, huh? Byron thought. The old Minotaur didn't look like he could make it to the bathroom on his own in his present state.

"Where is Master Halicut?" Morek looked at the second Human, who had not yet been named.

Wong's smile faded instantly as he shook his head.

"He has been taken from us, master Morek." He sighed, his voice turned to thick phlegm. "He was my most trusted and valued friend in life, but none of our efforts could heal his heart. He was simply too old. But in his stead stands the newest member of our board of elders, master Robert Spore."

The silver-haired Human stepped forward.

Spore, Byron thought. *Oh no.* Could David have been this man's son? If so, Byron had a terrible task ahead of him.

"Konichiwa." The Human master approached the company. Though aged, master Spore did not appear to have the burden of years on him that his colleagues suffered. He stopped only a few strides from Byron's massive form, his eyebrows twitching, his hands clasped behind his back. "You are known to us for your deeds in the southern cities, Byron. Your struggle against the madman Richard Vandross is told of far and wide. Yet I sense you are troubled, despite your victories. What bothers you?"

Byron fought to keep his composure, to remain calm, and to be ready for the worst reaction.

"Master Spore, did you have a son by the name of David," he asked hesitantly.

"David? No, David Spore is my nephew. How do you know him?"

Well, at least it wouldn't be as hard now, Byron thought with an inward sigh.

"He traveled with us from Whitewood, master Spore. He fought at our side valiantly in the Elven capital, and on our way here. But, Richard Vandross and one of his minions set a trap for us. There was a particularly fierce battle, and we were victorious over our enemies. But, David didn't make it." He related the entirety of the battle and the events that brought David to his ruin.

The old Monk stood still as Byron related how Phazion Lurik had worked his way into the company, gaining their sympathy and trust, and finally how the Lizardman assassin had betrayed them all. When the telling was done, Robert Spore nodded, a severe frown creasing his lips. He placed one soft hand on Byron's shoulder, reaching up almost as far as his arm could go to do so.

"The fault is not yours, Byron. Nor was it David's. He only had one arm, and still he managed to be one of our best and brightest. No, the fault lies with the conniver, Richard Vandross. The day you destroy him, as I am certain you shall, we shall properly mourn the loss of my nephew. Now, he is in Nirvana, with his mother and father. For the time being, we must be satisfied with that knowledge. Come, master Wong, we have matters of business to discuss, and our guests have not yet been given a place that they might rest and ask their questions."

Wong bowed to the silver-haired Spore, and guided Byron and his companions away from the council hall. Up the street, to the north, he pointed out a quaint, two story family house.

"This is the home reserved for our most honored guests. There are several bedrooms, a small study, two washrooms, a den, and a kitchen with dining room. There are foodstuffs inside, but if there is anything you want specially prepared or brought for your own cooking, you need only ask Daikatsu. He is the caretaker, and he resides over there." Wong pointed across the road to a well-made cottage. "If he is not in the guest home or his own abode, he is likely at the library, which is at the end of the street, down there." He pointed back the way they had come. "Have you any questions, honored guests?"

"We have many, old friend," grumbled Morek. "But they may wait for a few hours while you finish your business with the board. Come see us as soon as you can, for the matters we need to discuss are grave." Morek bowed to the old master as Wong turned and shuffled away on his wooden sandals.

"Well, all those in favor of going in and having a real meal, say aye," he said to the group with a wide grin. Nobody argued, and the Dwarven Boxer led them into the main entry room of the guesthouse. Opposite the main door was another sliding door, and the entry room appeared to be for hanging coats and removing shoes. Morek took his boots off, and the smell of his feet nearly knocked a couple of the others to the ground. He slid the other door open, and walked into the den.

James Hayes, Selena, and Ellen all removed their own boots and greaves, leaving only Byron fully armored and clothed. As they entered into the den in a single file fashion, the Dread Knight took a good look at their arrangements.

The den had a decided martial arts theme, with wall scrolls hung everywhere, rugs of austere design draped on the floor with care, and the furniture arranged in a fashion he had heard referred to as *fung shui*. He personally didn't care for it: it was too precise, too elegant for his taste. He had become accustomed to a soldier's home, one with a family, where the furniture was arranged to allow for family closeness and conservation of space. There were no toys or footwear scattered about, no tankards of half-drank ale or tobacco pipes laid out and forgotten. If this was how guests kept their living quarters among the Monks, what would a resident's home look like? He shuddered involuntarily at the idea.

James Hayes, however, didn't appear to have qualms with the appearance or layout of the room. He had already plunked himself down on one of the chairs with a heave, the sound of creaking leather chair cushions grinding in Byron's ears as the Paladin made himself comfortable.

Shoryu was admiring one of the weapons on a display pedestal, carefully enclosed in glass.

Selena seemed to be scrunching her nose up at the smell of the potpourri bowls that hung from the ceiling. Byron agreed with her mentally; he didn't care for the aroma of the room either. Morek had disappeared, presumably to have a look around. And Byron couldn't see where Ellen had gotten off to. Probably ran off to find a bathroom, he thought with a silent chuckle. The poor Elven girl was still combating the effects of Munda berries when they had arrived in town, and hadn't hit a toilet the whole time.

From an archway in the back left corner of the room, Morek popped his head into view. "One of the washrooms is down at the end of this hall, along with a pair of bedrooms. I'm gonna have meself a bath," he announced, much to everyone's relief.

James Hayes and Shoryu both sighed as Morek disappeared from view, relieved that the Dwarf was going to clean himself.

Ellen returned to the den a moment after Byron settled himself into one of the huge chairs by the fireplace, a small earthenware bowl in her cupped hands.

"Friends, I have prepared a soup in the kitchen, if you wish to have a hot meal. Also, there is a bathroom just upstairs from the kitchen. It seems there are several ways to get to the second floor, most thankfully," she added, blushing. They all understood what she had to do as soon as they were inside, and Morek had already claimed the other washroom for his own purposes.

"This place seems awfully big for guests, my lord," squeaked Alex in Byron's 'ear'. "I'm guessing they don't get company very often."

"Yes, well, they are Monks, after all, Alex," Byron whispered. He had finally gotten comfortable, and intended to knock off for a couple of hours' rest, or at least until master Wong returned to speak with them about the Orb. He would handle the questions, he decided, for Morek seemed a bit too friendly to press the matter if it needed to be pressed. The Boxer had too much respect and acquaintance with these people to drive a hard line if they hesitated to answer their questions. Besides, Byron thought, if they truly respect us and what we're doing, they'll help us quickly, for time is of the essence. Without a second thought, he lapsed into silent, empty sleep, enjoying the nothingness of simple rest.

* * * *

Richard Vandross stood before the assembled platoon that would dare Dwarves and Dragons in the hope that he might gain possession of the final Orb of Eden's Serpent. His top men, those who he had assembled to formulate the plan for this journey, stood before bunches of their own men and women, barking commands and giving speeches about the glory that would be theirs. The only one without his own unit was the Beastmaster, Sergeant Robin. He stood with Talus Cur, the Illeck Q Mage, before a handful of mages who were locking spells onto their robes and weapons. An interesting and useful trick, Vandross thought with a smile.

Locking spells allowed magic users to expend double the amount of magical energy on a spell in order to secure the spell to a weapon or body part. On command it would be automatically cast from its anchoring object without the need for the caster to expend any energy at that moment. It was a tactic used primarily by mages enlisted in armies, such as these.

Most of them sagged and wobbled after the expenditure of so much mystic force, but they would be better off later on down the road, as walking would not require too much concentration or effort. Spells that took a long time to cast, perhaps a fatal amount of time in a confrontation, would be at their instant command, and with the right combination of spells, even a Dragon could be humbled.

Major Tamriel stood with his Sergeants, Moran and Doran, discussing something in their unique tongue, their tones low and secretive. Being overheard was inevitable, however, as they were huge and deep in voice. Vandross walked up and down the line before them, inspecting the ranks as closely as he could without making anyone nervous. Colonel Molis had begun a conversation with General and Shadowbeast Prime Vilec Roak, apparently about the Colonel's choice of men. Molis had selected combatants from each walk of life available in Vandross's vast and still growing army; Black Fur Werewolf Berserkers, Human Alchemists, Shadowbeast warriors, Human Hunters and Knights, a handful of vicious-looking undead creatures called Revenants, and a pair of Vandross's recently created Dreadnaughts. The

Revenants, Vandross thought with a smug smile, were not the most effective creatures, but their touch turned everything to decay, rotting away even metal if it were exposed to their fingertips for long. They moved swiftly, and some were even capable of speech and coherent thought, an ability that had earned them the nickname of uberzombie.

Dreadnaughts were essentially a collection of body parts from various different beings and Races pulled together and held tight by magic. The flesh and blood of their structure came from dead creatures, and so Dreadnaughts were considered an affront to anyone who valued life. What species, exactly the pieces came from didn't matter, for they could all be held by the magic required to create one of these monstrosities. The four that Molis had hand picked were the best of the two or three dozen Vandross had constructed, for much of their makeup had come from beings that possessed magic. The Dreadnaughts would have access to a limited number of the spells wielded by the former owners of its flesh, and thus they would be a great force to be reckoned with, both physically and magically.

His expedition's forces looked to be quite capable of taking on an entire nation just by itself, he thought. But they would be dealing with two of the land's greatest defenders: Dwarves and Dragons. He would need every last advantage available to him when they sought the final Orb of Eden's Serpent.

Richard Vandross finished his inspection, and turned toward the northwest, focusing his inner eye. To teleport the entire unit to the mountains, he would have to tear a rift in space and sustain it long enough to get through himself. Doing so would require a colossal amount of energy, but he would be aided by Talus Cur, who would temporarily amplify the effectiveness of Vandross's magic. The Q Mage would then set up a magical barrier around the unit on the other side of the rift, to protect them from anyone or anything that might descend on them right away.

Vandross sincerely hoped there would be no confrontation right away; he would be physically drained when he finally passed through the rift, and might not be able to defend himself properly. He refused to show any sign of weakness before his top commanders, though, lest they decide to mutiny against him. The only one who simply could not fight him was Grigory Molis, whom he had created.

He closed his eyes and sought the exact position he wanted to arrive at with his forces. After a moment, his mental vision cleared. He saw that it was snowing heavily at the base of the hills leading into the mountains. He swept his mental eyes around the area, looking for a good opening that might offer some shelter from the cold. The Khan, Shadowbeasts and other demons would be fine, but the Humans and Illecks would not do well in such a rapid climate change.

As he cast his gaze around, something caught his eye. He turned his attention to it and saw the remains of a camp, a couple of days old. The aura of the Morning Glory hung heavily in the air, as well as that of Byron of Sidius himself.

The Dread Knight's Redemption

Blast it all, he thought with a scowl. *The Dread Knight is ahead of us.*

Vandross summoned forth his power, and brought his palms together before him. As chaotic spasms of energy ripped through his arms, he clutched at the empty air, finding purchase on solid reality after a moment of grasping.

Taking solid hold, he tore his arms back in a sweeping gesture, feeling the fabric of space and time rupture just before him. As he opened his good eye, he saw that he had created rift large enough for swift movement of his men. The time required would be shortened.

"Cur," he yelled, keeping his eye fixed on the rift, channeling energy into it from his palms.

The Q Mage sprinted toward him, and as he mumbled strange incantations under his breath, a ring of yellow energy enveloped Vandross's feet, swirling up in a spiraling pillar around the warlock, sustaining him and feeding his magic.

Without any further order, Amon, Molis, Robin, Vilec Roak and Tamriel motioned their men forward, moving into the rift and disappearing from sight.

As the last of them surged through, Vandross stalked forward, holding onto the power flowing from his body as he crept closer to the rift. When he felt his arms would be torn from his body, he lunged through the gap, and came out of the other side onto a snow-covered slope. A slight miscalculation, he noted, but Byron's campsite was only a few dozen yards away.

Colonel Molis, his breath misting in the cool northern air, snapped off a smart salute. "Your orders, my lord?"

Vandross looked out across the unit, seeing that the transfer from one side of the continent clear across to the other had not just drained him, but most of the soldiers. Even the magic users, except for Talus Cur, looked like they were on the verge of collapse.

"Set up camp, Colonel. We shall rest here until nightfall. Under cover of night we shall move north and west. Have Amon send Khan scouts up into the hills to survey the area. I don't want any surprises."

"My lord, I can use some of my own men for the task," Vilec Roak rasped as he approached from behind.

Had he come through after Vandross? the one-eyed warlock wondered. That didn't matter at the moment, however. He had to establish control now that they were away from Mount Toane.

"No, Vilec. Amon's Khan are from the Allenian Hills, and are very accustomed to such tasks. They should scout and hunt this terrain. Besides," he added in a conspiratorial whisper, "they are much more expendable than your Shadowbeasts."

Vilec Roak grinned maliciously, nodding his agreement to Vandross. The Shadowbeast General darted off to issue his lord's will to Lieutenant Amon, who turned and barked orders to two slender Khan women.

Molis had moved away to give the order to set up camp, for nightfall was four or five hours off.

The camp would not be large or complicated: this wasn't a siege, just a rest stop. Vandross suddenly felt very tired, and unslung his rucksack to pull out a bedroll. He unfurled it on a clear patch of frosted grass, and tucked himself inside for a nap. The cold didn't bother him, for the Orbs of Eden's Serpent protected his body from the elements. But, he thought before passing out, it might eventually take a toll on some of the less hardy men and women of his unit.

"Feh," he grunted as he rolled over to get comfortable. "It doesn't matter. As long as I attain the last Orb." With these words on his tongue, he drifted off into a deep, and thankfully, dreamless slumber.

* * * *

As dusk settled in, Richard Vandross roused himself from his bedroll, listening to every sound around him. The conversations around him consisted mainly of what each man or woman in his army wanted out of being with him. Several of the higher-ranking females, to his surprise, admitted aloud that they wanted to feel the heat of his loins in their own—until they noticed he was awake. At that point, all conversation between the ladies of his unit ceased.

Still, a couple of them weren't half bad looking, he mused. He might take one of them on a colder night, help them keep warm. Vandross passed directly by them, stalking toward Colonel Molis, who had a pot of some black sludge brewing.

"Coffee, my lord?" Molis held up his own earthenware mug.

Vandross grabbed a nearby drinking cup made of pewter, dipping it into the pot for something to wake him up further. The liquid was foul but potent; he felt like he'd had a shock of lightning rip through him for just the briefest moment.

"You'll be wanting a report then, sir?"

Vandross said nothing, staring into the mountains but nodding just slightly.

"The two Khan scouts returned an hour ago, having ranged far ahead of us, my lord. The one who traveled east discovered signs of a small company, lord Vandross, most likely the Dread Knight and his fellows. The Khan who scouted west found no signs of their passing, but nearly came upon several Dwarven sentry patrols. A village lies not far from the top of these slopes. Traithrock is to the east of our current position, my lord, and we needn't worry about their capital forces if we avoid traveling that way. Thoughts, my lord?"

Vandross considered his available options; the capital of the Dwarven territories would be the most difficult to assail, but thankfully, their path would most likely keep them away from the walled fortress city. But other Dwarven cities would lie in their way to the west, and could not be assumed to be any less a threat.

"We should get going. By the time we get to the upper reaches and have a way into the west, it will be dark. Give the order to pack up and prepare to march, Colonel. And find Vilec Roak for me. He and I have something to discuss."

The half-demon saluted stiffly and shuffled off to carry out his orders.

Definitely a strange one, he is, Vandross thought. The half-demon seldom removed his armor, including his helmet, even to partake of meals. Without any fully visible face most of the time, Vandross found him difficult to identify in a pack of the Shadowbeasts, since his armor was a dark steel. Yet the half of him that was demon could not be Shadowbeast: he would defer to Vilec Roak much easier if such were the case.

Roak appeared at his elbow a moment after his latest musing, and cleared his throat to get Vandross's attention.

"You sent for me, lord Vandross?" hissed the Shadowbeast Prime.

" Indeed I did. But before I come to the true question I called you for, do you recall when I ordered Molis to come with us to Fort Flag? I don't regret the decision. I recall quite well his ability to slaughter those pew-hugging fools. But do you remember me ever actually ordering him to follow us?"

"No, my lordship, I can't say as I do."

"Hmm." Vandross rubbed his chin thoughtfully. "A mystery best left for another time. Now, to the heart of things. We will make our way toward the Dwarven village the scout spotted. Let Tamriel and his compatriots be on point as a vanguard. If he is correct in his analysis of the Dwarves' fear of his kind, we can use their village to stock up on supplies and get a feeling for these mountains. Perhaps even some information might be gathered from them. Prepare the ranks to fall in." He dismissed the General with a wave of his hand.

As the columns were formed and elements shifted to present a fighting force, Vandross swooped alongside the regiment. Every man and woman here was ready for bloodshed, eager for conflict; even the Illeck Talus Cur and his mages seemed spoiling for a chance to make vulgar displays of power. He would grant them their wishes if the Dwarves put up any resistance. He would likely incur some casualties on his side, but a few heads in exchange for glory seemed a paltry price to pay. The morale of the troops would be on the upswing in any event, and he would have even more committed soldiers at his command. Though he had little more than a hundred assembled, they would be a force to be reckoned with.

Despite the cold and wind, the troupe made good time up the slopes and foothills into the higher mountain range. The air became thin and stinging on reaching the upper heights, however, and progress slowed to a near crawl by midnight. Having the cover of night would do little good if they couldn't reach their destination before sunrise, which in these parts of the continent, came mighty early.

As he grumbled to himself, Vandross saw Colonel Molis issue a hand signal to Talus Cur, who sent two of his mages to the front of the marching elements. With a few hand gestures and garbled words, the mages seemed to part the wind coming at them, leaving clean, unmoving air for the troops to move through.

Aeromancers, Vandross thought with a smile. Masters of wind. Talus Cur had come prepared, much to Vandross's approval.

With the Aeromancers at the front of the main body, and the Renkas ahead of them to further shield them from the elements and any pitfalls, Vandross's company made better progress. Within two hours' time, they were atop a high ridge that led down into a valley. In the center of the valley, structures of stone, laden with snow and ice, sat arranged in a quaint pattern: the Dwarven village the scout had seen.

Vandross focused his energy, using his mental vision to see down into the village. Sentry posts were set up on each side of the village, giving the impression that even in this isolated town, the Dwarves expected trouble.

An ambush might be out of the question, Vandross realized, for the stout people of stone and rock lore were much more accustomed to their chosen environment than were any of the members of the expeditionary force at Vandross's command. The Khan might be able to maneuver their way down the slopes into the village undetected, but not for long, and not without difficulty. The Renkas, impervious to the wintry conditions, could stomp into the village, magic at the ready, razor-sharp claws rending the foremost guards with ease, but the entirety of the village would come to the aid of its guards. Neither tactic would be advisable.

The guards at the closest post appeared to be Dwarven gentlemen of middle age, their long, brown beards beginning to take on the flecks of gray that come with elder years. Their armor appeared to be wrought iron, uncolored and battered from time and use. These Dwarves obviously valued their money reserves, or else they'd have bought themselves some new equipment. But such was the nature of their Race: frugal, practical, and lethal.

Ah, Vandross thought with a smile, *but don't forget, superstitious.* The appearance of Renkas would surely frighten them, but not as much as the shadowy, slippery and conspicuous movements of a handful of Shadowbeasts. A few illusions, too, might go a long way.

"Roak," Vandross whispered to his General, who had taken up his usual position at Vandross's elbow. "Tell Talus Cur I want his best Illusionist over here now." Not many plans made in haste succeeded, he knew, but this one had the makings of greatness.

A minute later, a frail looking Human woman was brought forth, her robes flapping around her as though she had no more substance than her shadow.

"Sweet gods, woman, do you feed yourself," he rasped, raising an eyebrow.

The woman said nothing, simply staring at him in an unnerving fashion; it was as though she had no soul, that she merely existed to be used in such ways.

No matter, Vandross thought with a mental shrug. "Now, Roak, pick a couple of your more imaginative and stealthy Shadowbeast grunts. I have an idea."

The plan that Vandross laid out to Roak was simple, but would be effective.

First, the Illusionist would summon a fake maelstrom of spirits, unleashing inhuman howls and banshee wails. Gaiamancers would make tremors in the earth, just enough to spook the hardy mountain folk further. The Illusionist's lights and explosions would thunder and crack above the village, followed by a booming, ominous voice. It would say, 'thou foul creatures. Too long have I abided thy presence in my domain. I am the demon Secenterock, Renka Lord of the Fifth Ring of Hell. I have sent an envoy to clear you out, if you do not leave this place now.' On cue, Tamriel would lead Moran and Doran down into the village, and the Illusionist would provide just enough light to illuminate the Shadowbeasts already in the Dwarves' midst.

Vandross felt certain they would turn and flee, abandoning their homes in less than an hour's time, and no one would be lost on Vandross's side. Unless, of course, there were a few fools brave enough to try to play the part of the hero.

Doubtless some of the guards would try, he thought with a grin. Let them. We will crush all who oppose us. He felt the Orbs jitter inside of his soul in pleasure, savoring his cunning and deception, his unequaled guile.

"It is a most excellent plan, my lord," rasped Molis from somewhere nearby in the shadows. A glint of metal gave him away among the darkness, but Vandross was uneasy that the Colonel had crept up unannounced. He had always detected Vilec Roak, always knew when the Orbs were creeping toward the surface of his consciousness. *Mighty Hell,* he almost spat, he could even tell that Byron of Sidius was two or three days' travel east of his current position. How had this half-demon gotten so close to him? Especially since Vandross himself was responsible for his creation.

No, he thought vehemently, *this is no time to be paranoid.* Paranoia unseated more rulers than wars ever did, he realized. Best to just take comfort in the fact that if he needed someone who could go undetected, he had him.

"How long have you been standing there, half-breed?" Tamriel growled.

"Long enough, Major." The Colonel showed the first clear sign of anger Vandross had seen from him. "I would remind you to remember your rank, Tamriel. Full blood or not, you are beneath me, and beneath my scorn. And if you test me," he growled, his eyes flashing a deep blue. "I will return you to your home in the Hells."

The hulking Renka extracted his claws, crouching low to the ground and stamping the ground with his rear foot. A conflict was about to come to a head, and Vilec Roak moved to intercept the coming blows from being thrown. But Vandross held his General at bay with one thick arm.

"Hold yourself, General," he whispered to the Shadowbeast Prime.

Roak gave him a puzzled look of dismay, but Vandross nodded in Molis's direction; swirls of blue and purple energy lashed about the half-demon's fists, and his helmet flashed a mix of red and yellow as flames erupted from within the darkness of its visor.

Clearly unafraid of anything, Tamriel launched a huge arm, claws tearing through the air, at Molis.

A vapor trail followed the Colonel as he shifted position in the blink of an eye, leaping up onto the Renka's arm and running up the length of it to his shoulder.

As Tamriel attempted to grasp at the half-demon, Molis clasped both hands around Tamriel's face, and a surge of energy burst through Tamriel's body, making him writhe and quiver in agony. The entire assault was committed in utter silence; it was as though Molis's aura absorbed all noise around him.

Tamriel's eyes rolled back, and he fell to the ground, heaving and unconscious.

With a snap of his finger, Molis awakened the bear demon, and returned his body to its original appearance.

Tamriel quivered once and backed away swiftly, backpedaling on all fours.

Vandross clapped his hands, but no sound issued from them. He turned an up-raised eyebrow to Molis, who clapped his hands once. The sounds of the wintry wind blew past once more, and the mutterings of all assembled grew.

"My apologies for this unpleasant display, my lord," the half-demon said in a humble tone, bowing deeply to Vandross.

"No need for an apology, Colonel," Vandross said, walking to within a few steps of the half-demon. "Your display here is actually appreciated. It finally gives me a first-hand account of your power and skill. Major, I trust you are whole?"

Tamriel mutely nodded, and remained on his hands and feet.

Molis made a hand gesture, which was not lost on the Renka. Tamriel approached Molis, walking on all fours like the animal his body resembled. A few whispered words were exchanged, after which Tamriel bowed once more to the half-demon.

Vandross would like to have heard that little exchange, but he had already busied himself with Vilec Roak, making the final preparations for the attack. He would feel much better once he had control of the village, and from the looks of things, even if things went poorly, he had a new trump card in his hand.

* * * *

Byron groaned as Shoryu nudged him awake, and as the Dread Knight opened his eyes, he saw the squat form of master Wong sitting across from him.

"Even the dead need rest, I see," the old martial artist chided with a wrinkled grin.

Byron chuckled softly as he stretched his arms and legs, shaking off the last vestiges of drowsiness. "Indeed, we do, master Wong. Given those age lines, I'd say you haven't long before you join the ranks!"

"These are laugh lines, young whelp," Wong chided. "I am told that master of fists Morek Rockmight is resting at the moment, and seeing as the others defer to you, I figured you have some questions for me. Am I wrong?" He took a sip of some sweetly scented tea.

"No, you are not." Byron cleared his throat. "We have but a few questions, and a few requests. Firstly, we are in search of an artifact of dark magic, an item known as an Orb of Eden's Serpent. Do you know of it?"

The look of abhorrence in the old Monk's eyes told him everything he needed to know.

"Indeed, I know of this, thing," the Monk spat. "Its protection and concealment were entrusted to us by the Paladin, Rimzan of Grey. We took it in, though we knew the risks. Such evils should not be allowed into being, Byron. But we believed in our hearts that our monastery, on the other side of the tunnels, would be a safe place for its storage. But recently, we felt a shift in the balance of nature." Wong took another sip of his tea. His long, green tunics and robes hung loosely off of him, as though he were merely bones beneath his garments.

In a way, Byron thought bemusedly, the two had much in common.

"We determined that the other artifacts had been reclaimed by a new master, and that he would eventually come for this one. So, we sealed it in a Sokchi, which is a crate enchanted with Monk sutra magic. It conceals all forms of power within it, and was the perfect choice for what we had in mind. The Dwarves would be better prepared for any assault made in an effort to take the artifact. But it isn't guaranteed that the little people of the west will take it in; they are superstitious folk, and are just as likely to tell us to go away with it as take it in. If that is the case, we have a second destination in mind."

"And where is that, wizened master?" Byron asked in a hushed voice.

"Farther west, in the Dragon territories. We have a truce with the Dragons, and they are more than capable of protecting the Orb of Eden's Serpent, Byron. In either event, this Vandross may still be able to reach it. You are five days away from those places as of now, and the going will not be easy if you take the known roads. Master Morek shall have to be more choosy when making the return trip to the west. What are your other questions?"

Byron requested the provisions they would need, in the form of dried foods, new bedrolls, and some other sundry goods for traveling. Master Wong acknowledged the company's needs with a barely perceptible nod, and shuffled away from the guesthouse in order to secure them.

After an hour or so, Morek came into the main den, and everyone was assembled, either seated on the comfortable furniture, or standing as James Hayes was by the fireplace. Byron stood in the center of the room, looking around at the others with a grim set to his stance. "Listen up, everyone. Master Wong has informed me that the Orb of Eden's Serpent is most likely in the Dragon territories, in the farthest reaches of the northwestern mountains. We are five days' travel from them, and I have a sneaking suspicion that Vandross may already be ahead of us. Don't ask me how he could be, just remember this: everywhere we've been, everything we've done, he has only been a step or two behind us. This time, while we came east, he may very well have gone straight west. We have to hope that the Dwarves and Dragons can hold him off for the time being. We must gain the Orb of Eden's Serpent before him. I have discovered a way to destroy it," he said, almost in a whisper, with his head lowered. "But it will take all of us to do it, and we will be in no condition to defend ourselves afterwards. We shall have to secure it, and then take it away to someplace secretive, someplace where we can gain aid in our cause against Vandross."

"My people might be willing to take us in if they know we mean to destroy the Orb," Morek offered from his wicker seat. "They will be suspicious, but if they recognize us for what we are, they won't hesitate to let us in and dispose of the thing. It should work."

Byron gave them a basic summary of what Voice had told him, leaving out the fact that he was speaking to some apparition in his head. He didn't want to come off as crazy, or somehow overly stressed. In addition, Voice had warned him not to make the others in his company aware that each had their own Keeper in their soul. Apparently, awareness of the Keepers' presence would put them at risk for expulsion from their respective hosts. That was the last thing that Byron wanted to do; the Keepers, while trustworthy, seemed somehow capable of unfathomable measures of violence. He had garnered this impression of them by his encounter with Locke, and his continuing conversations with Voice. He didn't want to risk the company to beings beyond their comprehension, when they had real threats to deal with in the physical world.

"And that's the basic premise," he said, letting out a sigh of relief when none of the others questioned him. "It will require more than mere spells or trickery. It shall require the expenditure of energy from our very souls. The risks are great, and if one of us is taken by the Orb, the others may have to subdue the afflicted member of our party. Is that understood?"

A general murmur of acceptance ripped through the company, and they stood to their feet as one. Shoryu put his hand forward, into the center of their circle.

"On my life, I swear this," he said, his tone unusually formal and grave. Ellen placed her hand atop his next.

"In the name of Mother Gaia, I swear this," she intoned.

"With the power granted me, I swear this," Selena said, adding her hand.

"By the honor of my people, I swear this," Morek reached his rough fist underneath the pile.

All eyes turned to James Hayes, who had a glossy look in his eyes.

Byron couldn't immediately read what the Human Paladin was feeling, but a soft grin graced his now stubbled face. He placed his hand to the group, his features sharpening as he clenched his jaw.

"In the name of mighty Oun, I swear this," he proclaimed loudly, his voice echoing through the guesthouse's den.

Lastly, Byron removed his gauntlet from his left hand, flexing the flesh and bones of his mortal hand. He added it lastly, atop the hands of his comrades.

"With all my soul, I swear this," he said, sealing the pact and gazing into the faces of his companions. They were his closest, and only friends, aside from Alex, who hadn't added his hand, but sat, perched with an impish grin, on Selena's shoulder. He would protect them from harm where he could, and ensure a victory in the name of their cause. The warlock Richard Vandross would not be allowed to win.

As they withdrew their hands, a comfortable silence wrapped around them. A knock came at the door a moment later, and Shoryu crossed the room and swung the door open.

There stood master Wong, along with three large Monks, each carrying a rucksack filled with provisions for their journey.

This was odd, Byron thought as he looked past Shoryu, considering that they would not be leaving until morning. He and James Hayes approached the door and master Wong as Morek and Shoryu hauled the sacks into the room.

"Is something wrong, goodly Monk," Hayes asked as he looked into the old man's face. There was a clear mark of concern there, and master Wong was doing nothing to conceal it.

"Indeed there is, kind Paladin. One of the three young Monks sent to hide the artifact has returned, with ill news. It seems that the Dwarves of one of the western cities refused them, and they were forced to turn to the Dragon territories. They thought they had found an empty cave, but as they were leaving, a great, metallic Dragon of midnight hue assaulted them. Two of the three were slain, and this one who has returned is not in good shape."

"So a Black Dragon has the Orb in its lair," asked Morek with a wry grin. "Let him keep it then. I'd like to see Vandross get it from him."

"Therein lies the problem," master Wong said with a serious look at the Dwarf. "If this warlock cannot reach it, what chance have you, master of fists? Black Dragons are fierce, magically potent, and able to change shapes at will. It may not know what it now possesses, but if it finds out and takes the Orb for itself, it will be even more powerful than before. You must make haste, master Byron, for our young Monk also told us that a large force was making its way into the mountains when he was returning to us. A day and a half has passed since then, and night is upon us. That will put the warlock a full two days' time ahead of you if you do not leave now."

Byron understood the urgency of the situation immediately. They could not afford to fall too far behind Vandross in the search for the fifth and final Orb of Eden's Serpent.

Shoryu and Morek rifled through the provisions, placing aside those things they didn't need, or didn't foresee needing. All of the foodstuffs, however, were kept and collected into two of the rucksacks, while the third was filled with the travel goods they would require. A length of rope, oil laced torches, new bedrolls, and even a pair of simple tent tarps. An old bronze compass rested atop the travel supplies, a small pocket sized number that opened like a pocket watch. A small button atop the circle of gold that lined the outside of the compass could be pressed to pop open its cover, revealing a simple cross with the directional letters under the glass. The arrow, however, was a lightning bolt, with the small, striking tip pointing in the direction the holder faced. Byron lifted the compass out and held it in front of master Wong.

"Shoryu is a skilled Hunter, trained in the lay of the lands he passes through. And Morek Rockmight is the best guide we could have for these mountains. What use is this trinket?"

"It is no mere trinket, my undead friend. It will guide you when you are most lost, even when physical direction is not your issue. Come closer," the old Monk whispered, and Byron bent down enough to put his head next to Wong's mouth. "I do not foresee that you who shall require its innermost use, good Byron. Rather, another in your company shall need it. Be prepared for the moment that occurs, for it shall be a true test of all of your characters."

Byron stood and nodded, thanking Wong under his breath for the heads-up. If he wouldn't need it, then who? James Hayes seemed to have regained his faith, and aside from the Human Paladin, nobody in the company seemed to need further guidance. For the time being, he would let the matter drop, and concentrate on getting things moving. The company had a great deal of distance to cover, and little time to cover it.

"All right everyone, gather up your own things. We head out in one hour. Take whatever comforts you can, a quick bath or a nap, and let's get moving after that. Shoryu," he said, pulling the Cuyotai Hunter aside after his announcements. "Do you remember the way we came here?"

"Of course," Shoryu said with a hint of pride, puffing out his chest slightly. "I am a Hunter and a Cuyotai. I can recall every step of our journey here, including the footfalls, the faulty passages. Why?"

"Because Vandross may have sent some of his cronies our way when he entered the mountain ranges. I want you to range ahead of us as a scout. If you come across a patrol, do not engage them on your own, under any circumstances, do you understand? Report back to us immediately, and relay information regarding their numbers, their Race, their equipment, and their apparent strength. Got that?"

"Of course, my friend." Shoryu gave a sly grin. "Such activity is what I was trained for. It will be a nice change of pace from running for dear life and outright battling creatures of darkness. I welcome the opportunity, good Byron."

Byron nodded, and moved off to speak with Morek. The taciturn Dwarf wouldn't like being informed that he would not be taking the lead for about half of the march west, but Byron was sure he would understand the Dread Knight's reasoning.

"Morek," Byron said as he came upon the Dwarven Boxer securing his silver-studded gloves over his gnarled fists. Years of handing out brutality with little more than some leather padding over his hands made it impossible for even the thickest gloves to hide the deformed and busted appearance of his hands. Byron seldom understood Boxers: they were akin to Monks in that they preferred unarmed combat, but even Monks admitted that sometimes a weapon was a sensible thing to use. After all, Stone Golems tended to hurt when one struck them with a bare hand. Morek obviously hadn't learned that lesson yet.

"What's up boss?" Morek grunted as he secured the lacing on his gloves.

"Shoryu will scout ahead on our way back to our point of entrance into the mountains. He is trained as a Hunter, and they make the best scouts. I wanted to tell you myself."

Morek turned and raised an eyebrow at the Dread Knight, silently requesting further explanation.

"I know how you feel about this region. It is your homeland, your territory. You are one of the most revered leaders of Traithrock, and thus, of the Dwarven territories. These are your lands. I don't want to offend you."

Morek let out a hearty laugh, throwing his head back and guffawing.

"Byron, Byron, Byron," he chuckled, shaking his head and putting his hands on his hips. "I take no offense from this. The lad is as you say, a fine Hunter and a worthy scout. No, my friend." He patted Byron on the lower back. "I would only take offense if you said that my mother had no beard. Ha hah ha ha!"

Byron tried to understand the humor in Dwarven jokes, but never succeeded, and this was no exception. The joke was simply lost on him.

"Good," he continued. "Now, take that hour of rest I suggested. It isn't much, but it shall be all you get this night. We have a great deal of ground to cover, and will not rest until we are on the verge of collapse. I know that such action is extreme, but it is what is necessary if we are to catch Vandross and his forces. We must not engage them in a direct confrontation, but it will be easiest to skirt around them if we know where they are located. If we come in direct contact, we must harass them only, and then disengage. So no plunging headlong into battle Morek." He wagged a finger at Morek like he would an obstinate child.

"Roit, roit, roit," Morek said, waving him off. "Nothing foolish. I'm gonna go rest up. See you in fifty or so." Morek moved down one hallway, picking out the smaller room to sleep in.

Shoryu and Ellen Daires had gone upstairs, presumably to sleep, though Byron wouldn't be surprised if they were doing, well, something else.

James Hayes had passed out on one of the comfortable couches in the den, and Selena and Alex played a card game at a small, round wooden table off to one side of the room. Alex levitated his cards in front of him, while Selena held hers with her hands.

Of course, Byron thought rather amusedly, the cards were half Alex's size. He decided to prepare his own magic in the hour before the company moved out, not wanting to be caught unprepared. If they came across a scouting band and were forced to fight, they would not have time to rest afterwards. They would have to rely on Shoryu's abilities as a scout to carry them through without conflict. If that somehow failed, they would have to rely on their own combat strengths and tactics.

The first plan of attack was always a simple one, Byron thought, recalling his training in tactical warfare. The lessons his father had given him seemed full of harsh laughter and cruel jokes, his father always reminding young Byron that in war, casualties were inevitable. No fighting force, regardless of size, went forever without losing at least one man. Byron and his company had lost one man, young David Spore, the one-armed Monk. He didn't want to think about how many of the others might not make it through this quest. However, he had to admit that a couple were at higher risk than the others, and one or two of them were nearly certain to see this through to the end. Byron saw Shoryu, Ellen and Alex all making good lives for themselves after Vandross's defeat, if he could in fact defeat the warlock. But Selena Bradford, and perhaps James Hayes, he felt, were at the highest risk of not returning from their current mission or the necessary and eventual trek into Mount Toane. Of course, any error of judgment on his part might very well doom them all. He would have to plan every step of their journey, including contingency plans.

After locking a few spells on his armor, Byron looked at the grandfather clock in the corner of the den, and saw that the hour was nearly passed. He heard the creak of stairs, saw Shoryu and Ellen come from the direction of the kitchen, holding hands as young lovers do. Byron gave them a grin, or at least as best a facsimile as he could manage, and they half-bowed to him.

The gesture seemed oddly formal, and they did not move from where they stood, near the doorway to the kitchen.

Morek, Selena, James Hayes and Alex all gathered near Byron, who looked up in surprise. James had a tarnished Order of Oun bible in his hands, and Morek and Selena stood to either side of him and slightly closer to the Cuyotai and Elf.

What was going on here, Byron wondered.

"Byron Aixler," James Hayes began, his voice ceremonial.

Byron finally noticed that he had donned his church garb over his armor, giving him the appearance of a Priest made of blocks. When had the Paladin changed? *Probably while I was preparing spells,* the Dread Knight thought.

"Please rise and bear witness, for Shoryu Tearfang has declared that he wishes you to be Honored Witness, as is Cuyotai custom," James said, and Byron stood to his feet, sheathing the Morning Glory.

"Actually, keep that out. We'll be needing it."

Byron leaned in close as Hayes positioned him at his left side, whispering in his ear.

"What is going on, James?"

"I am performing one of my duties as an ordained member of the Order, Byron, which you should realize. Shoryu wanted to do some of his own people's customs for this grand event, and though it must be rushed, I didn't want to do it half-assed. Byron, they are to be wed, now."

Marriage? Now? It seemed rather an odd time for such an event.

"Trust me, I don't understand what this has to do with the overall plot either," Alex commented as he buzzed by Byron's head.

Well, Byron thought, *the company had everyone they needed for it.* He drew the Morning Glory once more. A Priest could be substituted with a Paladin, one male and one female witness, preferably well-known people with posts of authority, and as the Cuyotai custom required, an Honored Witness—Byron himself.

The position of Honored Witness was typically reserved for the Cuyotai groom's father, brother, or best friend. Byron supposed that Shoryu viewed him as a bit of each, given their time together and circumstances.

As he took his position and stood upright, Shoryu Tearfang and Ellen Daires moved forward, standing before James Hayes and Byron, and between Selena, Morek and Alex. The taciturn Dwarf had a grin on his face that threatened to split his head, and Selena had the vaguest shimmer of dampness in her eyes.

Was she going to cry? Byron wondered. She hardly knew these two; then again, neither did Byron, when he thought about it. But sometimes the strongest friendships were forged in the flames of battle, the pits of mutual strife.

Shoryu began the ceremony as soon as he and Ellen came to a stop, half turning to face Ellen. Their eyes locked then, and did not waver. "I, Shoryu Tearfang, do swear to love and protect you for all the days that remain to me. My oath to you is one of honor, for I have no ring to offer at this time. But know this: I love you as I have loved no other, and I shall never love another so much as you." His voice filled with tension, apparently from trying to remember the words he had recited for this moment.

"Let it be known," James Hayes held up the bible with one hand and pointed skyward with his other, "that you have been heard by mighty Oun, and your own deity, and both shall protect you so long as you hold to your oath to this woman. Ellen, what of you?"

The Elven Gaiamancer turned to glance at Hayes, and she nodded. "I, Ellen Daires, do swear to wrap myself in your love and adoration, and to return these things to you as best I can, for my heart beats only for you."

"Then will the bride and groom now face me?" Hayes's tone was serious and at the same time, light as a feather.

He was, Byron realized, enjoying this entirely too much. Perhaps the paladin had chosen the wrong profession, he thought. But his inner laugh stopped quite abruptly. What if that was exactly what had been gnawing at the Paladin over the weeks since Desanadron? Had he been trying to figure out which role to take, the Priest or the Paladin?

"Before I make my declaration that this marriage is complete, we shall hear from the Honored Witness, as is Cuyotai custom. Byron?"

The Dread Knight was caught off guard, and rubbed his skull with his free hand, searching for the right words for the occasion. It didn't take long: memory was the best source of inspiration. Byron stood at attention, and bowed low to Shoryu, then to Ellen.

"Celebrated groom, celebrated bride, hear me well." He recited the words his father had said to him at his wedding. "This pact of marriage you make of your own free will, with your hearts filled with that which the gods most cherish, love, and honor. Let nothing, man, beast or otherwise, come between you from this day forth. Hold close to your heart the joy of such kinship, for no closer or stronger bond can be formed in this life. Know that you are no longer two separate individuals, two distinct souls, but you are now joined as one. The power of one soul, made of two joined souls, is beyond measure, for no other being in this life, or force in this world, can create the beauty and rapture that you now can. May your lives be filled with joyous memories, and times of hardship to strengthen your bond." He held the Morning Glory high in the air, its tip pointing straight to the sky, its surface shimmering with white light. "And lastly, may your children be just like you," he said, using the same joke his father had on him. "So that they might drive you crazy as fools."

Everyone shared a good, heart-felt guffaw at this jest, including Alex, who typically would have made a sarcastic comment by now.

Perhaps the Ki Fairy realized how honest and sacred this ritual was, Byron thought with gratitude.

"Heed your Honored Witness's words, Shoryu Tearfang and Ellen Daires," James Hayes said, clutching his bible to his chest. "The gods and these friends to the now joined have heard all, and will attest to the honesty and strength of this marriage. Shoryu, you may now kiss your bride."

The Cuyotai almost moved ahead of James, and the company hollered and hooted as they locked lips for a minute, Shoryu dipping Ellen toward the floor. They stared into each other's eyes afterwards for a moment, and then stood arm in arm. The others of the company clapped their hands, smiles beaming from their assembled faces.

Alex flittered over to Byron's shoulder, whispering in his 'ear'.

"Well, now we can at least get back to the rest of the story," he commented, gaining a confused glance from Byron.

"What are you talking about?"

"Oh, nothing. Just remember Byron, every life is but a story, written by some author who exists beyond our knowledge."

As the Ki Fairy fluttered away, Byron thought his words over. What sort of story would be written about this journey? Would the recorders of Tamalaria's history cast him as the tyrant he had been, or the confused soul who struggled against Richard Vandross? Perhaps both, he mused, clapping his hands and favoring the newly married couple with as gracious a smile as he could make with his fleshless skull. They had lost one of their comrades, but new hope sprang from the Cuyotai and Elf's joining.

"All right, we have lost time in this ritual," Morek said, always the pragmatist. "We must head out now, while we have only lost a few minutes." He hoisted his rucksack, slinging it over his shoulders. "Shoryu, you will be taking the lead, right?"

The young Cuyotai Hunter nodded his confirmation, drawing his bow from his back, and picking up his own belongings.

Without further ado, the company left the guesthouse and the village in peaceful silence. As they passed from the barrier to the wintry mountain air, they collectively shivered for a moment, except for Morek, who had taken the lead twenty paces or so behind Shoryu.

James Hayes, having taken off his priestly robes, provided a rear guard, and in this manner they struck out west.

Byron prayed inwardly that Vandross would be too arrogant to send forces their way, at least for the evening. He wanted the wave of warmth flowing through him to remain for a while longer, just to offset the many hardships the company had already suffered. They were due a little happiness, he thought.

Chapter Three
Glory

The plan had gone off without incident, which pleased Richard Vandross to no end. The Dwarves hadn't even bothered to pack their belongings in their terror, fleeing the village in droves, in all directions. Some of the guards had mustered enough courage to defy Vandross and his minions, but only long enough to be torn apart by Tamriel's enormous claws and the swords of Khan grunts. Vandross hadn't lost a single man in the effort, making the pillaging of supplies much easier.

The one-eyed warlock called a halt to the night's travel, declaring that they would rest for the whole of the daylight hours in the village. Vandross himself slunk off to a modest one-story home, navigating the small rooms until he found a bedroom. The bed itself, thankfully, was just big enough for him to lie flat on his back (his feet dangled over empty space, however), and he passed into slumber in an instant.

A few hours later, at around noon, he was roused by a gentle nudging at his shoulder.

He opened his good eye and looked into the darkness of Colonel Molis's helmet, the demon's gimlet eyes shining darkly at the warlock. Vandross buried his face in the pillow, and managed to say in a muffled voice, "Shall I ever have a decent rest again? What is it, Colonel?"

"My lord." The half-demon stiffened to attention and snapped off a smart salute. Standing upright, the top of his helmet scraped the ceiling. "One of Lieutenant Amon's men has discovered something you may find interesting." Molis motioned someone into the low room.

A Khan, stooped almost in half, came forward with something wrapped in a blanket.

Molis unveiled the object, which appeared to be a huge, wicked scimitar, much like the one Vandross had once wielded. The blade was inscribed with several Dwarven runes, and it shone in the sunlight filtering through the window.

Vandross rather liked the look of it, and wondered what sort of Dwarven enchantments had been placed upon it.

"May I present this to you, my lord, as a new weapon."

Vandross swung his legs over the side of the bed, grasping the hilt of the weapon and testing its weight and balance. The weapon almost seemed too large for a Dwarf, but Vandross knew that the stocky mountain people of their Race tended to be stronger than any Human. Such weapons were not uncommon among their people.

"I sense magic in this weapon, Colonel," Vandross said, still eyeing the weapon. "But I must admit that I cannot tell what sort of magic it is. Would you be so kind as to tell me, if you can?"

Molis nodded, and reached for the weapon, which Vandross gave to him. A patch of shadows reached from inside one of the half-demon's gauntlets, and wrapped around the blade. There was a slight shimmering, and then the shadows recoiled back within the Colonel's glove.

"It will not break, my lord," he handed the weapon back. "It is an extraordinary weapon, lord Vandross. Not even adamantite will break it. And, from what I can sense, it cannot be removed from your hand once you wield it, if you do not wish it. No warrior, regardless of skill, can disarm you with that blade in hand." A hint of jealousy touched his voice.

Vandross made a noise of approval and ordered the Khan to find him a sheath for the weapon.

The soldier saluted and moved off to do as his master bade him.

Molis saluted as well, and was about to leave when Vandross called him back.

"Wait a moment, Colonel. I have something I must ask of you," the one-eyed warlock said, motioning the half-demon to one of the wicker chairs near the corner of the room. Molis sat obediently, his frame and posture still militant. "Why are you here, Molis? Honestly, I mean."

"Sir," Molis asked, and Vandross could almost see an eyebrow rise in query.

"I mean, Colonel, that you seem able to have accomplished much of what I have done, and without much difficulty. When I began this undertaking, you were often silent and a bit sullen. You joined our assault on Fort Flag, but up until then, you had been sort of hanging back in the shadows. You are mine to command, have been since I first awakened the demon within you," Vandross said in a hushed whisper, leaning forward with one hand on his left knee, his tone and look gaining intensity. "What are you?"

"I am a half-demon, my lord, as I have said."

He was being evasive, Vandross realized. The Colonel hadn't been prepared for such questions. And if Vandross wasn't careful, he might experience a fair amount of agony before he could do anything about it. He had to be careful with this half-demon: more careful than he would be with Vilec Roak or any of his kind. Though the half-breed was strictly forbidden to directly harm Vandross due to the magic that summoned him, he could certainly make things difficult for him.

"What precise type of demon I am is of little or no consequence. I am your third-in-command, your left hand man. You needn't concern yourself with anything other than my performance in the field, for little else about me truly matters."

Damn it all, Vandross thought, this man was hiding something from him, something vital. What was it? He dismissed Molis to tend to his duties, since the half-demon never seemed to sleep. He would get answers from the half-demon, but not by directly questioning him. He had to lay a trap for the Colonel, get him to reveal something to someone else in the expeditionary force. He had been foolish as an apprentice under Tanarak to release that unseen demon from its hold in the bowels of Mount Toane. He would discover more about its nature, its exact origin in the Hells, if he could. He would also try to figure out who the original host mortal had been.

The Dread Knight's Redemption

Too restless to return to sleep, Vandross negotiated his way out of the squat dwelling and into the noon light. His men stood around smoking pipes, talking in their own native tongues, and barking harsh laughter at each other's jests. He spotted Vilec Roak just outside of a tavern, drinking something from an earthenware mug, and guffawing at some secretive joke one of his men whispered into his ear. The one-eyed warlock, cloak whipping out behind him, stalked through the snow-laden street to stand before his General, who tried to stand and failed.

"No need to get up for my sake, Roak," Vandross said, observing the reek of hard liquor on the Shadowbeast Prime. "I have a request to make of you. Find out what you can about Colonel Molis, and come to me when you've learned something of value."

"What sort of information do you need," the Prime asked, sobering up slightly.

Disciplined, Vandross noted. Much as Bael had been.

"I need to know where he comes from, what his demon lineage is. I need to know who he is, exactly, the mortal host. He has great power, Roak, and his origins might reveal to me the source of his abilities. Go about this with caution and care, however. I don't think he'd be too appreciative of people snooping. He wouldn't even give me any straight answers, so he's likely to be withholding of others."

Roak nodded and grunted his acquiescence, then put his mug down and began walking here and there, joining conversations with an ease that came to Shadowbeasts as clever as him.

Vandross walked into the tavern himself, taking a glass and a bottle of Dwarven stonegut, a harsh drink indeed. He needed to relax, and this might just do the trick, he thought. Let Roak handle the investigation. After all, if Molis decided to become hostile, at least Vandross himself would be clear of the line of fire.

* * * *

For Byron, the first twenty-four hours after leaving the Monk village passed in a blur of snow and blowing wind. However, he didn't have the same perception as Shoryu enjoyed.

The young Cuyotai ranged a good ten minutes ahead of the rest of the company, keeping his wits about him. He didn't let his recent rapture cloud his judgment, keeping his mind focused on scouting. Even in the heavy snowfall, he was able to tell that a small search party had recently come close to his current position. From the size of the tracks, and the general scent, he guessed they were Khan. Vandross had indeed sent a group to search for them.

Using what little bit of the tracks was left, and placing it against the rate of snowfall, he estimated that they were about four or five minutes ahead of him personally, fifteen ahead of the party. And they were heading back to wherever they had come from, perhaps to lay an ambush.

Shoryu sprinted ahead, leaving a purposeful trail for the others to follow. He would only go ahead enough to estimate the war party's numbers and strength.

Using the twisting mountain paths as cover for his approach, Shoryu kept himself pressed against the cliff faces as he moved. The tracks became fresher and fresher, and soon he looked at tracks that were only a minute or so old. He heard the crunch of snow under heavy feet, and in the whipping wind, that meant he was practically on top of them.

Keeping low to the ground, Shoryu burrowed through the snow, so as not to make any noise. Peering around the corner of a turn in the path, he spotted a pack of four Khan, gathered around a pile of stray branches and brush, as well as some casks of lamp oil. Apparently they were stopping to make a fire and perhaps a meal.

It made sense, Shoryu thought. They were still a full day and a half from the entry paths to these particular mountains. Their path back to Vandross probably made it another day or so before they reached their final destination. They would need to keep themselves fresh, even if they were accustomed to an environment like these mountains.

Perhaps he could dispatch them, if he was quick about it. But they would likely survive a bowshot or two, and there were exactly four of them. Four on one, eh? He didn't like the odds, regardless of how swift he was. Perhaps if he could lure them closer to the edge of the drop, down a few hundred yards to a crushing death. A sound, he had to make a sound to get their attention.

He decided to take one of the arrows that Ellen had given him, one that held a spell on it to shatter the ground beneath the arrowhead. However, if he did it now, and here, the company would have to find another way back. *Wait a minute*, he thought, looking at the jut hanging over the Khan party. If he could get that to come down, the Khan would be buried under roughly half a ton of snow.

Rolling slowly onto his back, he took aim at a diagonal, staying out of plain view. He redoubled his efforts to focus his eyes, and found a small goat standing on the jut. Taking aim slightly to its right, he let one arrow fly. As his bowstring twanged, the largest of the Khan looked directly at his snout and hands, the only parts of him in any measure of view.

"You there," the Khan bellowed, lumbering to his feet. "What are you doing?" The Khan looked up at where the arrow had landed, and smiled viciously. "Your shot is pathetic, Cuyotai whelp. Your meal escapes you even now." The tiger-man pointed up at the retreating goat.

Idiot, Shoryu thought.

"Sir, didn't the Lieutenant say that one of the Dread Knight's companions was a young Cuyotai Hunter," one of the smaller grunts asked. As the mountain shook from the arrow stuck in the jut, the Khan leader's eyes widened in revelation.

"That's right. Shoryu Tearfang, drop your bow and surrender to us now, and we may be merciful. Perhaps," he added with a chuckle to his fellows.

Shoryu smiled like a madman, one eye twitching and squinting as he tried to contain his mirth. But it was to no avail.

"What is so amusing, you scrawny Cuyotai faggot? Do you not realize you are doomed if you resist us?"

Shoryu threw his head back and laughed, the derisive laughter of a lycanthrope on the verge of rage. Before he'd met Byron, he hadn't often found pleasure in taking life, but these Khan had threatened and insulted him. For all he knew, there was more blood on their hands than those of his entire company, who would be arriving at his current position shortly.

"Perhaps if you changed your point of view, sir," Shoryu said, pointing to the slabs of mountain granite that would fall on top of the Khan in five or six more seconds.

As one, the Khan turned their attention skyward, and all had the same general reaction; the smell of Khan urine stung Shoryu's nostrils for only the briefest of moments.

"Ah, shit," grumbled their leader, as nearly a ton of mountain rock crashed down atop the Khan, making instant burial stones as they filled the small niche in the mountainside.

Blood oozed out in rivulets from beneath the pile. Shoryu spat on the pile of rubble, and picked a nice, settled spot after visually assuring himself that nothing else would drop on top of him. There, he waited for the rest of the company. After about five minutes, he saw the blurred and snow-covered forms of Morek Rockmight and Byron come through the veil of snow, the others following.

The great, massive Dread Knight looked around, and eyed the pile of rubble suspiciously.

"This wasn't like this when we passed through the first time, Shoryu. What happened here?"

Morek Rockmight raised an eyebrow at the Cuyotai Hunter as he snickered under his breath.

"Not much, really. The matter is dealt with, good Byron," Shoryu said matter-of-factly. "Nothing at all to worry about. Would anyone care to sit a spell and rest? I think I need a few minutes."

Ellen sat next to her husband, and the two wrapped their arms around each other's waists.

Byron fixed the pile of rubble with a steady glare, and sensed the last traces of a quickly ebbing life. He focused his efforts, and his magic streamed from his eye sockets into the cracks in the pile. Beneath all that stone, four Khan lay dead, all in military uniforms. *Vandross's flunkies*, he thought. Surely one arrow couldn't have caused this destruction. But Byron realized it must have been one of Shoryu's enchanted arrows, further enhanced by having Ellen's spell.

He looked up, and saw a billy-goat sticking its tongue out at him. Well, he had seen stranger things....

* * * *

Richard Vandross couldn't quite explain what happened when he walked through the former Dwarven village, but it went something like this: as he roamed the streets, looking over his men, a blanket of shadows spread from his body, writhing about like it was a living skin. His troops shuffled aside, keeping back from the serpentine darkness, and he felt heat gathering behind the patch over his right eye.

Something was shifting, changing inside of him, and for reasons beyond his knowledge. He didn't feel threatened, didn't sense the Orbs' will in this. It was as though his body and magic were reacting to a perceived threat beyond his normal field of perception.

After reaching the opposite end of the village, he was fairly certain he saw what it was he had reacted to; a huge Black Dragon flew past, heading northwest. Something in his very blood boiled at the sight of it, and he knew he would see that creature again.

As soon as the Dragon was out of sight, his body returned to normal, and Vilec Roak approached. "My lord, evening is nigh, and the men grow restless now that they are fed and have slept. We should be heading out."

"Hmm, agreed. Has there been any news from the party we sent in Byron's direction at the foothills?"

"None, my lord. But do not forget, if they found Byron and his people, they would be heading back with caution, so as not to leave any trace of themselves. They are Khan, my lord, quite adept at survival in climates such as this. Also, my lord," Vilec Roak whispered conspiratorially. "I have discovered where the Colonel comes from."

Vandross shot Roak a look that was unmistakable: come here and tell me.

He led Roak into a small traveling goods store, stooping down to ensure that he didn't brain himself on the ceiling.

"Lord Vandross, one of my own, a Shadowbeast by the name of Gurik Luran, used to reside in Mount Toane. He dwelled there after the fall of Tanarak of Sidius, the warlock who formerly possessed the Orbs of Eden's Serpent. Gurik survived the wrath of Rimzan of Grey by hiding in one of the deeper tunnels. One day, while debating if he should continue his residence there, he came upon a chamber that would not admit light. He described it as having a wall of darkness much like his own skin, right at the entrance. This, he said, made no sense, for the inner fires of Mount Toane lit all of those tunnels and chambers as brightly as the sun does the southern plains. Furthermore, that very chamber had been lit the day before, and he became curious. When Gurik tried to pass through the veil, a voice told him, 'Get thee back. I have need of rest, for my rebirth is most recent.' The creature came out some time during that night, Gurik relates, and approached him in his sleeping quarters. He knows it was Molis, for the half-demon has not changed one bit since that time, either in appearance or demeanor.

"It was the same day that we moved our forces into Mount Toane, my lord. Molis was already there, apparently waiting for you to command him," Roak finished in a final rush of slurred words. There was a hint of panic in his voice, as though he had read something terrible in the tale he had been told. "I dare say, my lord, that he was waiting for you specifically."

Vandross thought over this information for a moment, trying to process it all.

"That's as should be, Roak. I released the demon that was within one of the lower chambers when I was still an apprentice, though it did not immediately take a host. What of his composition? Do we know precisely what he is yet?"

Vilec Roak cleared his throat awkwardly, his yellow eyes darting back and forth.

"Not yet, my lord. His mortal half, we know to be Human, my lord. But the demon within him is something I do not recognize. Regardless, this half-demon was not born so, I believe. Sometimes, when a full demon surfaces on its own from the Hells, it requires a host to maintain its existence on the mortal realm. Usually, this simply results in the fusion of the mortal body with the demon, making either a demon possessed mortal, or a demon with a mortal body. But, once in a great while, the two elements, the two souls, collide, and create a whole that is one half of each original. That, my lord, is what Molis is. He is no child born of a mortal and demon's coupling."

Vilec Roak was actually sweating, and had almost become delirious, Vandross realized. Apparently, such creatures were a big deal. But again, this wasn't exactly new information for him.

"So, what's the difference between a half-breed like Molis and one born of a mortal and a demon parent," Vandross asked, keeping his voice low. He wasn't so much afraid of being overheard as he was that Vilec Roak was going to bolt from him.

"There is a great difference, my lord. Those born of two parents possess only half of their demon parent's power. They have mortal weaknesses, mortal emotions, and mortal concerns. There is little about them that causes concern, sire. They are shunned by both worlds from which they come, and are often discouraged from an early age in all things. They do not become heroes or villains, do not reach grand stature. They do not become hostile, for the most part. Half-breeds like Molis, however, retain all of the powers and skills of the demon half of the fusion. They retain the knowledge of their mortal host, as well as their skills and training. They have the best of both worlds." He nearly screamed, gesturing wildly with his hands. "And at any given time, they may take on the visage of either half of their being, though Molis has never done as much I suspect. My lord, he must not be allowed near the Orb of Eden's Serpent. If he is, he may become a threat to even you."

Vandross, out of instinct and insult, slapped Roak hard with one gauntleted hand, knocking his General to the floor.

Roak looked up at him, fear in his eyes. He crouched on his hands and knees before the one-eyed warlock, groveling. "I am sorry, my lord. I have spoken out of turn. I will not do so again. Please pardon my behavior."

Vandross brought the tip of his left boot under Vilec Roak's chin, lifting his face so that their eyes met for a moment. Fire blared behind his mangled eye.

"You are forgiven, General. Do not forget, you are a Shadowbeast Prime, and my General. And he can never be a threat to me. I summoned the sealed demon that is half of his soul, if what you suppose is the truth. By binding magical laws, he is forbidden to harm me. Regardless of power or fear, Molis is a Colonel, and is below your rank. Remember, this is an army, and any army worth its weight in salt keeps discipline within the ranks. Isn't that the lesson he taught to the Major," he said, referring to Tamriel, the hulking Renka.

Vilec Roak stood and brushed himself off.

"Yes, of course." He got a grip on himself. "Discipline. Every army needs discipline. Thank you for balancing me, sire. Come now, we must prepare to march." The General was now fully in command of himself.

He had spent too much time among mortals, Vandross realized. The emotions that Roak had mentioned were filtering through his demonic aura, giving him a taste that no demon knew in the Hells—fear, apprehension, distrust, and confusion.

With the power of the Glorious Mother of Destruction, Vandross might be able to sweep those feelings away from the Shadowbeast. If not, he could always destroy him. With that thought in mind, whistling softly to himself, Vandross walked alongside his marching forces.

* * * *

When they finally reached their entry point to the mountains, Byron and his company nearly collapsed from exhaustion. They had pressed on without rest or a real meal for nearly two days, and they all needed sleep. Even the Dread Knight felt himself slipping into slumber as he flopped to the floor of a small cave that Shoryu had found. He felt most grateful that James Hayes volunteered to keep the first watch, and slipped into sleep.

Evening was approaching, and what little sunlight had penetrated the general fog of snow and gloom outside of the cave quickly disappeared, leaving only the darkness of night. The weather had improved over the last couple of hours, letting the company arrive at the cave earlier than expected. That was well, Hayes mused as he looked around the cave, seeing everyone slumbering peacefully.

They had gotten lucky, he thought to himself. Only Shoryu had been forced to deal with opposing forces, and he had done so quite effectively. And, from the way the young Cuyotai had laughed at his handiwork, he had enjoyed himself. James hadn't seen this side of Shoryu, the primal lust for combat that all lycanthropes suffered on occasion. The group already had to deal with Morek Rockmight's battle-lust, and to have to deal with both the Dwarven Boxer and the Cuyotai Hunter might prove difficult. Together, the two of them could probably take down a small battalion, but they would eventually draw too much attention for the company to deal with. He prayed silently to Oun for guidance, and strength.

His watch passed slowly, for he too was in great need of rest, and it was only in times like this that time seemed to crawl for him. A Paladin's training gave him great endurance and resilience, but almost forty-eight hours of marching had drained him considerably. He barely had the energy to stand upright, but decided that doing some menial task might wake him enough to last his entire shift. He removed the iron cooking pot from his rucksack, and placed it over the fire Selena had created to provide warmth and light. Pouring in some snow to melt for water, he began adding some of the cooking ingredients he had taken from the guesthouse kitchen, blending in vegetables and strips of dried meat to give the food some body and flavor, making a good stew. When it was prepared, he had a small bowl for himself, and let the pot simmer as he awoke Selena for her watch.

The Pyromancer looked at the food with a savage glare, and thanked James with a grunt before pouring herself a bowl and devouring it.

Selena felt bolstered by both sleep and food, and prepared some of her best spells, locking them on her hands and robes. The effort drained her slightly, but she felt much better having some protection. She had left the Monk village without properly preparing any defenses, and was as thankful as Hayes that no encounters had come their way. She might have acted foolishly if they had encountered anyone past the twenty-four hour mark. At that point she had gone numb to the world around her, sealed within the tomb of her mind, the only thoughts that passed being left, right, left, right, don't trip, don't look over that ledge. A fairly useless litany if they had come upon opposing forces.

She'd felt disgusted at her lack of endurance. She was Selena Bradford, damn it. Sorcerer Supreme. A trek like this should be nothing to her. But she had never been so physically taxed, except in combat, and even then she had been allowed proper rest afterwards. This forced march had been paced by Shoryu, and insisted upon by Byron, both of whom seemed to have more stamina than anyone else in the company. Byron, for obvious reasons. He was a Dread Knight, despite a body that appeared to be mortal beneath his armor. And Shoryu was trained as a Hunter, and Hunters had to be accustomed to trips like this. Selena liked the Cuyotai, and managed a faint smile when she thought of the wedding ceremony she had been part of. It had been quick and simple, for they hadn't had the time to do things properly. And Selena wasn't a fool; she knew why they did it there in the Monk village. Both feared that one or the other would not survive the struggle against Richard Vandross and his armies. They were smart to be afraid, she thought grimly.

Near the end of her shift, a sudden movement just outside of the cave startled Selena. Had Vandross sent lackeys to search for them? Had her fire given them away? She wasn't sure, and didn't want to take a chance. Summoning her magic, she let the heat of her power reach through the cave, rousing the others to consciousness. Crimson and pale yellow light shimmered off of her robes, and fire rimmed her eyes as she wove arcane symbols in the air, speaking in the dead tongue of mages.

She desisted just before completing the spell, and risked a quick glance about, just to make sure the others were getting to their feet and were aware that they had a visitor.

"Who goes there," she bellowed at the vague silhouette standing in the entrance of the cave. The figure, she could tell, was both tall and thick, massive in the way of Khan. Another war party could be coming, but she doubted it; the sounds of the creature's movements didn't indicate what it was, but it hadn't drawn a weapon on her and her companions yet.

The creature muttered something, then turned its head to their left, and rasped something in a strange language, rough and guttural. Were those, horns, she thought. A moment later, another of the creatures appeared in the entry, and both walked into the firelight, hands held before them to show they were unarmed. Two Minotaurs, dressed in primitive clothes made of pelts and crude weapons made of what appeared to be bones slung across their backs, came forward.

"We are not your foes, fiery one," the first Minotaur said, his bull head sweeping left to right to take in all of the company members.

Byron, Selena noticed, had not even drawn the Morning Glory. Had he known that there was no threat here?

Perhaps, she thought. The Dread Knight's abilities were beyond her ken, but she trusted his judgment. She undid the spell, letting her hands drop to her sides.

Byron came forward and put a solid hand on her shoulder, squaring himself to face the Minotaurs eye to eye, so to speak. They were the same height as Byron, standing at six and half feet roughly, and had an aura of silent pride about them.

"Please, let me introduce myself and my companion. I am Adrian Fistcrush, and this is my cousin, Brock Swordslash," said the Minotaur.

Byron had to suppress the urge to laugh aloud. Ah, Minotaurs. Their names never ceased to amuse him. He even recalled one Minotaur, who had served in the Final Push, whose name had been Punch Rockgroin, and he almost burst into a cackle just thinking about the oddball Minotaur Shaman. Somehow, he retained his composure, and offered a slight bow.

"I am Byron," he said, and gave Selena a nod. "This is Selena Bradford, and I apologize if she seemed a tad bit hostile. With us are—"

"We know who you are, Byron of Sidius." Adrian held up a hand.

Byron gave him a curious stare, and kept his hand at the ready, in case the Minotaurs proved to be hostile. Then, he saw it; both Minotaurs wore a black armband, with a skull on it. The same armband had been worn by the bordermen of the Elven Kingdom. "

We have been sent by our elders, who have received word that an army assembles in the city of Desanadron in order to resist the warlock Richard Vandross. The army also gathers in secret in the city of Ja-Wen, deep in the tunnels and caverns beneath the city."

"How did you find out about us," Byron asked, still wary of the Minotaurs. They were, after all, quite large, and probably capable of massive amounts of damage.

"An emissary from the Elven Kingdom came to us two days ago, lord Byron." Brock's voice was surprisingly deeper than his slightly taller cousin, who had done all of the talking to this point. "He told us of your victory in Whitewood. Large numbers of soldiers and concerned free warriors have joined ranks, in the name of a common cause. They all, like you, seek to resist this madman, for the memory of Tanarak of Sidius is still fresh in their minds. Though this Vandross and Tanarak share no known common bond."

Byron thought, *Oh, if only you knew.*

"It is apparent," the Minotaur continued, "that he will be a tyrant just like the warlock who came before him. The peoples of the lands of Tamalaria remember that dark age, and have no wish to repeat it. Do you approve, lord Byron?"

Byron stood dumbfounded. All of this, all because he had done what he thought was right. He could hardly believe it, but it seemed that his recent stand against Richard Vandross had erased all memory of his atrocities from the land and its people. Most likely, however, the Elven Queen had made her own opinion known, and let her stature influence many thousands in his favor. And whoever ran Desanadron now had surely witnessed Byron's leadership in the defense of the city-state.

He nodded slightly. "I approve, Brock Swordslash, Adrian Fistcrush. You have been sent to join the ranks of the armies who oppose Richard Vandross, correct?"

A barely perceptible nod.

"Good. You both appear to be capable young men. May your gods bless you, and may mighty Oun bless you as well, even if you should not worship him." He made a gesture, the motion priests of Oun use to bless the members of their congregations, before each of them.

The Minotaurs smiled at him, and saluted. Without another word, they turned to walk away, but Byron stopped them with a hand on their shoulders. "Wait a moment. Why did you come here? How did you know who we were, and where we were?"

"We didn't," said Adrian. "We thought you might have been another patrol of Khan, like the one just up the pass. Do not worry, lord Byron. We have already dispatched them."

Byron took a step back in surprise. Just up the pass? Had they camped so close to potential foes?

"There were three of them, and they appeared to have been readying themselves to head back to a larger group. We have sensed that there is a vast force further west, but they are not our concern, lord Byron. We apologize for the disservice, but we must go join our new unit."

"No need for apologies," Byron said, waving them off. "Go with your gods."

Without another word, the Minotaurs left Byron and his company staring after them, silence thickening into a total absence of noise.

Byron turned to face the others. "Grab your things. We might be closer to Vandross's forces than we thought. We head out, now."

Groggy and worn, the company shuffled about the cave, collecting their belongings and hefting their rucksacks onto their backs.

I'll have you yet, Richard Vandross, Byron thought. *I'll have you yet.*

* * * *

The one-eyed warlock stalked ahead of his marching elements, a full two days ahead of Byron and his companions if his perceptions were accurate. He could feel the Dread Knight closing on them, however, with each passing few hours. It was as though the undead warrior wasn't taking time to rest. Vandross had sent two groups of Khan to patrol the path behind the main body of the company, perhaps slow Byron and his men down, but he had received no report from either group. The Dread Knight's pace only seemed to have slowed for about five hours during the night. But Vandross sensed that he was on the move again.

It came as no real surprise that Byron was gaining on him, when he thought about it. The Dread Knight had a group of less than ten, whereas Vandross led an entire unit of just over one hundred men and women. The one-eyed warlock signaled for Vilec Roak to join him at his side.

The Shadowbeast Prime and General swept over to Vandross's side, and fell into step. "Yes, my lord?"

"Send a couple of your people ahead. Make certain that they know they can move however they need to, including through the Shadow Realm. I need an idea of what direction we're heading in, so that we can make better time. Byron and his company are gaining ground on us as we speak. We have only a couple of days before they catch up with us. Do you understand?"

Roak moved away without a word, and conferred with a pair of Shadowbeasts among the rank and file. The two of them disappeared into the shadows of an overpass, and did not emerge on the other side.

Vandross smiled to himself, and when Vilec Roak returned to his side, said, "Thank you very much General, for your help. Remind me to give those two promotions when they return."

"My lord, I told them to not only to find the best path, but to try to locate the Orb of Eden's Serpent as well. If it can be detected, they will find it. Also, I have warned them to be wary of Dragons, and report back immediately if they spy any in their lairs."

"Very good, General," Vandross said, folding his hands behind his back. "By the way, what sort of Dragons live in these mountains? If you know offhand, that is."

Vilec Roak rubbed his chin a moment in concentration, then held up a finger in revelation.

"I do recall, my lord, for I have been here on a few occasions. For the most part, Red Dragons, White Dragons, and Black Dragons, my lord. White Dragons are not a major threat, sire, for they are the weakest of the chromatic-type Wyrms. Red Dragons I do not deem much of a threat either, for their views of the world are much like your own. One might even be persuaded to aid us in our efforts. But Black Dragons, my lord, are another matter entirely."

"How so?" Vandross raised an eyebrow at his General.

Roak took on a speculative stance once more, his eyes darting back and forth as he searched for the right words.

"Well, my lord, they are physically mighty, and magically adept. They are cunning, and greedy beyond measure. They find all life forms other than Dragons and Draconus—you know, Dragonmen—to be beneath them. They even disdain Lizardmen, who are not unlike them in many ways. And, my lord, Black Dragons covet one thing above all else."

"And what is that, General?"

"Power, my lord. If a Black Dragon has an Orb of Eden's Serpent, even if it somehow doesn't know about it at first, it will find a way to put it to use. We know that Monks took the Orb in a cask of some sort, an object that makes it undecipherable. But Dragons are large, and not exactly known for their grace. If the Monks took the Orb to a Black Dragon and left it with him, he might accidentally knock the cask open, and discover the Orb for himself."

"And absorb it," Vandross said bitterly. "No matter. I doubt that any Monk would be brave enough or foolish enough to try to secret something in a Black Dragon's lair, or any Dragon for that matter. We will find the Orb of Eden's Serpent for ourselves, Roak, I have no doubt of that. We simply need to find any unoccupied caves or secret lairs among these mountains. Besides," he said, feeling a slight pulse from within his body; the other Orbs were reacting to something nearby. "I don't think those Monks' efforts will work. I believe I can feel the Orb. It is somewhere nearby, within perhaps another day's distance. We will find it, and I shall have it."

Roak saluted and fell back into line with his ranks, and Vandross continued to walk alone alongside the elements and ranks.

The rest of the day seemed to drag in a sequence of non-events. Near evening, the unit stopped briefly for a meal near evening. Vandross called a halt to their progress when a section of a narrow pass collapsed, taking several of Talus Cur's magic users with it. The fall, when he peered over the edge of the crumbled path, was about three or four hundred yards long. He could just make out four or five limp forms on the hard packed ground below, and marked them off mentally as necessary casualties. *Ah well*, he thought. *At least it wasn't anyone important*. But the collapse of that passage meant they would have to find another way around, and he didn't want any delays.

Before he could turn to call on Vilec Roak, two Shadowbeasts, the ones that Roak had dispatched earlier in the day, stood before him, saluting.

"Report," he snapped at them.

"My lord," began the one on the left, bearing the stripes of a Sergeant. The other, though larger and more brutish, was only a Corporal.

Ah, discipline, Vandross thought. *Good to see something's working around here.*

"We have found a series of pathways that will take us to the same place as that passage. And, we believe we may have found where the Orb is," the sergeant said with a wicked grin.

"Really?"

"Indeed, my lord. There is another small village, just to the west of here about half a day's travel. It is a Monk village, from the appearance and activities of the inhabitants."

Of course, Vandross thought. Why would the Monks risk leaving something like the Orb of Eden's Serpent with a Dragon, when they could simply move it among their own kinsmen?

"Gentlemen, give your findings to the General, and have him lead the unit to those pathways! We do not rest until we are a few hours away from that village. Then I want all of the men to be well fed and rested, prepared to storm that village and take the Orb. Men," he yelled, addressing everyone in his force. "We needn't bother about with Dwarves and Dragons. These scouts have found the Orb's location for certain. We march onward now, to victory, and glory."

A resounding war cry issued from the unit as a whole, and weapons and armor clanged with anticipation.

"How many are there in the village," he whispered to the Sergeant.

"Nearly eight hundred, sire," the Shadowbeast replied.

"Ladies and gentlemen," Vandross bellowed again, addressing the unit once more. "There are eight hundred Monks and warriors in the village. Blood shall be yours to spill, and lives yours to rampage over. I, Richard Vandross, charge you to destroy all those who oppose us with extreme prejudice."

Another roar of bloodlust escaped the gathered warriors and mages, and Vandross felt a warm glow moving through him, a serpent of joy slithering its way up his spine and into his insides. It was a grand feeling, indeed. "We march! Now!"

With Vilec Roak in the lead, and Vandross staying on the side as usual, the expeditionary force moved with renewed vigor and determination, each member of the unit thirsty for the taste of real battle. Monks would be able to provide them with just enough of a challenge to make their efforts worthwhile, as far as they were concerned. And to think, Vandross mused, we had a complex strategy prepared and everything. It was nice to know that for once, things were simpler than he had planned on.

Meanwhile, in a cave just a short way away from the four fallen mages, a Black Dragon chose to ignore the strange container the Humans had left with it...

* * * *

Shoryu sniffed at the air, his lupine snout twitching as he took in the surrounding scents. Vandross's smell wasn't one he'd soon forget, and when the company followed his nose over the crest of a slanted passageway, they looked down into what looked like a ghost town.

Morek Rockmight drew breath between his teeth in a harsh rasp of either fury or disgust.

"The warlock was here, but there has been no battle. I smell little blood here, other than that of a few animals," Shoryu reported, returning to the company.

Morek punched a nice sized stone, shattering it on impact; the rest of the company took a step or two back out of caution.

"He must have tricked the Dwarves who lived here. More black magic and witchcraft, more trickery. I tell you Byron," Morek growled through grated teeth. "You want him to yourself, and that is fine, but I want one shot at him. One glorious uppercut."

Shoryu stayed ahead of the company, leading them down into the village.

Byron looked around at the squat buildings, each hewn either of sturdy redwood trees or stone. None of these homes was exactly like another, and the overall atmosphere was quaint and homey. Judging from the bodies of a few guards, Shoryu had guessed correctly. The bodies numbered less than one dozen men. The struggle here hadn't been large, and there was nothing to indicate that Vandross had suffered any casualties.

"Byron." Shoryu sniffed the air and ground. "I believe we are losing ground on him. And I estimate from the tracks that he leads about one hundred men or so. There are some women among the ranks as well," he said, his nose twitching again. "Shall we investigate?"

Byron thought hard on this point; he wanted to ensure that no one had been left behind, Dwarf or otherwise, but checking the village would only waste valuable time. A moment later, he shook his head.

"No, Shoryu, we shan't. We already have enough to deal with. How far away from them do you estimate we are?"

"Well, good Byron," the Cuyotai Hunter tested the air once again. "We had gained a full day on them, and were perhaps eighteen hours behind. Now, we are a full day behind again. If we continue at our previous pace, we may catch them before they enter Dragon territory."

"Too late fer that," Morek stated flatly. "This is the border village. We passed by all of the other Dwarven cities by coming along these routes. I didn't make any corrections to our course because I didn't fink that we'd need to stop anyplace. I figured we might catch him here, fighting with the townspeople. Looks like I was wrong."

Byron tried to cycle through their options, and decided finally that following directly behind Vandross's force might not be such a good idea.

"Shoryu, take the lead once again, but parallel Vandross and his men. I'd rather not confront them whilst they're on the move. I want to dictate the pace and location of our meetings from here on, not him. Everyone, come on," he said, trying to sound upbeat, but knowing that he had failed. "We'll have our query yet."

The young Cuyotai Hunter gave his new bride a quick kiss, and ranged ahead of the group, finally reaching the edge of Byron's vision.

Shoryu led them into a series of pathways so narrow they were forced to march single file, with Byron in the front, and James Hayes serving as the rear guard. In this fashion they traveled for ten hours straight, without so much as a stop for food or water.

Though Byron didn't know it, another Monk village was about to fall under attack at that moment.

"Byron, come here," Shoryu called back at him as the passage opened into a field of snow on a flat cliff top. Across from him, Shoryu stood on a path that skirted the rim of a mountain, and it didn't appear trustworthy. He stomped through the ankle-deep snow until he reached the Cuyotai, and raised a proverbial eyebrow. "Look," Shoryu said, pointing to a point about a dozen yards ahead. The path had fallen away from the mountain, effectively barring passage around the mountain.

Byron had seen another path open from the field behind him, a path trampled flat from scores of feet; they had gained ground on Vandross once again, but he didn't like being forced to come right up on the one-eyed warlock.

Shoryu, curious as ever, crept slowly to the edge of the drop off, and nearly fell back when he looked down. "Byron! Bodies! Four of them!"

The entire company rushed over to the Cuyotai, being cautious not to make the same mistake as the four Illeck mages who lie dead three hundred yards below them. "And Byron, that isn't all," Shoryu said with a broad grin.

"What do you mean," Byron asked.

"I think I know," James Hayes said with a hushed voice. He too, was smiling from ear to ear. "Byron, I believe I can sense what young Shoryu smells down there. A Black Dragon, Byron. Just like master Wong told us."

Byron did a double take, and peered down the drop to the surface below. It did look like there was a cave mouth down there.

He reached out with his mystic feelers, probing into the shadows of the cave he mentally viewed through his magic.

Inside slumbered a hulking, black-scaled Wyrm, smoke steaming from its gigantic nostrils. Near its hindquarters, sat a cask, its lid sealed tight. The exact same sort of cask the Monks had used.

They had found the last Orb of Eden's Serpent.

* * * *

Richard Vandross had marched for almost ten more hours before calling the unit to a halt. The Shadowbeast scout had given Vandross the head's up that they were within forty minutes of the Monk village they sought, and the one-eyed warlock could hardly contain himself. He would finally have what he had come so far for. And without encountering Byron.

Something had happened, almost at the same time they had decided to go to the Monk village, and the Dread Knight had ceased to follow. Perhaps they had been unfortunate enough to encounter a Dragon? If a Dragon had attacked them, they would likely defeat it, but not without injuries and delay. They would have to take the time to set up a camp and lick their wounds, time enough for Vandross to claim the Orb of Eden's Serpent, and take himself and his unit back to Mount Toane without so much as a sighting of the Dread Knight.

His ranking officers, Lieutenant Amon, Major Tamriel, Talus Cur, Colonel Molis and General Vilec Roak all approached as he had requested, and snapped off salutes to their leader. He actually returned it in style this time, his optimism for the situation glimmering in his good eye.

"Gentlemen, I called you all here for a very good reason. The time is nearly upon us, when I shall receive the power of the fifth and final Orb of Eden's Serpent, completing the chain of artifacts within my body. When this is done, I shall have the power of the Glorious Mother of Destruction, and shall become a one-man army. And all shall be made to grovel in terror at my feet," he said, his tone of voice shifting into the dual harmony of possession. "When the time comes, and we return to Mount Toane, you shall each be given a reward for your loyalty, and command over new regiments. And you shall each be assigned to take control of a region of the land, and keep it in my name. The weak shall be tossed to the wayside as slaves and food for my beasts. The ignorant masses shall weep as they see me approach. And I shall revel in their despair." He threw his head back and cackled like a hyena, half-crazed with power and the promise of what was to be his.

Vilec Roak stepped forward, and caught Vandross's attention. "My lord, the men must rest, though they pretend they do not need it. Their thirst for blood must be slaked, but I fear that if they charge in now, they may not perform up to par. A good number of them may perish in the process."

Vandross nodded. Though he didn't give a damn about any of the lives of his men, he did care about their numbers. He would have to return through the mountains until he found a clearing of some sort to open a rift to teleport through. If they were attacked in the interim, he might still be too fatigued from unlocking the Glorious Mother of Destruction to defend himself. He needed as few fatalities on his own side of the battle as he could manage.

"Issue the order, General. Every soldier is to take food and rest. Have Talus Cur help them get to sleep with a spell or two from his men. We've already lost four to the mountains themselves, through their own folly. Had they not ranged ahead of us, one of the Gaiamancers might have detected the weakness in the path," he said, rubbing his goatee thoughtfully. "Get it done."

"Yes, my lord." The Shadowbeast General saluted before he moved off.

Vandross set up his own bedroll and curled into it, a smile plastered onto his face as he lay down to catch a few hours' sleep.

When he awoke two hours later, he felt refreshed and ready for anything, rolling up his bedroll and putting it back in his rucksack. He summoned his officers to him, and was immediately troubled when Colonel Molis didn't respond. Everyone else, including Sergeant Robin, the Human Beastmaster, had answered his call, each of them looking groggy but better off with the little sleep they'd gotten than before.

"Have any of you seen the Colonel?" he asked a tad more harshly than he had intended. He feared that the Colonel might be doing something foolish, like going into the village on his own to take the Orb for himself. He might be a half-demon, but he had a demon's blood, and a demon's ambition. He might try to claim the Orb for himself, and Vandross wasn't sure if his hold over Molis would remain if that happened. Nor was he certain that if he lost control, he'd have such a large advantage over Molis anymore. Probably not much advantage at all, now that he thought about it. Without the Orbs he already had, surely the Colonel could have laid waste to him; one Orb in the half-breed might make him a thousand times more dangerous.

"I am afraid not, my lord," Roak said with a stiff salute. "I noticed he was missing about twenty minutes ago, when I first awoke. I cannot sense him without great effort in the best of cases, but now, it is as though he never existed, my lord. However, I am certain it is not important that he be here now, my lord. If he returns too late to partake of this meeting, I can relate any information he might need."

Vandross harrumphed and went on to lay out an attack plan with his officers, all the while wondering what his enigmatic Colonel was doing. Perhaps something had called him back to Mount Toane? It seemed entirely possible that the half-demon would drop everything to go back to his place of origin. Some demons were territorial like that, and he wouldn't be surprised if his domain had been attacked in his absence. As a point of fact, he thought, he would feel better if that were the case. At least then he wouldn't be so worried about the Colonel's loyalty and intentions. With a brief shake of his head, he brushed the thought aside.

He did not know that the Colonel was closer to Byron of Sidius than to him or Mount Toane.

* * * *

It took a while, but James Hayes successfully lashed several of their lengths of climbing rope together, and volunteered to be the first to attempt the climb down to the cave entrance below.

As Byron anchored the rope by tying it around his waist, the Human Paladin made a slow, steady descent, reaching the end of the rope after about ten minutes. He gave a thumb's up to the others above him, and waited patiently as each of the members of the company descended in the same manner.

Lastly, Byron secured the rope to rock outcropping as best he could, and risked the climb himself. He had about fifty feet left to go when he felt a strange tug on the rope. Probably an animal had decided to investigate the rope, a mountain goat or lion, he thought grimly as he jumped off of the rope, landing awkwardly and falling on his face.

Shoryu and Ellen had nearly been bowled over when Byron fell forward, but helped him to his feet as he looked up. There was no sign of anyone being there, but the rope suddenly dropped down in a piled coil to them. James inspected the other end, and shook his head.

"Good thing you jumped, Byron. Looks like it pulled out from the rock." He showed the frayed loop to the Dread Knight.

At least it hadn't been foul play, Byron thought with a sigh. "Question now is, how do we get back up without the rope?"

"I think I can be of some assistance there," said an unfamiliar voice from the entrance to the cave. The company whipped their heads around to see a man in full silver plate armor stalking toward them. His features seemed obscured, and Hayes made the sign of Oun before himself as he realized what they faced: a demon.

"Who are you?" Shoryu leveled an arrow on the creature's chest plate. "I smell Human blood in you, and something else, something sinister. Give us your name."

Byron looked closely at the metal collar around the man's neck. On his left side, a small golden eagle connected to the collar. A Colonel, probably in Vandross's army.

"My name is Colonel Molis," said the half-demon in a calm, level tone. "Byron Aixler, tell this boy to lower his weapon, lest I be forced to make him lower it." The half-demon's voice filled with potential violence.

Byron sidestepped next to Shoryu, and lowered his weapon.

Shoryu kept the arrow notched, though, in case he had to open fire.

Byron then did a double take. The half-demon had used Byron's proper name. Did he know this man, this demon?

"I am a half-demon, in the employ of Richard Vandross the warlock. You all have good reason to abhor me, but please, trust me for now. I mean you no harm." The half-demon removed his broadsword, laying it on the snow covered ground, then kicking it over to James Hayes, who hesitated before picking up the weapon.

"Why should we trust him, Byron?" Shoryu whispered to the Dread Knight.

"Go stand with your wife, Shoryu," the undead warrior whispered back. To Molis, he said, "The Hunter raises a good question. Why should we trust you?"

"I, like you, was once Human, mortal, Byron Aixler." Molis once more referred to Byron by his mortal name. "I stand by the one-eyed madman for reasons of my own, which I feel no need to reveal to you at this time. But know this: I have taken a great risk by coming here to help you. Surely Vandross has realized I am not with him by now. He and his forces march on a Monk village farther north and west of here, thinking the Orb of Eden's Serpent to be there. But I knew you would find it. I also knew that you would need my help." Colonel Molis took one step forward, his hands open and out at his sides. "What say you?"

Byron thought on his choices. Had this half-breed been under his command once, perhaps when he was a Paladin in the Order of Oun? It was possible, for he sensed that the Colonel was telling the truth about his former status as a Human. But this might be another one of Vandross's traps. He didn't want to run that risk.

"Shoryu, Ellen, come here," he said.

As they looked into his eyes, he could see that they were anxious to be of some help in this situation, and to share the duty. "Stay out here with him, keep an eye out for anything suspicious. If you have to, kill him. I shall take Selena, Morek and James inside to retrieve the Orb. With any luck, we won't have to deal with the Dragon directly, for he now rests. Alex, go inside quickly and check to make certain."

Without a word, Alex flew out of sight.

"Remember, take no action lest you must. If this creature truly means to aid us, it will be invaluable assistance. Do you understand?"

"Indeed, we do lord Byron," Ellen said.

Now there was a title he hadn't heard for some time, he thought with a smile.

"We will not fail you. Come, husband." She took the Cuyotai's hand and walked over to Molis.

"Morek, Selena, James, let's get ready." As Byron drew the Morning Glory, he snuck a look at the half-demon out of the corner of his eye, but the man didn't even flinch at the sight of the blade. The Shadowbeasts in Vandross's employ generally had some negative reaction to the weapon, but the Colonel sat down and engaged himself in conversation with the Cuyotai Hunter and Elven Gaiamancer.

"Byron," James Hayes said as he returned his weapon to its scabbard, approaching the company's leader slowly, looking over his shoulder at the half-demon. "I do not like this. I sense great demonic power in him, but no malice. And he seems to know you. Will Shoryu and Ellen be enough should he prove hostile?"

Byron nodded, confident in Shoryu and Ellen's powers and skills. They had surely faced greater threats over the course of their service with the Dread Knight.

"Alex returns," James Hayes reported as the Ki Fairy joined them.

"Byron, the Dragon sleeps lightly. The slightest noise will rouse him, so I suggest we tone our volume down to a dull roar out here," Alex squeaked. "The cask the Monks described is near the tip of his tail, and though you might not know this, Black Dragons have a second set of nostrils on their barbed tails. He will surely smell you or the Dwarf," he said, dodging a swatting hand from the Boxer. "But Selena and James are freshly bathed and carry no natural reek of their own, like your flesh rot odor or the, well, whatever of master Morek here." He evaded the angered Dwarf's grasp once again. "Hey, at least we don't have any Jafts in our group."

"Keep movin', you smarmy little barstard," Morek said around a mouthful of dried meat from his supplies. "It's good practice fer me."

Alex darted over to Selena's shoulder, and the Pyromancer raised an eyebrow at Morek as the stout Boxer stamped up to her. His eyes barely reached her ample chest. He gave her an awkward smile, and turned away, grumbling under his breath. "Shall we get this over with," he snapped at Byron and James, who shared a broad smile at his expense.

Walking slowly, cautious and aware of their own noise, the four companions, five including Alex, crept into the Dragon's lair. They were not privy to Molis's conversation with the Cuyotai and Elf woman.

"So, you two are recently wed," the half-demon asked with an ease to his tone that made Shoryu instinctively relax a little. He gazed into Ellen's eyes for a moment, and turned his attention back to the Colonel.

"Indeed. We met in Whitewood, while defending it from your master."

Molis put up a hand reflexively, stopping Shoryu in his tracks. "No man is my master, Shoryu. I serve him as a means to an end, and nothing more. I tried to manage the casualties of that battle as best I could, but lord Vandross had an entire army there, you understand. It is difficult even as a man of my rank to control everything. I did not serve him when your village was attacked, but I have heard much of it. I understand why you both may feel a grudge toward me, but do not. Grudges are foolish." He took a water skin from his rucksack.

Shoryu peered into his open helmet, but saw only shadows and yellow, glimmering eyes like Byron's. There were no distinct facial features there, probably as a result of his demonic nature.

"So, why are you doing this?" Ellen asked, hesitantly. "Helping us, I mean."

"You do not know Vandross's plans," Molis said after taking a swig of water. "He cannot be allowed to have all of the Orbs. They already cause a great madness in him, and will do more damage still to his fragile mind if he is allowed to possess them all. Have you heard of the Glorious Mother of Destruction?"

The couple looked at each other questioningly, then shook their heads.

Molis leaned back against the mountain wall, and removed his helmet, setting it on the ground. Wisps of darkness writhed like snakes around his darkened head, and he scratched the back of his neck with his free hand. "It is a spirit creature, only capable of being called into being by the spirits within the Orbs. When all five are joined, they can perform a ritual within their owner's very soul, awakening the spirit. She is a volatile being, whose strength resides in the Orbs' manifestations. She has a single purpose; destroying all life around it, and absorbing the souls of those slain."

"Their very souls," Ellen gasped, her hand over her mouth. "Is such a thing possible?"

"Oh yes, it is dear lady," Molis replied, offering Shoryu his water skin.

Shoryu decided to give Molis a show of trust, and accepted.

"Don't worry, it isn't poisonous or anything. Vandross's intention is not to destroy the lives of the peoples of Tamalaria, however. He wants to feed on their fear for all time, using Eternal Rest to prolong his life, that he may rise again in centuries from now and repeat this terrible war. He is a tyrant of the worst sort, and with the Glorious Mother of Destruction, he will be able to spread fear and madness everywhere he goes. His dream can come to fruition if he has all of the Orbs."

"So without all of the Orbs, he can't raise this spirit," Shoryu asked with a hopeful grin.

"Actually, yes, he can," Molis said flatly, and Shoryu's face fell. "But the spirit's power would be a great deal less, and using the power would deplete Vandross's reserves entirely. He would be left defenseless for a short time, which could then be used to your advantage."

Shoryu gave Molis a concerned look, a question hanging on his lips. He finally mustered the courage to ask it. "Why exactly are you doing this? As a half-demon, do you not seek similar goals to those of the Shadowbeasts and other creatures of the Hells under Vandross's command?"

Molis laughed harshly, the sound of it scraping Shoryu's nerves raw. Streams of darkness shot from Molis as he chuckled, although the joke was lost on his two companions.

"Not all demons are made the same, young one." He put his helmet back on and stood to his feet. "I do as I do for reasons that are my own. But to ease your troubled mind, I will tell you this much. It is because of Richard Vandross that I am the way I am now. Otherwise, I would be a Human of upper middle age, possibly enjoying the company of my grandchildren. He took that from me, and I intend to make certain that he rues his actions. Now, let us make ready, for I can sense that there is soon to be trouble."

* * * *

Byron had let James Hayes and Selena Bradford range about five paces ahead of him and Morek. The group moved forward in a loose semi-circle, their eyes constantly adjusting to the surroundings, preparing for the worst.

One hundred yards away, a huge, black-scaled Wyrm, or Dragon, slumbered fitfully, its front claws twitching every so often. Its hulking upper body heaved up and down as it breathed deeply of the air, and its eyes moved rapidly beneath its scaled eyelids.

The Black Dragon stretched about twenty feet from snout to tail base, with a whip-like, spiked tail that was nearly twelve feet long on its own. This prehensile tail was curled now against its side, almost gracing the Dragon with the appearance of a large cat, not a creature capable of destroying entire cities or villages.

The group took small, hesitant steps forward, only moving about a yard every minute or so, trying to watch their step. Heaps of gold and silver pieces lined the floor of the cave, and if they made any sound, they were sure to rouse the Dragon from its slumber, a prospect none of them liked.

With his hand on the hilt of the Morning Glory, Byron gazed about the chamber and marveled at the treasures and items the Dragon had plundered. He could detect traces of magical enchantment on some of the weapons and armors, as well as a few shields that lay tossed about in disarray. Black Dragons, he had read, weren't big on presentation or appearances in their personal hoard. Blue Dragons, on the other hand, typically metamorphed themselves into large humanoid forms in order to give their lairs a sense of order and cleanliness. Then again, Blue Dragons didn't plunder townships—they weren't aggressive like their Black Dragon cousins. They only took from those foolish enough to insult or attack them for their treasure or scaled hides.

It happened when the four of them, Byron, Morek, Selena, and James Hayes had nearly reached the cask. Morek hadn't seen the perfectly round gold piece, standing on its edge, and he kicked it as he stepped forward. The coin rolled for a few moments, each of them locked on it with a sense of dread. Finally, it connected silently with the Dragon's left front leg—and its eyes immediately fluttered open.

Yawning, the Dragon heaved up and stretched its legs and back, its eyes blinking rapidly to clear its vision. It didn't seem in any rush to identify the source of its awakening. For all the group knew, small animals from the mountains might come in all the time. But as the Black Dragon looked lazily at them, its mild interest turned immediately to rage. Leaping back and to their left, the Black Dragon cornered itself, squaring off with the company.

"Who dares," the Black Dragon bellowed, the cavern vibrating with the echo of its voice.

Byron heard rushing footsteps, and looked over to see Molis, Shoryu and Ellen charging toward them. Had they known something was going to happen? They were already only a score of yards away, which meant they had to have entered about five minutes ago. Most likely, he mused silently, the half-demon sensed this would happen.

"Name yourselves," the dragon continued, "that I might know my next meal!"

"I am Byron, great Wyrm," the Dread Knight bellowed back, drawing the Morning Glory from its sheath, its length pouring holy light into the cavern, flooding every shadow with illumination and warmth. "With me are Selena Bradford, James Hayes, Morek Rockmight, Alex, of the Fairy Clan Ki Shoryu and Ellen Tearfang, and Molis. You have something that does not belong to you, and we intend to take it with us. "

The huge, reptilian beast laughed derisively.

"I suppose you think yours are the right hands, Dread Knight," the Black Dragon rasped. "Tell me what this object is, and if I have no use for it, you might be able to take it from me. Provided you play my game, and play it rightly. Do you want to hear the rules?"

Byron looked around to the others, taking special notice of the subtle signs and shapes that Colonel Molis wove at his sides. Clearly, the half-demon had decided that no matter how many games were played, the Black Dragon was going to want to play the only game that mattered to such creatures—the same game cats played with mice before eating them.

"Mine are *not* the right hands to own the object, Dragon," Byron shouted, so that his voice reverberated off of the cave walls. "But I do not intend to use the object. I intend to destroy it. As for games, certainly." He spread his arms wide in a gesture of mock friendliness. "Explain your rules, beast. I would enjoy a little challenge from an intelligent foe. Provided you have a brain sized to match that thick skull of yours."

The Dragon growled deep in its chest.

"You certainly know how to raise my ire, Dread Knight. Very well, Byron. Gaze about my cavern, and take it all in. Had a good look?" the Dragon asked, smiling toothily. "Very good! A series of riddles, my tiny, bony friend. First, 'I am what men and women of greed seek, though I am also owned by the poor and meek.' What am I?"

"Simple," said Byron. "You are gold!"

"Very good," the Dragon bellowed. "You have made a simple question quickly. Now, to make things a tad more, interesting," the Dragon mused, still grinning. "Next riddle. 'Though I have eyes, I cannot see. The world around me continues on, while I remain as I am. Through all seasons, whether winter or summer, I feel no heat, though once I did.' What is it, Dread Knight?" Byron scanned the cave's confines once more, searching for some sign of what the

Black Dragon spoke of.

"A question, Dragon. Must I be the one to answer?"

"No," boomed the Dragon, smiling once again. "If one of your companions is foolish enough to test their mental mettle against me, they may try. Though, I must be frank with you, Dread Knight, they are not as uniquely qualified to answer this riddle."

Shoryu stepped forward, his bow still in hand with an arrow notched and ready.

"A skull," he said, baring his teeth at the Black Dragon. "That is the answer."

Byron whipped his head over to the left, seeing a vacant skull amid the charred remains of lost adventurers.

Most of them, curiously, were Dwarven. Hadn't there been a truce between the stoic mountain people and the great Wyrms? Apparently, that truce ended at the entrance of this Dragon's lair. Yet, none of the Dwarven remains appeared to have armor, or weapons—all of the armor and weaponry were sized for Humans and other taller Races.

Had this Black Dragon been preying on defenseless Dwarves? Byron mentally logged this bit of information away.

"Very good guess, Cuyotai, and correct," the Wyrm boomed, his smile fading fast. "Only a couple more riddles, little ones, and the object in question is yours. Now, the third riddle. 'I am beaten, burned, and stabbed, yet feel no pain. I am as necessary to war, as I am to peace. I am a body, without a body.' What am I?"

"Armor," said James Hayes without thinking. It was almost an automatic response, for his seniors in the Order had used a similar set of riddles to test his knowledge of warfare before graduating to the ranks of an officer.

"Once again, you are correct, little creatures. And now, for the final question, one that shall give both you and I something we want. You seek to have the object within that cask, and I do not know what it is."

Byron felt a chill run up the length of his spine; if the Dragon learned what was within the cask, he was likely to set aside his rules and traditions in order to claim the Orb for himself.

"The last question is this! 'I am inside the cask thou so seeks.' What am I?"

Byron wasn't surprised by the question, though it was no riddle at all. Then again, the Dragon had used the question in the form of a riddle, and so hadn't broken its own rules. Dragons as a whole tended to adhere to their own rules and customs very carefully, as a breach of their laws would sever them from the rest of their collective species: a Dragon who broke rules or oaths, was branded a traitor to all Dragonkind. If another Dragon, regardless of their specific Race, came across such an outcast, they were allowed to attack without provocation, and the death of a traitor meant nothing.

"I shall answer this question, but you shall have to answer one in return," Byron called out. The great Wyrm turned about, and squared its body to the Dread Knight, obviously offended.

"It doesn't work that way, little man." It turned its head to bare its teeth at Shoryu, who hadn't closed his lips yet.

After a moment's hesitation, the Cuyotai backed down, his anger put quickly in his back pocket.

"You will answer the riddle now, or be destroyed. You can't have the object if you're dead, after all. Answer, and you have my word that no harm shall come to you."

"The object is an Orb of Eden's Serpent," Byron snapped, the blade of the Morning Glory blazing brightly.

The Black Dragon's eyes went wide, and it tore the cask open, dumping the Orb onto a pile of gold. Its breath came in heavy gasps as it marveled at the artifact of darkness, a thin line of drool escaping its lips.

"Marvelous," it said, crouching low to take it in its claw.

"Halt," Byron shouted, brandishing the Morning Glory at the Wyrm. "You said that we would have the object when we completed your little game!"

"Wrong, little Dread Knight. My words, exactly, were that you could have it if it were of no use to me. I owe you nothing, for I fully intend to make use of this artifact. I know of its power and uses, and to destroy it is not only almost impossible, but a waste of such glorious power."

The Black Dragon attempted to pick the Orb up, but Shoryu launched a volley of four arrows, rapid fire, into the Dragon's claws. The Wyrm howled in pain as the magic projectiles exploded on contact, ripping half of its front right claw off. "I gave you my word no harm would come to you. And you assault me?" Byron stalked forward, now only twenty or so yards away now from the Dragon's face.

"We gave no word that we would not harm you, Dragon. And we already know that your word is worth less than a pound of dog shit! Those corpses," he yelled, pointing to the Dwarven cadavers. "They wear no armor, bear no weapons, only torn and singed clothes and beards. Do you not have a truce with the Dwarves of these mountains? What happened to your word then? "

The Black Dragon looked at the corpses worriedly, and then back at its ruined claw, its mouth agape, stuttering.

"I, I, I can explain that. They, they came into my lair, without warning or welcome."

"That's horse shit!" Morek brandishing his fists at the Black Dragon. "Five years ago, the Black and Red Dragons joined the truce with the Dwarven territories. We swore there would be no exceptions, no breaches. You have clearly broken the truce here, Dragon. You know damn well what that means for you."

"No," the Dragon sputtered, his face falling into a panic, his voice laced with fear. "You can't do that. I told you, they came to me."

"Dwarves don't leave their cities without equipment," Ellen observed from behind her husband. "Many do not even leave their homes without a weapon."

The Dragon hung its head, and closed its eyes. Deep in its chest, it growled and rumbled.

"Traitor," Byron rasped, just loud enough for the word to echo throughout the cave. He pointed a single, accusing finger at the Black Dragon. "Traitor. You are to be branded a traitor to all of your kind, Wyrm. We shall bear you no more grudge." He sheathed the Morning Glory.

Molis gave him a look that seethed with frustration. The half-demon had apparently expected some combat with the creature, and was dissatisfied that Byron would give up on the Orb of Eden's Serpent so easily.

"No." The Dragon lurched forward and blocked Byron off from the entrance and exit of the cave. "I, I will give you the Orb. Take it, and leave me be. Speak no word of what you have seen here, and I shall forget you ever came. Please! If the others know of what I have done, they shall surely favor me with a punishment worse than death. What say you, great Dread Knight?"

Byron smiled like a devil, and made a gesture back to James Hayes and Selena Bradford, who lifted the Orb and placed it back in the cask, covering it up and carrying the cask between them to Byron.

"Agreed. You have our word, Dragon, which is apparently worth more than yours. This man," he said, indicating Morek Rockmight. "Is one of the leaders of Traithrock, and has easy access to your brethren for a meeting. Take any more of his people, and he shall reveal all that has been learned here today. Your fellows will learn quickly, and hunt you down. Do you understand?"

With a miserable look, the Dragon nodded, and moved out of their way. "Excellent. Let's go, folks. We're done here."

Without another word, the company left the cave. Once outside, Molis created a rift in the air, and the company stepped through, teleported to the entry path into the mountains.

Byron recognized the area from the remains of their campsite, and tried to manage a kinder smile for the half-demon than the one he had graced the Dragon with. "We owe you a great deal for this, Colonel Molis. I thank you for your aid."

The half-demon stepped forward and clasped Byron's hand unexpectedly.

"You owe me nothing, Byron Aixler." His crimson eyes flared for a moment, then turned into a shimmering blue. "Just don't curse my eternal soul, or any other Paladin nonsense." The half-demon disappeared in a cloud of smoke.

Strange, Byron thought. Someone said that to me once before. Who?

"I know him," he muttered half to himself.

Morek nodded his head, trying to remember something similar he, too, had heard a long time ago.

"Well, you have met a number of folks like me who were with you at the Final Push," Morek said. "Could be he reminds you of someone important."

As soon as Morek fell silent, Byron stood shock straight, fire dancing through his soul. *Of course*, he thought, turning and facing Morek.

"He doesn't just remind me of someone, Morek. He was someone. A Knight, and a great leader of men."

"Who was he, then?" Morek folded his arms in suspicion.

"His name," Byron whispered, looking to the sky for answers that weren't there. "Was Edgar Cesar."

* * * *

Poised high above the Monk village, Richard Vandross scanned the layout of the buildings as best he could, trying to mentally gauge which building would serve best to house the Orb of Eden's Serpent. One in particular attracted his attention—a smallish building, squat, one story, and heavily guarded by fierce-looking martial arts masters. Perhaps the Orb wasn't in there, but it drew his attention an awful lot.

"Roak," he whispered, waiting for his General to slither up next to him. When he felt the demonic presence of the Shadowbeast, he put an arm around his shoulders and pulled him close. "It could just be me being paranoid, but I suspect that there is something of value in that little hut there." He pointed out the guarded building.

Roak nodded, and squinted his eyes.

"Indeed, there is, my lord, but it is not the Orb of Eden's Serpent. The energy within that shack is not demonic. The very fact that I can detect it tells us that it is not what we seek. Remember, the Monks are capable of masking the Orb's power with their casks and containers. Although," he hissed, morphing his body shape to resemble a large serpent. "If you wish it, I can take a closer look quickly and see if it might be a nice bit of added treasure to our total."

Vandross shook his head to silence him, and gazed about some more.

"When we go in, we go all in, Roak," he whispered, still searching for something out of place, out of the ordinary. "If we have to, and I have a sneaking suspicion we will, we can raze the entire village, turn everything into ashes in the process. If we see something, shiny, we will, ah, procure it for our own."

He spied a robed individual exiting a common looking home and gave a toothy smile. The person, man or woman, was carrying something large and heavy, heaving it directly across the street, where she was helped in by what appeared from the distance to be a Jaft, or some other taller Race. They disappeared into the house after some words.

"My lord," a familiar voice rasped through the darkness.

Vandross swiveled on his knee to see Colonel Molis approaching, his eyes blazing brightly. Was that anger, or anticipation in his eyes? Vandross didn't want to hazard a guess just yet, and opted to wait with his eye and ears open, and his mouth shut.

"My apologies, my lord, but I felt it necessary to check on something. I sensed that the Dread Knight was gaining on us, and had to create a, diversion, shall we call it."

Vandross smiled again, and relaxed, breathing a sigh of relief.

"Well done, Colonel." He motioned him to come to his left hand side, opposite Vilec Roak at his right. "Roak and I are not certain where the Orb of Eden's Serpent might lie within the village, Molis, and since I only have one good eye, I'd like you both to take a look. " He excused himself to go around a rock outcropping to take a piss. After drawing a yellow skull in the snow, he returned to the Colonel and General.

"We believe we've found its location, sire," said Roak, taking the lead. "There is only one building with a storm cellar entrance. Three Monks checked their surroundings before opening the doors to enter. They were acting suspiciously, and between them carried a crate of some sort. We are pretty certain at this point, my lord."

"The house is at the farthest point in the village from us, lord Vandross," Molis chimed in, saluting. "We will have to get through the rest of the residents before we reach it."

Vandross almost laughed aloud at the tone of concern in Molis's voice.

"Excellent," he rasped, still trying to maintain the element of surprise. "We shall storm down among them, and tear them asunder. We shall leave no man, woman or child unscathed in our wake, gentlemen. We shall tear their souls apart. We shall bathe in their blood, and take rapture in their agony. No more waiting, no more plotting. The time is ours." He gave the signal to charge.

With a roar, the entirety of Vandross's unit stampeded down the slope into the valley with the Monk village. The first wave of marauders crashed into the guards closest to them, mowing them down in a splash of crimson, liquid fury as Khan claws tore through Human, Elven and Jaft flesh.

Shouts of terror and shock rose up through the rest of the village, as various Monks, armed with a plethora of martial arts weaponry, charged from their homes and places of work with their own war cries.

Vandross leapt into the fray, his scimitar flashing and dancing in the moonlight, the blade soaked through with blood in only a few minutes. After a few minutes of physical combat, he took a hard hit to his left ribs as a Jaft Monk, garbed in a black karate uniform, swung a stone war hammer into his side. As Vandross skidded to a halt, he leaped at the Jaft, who deftly dodged and blocked the stabs and slashes the warlock flung at him. *Damn it all*, Vandross growled in his mind, *this one is good*. The natural stench of the blue-skinned humanoid made his eyes water, and unlike many of the other Monks, this one showed little or no emotion. From the blue tiger patch on his left shoulder, apparently this man was a grandmaster or other important person in this Monk order.

Vandross stopped trying to wound the Jaft, and began playing a game of standoff, making each blow and each block a draw on purpose. But the Jaft didn't get flustered, or try to press any advantage. He played the game right back.

All right, Vandross thought, *let's see him deal with this*. He took a leap back, near to an ongoing battle between Lieutenant Amon and a lithe Elven woman, and launched a streak of lightning at the Jaft. *If I can't beat him down, I'll fry him.*

He watched the world around him slow to a standstill, and the Jaft's right hand left the handle of his weapon, sweeping in an upward arch.

As his outstretched fingers pointed directly in front of him, he repelled the streak of magical lightning, deflecting it harmlessly into the sky with a crack of thunder.

"What in the Hells?

The Jaft lowered the head of his weapon to the ground, muttering and chanting as he spun his hands in a circle in front of him.

Chi magic?

The Jaft Monk was obviously preparing to return the favor of Vandross's spell. He could easily defend against a chi spell, but he didn't want to dilly dally with this martial artist. The Jaft had proven a worthy opponent, and Vandross didn't want to call on the vast powers at his disposal from the Orbs. It would surely drain him, and he needed his strength to take in the last Orb.

Improvise, improvise Richard. And then, he had it. He looked up to a high point in the sky above, focusing on it for just a moment, calculating.

As the Jaft finished his chanting, Vandross lashed out with his free hand, and created a teleportation rift directly beneath the Jaft Monk.

The Monk's eyes went wide and Vandross looked up to see him fall hundreds of feet through the air.

He landed in a sickening crunch of bones and splashing of blood from ruptured eye sockets and organs.

All around him, his men and women crushed Monks underfoot, ripping limbs from bodies, tearing gaping holes in throats and chests, leaving only the harsh cries of agony and the thick, wet noise of bloody gurgles audible in the night air. Vandross's vision blurred with a cloak of crimson rage, and he stalked like Death incarnate through the waves of bloodshed and battle all around him. He randomly sent shock waves of energy ripping through the throngs of defenders where they seemed to have an advantage over his own men. The few Monks brave enough to attack him head-on met dancing death as his blade cut them cleanly into thrashing, writhing chunks of meat. It was as it had been in the Cuyotai village, in Koreindar, in Fort Flag. All of those victories, and now his goal was within a hundred or so feet.

He stood before the storm cellar doors, Vilec Roak and Colonel Molis with him. Each grabbed a door, and flung them open for their lord and master. He descended into a dimly lit chamber, where three robed forms huddled together, shivering in fear.

"Roak," he rasped.

The Shadowbeast darted through the shadows, ripping each of the Monk's throats open. Blood trailed behind him as he joined his master before the crate.

Vandross savored the moment, and with a grandiose gesture, kicked the lid open.

As he looked inside and found nothing, the warlock let out a scream of fury that could be heard across the whole of the land.

Chapter Four
If You Want Peace, You Must Prepare For War

The world around him turned into a blur of ashes, flames, and rubble as he tossed magic and bursts of arcane power throughout what remained of the Monk village. Crimson fury blazed in a stream of fiery smoke from his mangled eye, and as he searched under every pile of rubble and corpse. Had they come the wrong way? Had the Orb indeed fallen into the hands of a Dragon? Did they have a chance of finding it before Byron and his company? Molis had informed him that he had created a diversion for the Dread Knight and his group. That might buy him the time he needed in order to catch up, locate the Orb, and if the Dread Knight had it, wrest it from his broken body when he was done toying with it.

"Roak! Now," he screamed.

The Shadowbeast General appeared almost within a blink of an eye. For once, he gave a stiff, formal military salute, his knees almost visibly buckling with fear. Vandross might just decide to destroy him to get rid of some aggression, and Vilec Roak didn't want to think about how cruel the one-eyed warlock might be about it.

"Roak, I have to know something, and be brutally honest," Vandross said, his voice now locked into the twin harmony of possession he had used when engaged in combat or ranting. "Just how fucked are we?" He turned to face Roak full-on, his scimitar gleaming with drying blood.

"Well, that is," Roak sputtered, nervous as all Hells but knowing that honesty would, for once, serve him best. "We're pretty screwed. Um, my lord," he added, almost as an afterthought. "But all is not lost. We need now only get a fix on the Dread Knight's location, and we will have the Orb within sight. I can send a couple of scouts ahead, through the Shadowrealm, point them in the right direction if you can locate the Dread Knight as you have before. It can be done, my lord. "

"Give me but a moment." Vandross sheathed his weapon and tried to regain his composure. He focused his efforts on attempting to feel outward with his magic, sense Byron's energy, his soul. He found scattered remnants of where the undead warrior had been throughout the mountains, from the monastery to the east, to the path his own men had avoided due to the collapse. More concentrated where the bodies of four of his own magic users had fallen to their deaths. And on that small jut, in the side of the mountain, was a cave opening.

Inside, he mentally envisioned a Black Dragon, hanging its head in shame and disgust. It held its right claw up to the dim light filtering down through the cracks in the cave ceiling, to reveal a mangled, nearly destroyed stump.

Vandross whipped his energy back into his body. Somehow, Byron and his group had found a way down into the Dragon's cave and bested it in a confrontation that clearly wasn't entirely physical. If it had been, the Dread Knight would not have left the Dragon alive. However, Dragons were often fond of playing games with their intruders, and this game had obviously gone sour. Most likely, the Dragon had broken one of his own rules, and Byron had rather violently objected to his breach. More important was the lingering trace of magic on the jut. Byron had teleported himself away from the jut, but he hadn't gone far.

Vandross cleared his mind's eye, attempted to get a lock on the energy, and when he had it, he followed it as far as he could.

Byron had reappeared at the entrance to the mountains, where his company had camped before. Perhaps someone in his company had taken a severe injury from the Black Dragon. That would please Vandross greatly.

He followed Byron's aura another half-day's travel in the blink of an eye, and found him and his group resting in a wooded area. The Dread Knight only interested Vandross for a few moments; the cask in the middle of the company, next to the fire they had burning for warmth, drew his primary interest.

He watched as Byron opened the lid for just a moment, only long enough to shake his skull in what appeared to be disgust.

For that brief moment, Vandross felt the Orb of Eden's Serpent.

"Son of a bitch," he muttered as he drew himself back into his body and surroundings. "Son of a bitch!" He hurled a spear of black vitriol through a pair of Khan warriors scrounging for loot.

Their bodies shivered and their mouths foamed with saliva and blood, their veins showing black through their thin orange fur. They quivered for a moment longer, then erupted in a shower of blood and some tar-like substance. A single rib clipped Vandross's shoulder, but he didn't take notice of it, or the welt it left. He only had room in his mind for one thing: murder. Byron would not be foolish enough to keep the Orb with himself. As long as it stayed in that cask, Vandross would not be able to track it. If Byron had someone else take the orb, Vandross would have little or no chance of ever finding it. He had run out of options. He decided to take the one risk he had been truly afraid of.

"Roak," he shouted.

The Shadowbeast General was immediately at his side.

"Never mind the scouts, and never mind the last Orb. It is lost to us. The Dread Knight has it in his possession, and will no doubt have it taken away if he reaches friendly territory."

"Then, my lord, what is your intent?" Roak took note of the tense stance the warlock had taken, and the concern reflected in his wrinkled brow.

"I will consult with the other Orbs, and they shall undertake the ritual necessary to awaken the Glorious Mother of Destruction. When that moment comes, I will have enough power to crush all who oppose me and my armies. There will be nothing, no one, who can stand against us Roak. Now, leave me be. I have to concentrate, focus on this. It will be dangerous." He gave Roak a murderous glance. "Take all but a select few, those who have a good deal of blood in their bodies. I may need some sort of collateral for this ritual. Better somebody else's blood than my own."

Vilec smiled in response to the hint of insanity in the warlock's grin. Roak would gladly make a few sacrifices if it meant he could get away from Vandross. For perhaps the first time in his entire, eternal existence, Vilec Roak, Shadowbeast and demon, prayed for the mercy of the heavens, and he didn't care which god answered his call. No mortal in existence had ever left him feeling so afraid and ashamed of what he was as the warlock Richard Vandross. Even Tanarak of Sidius had possessed a veil of sanity and control; with the Glorious Mother of Destruction, Vandross would tear the entire world asunder just to get at the Dread Knight Byron of Sidius.

The General darted away, leaving the task of hand-selecting the unfortunate few to Colonel Molis, who immediately chose three Khan and a pair of pudgy mages from Sergeant Robin's troupe. Roak nearly had to drag them away, because Molis informed them that they were required to be "honored sacrifices to the will of lord Vandross." He had even lashed one of the huge Renkas with an energy whip until the groveling demon huddled in a heap next to the other panic-stricken warriors.

Molis encased them in a huge cage of glowing red iron, bars levitated out of the surrounding rubble.

Vandross nodded and thanked Molis, then ordered him to return to Mount Toane with Roak and the rest of the force. The half-demon approached Vilec Roak, whose only thought was once again escape. He feared the half-demon Colonel on the same primal level as he did Vandross, though now that he had time to think it through, Molis was safer at the time. He flashed a fake, toothy smile at Molis nervously, and the Colonel stood straight and saluted.

"General Roak, sir," rasped the half-demon. "Your orders?"

A military man to the core, Roak thought with an inward sigh of relief. *Follow orders, keep your nose clean, and don't draw too much attention to yourself.* He liked that about Molis. The half-demon, as long as he was employed in a rank beneath his own, would not be a threat. He had control so long as Vandross kept an orderly army around him. But what would happen to the order of things once the warlock achieved the Glorious Mother of Destruction? He shuddered to think about what would happen. Molis would likely mow him down just to prove that he was the most valuable slaughterer in the army, and curry favor with his lord. Then again, without structure, perhaps the half-demon would seek some other organization to assimilate himself into. Yes, thought Roak, that would make sense. And it would let him live longer on the mortal coil.

"Can you create a teleportation rift large enough to pass all of us through, get us back to Mount Toane, Colonel?"

Molis nodded.

"Good. Make it so."

He received another sharp salute, then Molis muttered in an ancient and dead tongue under his breath, opening a breach in the air before him.

Through the rift, Roak could see Mount Toane, his home. And, perhaps he thought, the good Colonel's birthplace. He would do some more digging when he returned, find that chamber he had been told about, try to unveil the secrets of Molis's existence. Of course, he would have to distract Molis, but he had a dozen choices where that was concerned.

Without another thought on the matter, he ordered the expeditionary force through the rift, going through only when all others, including Molis, had left.

The rift wouldn't hold for long, but he had to take one last look at the man he had chosen to serve.

Vandross had knelt on the ground, his head resting against his chest.

In a way, Roak hoped that Richard Vandross would fail in his efforts to awaken the Glorious Mother of Destruction. As silently as a shadow, he slipped through the rift, and was gone.

* * * *

The mirrors in the grand entrance hall of his soul had become of the variety one might find in a modern funhouse, warping and distorting Richard Vandross's reflection beyond recognition. In a few, he even had sprouted black, angular wings like a fallen angel, and his entire visage had become blurred and vaguely inhuman. But Vandross passed through with single-minded intent.

He had a mission, an objective, and he would not spare time to notice such subtleties. He wanted only one thing now, and it lay on the other side of those huge, obsidian double doors.

Wait a moment. He came to a stop a few steps from the doors. They had been wooden before: now, they appeared to be two huge slabs of stone, arcane symbols etched into their surfaces and glimmering the same crimson light that emanated from his ruined eye when the Orbs and his fury took hold of him. What was this? Some further alteration to his soul?

Shaking his head to clear his mind, he thrust the doors open and stalked across the narrow bridge, over the pit of fire, to the central dais.

The Orbs' manifestations were gathered, and they had used a series of chains to pull the casket upright. Within, something rattled and groaned, almost like a rabid animal awaiting prey foolish enough to get close.

"Gracious host." Power lifted the thin black veil from her face.

It too had changed since his last visit: she now looked more like a hag than the visage of beauty. Was this her true appearance?

"We have heard your thoughts, and acknowledge your wishes." She waved her arm before herself.

Once again, she appeared to be the young vixen he had first seen in the Orb of Eden's Serpent's manifestation.

"We are prepared to begin. You need only give the word."

Out of the corner of his good eye, Vandross saw that the other manifestations returning to their first appearance. Vengeance, the spider-like Orb, had been rotted and grotesque, more so than usual. Spite, the man-serpent, had appeared for a moment to have four or five heads, each biting at the other. And Deceit, the shadowy form of himself, had been black-winged and gangrenous, with boils festering all over his face.

He should have felt ill at ease; he didn't care anymore, though. What he wanted more than anything now was only a few feet away from him; in actuality, within his very body and soul. He needed only gain access to it.

"Then let's get to it." Vandross tossed off his cape and removing his upper armor. He knew the armor wasn't really there, but he had to immerse himself in the experience. If he lost himself in the ritual, he would be able to help the other Orbs' manifestations do whatever they needed to in order to awaken the Glorious Mother of Destruction.

"Where should I stand," he asked Power, who graced him with a coy smile.

"Right there, great host." She pointed to a spot only a foot away from the rattling casket.

Vandross stepped in front of the object, his dark blue tunic shirt clinging to his sweaty chest. He felt a little nervous, but he wasn't about to stop now.

On the front of the casket were various strange symbols, one of which in particular held his interest. It was a single crimson, baleful eye. The sight of it did not make him think of his own eye, however. That eye made him think, strangely, of other worlds. *What other worlds,* he thought? *There is only this world, here and now.*

"Now, Richard Vandross, cross your arms over your chest, and free your mind, your heart, your body. Let the Glorious Mother know what it is you desire. Let the hatred for those who oppose you burn through your veins, and let that fury be known." Power's voice turned cold and steely. She sounded almost distant in his ears.

He closed his mind's eye and crossed his arms, digging into the darkest places of his being. He saw there the potential for rule, the lust for power and hunger for the fear of others, and for the briefest moment, he inwardly shuddered. Had he always been this way, a small voice seemed to ask.

Yes, I have been, he thought in response, grinning from ear to ear. Those too weak to rule must be ruled. Those weak enough to fear should have something to truly be mortified by. And why not him?

"What, about, blood, Power," Vengeance shlurped.

Vandross hadn't realized just how annoying the spider-beast was when it was speaking.

"There is plenty available, my brother," she rasped to the spider-beast. "Can you not sense them huddling near us? Lord Vandross has prepared an ample supply for the ritual to be carried out. Now, let us begin."

The four Orbs' manifestations stood in a semi-circle around Vandross and the Glorious Mother of Destruction. They prepared several pots of a strange green substance and set them before them, chanting in a low, guttural language while weaving arcane symbols in golden and crimson light in the air. The dais upon which they stood rumbled and shook, and small portions dropped off into the magma below.

Richard Vandross felt bits of himself dropping like those chunks of stone, peeling away like an inner shell, and he realized that it was his last line of magical defenses dropping away. He would be completely vulnerable not only here, but in the outside world. Had he requested any guards, he wondered.

No, he hadn't, and from the strange way Vilec Roak had been inching away from him, he doubted the Shadowbeast General would have been willing to take on that duty. Perhaps if he had asked Colonel Molis...

No. He tried once again to clear his mind. Something had begun to severely bother him about the half-demon, as though he were somehow directly responsible for not only the demon portion of Molis, but the mortal host as well. But once again he cleared his mind, opened himself to the Orbs.

The first wave of energy that came from the Glorious Mother of Destruction struck Vandross like a stone church or castle wall falling on a rat. A small, undernourished rat at that, he thought as he nearly fell flat on his back.

For a moment, as he opened his eye, his vision blurred into a blend of his inner soul and the outside world. The sacrifices Molis had arranged were already being torn apart by strange black, wraith-like beings who seemed to be attached to his own chest.

He closed his eye and brought himself back within his soul's inner sanctum.

The volume of the Orbs' chanting had risen to echo through the chamber like a marching cadence barked by a maddened beast. Vandross risked a quick look up at the chained casket containing his ultimate prize, and saw that the chains were whipping back and forth. Another shock wave slowly erupted towards him.

He attempted to brace himself for it, but had no magical defenses. If he survived this ritual, he would hardly be in good enough shape to eat a bowl of soup.

Something like a banshee wail ripped through his ears as the second wave of power tore through him, and he felt the slow trickle of blood leaking out of them.

He clasped his hands to the side of his head, trying to block out the otherworldly noise—to no avail. Instead, he threw his own head back and let out a shriek of his own, one of pain and fury, predator and prey.

After roughly three minutes of listening to his own wailing, the noise stopped.

He prepared himself once again, but all had gone silent.

He opened his eye, and saw that Vengeance had scuttled forward on all eight legs, and was removing one of the chains from the casket. There were five in all, one for each Orb.

Vandross himself, the warlock realized, would have to take care of the fifth one in Despair's place.

There was little he could do to get ready for the third shock wave of power.

A blue streak of lightning shot from the lid of the casket and struck him squarely in his mangled eye.

In both his inner sanctum and the outer world, his body was wracked with convulsions, and foam drooled out of the sides of his mouth. He smelled the small hairs on his neck burning, singed into small, curled wisps. Thankfully, the energy lasted only a few seconds. Then his body slumped forward, his head striking the stone dais hard.

He pulled himself upright again, and saw Power removing a chain. The casket trembled, but had otherwise remained still since the first wave of energy.

Had reason held any grip on him, he would have worried. But the hits from the Glorious Mother of Destruction had given him no reason to believe that it was dormant. Rather, it seemed that with each expulsion of energy, the casket and the power within was calming.

Vandross reached down within himself for a moment, and detected the power he had felt strike him waiting inside, scrambling to be released for the slightest reason. He was indeed receiving the power he sought: it was simply much more painful than he had imagined. He could survive the pain.

The fourth shock wave, the fourth chain removed.

As the fifth wave of power ripped through Richard Vandross's body and soul, he hardly felt anything more than a slight buzz, as from drunkenness.

He rose to his feet, his body wrapped in a shroud of blue and red magic, his eyes burning with hellfire. The patch over his right eye had been burnt off, and a single point of darkness marred the yellow and crimson heat escaping from the socket. His body felt feather-light, and he stalked forward to the casket, grabbing the only chain attached to the casket's lid. With a single heave, he tossed the lid over the edge of the dais.

As it splashed into the magma below, a spear of darkness ran Vandross through.

For a moment, he thought he was being attacked, that he had loosed some sort of trap. But as the shadow weapon pulled itself into his flesh, he realized that this was the final step, the ultimate moment. It had worked!

He now possessed the power of the Glorious Mother of Destruction. With it, he vowed inwardly as he looked at his real world surroundings, laughing at the sight of the destroyed sacrifices, he would bring such horror to the world that none would go unscathed.

He looked down at his armor where he'd left it. Upon his breastplate now stood a new emblem. It was a set of blue claws joined by a single line connecting their tops. As if grasped in those claws, a crimson eye stared sightlessly from his armor.

* * * *

Perhaps it was the breeze blowing in from the northwest, or perhaps it was the sensation that an eye was upon him; regardless of the reason, Byron wanted the Orb destroyed more than ever.

The others in the company slept restfully, perhaps for the first time in a long while. They had been harassed, harried and rushed into conflict and confrontation ever since meeting the Dread Knight. One of their party members had died in the process, and two had found eternal love in one another. Alex, the Ki Fairy, had found a friend he could continue on with after Byron's inevitable departure from the mortal coil. It seemed that despite the damage done to their company, they would all see this battle to the end. The fate of the lands of Tamalaria, and perhaps even those lands that lie across the great blue seas, rested in their hands.

Good lord, Byron thought with a sigh, *what a cliché.* Such words could be read in the corny fantasy tales he had pursued as a youth. But they might, in his circumstances, be true. If he didn't stand against Richard Vandross, would anyone else in the land be able to defy him? Possibly Rimzan of Gray, but the Paladin had been injured in his battle with Tanarak of Sidius, and hadn't gone into battle since the day he exited Mount Toane with Tanarak's head gripped in his scorched gauntlet.

Another chill breeze blew through the camp as he turned his thoughts aside to a more personal matter. What of his relationship with his lord, Oun? Could he atone for his crimes as Byron of Sidius? Or was he doomed to suffer below in the Hells, forever banished from any god's domain? Would his questioning of his own faith bite him in the ass? He believed that other gods existed aside from Oun, but he had never accepted any of them as his own, never vowed allegiance to them. Would they in turn condemn him? What were the right answers, and furthermore, was he even asking the right questions? He had no way of knowing anymore.

The hulking Dread Knight rose and approached Shoryu and Ellen, waking them for their watch shift.

The couple dragged themselves groggily to their feet, rubbing the remnants of sleep from their eyes. The company would be well protected and warned should anything occur, and so Byron let himself lie near the fire and drift into slumber.

Even before he fell fully asleep, he knew that he would have another conversation with Voice this night. As he regained his senses in the cemetery, he saw that the burial plots were well tended and groomed, and the headstones looked new.

In the black void above him, he thought he made out a hint of light streaming down to cut through the fog that usually blanketed the cemetery grounds. "The place looks good," he whispered, almost to himself.

"Thank you," said Voice from the air around him. "I have attempted to make things more hospitable for your arrival. We have something to discuss, Byron."

"I would assume as much." Byron sat cross-legged by the lone tree in the whole cemetery. The ground was still fresh from his battle with the Dreamstalker, perhaps because he wanted it to be. A reminder that he was no longer the fearsome General of Tanarak's armies. "We don't exactly have tea and biscuits when I'm here, now do we?"

Voice chuckled softly in the background. "You do not often use humor, Byron. You are good at it. It is something I have never been very adept with. Perhaps we should discuss that which I summoned you here for."

"Yes, let's."

"The one known as Vandross has unleashed an incredible power unto himself, with the aid of the Orbs of Eden's Serpent already in his possession. But his control over it is hazardous. If he obtains the fifth Orb of Eden's Serpent, he will gain full control over it. That must not be allowed to happen, Byron. You must destroy the Orb when the sun rises. It is the best time to do it."

Terrific, Byron thought grimly. *We'll just be awake enough to risk destroying ourselves for this thing.* He had taken a short peek at the Orb before rousing Shoryu and Ellen from their slumber, and knew that the company could indeed destroy it, but the effort would leave them as weak and vulnerable as newborn kittens.

"Let's just get one thing straight. When we do this, the power of this Orb of Eden's Serpent will be utterly vanquished, correct? No chance it's going to flow through the realm to Vandross, right?"

"Of course not." Voice sounded almost indignant. "I know about these things, Byron. I am a Keeper, and have been in existence since long before your birth. I have served many souls, some I am not so proud of. I have experience in the Orbs of Eden's Serpent—from both sides of the struggle."

Byron nodded, reassured. "Well then, what else is there to talk about? Unless that was all, because trust me, I've had a bad feeling about Vandross's progress for most of the evening."

"I have sensed this. Your emotions are well placed, Byron. You will see the results of his newfound power before you reach Mount Toane, Byron. Cities shall be razed to the ground, and many thousands shall die before you put Vandross in his grave. But rest assured, there are armies forming to defend the land, and aid you in your march on Mount Toane."

"I seem to recall that not helping much the first time I marched into Mount Toane. In point of fact, that's exactly how I ended up this way." He spread his arms wide to indicate his undead condition. "What have you to say about that?"

"It is possible that you were always meant to become thus."

"I beg your pardon? I was a faithful follower of Oun! Even now I attempt to serve my lord, but I receive little more than more pain for my troubles. One of my allies lies dead in a shallow grave because of this quest. Was that meant to be?"

Byron took a deep breath, trying to calm himself. Voice hadn't done anything to him, after all. He shouldn't lose his temper with the Keeper. "My apologies, Voice. I have seen much that tries my patience and faith."

"Yet both you retain, Byron, and that is well. It proves you to have great wisdom, for few greater tests can be made for you."

"Well, pardon me if I harumph at that, my good friend," Byron said with what ire he could muster, trying to remain friendly. "I feel like I'm tilting at windmills out there, Voice. I have regained the flesh on my hands, the sensation in my nerves, yet not my true nature, my whole body. So long as Vandross lives, I cannot be whole. Yet when he dies, so too, do I die."

"Yes, that is quite a conundrum. I believe that is what you mortals refer to as a paradox. You know, damned if you do, damned if you don't?"

Byron chuckled softly to himself. "And you say you have no sense of humor. I simply want this all to be over with, Voice. I am prepared for my judgment before my god." He stood. "And by the way, Voice," he added as he began to fade, his shoulder being nudged by someone so as to awaken him for the trial ahead of destroying the Orb of Eden's Serpent. "I have a better paradox for you."

"Truly? And just what is that?"

Byron walked toward the entrance gates of the cemetery, his figure becoming translucent. "If you want peace," he said, unsheathing the Morning Glory as he stood to his feet in the waking world. "You must prepare for war!"

* * * *

The members of the company stood around the Dread Knight, staring at him with puzzled gazes. "Um, you feelin' all right gov," Morek asked with a raised eyebrow.

"Just fine, master Morek. I know you're all probably very tired still, from the struggles we have encountered, and the terrain we have most recently slogged through. We have been tired before, however, and now is the time to take action. We must destroy the Orb of Eden's Serpent."

Byron placed the cask in the center of the group. He quickly removed the lid and stepped back, and all of them watched as the black artifact of arcane power and knowledge hovered in the air.

"We must all use every resource at our disposal, but we must be careful not to harm one another. For those reasons, James Hayes and I shall stand across from one another. Our Paladin powers are great, but each of us is defended against them by having them ourselves."

"No, Byron," Shoryu said, shaking his head vehemently. "You may have the powers and soul of a Paladin, noble and pure, but your body is still the product of Tanarak's black magic. The risk to you is enormous."

"The risk to the lands of Tamalaria and the entirety of the mortal realm is greater if we do not make this effort. Ellen and Selena shall take up opposite sides. And lastly, Morek and Shoryu. Ellen and Selena, you shall each use your greatest powers on the Orb. But remember, no spells that would put any of the rest of us at risk. I understand the difficulty in that for you, Selena." He looked directly into the Pyromancer's eyes. "Pyromancy is especially deadly against Gaiamancers, and many of your spells affect entire areas. Simply channel that extra manna into a single target spell, understood?"

Both Human Pyromancer and Elven Gaiamancer nodded, looking to each other for reassurance.

"Morek, you have several sets of enchanted gloves, right?"

Morek nodded.

"Any that will protect you against all the magic that's going to be getting hurled at this thing?"

"I'll have to put on two sets, but one is skin-tight. Shouldn't be any problem."

"Good. Once we begin, you start wailing on that thing as hard as you possibly can." Byron talked faster as he went. Something was stirring within him, some snake coiled in the shadows of his soul.

The Orb, he realized, was trying to call out to that which Tanarak of Sidius had created within him. It was trying to coax him into absorbing it, as he had feared all along.

Such wondrous power it could bring him, it seemed to say. *Power enough to reclaim his Human body, power enough to take back his home. Power enough to destroy Richard Vandross and take the remaining Orbs for himself.*

No, he thought, calmly, patiently. He continued speaking, slowing down, preparing himself. "Shoryu, from opposite Morek, you shall volley your arrows at the Orb. Make certain they are mystically charged before firing them. We have little or no room for error here, people. Let's get this done!"

"What else is there, Byron," Alex squeaked from Selena's shoulder. "I'm a pretty good judge of lies or half-truths. After all, they're the majority of my conversational repertoire. You're leaving something out here."

"You are right as ever about that, my diminutive friend. There is one thing more to be done, but I shall shoulder that responsibility myself. When the Orb begins to crack under our collective energies, I must take the Orb in my hands. I must channel the convictions of my faith, my energy, and allow my very soul to touch the Orb. When this is done, I shall reject the Orb, and all it stands for. That shall seal its fate. Now, are we all on the same page here?"

Everyone nodded.

"Very good then, my friends. Let us begin."

Without hesitation, Ellen and Selena began channeling blasts and concussions of their own respective schools of magic into the very core of the Orb.

Morek launched himself forward, gloves slamming into the Orb of Eden's Serpent, sweat pouring down off of his brow from his proximity to both the artifact's force, and the magic being focused at it.

The dwarf's blows hammered into the Orb, causing waves of force to blow through it and into Shoryu on the other side, pushing the Cuyotai backwards. But Shoryu's aim was exact, and each mystic arrowhead plunged into the Orb's outer surface.

Standing opposite James Hayes, Byron chanted low in his chest, summoning up the courage and strength of conviction he would need in order to resist the Orb's call to his darker nature.

Hayes himself blasted the Holy Cross spell into the Orb with as much magical amplification as he could muster.

With a Q Mage in the group, the effort might have been made easier, but the company had to do what they could. Thus far, it appeared to be working.

The Orb of Eden's Serpent had developed a single crack, and when Byron focused his shaft of holy light through that flaw, several more appeared, accompanied by the sound of glass shattering.

Slivers of the Orb clattered to the ground, and the company poured more of themselves into the effort with each passing moment. They pummeled the Orb as hard as they could, but it became clear that Ellen Daires was waning. Ellen struggled to keep striking at the Orb while defending herself from the overflowing energy on Selena's side.

Byron drove his cannon of power into the Orb with as much effort as he could, and then drew the Morning Glory. It was a weapon of enormous Paladin power: channeling his own power through it would absorb less energy from him.

With a war cry and a leap, he brought the blade down directly into the center of the Orb.

The waves of darkness stopped flowing off of the Orb, and as the others of the company fell to the ground, burdened with fatigue beyond anything they had known, Byron clutched the Orb between his bare hands.

For a moment, he felt nothing. Then, he found himself in the cemetery.

* * * *

"Voice," Byron shouted to the void above him. The sky in his inner sanctum had gone dark as pitch, and lines of crimson light stitched themselves back and forth in the air. "Voice, where are you? Is the Orb affecting you?"

"It is not," the Keeper said from the darkness. "I am quite fine. You must do what you need to, and do it soon."

Byron looked down, and saw that he still held the Orb in his hands.

"You needn't do anything he tells you, Byron of Sidius," another voice intoned, its rumble and timber coming from the artifact that Byron held tightly between his hands. "You are Byron of Sidius. You are the great and powerful General of the armies that once swept over this miserable land. Claim me, claim my power for your own. Together, we can destroy the one who hosts my brethren, and take them as well. You will be host to the Glorious Mother of—"

"No." Byron attempted to crush the Orb as he would strangle Vandross if the warlock were before him. "You cannot tempt me!"

"Why are you so adamant? Perhaps, because you know that what I say is true. Think of the power, Byron of Sidius."

"I am that foul creature NO MORE."

Byron screamed as he hurled the Orb skyward. As it hovered over his head, Byron was assaulted by a wave of images: images of his time in service to Tanarak of Sidius.

He stood atop a pile of bloodied, broken bodies, the flesh torn from the bones and fed to the lowly demons and beasts he commanded. A heart, still beating from the woman's chest he had torn it from, squeezed over his skull, the blood absorbed into his bones. The lust, the power, the rush of the kill, all flooded back to him. He heard voices pounding at him, rushing him from every side, commanding words of power.

"I am your master," he heard from his left. For a moment, his body was wracked with pain, and his arms flailed about his body as a surge of black lightning poured into him. His vision cleared just enough to see a vision of Tanarak of Sidius, his cruel, long face glaring at him from behind his darkened hood. "You shall obey, Byron. Now, kill them. Kill them all." A long, bone-thin arm, as pale as the Reaper's horse, pointed at a small stone church, dozens of armed Paladins standing out front to defend the women and children inside.

In a flash of light and nearly a loss of all forms of consciousness, Byron found himself looking at a smoldering pile of stone and blood. Bones jutted in awkward, unnatural angles from plates of ruined armor and scraps of flower dresses, the sort worn by young girls.

"Enough," Byron shouted, clearing his own vision and glaring once again at the hovering Orb of Eden's Serpent.

"How is it that you resist? Why?"

"We, who stand against the darkness, shall see it banished by our holy light," Byron exclaimed. "No matter the cost!" With a war cry that made several of the lesser gods shudder in their respective heavenly abodes, Byron thrust his left palm toward the Orb, and unleashed the most potent Holy Cannon spell he could muster.

Another scream, filled with hatred and pain, agony so acute that the world itself stopped for a brief moment in time, shredded the air. The smell of brimstone filled Byron's lungs with the scent of the Hells, and his mouth with the taste of curdled blood. A moment later, the entirety of his mental environment went black like the void around the cemetery, and he could hear, see, smell, feel and taste nothing.

Am I dead, he wondered. *Is this it? Is this the limbo to which my soul has been damned?*

"Do not worry, Byron. You are safe, you are alive. You are not dead," Voice said from the darkness. "However, you are, broken. The power you used has, backfired."

"What do you mean." Byron felt a tad worried, but he sensed a breeze over his body. He would be waking up soon.

"The dark powers you once possessed, are now less than they were. You shall not be able to fully rely on black magic anymore. Your powers as a Paladin, however, are returning more fully. Do you understand?"

"Understand? By Oun, yes I do. I am less the creature of Tanarak's design and more myself. This is excellent news!"

"It is a double-edged sword, Byron," Voice continued, not letting Byron take too much comfort in his revelation. "Without that dark power ingrained in your makeup, Richard Vandross and his followers can damage you more thoroughly than before. You shall have to be cautious, and you shall have to be completely merciless with those who deserve it. You understand, of course."

"Indeed," Byron said as Shoryu and James Hayes helped him to his feet. "I understand."

* * * *

It began as a twinge in his head, and grew into a roar as Richard Vandross felt the fifth Orb of Eden's Serpent's elimination.

It didn't matter, he thought with a wry grin. He didn't need the Orb, he had possession of the Glorious Mother of Destruction.

He had returned to the throne room in his home of Mount Toane and begun a sweep of the inner chambers after sitting in his throne a while, thinking of new methods of torture and cruelty. He was looking for something very specific, but he couldn't think about what it was.

Irritated that he had forgotten the purpose of his query, Vandross sought out a handful of Shadowbeasts and turned them to dust with a lash of a crimson energy whip. Nobody important, he thought to himself. Once again he set out to find the source of his continued discomfort.

But he couldn't get that thought back. *Perhaps,* he thought in a moment of clarity, *I should just get some rest.* He had been through an ordeal. He had taken the ultimate power of the Orbs of Eden's Serpent into himself, and done so without the fifth and final Orb. He had unleashed only a small fragment of that power into the world, and he hadn't rested or eaten anything since his return to Mount Toane.

Yes, he thought to himself, his vision clearing and his thoughts falling into order. *Yes, some food, a bath, and then some sleep.* That would do him good.

Leaving the tunnels of Mount Toane behind, he snapped his fingers and teleported instantaneously to his bedchambers. He opened the stone door and poked his head out, seeing a pair of Khan sentries posted near the end of the tunnel. "You there, you two. Come here."

The two tiger-men stomped up to the open door, and gave Vandross stiff salutes.

"M'lord," they said in unison.

"What do you require of us," the Sergeant said, being of higher rank.

"Food, my good man," Vandross said in as pleasant a voice as he could muster. "And some fresh clothes, if you could manage it. The same style and appearance as these," he said, referring to his own raiment.

"Of course, my lord." The Khan sent off his lower man. "Something troubles you of late, my lord," said the Khan sergeant, his tone indicating to Vandross that this was territory where he would rather not tread. But, the tiger-man was not accustomed to fear of any kind, it seemed; he bore the markings of a clan Chieftain, and Khan Chieftains were notorious for going into battles they clearly couldn't win. "I know not what it is, but it has made you rather, well, disagreeable for the men."

"What do you mean?" Vandross found himself curious to know what bothered so many of his minions. Even Vilec Roak had become distant, and afraid.

"I mean, sire, that you have become exceptionally frightening to all around you. Most of the Khan have requested that their quarters and assignments be shifted in order to keep their distance from you, and lessen the amount of time near you. The Illeck mages set up barriers to ward against you, to warn them of your presence. The Shadowbeasts, denizens of the seven Hells, do their best to avoid contact with you. And, to tell the truth, sir, even General Roak is disturbed by your powers and temper."

"Well," Vandross said, striding over to a full-length mirror and taking a good, long look at himself. He looked and felt like hell on earth, his hair disheveled, his skin the color of ashes, and his eye smoldering with crimson light. "I do suppose I'm not the man I once was. I thank you for your frank honesty, Sergeant." He pivoted slowly on his heels to face the soldier Khan. "It took courage to speak to me in such a fashion, and I commend you for that. There has been something on my mind, that much is true. Sergeant, you're a man of obvious strength of character. Does anything frighten you, as it does the other Khan and Shadowbeasts?"

"There are few things that intimidate me, sire," said the Khan, standing slightly straighter, his proud mane ruffling slightly. "But I am man enough to admit to one fear, my lord."

"And what might that be, Sergeant?" Vandross sat on the edge of his bed.

"Well, sire, I can't swim," muttered the Khan, half to himself.

Vandross tilted his head at the Khan and stared at him a moment, seeing the set of his jaw, the shame of his admission. Surely the massive, muscular Khan was joking, right? Vandross burst out laughing then, a rough bark that turned into a hyena's cackle.

"You have got to be kidding," he nearly shouted. "So you can't swim? So drowning is your greatest fear?"

The Khan nodded roughly.

"Well, that's actually a bit of a relief, Sergeant. We're nowhere near a large body of water, and I can't think of a stream nearby that you aren't tall enough to stand firmly in." Vandross poured himself a drink from a private flask under his bed. "Sergeant, I need you to do something for me. It's about what's been bothering me most these days, and it isn't Byron and his ilk."

"Sire?" The Khan raised an eyebrow.

"Hear me out," said Vandross, yawning. "Colonel Molis. You know him?"

The Khan visibly stiffened at the name, but Vandross could tell it wasn't fear; rather, it seemed to be disdain, for he heard the rumble of a growl from the Sergeant.

"Indeed, my lord, though I do not know why you allow him a position of such high command. May I speak freely, sir?"

Vandross indicated that he could.

"Sire, I do not trust him, or any of the demonspawn. I do not enjoy the company of Shadowbeasts, and Molis is a half-demon of a sort I have never even heard of. His powers are too many, too great, and too unknown. You should decommission him and send him scurrying back beneath whatever rock it is he came crawling out from under."

It struck Vandross just then what he had been looking for all day: the place where Vilec Roak had told him that Molis had been using as his personal quarters.

"That is an excellent idea, Sergeant, except that I don't know where that is, precisely. Vilec Roak tells me that the first time he saw Molis, the Colonel was coming from a darkened cavern deep within this very mountain." Vandross reached around the Sergeant to the other Khan, who had returned with a set of clothes over his arm and a tray of food. Vandross took first the food, setting it on the lone table in his room, then the clothes, laying them on the bed. "Speak to the General, on my orders. Find that chamber." Vandross turned away from the Khan sergeant. His eyes brimmed with crimson light, a fire rekindled from before. He was in command, damn it. Molis could not be a threat to him. He had the power of the Glorious Mother of Destruction! He had summoned and freed that demon. Yet there was doubt, subtle but very much there. "And when you do, come back and tell me what you find. I will know this Molis through and through."

"And if he turns out to be a threat, sire," asked the Khan, extracting his claws audibly.

Vandross turned to face the Khan, his eyes smoldering and smoking with power. His shoulders were set, his hair standing on end, and the sheen of grime and dirt on his skin seemed to mix with his own dark aura.

"Unlikely, Sergeant. I created him, and there is a condition to his existence. He can never cause me direct harm."

"What of indirect harm, sire?"

"If that becomes an issue," Vandross bit an apple from the tray and chewing slowly. "I'll just undo him. You are dismissed."

Chapter Five
The Long and Winding Road

For several days after the destruction of the fifth Orb of Eden's Serpent, Byron and his company did little more than trudge toward the closest town and sleep. Eating took little time, as they consumed almost everything they had the first time they stopped for a meal. As a result, they slept little, and spoke less, trying to reserve what energy and strength they had for marching.

It was noon of the fourth day when they finally spotted a village ahead of them, perhaps an hour away due to the pouring rain.

Shoryu shook his fur coat once again, groaning with the effort and trying to keep a smile plastered to his face. Only Morek Rockmight seemed entirely unaffected by the downpour, his Dwarven upbringing keeping him immune to poor weather. Selena Bradford, however, felt miserable. Her powers were severely hampered by the constant drenching she was taking, and her attitude was as foul as the skies above her.

Finally, they stood a stone's throw from the outermost abode, and saw that the residents were not all commoners. A small group of militiamen formed ranks, and a single Minotaur stood at the front of their formation, barking orders of rank and file.

As Byron and James Hayes ranged ahead to see what was going on, the Minotaur turned and saw them, staring wide-eyed in disbelief.

The hulking Dread Knight slowly moved his hand toward the hilt of the Morning Glory, but came up short as the Minotaur came to full attention and snapped off a smart salute. "Sirs," he shouted above the thunder and splash of the rain. "You honor us with your presence."

Upon closer inspection, Byron saw a black armband around the Minotaur's forearm. On it was the insignia of a single skull, the same as the Elven bordermen had been wearing. Byron looked around at the others of the company, and saw that for the first time in many days, they were all smiling. He quickly remembered the Minotaur, who hadn't moved his hand away from his forehead. Byron returned the salute, and the Minotaur lowered his arm.

"You would honor us, my good man, by offering some shelter, food, and a few changes of clothes. Also, an explanation would be good to have."

The Minotaur laughed roughly. He turned to the assembled men and shouted at them to get what 'mighty Byron' had requested of him.

"My apologies in advance, your lordship, for their lack of discipline. Most have never served in any sort of army." The Minotaur led them into what appeared to be the village library.

Over the course of the last few months, Byron and James Hayes had both become uncomfortable with libraries, as had Selena Bradford. They seemed to be the only buildings in the cities they had defended that offered sanctuary. Yet, nearly all had fallen.

"And to tell the truth," the Minotaur continued, "I am only assigned as Sergeant-at-Arms because of my post as head guardian of my tribe in the mountains. Our peoples' guardians do not have a typical rank and file as armies do, but it was lord Viper's recommendation that I take this post."

Byron felt something like a thunderclap in his ear at the mention of the name Viper.

"One moment," Morek Rockmight fumed before the Dread Knight could catch up. "You mean the leader of the Black Vipers? The mercenaries? Just how has he come into the title of lordship?"

The Minotaur put his hands up in resignation and sighed. "After the Final Push, in which our people fought beside you, Lord Byron, the Black Vipers escaped to the Port of Arcade.

Tea was poured for each of them, except for Morek, who requested hearty ale. "An' make sure it's good, strong stuff," he muttered to the attending Private at his side.

"As I am sure you are aware," the Minotaur said, "for many years, the Port of Arcade had been nothing more than a lawless refuge for rogues and bandits and the like. Murderers, even, and it was a seashore city without law. However, on the long trek from Mount Toane to the city, lord Viper realized something: he could not go on living his life as an outlaw. The defeat of his people and the armies at the hands of Tanarak that day made him realize that true power does not reside in the raiding and banditry.

"'What I want,' lord Viper said to his remaining men, 'is to establish the city as a true city-state, complete with law and order, and codes of honor and conduct. It is nations that rule and remain, not vagrants and vagabonds such as we.' And so, Byron, the Port of Arcade has been under the lordship of Thaddeus Viper since the year after the Final Push. He gained his post by rallying the people, telling them that the slate would be wiped clean, that by establishing a sovereign city-state, all the initial citizens would be forgiven their past trespasses. Most were eager to join the cause. That, little man," he said, his eyes swooping down to meet Morek's. The attempt failed as the taciturn Dwarf was taking a long pull of his ale. "That is why he has earned the title of lordship. And, as a lord, his word carries much weight in the formation of armies."

"But, Sergeant," interrupted Selena Bradford, her head propped up by her hand, looking tired and bored of talk. "We are nowhere near the Port of Arcade. Surely some other lord governs this region?"

The Minotaur gave her a kind smile. "You are correct. However, my father thought it best for me to serve under a lord other than the one he serves. The largest influence in this area is Desanadron, to the south and west. Prime Minister Ashton Wilts of Desanadron is my father's keeper and commander of most of the units here," said the Minotaur.

"Guess again, me bucko," rumbled Morek as he wiped his beard of the ale that had spilled into it.

"Ah, yes, of course," said James Hayes, already interpreting the Dwarven Boxer's response. Morek stood, cleared his throat, and opened a window to let air in and his bellowing voice out.

"Now hear this, and hear it well. I am Morek Rockmight, born to the Western Mountains, Dwarf of Traithrock, and Head Councilman of that wondrous capital to the Dwarven Race. If there be Dwarves, Minotaurs, or Gnomes from that region, or any other Race from that region for that matter, come to the front of the library now."

"My father will not be pleased," the young sergeant muttered, almost to himself.

Ellen Daires placed her hand consolingly on the Minotaur's forearm, and he thanked her with a nod.

"And why not?" grumbled Morek, taking another tankard from the Private who had been serving them. "I'm as good a man to lead the folks of this area as any. We are talking about people of the mountains, aren't we?"

"Oh, it isn't that," said the Minotaur Sergeant. "It's just that, well, he just got off of guard duty a couple of hours ago. When he is roused, someone will wind up with a bruise or three."

Byron and Shoryu shared a laugh.

The company stood as one, and went to the front entryway to the library, where many had already gathered, including a large, oafish-looking Minotaur who bore an uncanny resemblance to the Sergeant. *Daddy dearest*, Byron thought to himself.

The son had been right about the father, though: he half-carried a young Jaft soldier who had two black eyes and what appeared to be a broken jaw that would need a few hours to mend itself, even with the Jafts' gift of regeneration.

From among the soldiers gathered, a single Dwarf, outfitted like a small war engine, lifted the visor on his spiked helmet, pointing a finger up at Morek. "It is indeed Morek Rockmight of Traithrock. Hail, rockbrother. Hail, Head Councilman of beautiful Traithrock. Do you know me?"

Morek squinted his eyes deeply, appearing to be closing them altogether. Then, he smiled widely and approached the Dwarf who stood in the drizzle that the rain had weakened into.

"Hail, spellwarrior Hamin Crow," he said with a salute and a grin. "Head of the city's night watch! Have you no criminals back home to apprehend?"

"There is but one criminal from whom we must take the blood," growled the armored Dwarf. "And his name is Richard Vandross."

Several dozen loud cheers went up from behind him, and Byron felt his mind reel with memories. Things had been like this shortly before the Final Push, all those years ago. It had all began with a gathering together of smaller, independent armies, until all joined together before the ominous Mount Toane. Now, almost twenty years later, Byron was faced the same situation, save three major differences. Firstly, the enemy of the land was Richard Vandross, not Tanarak of Sidius. Secondly, Byron was now a Dread Knight, a creature of the undead, instead of the Human Paladin of fame. And then, he thought with a smile, there was the third, and perhaps, most important difference.

Tanarak of Sidius had possessed great power and guile, due to his possession of all five of the Orbs of Eden's Serpent. Richard Vandross did not.

One of those few instances, he thought, where less was more. He shook his head to bring himself back to the moment, and looked at the young Sergeant-at-Arms. "There shall be time for a pissing contest later, Morek," he snapped at the Dwarf, who shrugged his shoulders in deference to the company's undisputed leader. "Sergeant, go and fetch lord Viper. We have important matters to discuss, among them the march of these units toward Mount Toane."

The Minotaur saluted stiffly, his father joining him as he jogged away, slapping the younger man upside his horned head with such effect that the Sergeant nearly fell.

Morek continued to speak swiftly with those who had gathered before the library, while Byron slipped away from the bulk of the group, out into the open road. The rain had ceased completely, the slightest hints of sunlight streaming through the clouds above.

He heard Shoryu approaching before he saw the Cuyotai Hunter. Having spent more time with him than most of the other members of the company, he almost always knew where the young were-coyote was.

It was a comfort to him, he realized. He looked to the young Shoryu almost as if he were his own son, little Jacob. After all, had he lived, he would be around twenty years of age—a young adult like Shoryu. But rather than dwell on the comparison, he greeted Shoryu with the best facsimile of a smile he could manage. "Shoryu," he said, nodding.

"Good Byron," the Cuyotai responded in kind, taking a seat on a storefront's steps. "I must thank you once again for doing Ellen and I the honor of being the witness to our wedlock."

"It was nothing, lad," said Byron, putting a heavy hand on Shoryu's right shoulder. "I was more than happy to do it." Something still bothered Shoryu, he could see. Perhaps not bothered him, per se, but something surely sat on his mind. "What troubles your thoughts," he asked gently, taking a seat a step below Shoryu, so they were eye level.

"I have been thinking long about our travels together. You have protected me many times since first I joined you, or rather, since you first rescued me. To tell the truth, I still can't understand what made you take me away from there. I don't regret that you did, mind you," he said, waving his hands and trying not to be too defensive. "It's just that, well, I feel that I may have sometimes slowed you down, held you back. Made you hesitate when you would not otherwise do so," he finished, muttering the last words almost to himself.

Byron, looking sidelong at him with his head cocked at an angle, felt a flush of warmth spread through him. He threw his arm around Shoryu's shoulders and pulled him into a headlock, rubbing his coarse, tan fur as he might a child's hair.

The young Hunter struggled briefly, then laughed at the Dread Knight's antics.

"You have been an invaluable ally, Shoryu Tearfang," Byron proclaimed, his voice carrying a hint of pride in it. "Moreover, you have been a companion whom I would not replace if even given the choice. As for why I took you with me to begin with—" he leaned in close and whispered in a serious and conspiratorial voice. "I saw great things in store for you. If I had left you, you would have been lost for the whole of your life, perhaps. Or, you would have joined another tribe, only to be treated like a burden and outcast. Trust me," he said, turning away to see the Sergeant-at-Arms returning with a Human garbed in black and yellow robes. "Nobody deserves that." Byron offered the stranger in the hooded robes a moderate bow, keeping his eyes raised to watch for any sign of treachery. If Thaddeus Viper were beneath those robes, he would want to see exactly how the man would react to his presence.

A moment later, he received a pleasant surprise.

It should be said first that among the many Races that reside in the lands of Tamalaria, Humans are among the shortest lived. If they do not destroy one another or die in wars and petty squabbles with members of the other, more powerful Races, then time itself unravels the fabric of their mortality at a much swifter pace than it does with most other Races. Small hands, laced with scars and veins so varicose Byron thought the man might be a walking corpse, reached up to pull back the hood that concealed the wizened face within.

Thaddeus Viper, a man whose years now numbered somewhere in their late fifties, looked much different than he had only twenty years before.

The leader of the mercenary band, the Black Vipers, had been a strapping, well-built man of middle age when last Byron had laid eyes upon him. His eye had gleamed with the promise of battles to be won and prizes to be earned or taken away; his laughter had been maddened and bloodthirsty; his body had been a tightly coiled collection of toned muscles and animalistic instincts. But none of that could be seen in this humbly adorned elder. Thaddeus Viper, ruthless thug and mercenary, had become Thaddeus Viper, Prime Minister of the Port of Arcade.

His hair, always tied straight back and as black as the night, now hung about his head in gray wisps barely attached to his head. His eyes no longer held the steely glare of greed, but rather a soft sort of warmth, a glow of a sort that an elder or responsible politician might take on after years spent finding out just how difficult it could really be to maintain peace in one's own region. "Greetings, Byron," rasped the old bandit. "It has been a rather long time, and much has happened for each of us. Perhaps we shall have some time later to discuss those things, catch up on these last twenty years?" Viper's smile sent creases across his face, lines of age and worry set deep in the flesh.

"That would be most welcomed, old friend," Byron replied in a gentle tone. "But first, we must discuss our marching strategy. I do not wish to force your men into a sudden sojourn, but we should try to get going south by tomorrow. It is my intention that we join the regiments here, under yours and Morek's command."

The old man offered a slight bow to the master Boxer.

"We shall head to the borderlands of the Elven Kingdom, and see if they are preparing an army to stand with us at Mount Toane. From there we can calculate our first move."

Thaddeus Viper laughed gently, the kind laugh of an old wise man, patting Byron on the shoulder by reaching almost a full foot over his own head.

"Good and mighty Byron Aixler." Viper coughed for a moment. "Word had reached us yesterday that you were coming. A strange, conflicted creature, much as you are, I imagine, suddenly appeared at the Feather's Drop Inn, where I have been staying while the regiments prepare for the long march to Mount Toane. He gave me no name, but I sensed demon's blood in him." Viper's eyes became milky and unfocused as he recalled the memory. "He was clad in great, silver armor, and he bore a military uniform of some sort. He had a marking on his collar, an officer for certain, but of whose army, I do not know."

Byron had already guessed the identity of the creature. Colonel Molis, the half-demon. Or, as he would always know him, Edgar Cesar, second-in-command of the Final Push.

"We are ready to march out of this village at the drop of a hat," Viper said, signaling to a runner.

The young half-Elf man listened closely as Viper whispered something in his ear, then saluted and sprinted off down the street at top speed.

As Byron and his company were led to an inn to bathe, eat and rest, a loud horn sounded out over the village. Dozens of small platoons marched down the streets past the company as they walked up on the front porch of the quaint little inn, opening the twin oak doors and stepping into the lobby.

There a Gnome with the thickest glasses they'd ever seen smiled at them and handed each a room key without a question.

Byron thought he recognized the little man. "You are familiar to me, good master Gnome," he said.

The Gnome innkeeper smiled at him broadly. "I should think so, master Byron," the little man replied, tearing his attention away from his book. "I was once the innkeeper in Koreindar, before Richard Vandross attacked the church of Oun. You stayed there, though I didn't know who or what you were at the time you checked in."

Byron shrugged his shoulders and produced coins to pay for the rooms but the Gnome pushed them back at him, shaking his head. "Please, it's on the house, my lordship. You need only repay me by getting rid of that warlock once and for all. I've given you each your own room."

Shoryu handed his room key back to the Gnome. "We're together," he said, indicating his wife, Ellen Daires.

The Gnome grinned and winked.

The young Cuyotai Hunter flushed slightly, then turned. He and Ellen went down the hall with Ellen to their room, promptly locking the door behind them with a loud snick.

As they each headed towards their own chambers, Alex hovered in front of Byron for a moment.

"So, if those two, you know, have kids, what will they be? Will she have puppies, or what?"

He smacked hard into the wall as Byron flicked him with his index finger.

"I don't know, but that's a rather rude way of wording it, my diminutive friend." The Dread Knight entered his humble little room, removed his upper plate armor, and was unconscious before his skull even hit the pillow.

* * * *

Flames all around him, burning him, eating his very body alive, the only sound he heard were his own terrified, strangled wails of agony. A trap. It had been a trap, and he had been foolish enough to lead several hundred men headlong into it. How could he have not known?

And then, a single vision, something dark and foreboding, approaching through the haze of smoke and flames, straight at him. A strange, harsh voice, like claws scraping marble, speaking to him through the haze, its words as clear as thoughts. "Thy time is nigh at hand, and that is a shame, for I have need for one such as you. But thou dost not seek to embrace the sweet release of death, and I sense a greater strength in you than in many others. Doth thou seek to live?"

Yes, great Oun in heaven yes, he thought, his agony slightly dissipating in the odd creature's presence.

"Then so be it. You and I shall join as one, for I cannot achieve my purpose alone, as I am. Even summoned, freed into the mortal realm, I require a host. Do you accept that you shall be forever changed?"

Anything, he thought, the pain resurfacing, taking away all rational thought.

"So be it."

An arctic blast of power rushed all through his body, numbing every inch of his being, stunting his thought process. A different sort of pain came then, his bones snapping inside, his muscles and blood boiling and stretching, taking on a new shape. His mind reeled with pain, but he felt almost at peace, as though it was what was always meant to be.

There came a small point of light in his field of vision, the darkness receding around his eyes, turning into a recognizable tunnel of earthen rock and granite. His point of view was from the ground, on his stomach, and as he rose, he felt himself gaining strength, confidence. He was ready to fight once again.

"No," the voice spoke to him in his mind. "We need rest, and badly. We are not ready yet for any confrontation. We must take refuge. There is a chamber in which we can rest, where none shall find us. Move forward, host."

He immediately knew why the voice had suggested rest. He felt like a dozen Orcs or Ogres had hammered on him with cudgels for a day or so, and his new body was awkward, clunky. It seemed to have come fully armored, and larger than his previous body, more muscular and angular.

He half-dragged himself down twisting tunnels, noting how shadows seemed to pool around his feet, and how every little noise was discernable to his new ears. He heard a strange, rapid clicking noise, spun himself around to see if something was coming in pursuit of him.

What he saw was a medium sized spider making its way down the wall behind him, towards the floor of the tunnel. Its movements sounded crystal clear to him, and when he scrutinized the arachnid, he could hear its heartbeat and the rush of fluids through its bodily systems.

He shook his head and moved off down the tunnel once more.

"It's going to be an interesting day," he said, and marveled at how strange his own voice sounded.

After an hour of punishing movement, the voice in his mind spoke to him once more. "There, in that cavern."

The man who had become something more saw a chamber entrance, but noted how no light seemed to enter it.

As he stepped inside, he heard a whirl of air. Behind him, in the entryway, he saw a strange, light blue barrier. A small set of candles sat on what appeared to be an altar of some sort, perhaps twenty or so feet away from him. Upon this altar was a single symbol, one he didn't recognize, that neither he nor the creature inhabiting him knew—a set of hooked claws with a single blue line connecting their tops.

There were no other entrances or exits to or from the chamber, but there was a mirror next to the altar.

The man approached it slowly, wary of what he would see.

"Look upon yourself, once-mortal," the voice said. "See what we have become together. You are no longer the same as you were, but then, neither am I."

"What is your name?" the man asked, once again surprised to hear the dark and twisted sound of his own voice. Finally, he stood before the mirror, and his breath whistled through his teeth as he gazed upon his new countenance.

"My name is not important, but I shall tell you. It was Ezdareus, and I was one of Hell's rebels. My post was that of Tarum torturer. Those whom the god Tarum judged to be sinners, and who would not be vouched for by any other god, were sent to me and my men, in the third ring of Hell. But I could no longer stand to be the conductor of their eternal suffering. Thus, I removed myself from the Hells. Here, my essence was trapped, until a warlock inside this mountain released my energies, though he gave me no host. I required a host, and a way into the mortal realm. I found you, sensed your potential over all of those others. I also sensed that you are a good and noble man, a man of a god. Is that, correct?"

"Yes," said the once-mortal, adjusting now to his new voice.

As he looked into the mirror, he felt a mounting dread that he was stuck in his new body, instead of inhabiting it. He didn't feel entirely whole, a sensation that confused and frightened him. He didn't appear to have a face, but rather, a collection of shadows with two yellow, gimlet eyes set in it. "I was a follower of the great god Oun, though I must admit, I don't think he'll take me as I am.

"That is foolishness, once-man," the creature said. "You are the same, your soul is intact. We are simply joined now, two souls and bodies making one. Now, you shall give us a new name, one that we shall identify ourselves as to the world around us. It cannot be your old name; that name has no meaning now, as mine does not. Who are we now, once-man?"

The half-breed thought on this, and finally came up with a name that sounded fitting. It was a word in the ancient tongue of the Mystics, a word that meant 'sinner'.

"Our name, is Molis," the once-mortal said.

The half-demon Colonel sat upright from his dream-memory, soaked in sweat beneath his armor. He was back in that chamber, resting himself for the task that lay ahead of him. But even awake, the last bit of his memory played itself over in his mind. The demon had then asked him a question from within himself, before he had taken his first rest in his new body.

"By the way, once-mortal," it had said. "What was your mortal name?"

And the once-mortal gave him the same reply that Byron of Sidius would years later, standing outside of the lair of a Black Dragon.

* * * *

It is said that there is no rest for the wicked. How appropriate, thought Vilec Roak as a Khan Sergeant had just reported that he was to search for Colonel Molis's place of rest.

The Khan, a clever man in Roak's estimation, had asked the General to aid in the effort, as Roak's servant had been there to see Molis emerge from that chamber.

The Shadowbeast General had agreed to accompany the tiger-man, though he sensed a fair amount of dislike and discomfort from the Sergeant. Markus Triclaw, his name was, Roak had learned. A Khan who had began in the post of Sergeant, and who had refused promotions offered by Lieutenant Amon and Major Tamriel both, Triclaw seemed comfortable in the position of First Sergeant. After all, Roak thought glumly, Sergeants are very hands-on, whereas officers tended to only seem to be assigned managerial tasks.

Roak had, of course, been very hands-on. He was a Shadowbeast, and regardless of post or position, he refused to simply stand by and issue orders. That much, it seemed, he had in common with the Khan.

There was that, and the fact that he didn't trust Triclaw as far as he could probably throw the solid ruffian. Why had Vandross given such a task to the Khan when both the one-eyed warlock and Vilec Roak had already scoured the entire catacomb system under the mountain? Possibly Vandross needed rest and time to further plot against the peoples of Tamalaria, and this Sergeant was the only available body willing to undertake the task. Yes, Roak thought, that made sense. After all, Khan had keen noses, and a sense for anything that appeared to be out of place. Perhaps Roak would have better luck finding Colonel Molis's hiding hole with Triclaw at his side.

"I grow tired of these tunnels," the Sergeant finally said, breaking the ever-thickening silence between them. "We have searched this area already. We must go deeper down, into the very bowels of this place."

Roak felt himself twitch: such insolence!

The tiger-man was already heading down a tunnel that would lead them even further underground, not hesitating for even a moment.

The Shadowbeast General called out to the Khan to stop, making it a militant order. Triclaw, like a good little toy soldier, did as he was told.

"Do not forget your place, First Sergeant," Roak hissed at him from the deepening shadows. "I am the General of this army, and you will go no place and do nothing unless I say otherwise. Understood?" He glared at Triclaw with all the menace he could muster.

The Khan didn't flinch.

"Understood, sir." Triclaw's voice was slow and timorous, as though he had trouble controlling his reaction to Vilec Roak's reprisal. "Permission to speak freely, sir?"

"Hmm. Granted, but only for a minute."

"You attempted to intimidate me a moment ago, didn't you?"

The question was so abrupt and unexpected that Roak floundered for a response. Had he been so obvious? He had felt the deception and cunning of his kind trickle slowly out of him the more time he spent above the surface of the Seven Hells, and he'd developed emotions that would not even have a clear term to describe them where he hailed from. If the Khan could see through him, how far gone was he from the essential nature of a true Shadowbeast? Sure, he had been Prime in Hell, and now he stood as the General of Tamalaria's greatest power; but suddenly, he felt as weak and pathetic as the mortal creatures he had been summoned to crush under his heel!

"So what if I did," he retorted, trying to regain his composure.

"I am a Khan Chieftain, before all other things, demon," Triclaw said, spitting on Roak's foot as if the word were a curse. "I do not know fear from the likes of you. The moment this war is over, and Lord Vandross controls all things in the lands, he shall disband the need for ranks and regulations. When that time comes, bottom feeder, I shall have a headstone prepared for you. And I," he said, pressing his feline snout up against Roak's forehead, stooping slightly to do so. "I shall be the one to put you in the grave," he whispered, growling deep in his belly. "Sir," he added, returning to a strict, upright military stance.

He had been good to his word; he spoke quite freely, but only for the minute that Roak had given him. Disciplined, powerful, and most likely deadlier than even Lieutenant Amon, this Markus Triclaw was, Roak thought. He would keep a keen eye on the Khan for the remainder of the evening. When they came up empty once again on the search for Molis, he would slit the Khan's throat for being so presuming, and he would have his skull fashioned into an ornamental goblet. That, he mused, would keep any more of the tiger-men from getting lippy with him.

As they descended to a new level of Mount Toane, Vilec Roak sensed the slightest smell of rot and decay lingering in the air. He could hear Triclaw snuffling, using his fine sense of scent to guide him as Roak sparked a torch to light the way.

Bones and burnt out armor littered the tunnel for hundreds of feet in each direction. Apparently, there were a few ways to get to each level of the mountain, and they had come down one that had been used before, to a rather negative end.

Wait a minute, Roak thought. *I recognize this tunnel, I have heard of it.* One of the detachments of the armies at the Final Push, twenty years earlier, had come down one such tunnel and had all been burned alive by a set of spells that had been locked as traps for the unsuspecting regiment.

As he realized where he stood, knowing that Lord Vandross had set the spells, he looked up and found that Triclaw was moving off ahead without him.

Roak sprinted for a moment to catch up, and both men took their time looking at the bodies in their individual states of decay and rot. One or two of them had weapons and armor that were apparently magical in nature, for time had done nothing to them. One body in particular interested Roak, not because of any equipment it bore, but because of a familiarity in it. It was the body and bones of a large Cuyotai, a series of smears and demonic residue clinging to his fangs, claws, and the tunnel around him. He had slain many of the Shadowbeasts under Tanarak's control.

After what felt like an eternity, he heard a sharp intake of breath from the Khan.

Roak moved up next to him to look at what had drawn such a reaction from Sergeant Triclaw. "What is it," he rasped, trying to be quiet.

"This cave entrance," Triclaw said, pointing a few feet away from him where a perfectly circular portal had been cut into the gut rock of the mountain. "It allows no light through. When I tried to put my hand in, it was burned by a strange blue barrier." He showed his burned right hand to the Shadowbeast General. "This is a magic that is not familiar to me. I have never smelled such power."

Roak looked at the barrier, and felt his muscles constrict in panic. He recognized it immediately, for he had seen such barriers before. They were the sort that torture masters of great respect in the Seven Hells used to secure their personal quarters. His pride fell apart, abandoned and useless. Let someone else be proud, let someone else be fearless, for at that precise moment, he knew that he would never be a match for the half-demon Colonel. In all of Mount Toane only Richard Vandross stood a chance against such a foe, and the whole of the mountain would be brought down around their ears if a battle ensued.

Roak grabbed at Triclaw, who must have seen something in the Shadowbeast's eyes that made him suddenly very alert and on edge.

"Come, you fool," Roak screamed nearly at the top of his lungs, panic flooding every last inch of his being. He took hold of Triclaw by the wrist and began dragging the Khan away from the barrier. "We must flee."

As he turned, the light from Triclaw's torch sputtered and fanned enough to reveal the silhouette of a heavily armored figure before them.

Two red, gimlet eyes flared in the darkness, and Colonel Molis, sword in hand, slowly descended toward them.

Triclaw thrust Roak behind him with a grunt of disgust.

"Coward of a demon," he growled at Roak, turning with a vicious grin to face his opponent. "This half-breed shall be torn asunder in a few moments, and you can run sniveling to lord Vandross to explain why you had to have a Sergeant fight for your life."

Triclaw blinked, and as his eyes fluttered open, the figure before him became a silver blur of movement.

Molis, in an instant's time, stood directly before him, and horrible, stinging pain throbbed through the various appendages and inner organs of the Khan known as Triclaw.

"What happened?" he asked, his head twitching.

"I have cut through your arms and legs, Sergeant," Molis said, calm as a Monk in meditation. "They shall fall off shortly," he continued, his tone very plaintive and matter-of-fact. "But not before the seeds of dark magic I planted in your pressure points erupt. Actually," he said as blood spurted from various points of impact on the Khan's body, eliciting a shriek of such abominable suffering that mortal men would have gone mad to hear it. "They'll hit at about the same time."

Crimson life fluids burst like geysers from Triclaw's elbows and knees, as he fell apart into a mass of bleeding stumps and gushing holes. The life had been completely drained from his body before its various parts hit the floor of the tunnel.

Vilec Roak watched in mortified terror as Molis walked through the last bits of fountaining blood, his boots splashing in the already inch-deep pool of blood around the large Khan's body.

He tried to scurry away, but the half-demon Colonel made a dismissive wave with his free hand, and several dozen yards away from Roak, the tunnel collapsed in a massive and sudden cave-in.

As Roak sprinted ahead to the dead-end, he fell to his knees and began attempting to tear the very stones apart—anything to elude this mysterious yet now somewhat knowable figure. He stopped, pressing his back flat against the cave-in as Molis approached to within a few yards' distance.

The half-demon leveled his sword at Roak, who saw that almost no blood stained the blade's edge, just a few specks of crimson down its length.

"Please, I have learned my lesson," Roak pleaded, sounding like a weeping child. "Please, do not harm me!"

"Harm you, sir?" said Molis in an inquisitive tone. He sheathed his sword and snapped a quick salute at the Shadowbeast. "I wouldn't think of it, sir." He reached down, offering Roak a hand up, but the Shadowbeast General would have none of it. He stood up on his own, slowly, keeping a close eye on Molis as he rose.

"Keep your distance, if you please, Colonel," Roak rasped, trying to forget that he had just whimpered for his life like a dog. "I know of your kind, half-breed. I know what you once were. I watched how you slaughtered that Sergeant, and I intend to let lord Vandross know that you are too much of a threat to keep around."

Molis shrugged non-committally, but took another step forward, uncomfortably close to Roak, who pressed himself back against the caved in rock ever so slightly.

"That you may, Vilec Roak," Molis rumbled, his voice trembling with a movement of the mountain. Or perhaps, Roak considered, it was the mountain that shook with him? "I do not care what you do with regards to reports. *You* didn't touch my barrier," he said, pressing his own shadowy, formless face nose-to-helmet with the Shadowbeast General. "That's all that matters. In fact—" he jabbed Roak's upper left arm area once, very quickly. A moment later, Roak felt fire blaze through his entire arm, and it exploded in a shower of black blood across the tunnel walls and Molis's armor. He dropped to the ground, cradling his now decrepit arm, trying to gauge how long it would take to regenerate the damage, and realizing that it wouldn't take long. But also, he realized that the half-demon could easily have destroyed him. "That is the only reason I choose not to kill you," Molis said, once more in that cool, murderous tone. "At least, not here and now. I do not seek your position, nor that of Richard Vandross, my summoner and master."

Colonel Molis disappeared into the darkness of the tunnels above him, and Vilec Roak, Shadowbeast Prime, General of Richard Vandross's armies, didn't dare to move until the trembling stopped.

* * * *

None of Byron's company had realized just how badly they needed their rest.

It was late morning the next day when all awoke and went into the small dining hall of the inn.

Selena Bradford's hair once again shimmering crimson, instead of the dark, blotchy, blackish-red it had become from their travels. Byron felt good enough to try eating some more 'normal' food—though it should be said that Gnome cuisine is more an art form than a matter of culinary skill: there was nothing normal about it.

James Hayes had a fierce, determined set to his jaw as he silently gorged himself on platter after platter of exotic breakfast foods. Morek Rockmight, his body odor much improved after a long bath the previous afternoon, actually had a smile on his face once again—perhaps the first real smile he had cracked since leading the company into the Western Mountains. Shoryu and Ellen kept each other quiet company as they attempted to eat at a civilized pace, both of them shaking their legs with newfound energy and impatience, both making it very clear that they wanted to get moving again, while they were fresh. Even Alex, the Ki Fairy, hummed some little ditty to himself as he plundered bits and pieces of everyone's meals for himself.

No one much minded: Fairyfolk didn't tend to eat a whole lot in comparison to the lands' other Races.

Thaddeus Viper entered the dining hall, trying not to announce his presence, but as Humans get older, they become less able to hide their actions and movements.

James Hayes rose and offered his seat to the leader of the Port of Arcade, which the older gentleman happily accepted. The fierce pride and stubbornness that Byron remembered him once being possessed of had, over the course of his years as a diplomat, faded almost into nothing. He was willing to admit that he was no longer young, and would accept the kindness of youth, if they chose to offer it.

"Lord Byron," Viper said in a way that pretended a close familiarity that they did not actually enjoy. "As I said yesterday, we are ready to march. What is your final decision?"

Byron sensed a smattering of the old impatience in the Prime Minister, the urge to take immediate and hostile action. Such tactics worked fine for raiding bands of hoodlums and thugs, but for an *en masse* battle with Vandross's forces at the heart of their domain, they needed all the aid that could be mustered.

"We shall march south. A small handful of men shall detach themselves when we are one quarter of the distance away from the Elven Kingdom's borderlands. The rest shall redirect their march directly east, and begin the rather lengthy trip to Mount Toane. I highly doubt the Elves will have trouble catching up. They shall most likely send every horse at their disposal with the main force. They shall act as mounted or unmounted cavalry, while those assembled here shall be broken down into infantry and caster units, if you have any magic users. Does that sound about right to you, lord Viper?"

The older Human smiled and nodded, and waved his hand to indicate that a nearby runner come over to him. He whispered something in the young half-Elf's ear, and the youth saluted and sprinted out of the room at full tilt.

"Your suggestions have been ordered, lord Byron. The runner is going to update the head officers on the situation and our plans. We shall begin our march at noon, if that is acceptable." He made it more a question than a statement.

Byron nodded his approval, but not before looking at the other members of the company for any objections. Of course, he was given none.

"Very well, then. I have some preparations of my own to make, in that case." Viper moved his chair back from the table and stood. "I shall see you at noon."

Viper left the inn's dining hall, and a deep silence fell over the room like a pall.

The members of the company each finished their meal and left, one by one, until only Byron, Shoryu and Ellen sat at the table.

Byron leaning back slightly to get a better view out the window near his seat.

The common goings-on of daily life in the village seemed rushed, almost expectant; their parents, regardless of Race, watched the children closely but even they had nothing but smiles for the children. A celebration of life, it seemed, was taking place no further than a stone's throw away. He had been a part of that celebration, once, a long time ago. Twenty years, he thought. My son would be a fully-grown man by now. But wishful thinking wouldn't get anything done this day. He headed out of the inn.

He hadn't gone five feet when James Hayes approached him from across the street, his armor glinting in the early morning sunlight. His face held a grave look, as though something had troubled him all morning—which, Byron suspected, it had been.

Hayes stopped a few feet away from Byron, searching for an answer in his eyeless sockets.

"Something troubles you, my friend," Byron asked.

Hayes nodded gruffly, and motioned Byron to follow him as he walked off down an eastbound street.

"Indeed, there is. Byron, I need to ask you some rather, well, personal questions." He passed by local families and running soldiers, trying to keep clear of both groups of people.

"Go ahead, James. If you feel they bear any relevance to our current situation, I welcome any questions."

"Thank you." Hayes nodded in deference to the Dread Knight. "Byron, when you were, well, made what you are, what happened? Did you feel any pain?"

"Well, that's difficult to say." He wanted to answer Hayes's questions, but he didn't want to have to recall that agony in its truest form. "I would liken it to being forced into a very small, very dark room, so pitch black that you cannot see anything. You cannot hear anything, or feel anything, as if you were suspended in a pocket of numbing water. Then, a very small window is opened, and you can see yourself, in a mangled, twisted body. You know it's your own body, but it is doing things of such unspeakable evil that you cannot accept that it is such. I," he said, stumbling to find the right words, his feet slowing with his mind. "I remember, too, having a small voice tell me that I was indeed trapped. Some small part of myself, you might say, was trying to call out to the rest of my being. But I could do nothing, I could affect no change from where I was. That is what it was like, for me. Why do you ask, James?"

"Well, it's just that, if something like that happens to me, at Mount Toane, I want you to be the one to do away with me, Byron," Hayes half-whispered as they passed a small group of Jaft children, wrestling in their front yard.

Byron made a disapproving noise in his throat, but kept silent.

"Anyway, my next question. Are you bitter about it? I mean, with Oun?"

Byron stopped entirely, and after a moment, Hayes did as well, realizing that Byron was not with him.

"At first, I was incredibly enraged that great Oun would let something like that happen to me, one of his most devout followers. I recall shouting in my mind, 'How have I failed you? What have I done wrong?' But when I received no answer, I realized that I had not brought anything on myself, I had not wronged Oun. Even the gods themselves are powerless to aid us sometimes, James. That's just how things are. After a while, once I was freed from Tanarak's control, I came to appreciate the fact that I was alive."

"If it can be called living," Hayes commented, moving again. "No offense."

"None taken." Byron matched the Human Paladin's pace. "Most would have killed themselves at the first opportunity, I'm sure. But I knew there were things that had to be done. I could not simply give up on living just yet."

The two walked around in stunted silence for a while, returning to the front of the inn to await the remainder of the company.

Morek Rockmight showed up after only ten minutes or so, scowling and shaking his head.

"A problem?" Byron asked.

"The prices around here are highway robbery. It cost me twenty gold just to get some grappling equipment. And I don't want to tell you how much it would have cost me to purchase a horse from the stables. Three hundred gold! You show me a horse worth that much money, I'll sing and dance," he growled.

Hayes laughed aloud at the Dwarven Boxer's chagrin, unable to suppress his amusement.

Morek shot him a lethal glance, but said nothing more, content to sit on the inn's porch and growl at nothing in particular.

Shortly thereafter, the rest of the company returned in increments of five or so minutes apart, until even lord Viper showed up. The main roadway was filled with soldiers, members of many Races and Trades all assembled in organized rows and ranks.

"Lord Byron, we are prepared to leave," Viper announced.

Byron nodded, and took a position to the side of the battalions present. Nearly a thousand men and women, Byron thought. How this village had been able to sustain them was a mystery to him, until he saw the remains of a camp just south of the town, visible between a set of shops across from him.

Morek took up a position next to Viper, the three left-most rows of Dwarves, Minotaurs and Gnomes apparently his to command. The remainder of the company walked at a brisk pace alongside the battalion, as Viper and Morek counted marching cadences for the heads of each column to bark as they marched, in order to keep the soldiers marching in rhythm. They had a long march ahead of them, but they were well equipped and well prepared for it.

And so the journey to Mount Toane began in earnest.

* * * *

For five days they marched, a straight column of eager soldiers, waiting for the opportunity to do something other than march, eat and sleep. But they would have a good deal of time before they got the chance for a real battle.

On the sixth day, the Elven border patrol became visible in the distance, along with several hundred horsemen, apparently dispatched in preparation of their coming for aid.

Byron sprinted ahead of the rest of his company and the battalion, and was met by an Elven officer who gave him a stiff salute.

"Lord Byron, Prime Minister Viper sent a messenger bird several days ago telling of your approach. The cavalry units you've requested have been assembled and divided into squadrons, your lordship." The Elven soldier gave another salute before running back toward the border men. He gave a circular motion of his fist over his head, and the hundreds of assembled cavalry raised their gauntleted fists toward the sky, shouting out a war cry that shook the plains around them for miles in every direction. The horses stamped and reared, and pennants flew in the wind rising up out of the south, the symbol of the Elven Kingdom, a single arrow crossing a sword with a leaf behind them, hung proudly on almost all of them. A few were simple black cloth, with a single crimson stripe in the middle of the field, crossing horizontally: Dark Watch, Byron thought. Perhaps a handful of survivors of the assault on Whitewood. They would be most welcomed in the battle ahead.

The massed battalions looked more like an army than it had previously, the proximity of Elven military to that of Viper and Morek's troops making the facilitation of group shifting and assignments easier. However, in most 'civilized' armies, the officers did not chat or fraternize with the common rabble, the enlisted man. Here, however, with a common goal and a foe greater than most of these men and women had ever faced, those rules seemed left behind.

Privates and Colonels mixed company, sharing stories of home and why they had chosen to come with lord Byron, Prime Minister Viper, and Morek Rockmight, who had made it clear that he was to have no title.

"Commander works just fine," he commented to several of the men as they slowed their pace to get ready for the evening's camp down.

When the sun was perhaps a half an hour from setting, Byron, Viper, Morek, and the highest Elven officer present, a Colonel Woodwise, called their forces to a stop for the evening.

Supplies were swiftly moved about the encampment, and fires prepared by Pyromancers for cooking and keeping the troops warm in the bitter mid-plains night.

Byron and his company, along with Viper and Woodwise, made their fire near the center of the camp, so that any troops could get to them without delay.

"Besides," Viper had commented with a grin as he pulled a silver flask from his robes. "The heart of any army is its leaders."

A wise, and tactically sound argument, Hayes had commented.

The group sat in studied silence until Selena brought the flames to life under the cooking pots, and Ellen and Shoryu quickly set about preparing the meal for that night.

"Runner," Viper said, motioning a Minotaur soldier to his side. "Get the unit officers here for a meeting and report, to be held in two hours. That should give them plenty of time to eat and prepare for their day's summary, though I don't expect there'll be much to discuss. That's all."

The runner saluted and made off into the encroaching darkness and gloom; a thick fog from the nearby woodlands, which they would pass through on the next day, had drifted and settled in over the encamped army. Lunar light shone through clearly in spots here and there, giving the entire mass of soldiers and magic users an otherworldly appearance to Byron's ill-adjusted eyes. What sort of fog was this, he wondered, that even he was having trouble seeing through it?

"Parts of your being shall be no more," he remembered Voice telling him with a half-growl in his throat. Even if the fog had no magical origin, he might be having trouble seeing through it now, due to the changes to his body. He tried to assure himself that this meant nothing, but something about the fog nagged at him.

"James, tell me something," he asked across the now red-hot fire. "Do you sense anything amiss?"

The Human Paladin looked up from his musings and shook his head no, but said nothing. His eyes, however, seemed haunted, and Byron could vaguely detect something else in those deep blue orbs: fear. Hayes might not sense anything. Even so, the man was obviously uncomfortable with his surroundings. What was it, Byron wondered. But his mind went in other directions as the food was distributed, and Shoryu handed him a flask filled with the young Cuyotai's blood.

Byron poured the crimson liquid over his skull, absorbing the power and vitality of it, feeling renewed yet again. It was a dark ritual that he would like to avoid, but he would need all the strength he could muster for what lay ahead.

To ensure that he didn't have another sudden loss of control, Shoryu allowed his new bride to use a unique Gaiamancy spell to calm his nerves and ease his temper. This Ellen used at its utmost potential, but still it barely kept the Cuyotai in check. He would need to fight and kill something soon, or he might attack an ally, Byron feared.

For the duration of the quest, Byron decided, he could take no more of Shoryu's blood.

The meal was shared in near silence, the company members each speaking to each other in hushed tones, and only in pairs.

Byron and James, however, said nothing to anyone until the other officers arrived for the meeting that Viper had arranged.

After he had finished his meal, the old Prime Minister had gone off to find one of his allies and play a quick game of chess. When he returned to the circle, he had the officers with him.

Byron stood up straight, as did Morek Rockmight, and both saluted the lower officers. They all remained standing, and Byron could tell that this was customary for most of them; none even made a move to take a seat or relax. The Dread Knight waited for Viper to say something, but when he didn't, he took the initiative.

"All right," Byron said, clearing his throat and taking a militant tone. "Let's start from the lowest man on the totem pole." He fixed his eyes on the gathered men and women, and saw that one Elven woman, barely older than a girl, had a set of four stripes on her uniform sleeve, with a star above them: Sergeant-at-Arms. "Sergeant," he said, attempting to raise his eyebrow bone.

The faint reaction of confusion from the girl left him realizing he was probably quite strange to her, and so he let his 'face' go slack.

"My lord, Sergeant-at-Arms Cassandra Payne, sir," The military presence of mind had apparently sunk into this young woman at a very young age, her bearing that of a perfect, born-to-be-one soldier. "Mine is the Fifteenth Mounted Cavalry Division, sir. We have had no accidents to report, or pertinent discoveries, sir. However, three of our horsemen abandoned early on, sir. I believe they returned to the Kingdom. Shall I send a message to have them arrested, sir?"

Byron shook his head vehemently; after all, this was *his* war, not these people's. If they didn't have the nerve, let them go. He couldn't entirely blame them.

"Very good sir. Nothing else to report, sir!" She saluted once again, and took a step away from the firelight, back into the shadows and fog; the visual effect of her movement made her ethereal in appearance, like a specter on the verge of crossing into this reality.

Another Elf, a darker-skinned male with long, black hair down to his waist, tied in a ponytail, stepped forward.

"My lord, Lieutenant of the Second Grade Wilhelm Von Rook, sir." The man snapped a smart salute. "First Unmounted Cavalry Division, sir. We misjudged the heat of the day, sir, and several men passed out from heat exhaustion. They were carried in litters until we made camp, sir. They shall have their heavy leathers removed, that they might not suffer the same ill effects tomorrow, sir. No pertinent discoveries, sir. However, if we continue directly on our course, east and slightly north, we shall pass very close to Fort Flag, sir," the Elf said.

Byron realized with a shock what was bothering Hayes so much. They would pass only an hour or so south of the ruins of his former post, where so many of his allies had fallen.

"We understand that little remains of the fort, but several of lord Viper's men formerly served under Fort Flag, and would just as soon avoid it, sir."

"Understood," Byron said softly, putting an easy hand on Hayes's shoulder.

The Human Paladin gave him a small, brief smile of appreciation, then returned his face to that cold, steely glare of a soldier thinking through his priorities.

How like Edgar Cesar, he thought for a moment. The trace feelings of that thought left him feeling queer, uneasy. "Let us continue."

Down the ranks they went. Each reported only a few minor injuries and issues, then accepting the advice offered by the other officers, Byron, Viper and Morek, and the meeting adjourned. Each company set guards at watch over the encamped army, and everyone, save a few worried souls, found rest under the stars.

* * * *

"My rest, what little I get, is very dear to me," growled Richard Vandross as he opened his chamber door to find a quivering Vilec Roak standing there. "Where is Sergeant Triclaw," he asked, irritated at the interruption but inviting Roak into his quarters anyway. Vandross lay back down on his hard mattress, grateful for the little comfort it gave him. His dreams had been filled with imagery that made even his own skin crawl, nightmares that foreshadowed a future for Tamalaria bleaker than any he had ever read about in fairy tales. But with a shake of his weary head, he cleared his mental vision and allowed his enhanced senses to 'see' the room around him.

He kept his eye closed, careful not to doze off; he had never seen the Shadowbeast Prime so thoroughly shaken before, and he already had a sneaking suspicion as to what had occurred to the Khan Triclaw.

Roak's head spun on a swivel, snatching peeks up and down the tunnel, before he entered the chamber and closed the door quite securely behind him. "Triclaw is dead, lord Vandross," he half-whimpered.

Such terror, such fear, Vandross thought, drunk from the delight the waves of emotion were sending him.

"Molis tore him apart! He used some arcane blow, and severed the Sergeant's limbs with that blade of his before I even saw him draw it from its scabbard! And what's worse, he used that same blow on my arm."

Vandross opened his eye long enough to see that Vilec Roak's arm had not yet fully regenerated. He was impressed; common Shadowbeasts fell before the blade easily enough, but Primes possessed a strength of body and mind that rendered them nearly immune to mundane weaponry. Apparently, he thought with a good deal of inward mirth, the good Colonel hasn't been informed of that.

A heavy, thunderous booming came from the stone door, and Vilec Roak jumped a good six feet away, rolling away from the door as it opened and holding his good hand out, conjuring magical force. But when the door opened, it was Major Tamriel's ursine face pressed in the frame.

"My lord, General Roak, there are ill tidings," he rumbled, his voice echoing down the tunnels. "One of our scouts in the west has spotted a force marching north and east, in a direct line toward Ja-Wen. It is an army of moderate size, my lords, and continues to grow. Apparently, the militias of every major city-state and kingdom are being mobilized to march on us here, lord Vandross," he said, addressing the one-eyed warlock with this last bit.

"What is our state of readiness," Vandross asked with a yawn.

"My lord, of the twenty battalions, perhaps two or three can be spared to make a forward defensive. However, they shall require a measure of time to intercept the main force. I have been informed that Byron of Sidius leads the main force of their army."

Byron, Vandross thought, the name dripping like poison in his mind. Fury coursed immediately through his body, and he felt revived, regardless of his lack of sleep. He rose from his bed and began donning his armor and vestments.

"Lord Vandross, what are your orders?"

"Take two battalions to the entrance of Mount Toane, have them completely assembled and prepared for the first day's light," he said, securing his arm guards. "I shall begin preparations shortly for a mass teleportation portal. We'll send half a battalion through at a time, estimate a distance of five hours' march to intercept Byron's forces."

"My lord, that might not be enough to stop them," Tamriel protested, banging his heavy, fur-covered fist on the tunnel floor. "Allow me to take four full battalions through myself! We can delay the trip by a half a day's time, plenty of distance still between ours and their armies."

Vandross calmly finished securing his metal leggings, and gave Tamriel a sidelong glance, with a smile.

"We shall delay nothing, Major," he growled, approaching the large bear demon with his eyes glaring crimson. "As for you, you have disappointed me at every turn, and this is your final chance to redeem yourself. If you cannot do what is necessary with two battalions, then you are not worth keeping around. Take Lieutenant Amon with you, and if neither of you returns, then so much the better! I shall be rid of this inefficiency."

He took a deep, calming breath. Why was he behaving like this? It was irrational, and most of all, impulsive. Richard Vandross did not like to think of himself as a man given over to his impulses: in his mind's eye, he viewed himself as cool and collected, sinister, surely, but conniving and cunning. His blood ran cold for a moment, his sense of absolute control slipping rapidly away, a shimmer of gold attached to a string. At the precise moment he thought he could pluck that gold off the ground, it flew through the air, away from him, just out of reach. The overall effect left him feeling mentally fatigued, as though he was trapped in his own body. He enjoyed the power he now had coursing through his body, mind and soul, sure, but what cost had been exacted from him? At the moment, he could not, or rather, did not want to answer that question.

The mighty, bass-voiced Renka seemed to resign himself to his fate, letting out a heavy sigh into the air. "Very well, my lord. If that is your will, then it shall be done. I am confident that after you have quelled the threat to your dominion, you shall re-summon me from the Hells. I say that, my lord," he said, turning on his heel to face the direction he had come down the tunnel from. "Because Byron of Sidius and his allies are going to slay me, and send my soul hurtling back into the Pit. It is not a question of if," he said, moving now away from the open stone doorway. "But rather, a question of when." His voice echoed back at the one-eyed warlock and the Shadowbeast.

They stood in mutual silence for a long while before Vilec Roak departed.

So this is how it shall begin, Roak thought sullenly as he stalked down the tunnel. The final test of Richard Vandross's power, and of Byron's righteousness.

For a moment, a rather brief moment, he secretly hoped that the Dread Knight would bring Mount Toane crashing down around Vandross's ears.

Chapter Six
Immolation

Selena Bradford had held up better than many in the company could expect on the following day. The woodlands they passed through were dense and well covered with the high boughs of the maples that grew everywhere in thick stands, but they could not entirely keep out the torrential downpour that struck the mid-southern ranges of Tamalaria.

Her magical nature should have rendered her powerless due to the soaking conditions, but she managed to keep both her spirits up and her magic flowing through constant use. She kept her body layered in an aura of superheated temperature, evaporating the raindrops a few inches before they struck her delicate skin or tough, crimson robes.

Yet, unbeknownst to even her closest companions, her inner thoughts haunted her. Every step she marched, she felt more certain she was getting closer to her own demise. It was a sensation that she had felt vaguely during the assault on Desanadron, but the feeling had subsided when Byron and his company joined in the effort. Now, her fate seemingly lay right before her, spelled out quite clearly, but at such a distance as not to be discernable. The freezing rain and constant dampness did not add or detract at all from this inner sensation. Not even the eager gait of the soldiers all around her contributed to her mental condition. It came from within, from deep in the recesses of crimson fury that were so much a part of her being.

For as long as she could remember, fire had been her only friend. Her mastery of Pyromancy had come early, as she had told the others, but her powers had defined her as much as her name identified her as a living being. In her adolescence, she had strayed from social circles, never truly settling in with any friends or loved ones because the lure of her magic called so strongly to her. By the age of twenty, she had completed her own tome of spells, discovered through constant experimentation. By the age of twenty-one, she had traveled across and seen almost all there was to see in the west of Tamalaria. Yet she had never seen war.

Sure, she had been in her fair share of confrontations, leading adventuring parties into dangerous and unknown territory, plundering secret temples and dungeons beneath the surface of the earth. But war on this large a scale was something she had never been prepared to deal with—that, and the idea that she now had not just allies, but friends. People who had become involved in her life for reasons that seemed to stem from more than sharing a common foe.

Of Byron, she thought first. Of all of the company, she understood him the least. He was a Dread Knight, no matter how she looked at him. The tales of his savagery under the control of Tanarak had persisted in her mind from the moment she met him, yet she could do and say nothing about it. He did appear to be in this for the right reasons, and there had been changes in him, both obvious and subtle.

Shoryu Tearfang, she mused, looking over at the young Cuyotai Hunter as he strode hand-in-hand with his wife, the Gaiamancer Ellen Daires. A werecoyote and an Elf, she thought with a grin. Who'd have thought it could be? Shoryu appeared to her to possess a singular determination that she admired in one so clearly inexperienced in the world and its many ways of life. That he had find true love, if it were so, after losing so much at the hands of Richard Vandross, allowed her a small measure of pity and admiration both for the young man.

Ellen Daires, of course, came to her mind next. So gentle, so calm, yet so fragile at the same time. Her power over earthen magic was nearly a match for Selena's own over fire, but Ellen was not meant for conflict.

Morek Rockmight came alongside Byron for a moment, and the two exchanged words quietly. As the Human Pyromancer looked at the stout, rough-hewn brawler, she had to stifle a small laugh. So much courage and tenacity, so much strength, for one so small. The Dwarven Boxer moved and fought with a frankness and directness that reflected his taciturn personality. A few well-aimed punches from those enchanted gloves, and even Shadowbeasts turned to smoldering, bleeding piles of refuse. But he was not the smallest of them.

That was Alex, the Ki Fairy, whose sarcasm and razor wit had kept her good company in the last few weeks' time. He alone seemed to appreciate her brand of humor, and often played off of her jokes with his own. He was clever and crafty, and capable of much more than she figured most would attribute to him.

And lastly, there had been James Hayes, whom she had met before any of the others.

She recalled the crestfallen look that hung over his features like a death shroud when first he had received word of Fort Flag's utter destruction. Byron and his company had not yet arrived to lend aid, and the systematic defense and assault on Desanadron had been going on for two and a half days. A scout had returned from his survey, as requested by the Paladin, and she herself had stood near the steps of the library, going over defensive movements for the soldiers of the city with a Jaft Sergeant. The blue-skinned humanoid had turned his bald head to watch the scout approach Hayes, but he must have seen something in the scout's movements that told him to stay well away from the Paladin—he was going to take the news hard.

Selena had gone silent and watched as the stern, warrior-like face of James Hayes had transformed, for a few moments, into something so pitiable that it had made her want to weep for him. So many of his brethren slaughtered, while he had been trapped within the magical barrier erected around Desanadron. But he had regained his composure to reply to this news.

"Sacrifices must be made in the name of mighty Oun, our great god. We all knew the risks our titles and order would entail. I thank you, Martin. Now go see the healers. They shall tend to your wounds." As soon as the scout had darted away, Hayes had marched stoically into the nearby church, a temple erected for the worship of Oun.

Selena had crept to the large, ivory doors, and listened as Hayes sobbed and wailed up near the altar.

"Why, oh great Oun? How could our faith and service come to this? How have we betrayed you? Why have you let so many of your followers perish like this? It isn't fair," he had screamed, standing to his feet and striking the altar with the butt of his broadsword. "Why?" He had raged and moaned, alternately, for nearly an hour before he got up from his knees next to the altar.

Selena had ducked off, out of sight, so as not to be caught eavesdropping. James Hayes hadn't been the same since that afternoon. His faith had been shaken to its very core, but he seemed to recover some from his travels with the Dread Knight and his company.

But he was not the last, after all, she recalled. Oh no, there was also poor David Spore, the one-armed Monk. The moment he had become involved with the company, Selena had seen that he was doomed. Skilled though he was, he had only had one arm to work with. And he was a trusting soul, trusting enough to let an assassin close enough to deliver the killing blow. But they had all trusted the Lizardman assassin, and the blame for Spore's death lay with all of them, the group as a whole.

"Selena," a dark, rumbling voice said near to her. She shook her head to clear her thoughts, and saw Byron only a few feet away, concern somehow reflected in those twin orbs of glittering yellow light.

"I'm fine," she snapped, rather more brusquely than she had intended. "I'm just thinking about what lies before us."

"Aren't we all?" Without another word, he moved away from her, back toward Prime Minister Viper and Morek Rockmight.

Had he seen it too, she wondered. Had Byron felt the same disturbance that she had? She didn't know, and now, more than ever, she wanted to ask the mysterious undead warrior. But Byron kept his distance, like a con man who has spotted an undercover constable.

The army marched on, further into the forest, and she returned to simply following, building her magical force within her. Before the day was through, she would need all the energy she could muster.

* * * *

If Richard Vandross intended to send them to their deaths, Tamriel and Amon agreed, they would not leave the mad warlock their own people for his further designs. Tamriel, after having been rather bluntly dismissed, stormed through the tunnels of Mount Toane, swinging his huge, ursine arms at every Shadowbeast and Illeck that came within reach. The Shadowbeasts, for the most part, suffered only minor injuries, which they recovered from almost immediately. The Dark Elves, however, did not fare so well. Eight had to be rushed to healers, and nearly a dozen more perished where they landed against the rock walls.

Tamriel, leaving a wake of congealing and wounded soldiers and magic users behind him, took himself directly to the outside of Mount Toane's entrance, to the western front of the towering mountain. There, First Lieutenant

Amon was drilling his Khan soldiers adamantly, taking them through combat drills specifically designed for mass combat situations.

It was a curious exercise, and for a moment, Tamriel stopped in his tracks. Two Khan, armed only with their claws and fangs, wearing simple chain mail, stood in the center of a circle of nearly a hundred other Khan, who were all heavily armed. Three of these circles swirled and flowed as the training combat ensued, the pair in the middle of the circle forced to defend themselves from all sides under nearly impossible odds.

The Khan, though they were not true lycanthropes, had a decent regenerative system—none of the troops were slain in the exercise, merely rendered unconscious.

Though the conditions appeared quite brutal, Tamriel understood the logic of them.

If ever Amon's personal troops found themselves completely outnumbered, they would take down a large number of enemies before they themselves fell to their wounds. Of course, he added as a mental side-note, none of them appeared to be using magic of any sort, which would be present where they were going.

Lowering his lumbering head and sighing deeply, he set his back straight and stamped toward the Khan Lieutenant, who stood apart from the circles, his steel half-plate armor glinting in the fading sunlight. As Tamriel came within ten feet, Amon's ears pricked up, and he spun on his heel, sword drawn. Seeing the Major, he sheathed his weapon and whipped off a quick salute, which Tamriel returned with haste.

"Amon, there is no more time for formalities. We have been given orders from lord Vandross," the Renka boomed, his deep, throaty voice echoing across the field. The mock combat continued uninterrupted. "At dawn's first light, he is going to create a large teleportation rift, and we two are to lead two full battalions through to confront the army that marches towards us."

Amon stared at him, dumbstruck.

"Only two battalions," the Khan rasped, incredulous. "But the scout estimated the opposing forces to be a full five battalions in strength. Even my personal units here will not be enough for the task. And none of these men, proud and noble warriors though they may be, have what it takes to stand against a magical assault."

Tamriel gave Amon a smirk. "That is why we shall take *three* battalions. One of the Illeck sorcerer units shall accompany this battalion." Tamriel nodded his head to indicate the surging groups downhill from him. "And I shall bring a full complement of Shadowbeast and Human troops, along with my brothers. Combined, the three battalions should be able to hold off Byron and his army for long enough to do serious damage. When Vandross sees how effective we have been, he shall open the rift once more, for us to return to Mount Toane. Surely he is not so far gone in his madness that he won't see the wisdom in such a maneuver."

Amon agreed with a grunt and a nod, then turned to his troops and gave out a ferocious roar. The surging masses slowed to a standstill, then swarmed again as Amon raised his left hand in a fist, one finger pointing skyward. They were forming ranks and rows for marching, donning their armor and weapons as they moved.

Tamriel admired their structure and practiced movements for a moment, awed at the sight of so many brutal warriors brought under the command of a single Khan. Amon surely deserved better than his current rank, the Renka thought, but the Lieutenant had been adamant about leading only his own people, his own Race.

Vandross likely wouldn't raise him in rank due to this particular request, but Amon didn't seem to care so much about titles and ranks, or privileges. All he wanted was war, and Tamriel understood quite well the Khan's reasoning. He had been a Chieftain in his tribe, undefeated in combat: he saw his own people as superior to anything that lived in Mount Toane. He may have been right.

Tamriel took his leave and marched straight back into Mount Toane, locating Sergeant Robin after a sweeping search of the inner tunnels and chambers. He found the Beastmaster and mage in a large, spherical chamber high up in the mountain, where few of the troops ventured. Not even Vandross appeared to care much for the upper tunnels and chambers of the mountain, and so it made the perfect place for the mages to concentrate and train.

Several Human soldiers and stray Lizardmen, those who had not joined Bael when the former General had been left behind to die, stood about, getting spells locked onto their weapons and armor.

Robin, with a keen eye for anything larger than himself, came straight over to Tamriel from his meditation mat, a scowl darkening his already shadowy face. "What brings you here, Major? Can't you see we are, for the most part, occupied?"

Tamriel growled deep in his throat, and watched with satisfaction as the much smaller man backed away a step, his right hand drawing back into a fist. He wouldn't strike Tamriel physically, the Renka knew. He would surely have a spell prepared, but he would need a few moments to cast it, and with Tamriel being less than an arm's length away, he felt sure the mage wouldn't risk having his throat crushed.

"Be at ease, Sergeant," Tamriel said, putting his hands up in the 'no trouble' pose. "I come late in the evening, I know, but I must commandeer one of your units for tomorrow morning. We leave through a rift, at Vandross's command, to attack the marching army that threatens. You shall choose only those you think to be competent, but by no means send your very best. Some exceptional magicians would be nice, though." Robin raised an eyebrow at him, standing straight. "You do not have a choice in the matter, Robin. If you refuse me, I shall tear out your spine and leave you a loose collection of bones and organs." Tamriel smiled the whole while. He saw his own teeth reflected in the little man's eyes, and saw that to a lesser, mortal being, it must have been terrifying.

"O-of course." Robin skittered away like a cockroach when a torch is lit in a filthy kitchen. He sprinted out of the main chamber, and Tamriel gazed about the room at the assembled mages there.

These men and women, unlike the rest of the army, wore no uniforms, or any insignia on their personal garb that would indicate rank. Then again, perhaps it would be best this way, he thought. After all, the rank they might be assigned by officers in Vandross's army might not even reflect their true power or intellect. Surely there was a huge disparity between the half-breed, Colonel Molis, and General Vilec Roak. Tamriel had been touched by Molis's power: it shone above all others in Mount Toane. When he had confronted the Colonel, up in the northwestern mountains, he had been spared his life; he knew, however, that Molis could have wiped him off of the face of the mortal coil without effort.

How he accepted the role of only Colonel while one such as Roak remained General was beyond him. Then again, he thought, Roak is cunning and quite sly, even by Shadowbeast standards.

Robin returned just then, with nearly fifty Human and Illeck mages trailing after him, their robes of all materials and colors, like a shimmering rainbow of mystical force. Tamriel could feel the magic flowing off of them, and from the look of several of them, they had been training in combat magic with one another. "Here they are, Major. Forty-six of my mages, awaiting your orders. I have apprised them of the situation," Robin said, swallowing hard. "Some chose to remain above. They said that their powers would be best suited to the defense of Mount Toane."

"Good enough," Tamriel barked curtly. "All right, all of you," he said, thrusting a large, hairy finger at the unit assembled. "Get some rest. I'll be coming to collect you first thing in the morning."

After that, he went off to his own large chamber to speak with his brothers, who had agreed hastily to join him. They had become rather bored in the mountain, and were hungry for the taste of blood and flesh. He had gone off to his own cot to sleep then, to rest up for the following morning.

And now he stood outside of the mouth of Mount Toane, Richard Vandross off to one side of him, preparing to open the rift that would send them through to meet with Byron of Sidius's army. Vandross made no comment about the mages—after all, Amon had placed them cleverly throughout his own men, with a handful positioned strategically in Tamriel's battalion.

As the rift opened, Tamriel let out a battle cry that echoed across the plains, and led the battalions through the rift. As the opening in space clamped shut, Vandross sagged slightly towards the ground, but found that cold, steel-plated arm helping him back to his full height.

He turned to find Colonel Molis standing there, his strange, shadowed eyes peering out from the darkness of his helmet. Vandross shrugged the arm off, dusting himself down as the sun rose over the horizon.

"My lord, it is folly to send them after Byron's army. The Lizardman Bael has been spotted by several of my spies, leading a large force north to intercept and join the Dread Knight's forces. That was several days ago. Tamriel and

Amon's battalions, and the mage unit they tried to sneak through with them, are going to be utterly destroyed."

Vandross chuckled merrily for a moment, patting Molis on his shoulder plate as he stalked toward Mount Toane.

"I know, Colonel, I know. My own scouts reported the same sighting shortly before your men returned to inform you. Indeed, they'll be destroyed, but they'll also take down a nice chunk of Byron's army. Of that much, I am very certain."

Molis stared after the mad warlock for a moment, sprinting to catch up to him.

"And what of Sergeant Robin, my lord? Did he not betray you by sending magic users with Tamriel, when you clearly ordered the Renka to take only two battalions?"

Vandross spun on his heel, his face twisted up into a savage smile.

"He has already been dealt with. I needed to stretch my legs this morning, and test the edge of my scimitar." Vandross cackled like a hyena.

Molis saw the slightest hint of quickly drying blood on Vandross's scimitar hilt. He had known what was going to happen. He knew that Tamriel and his units would be backed against a wall. "Do not be mistaken. I intend for them to cripple Byron's army severely. I have secreted away into their midst a Necromancer, who is very skilled at quickly calling the recently deceased to her command. As the dead fall to the ground, she shall have them rising from it, in order to serve her."

"Is she to be sacrificed as well, lord Vandross," Molis asked, his tone taking on a hard edge.

Vandross turned to face him, and crimson light flared for a moment through his eye patch.

Molis took a defensive step back, clearly having enraged his master.

"Why, yes, she is. Of course, she wouldn't have agreed to go if I hadn't promised her a safe teleportation scroll to use when she's really in trouble."

Molis had stopped following Vandross, realizing for the first time how much like Tanarak this man had become since gaining the Glorious Mother of Destruction.

"Don't fret, Colonel," Vandross said, spinning to face him on one foot, arms wide open like a cajoling child at play with close friends. "I did give her a teleportation scroll! It just so happens that it will teleport her about a thousand feet straight into the sky." He cackled then, a maddened predator amused by his prey's pathetic attempts to run away or fight back.

The spider and the fly, Molis thought, watching the one-eyed warlock disappear into the dank gloom of Mount Toane. The spider and the fly.

* * * *

The army under Byron's command marched on through noon, not stopping to rest, as the sloping lowlands they had crossed into south of Fort Flag offered moderate temperatures and welcome breezes. The plains were not filled now, however, with the birdsong and small animals that made them their home. The wooded thickets did not appear to teem with any life—it was as though the whole region held its breath, about to sneeze at a moment's notice into full activity and life. Which was essentially what happened to the entire army when one of the forward scouts was seen atop a hill rise nearly a half a mile ahead of the army.

Though none could make out the physical appearance of the scout, everyone knew there was trouble coming. Only one scout stood there, and he was now blowing on a great horn made of carved elephant tusk. It was the warning sound for 'incoming attack.'

A moment later, as the Elven scout took a breath to make a second blow on the horn, a barely discernable projectile, a crossbow bolt Shoryu saw, flew through the back of his neck and out of his throat, smashing his jaw apart as he died where he stood.

Selena Bradford could barely breath, let alone move as just over a thousand armed men and women, warriors, priests and mages all, began to shuffle into complex marching and attacking formations around her. She had never involved herself in the middle of a combat of such magnitude; even in the Elven capital of Whitewood, she had been safely up on the walls around the outer perimeter, able to volley her deadly balls and cones of flames, her eruptions of magma, from a distance. The fire in her soul blazed yellow for a moment: cowardice? Could she be feeling a fleeting moment of hesitation?

No, she retorted mentally to the feeling of helplessness that had threatened to consume her. I am not a coward. I will not back down.

Moving herself into position near her traveling companions, who had already assembled themselves as a single unit, Selena Bradford prepared herself for use of short-range Pyromancer spells. There were not many, but enough that she could deal some hefty damage before retreating to her more comfortable distance.

"Any sign of them yet?" she asked Byron.

The hulking Dread Knight merely shook his head and shuffled forward slowly, trying to keep the little company from Whitewood and Desanadron behind the first unit, the Thirty-First Elven Infantry, and the third unit, Lord Viper's mages.

When at last they saw their enemies, Selena Bradford nearly choked on her sharp intake of breath. Three enormous, bear-like creatures, bedecked in full plate armor and wielding enormous maces, led a full complement of Khan warriors. The tiger-men had at their foremost lines a single man who stood out from the rest, himself wearing full plate like the bear-demons, while his soldiers were clad in much lighter braced chain mail.

While they marched head-on towards Byron and Viper's forces, the central Khan barked an order in the tongue of his kind, a harsh and guttural combination of grunts and roars. They broke stride and ranks, and from their midst came flowing dozens of magic users, each casting spells simultaneously on themselves and the warriors. A few of the first offensive spells were being hurled at the Thirty-first Elven Infantry, and men and women alike were being burned, frozen into crumbling shards, and bursting apart at the limbs, their blood already staining the ground.

"Forwarrrrrd," Byron shouted, charging ahead of the company into battle with the first set of troops.

Morek Rockmight leapt into the fray, his men joining the first troops.

Within less than two minutes, Selena could see, the battle would begin in earnest, and the body count would really begin to mount. She might be included in that body count if she weren't careful.

Around her, the world morphed into a cacophony of sounds and flashes of steel and light, and as the first rows of opposing forces collided, she realized that the flow of the army was dragging her into battle.

The clash of metal weapons on armor pierced through the haze in her mind, and she looked around frantically to discover how the first few minutes of the raging battle had gone for her friends and allies.

Shoryu and Ellen were each standing high up in the trees nearby—he picking off Khan and Illeck one by one with his enchanted arrows, she providing protective wooden and stone warriors from the ground and woodland itself.

Morek, in the thick of the fray, was throwing his fists around as though they were the tools of Armageddon, the mystic gloves he favored so crushing chain mail and bones as surely as a felled tree might. As she focused her attention on the smallest of the three bear creatures, the Renka, she noticed the comparatively small forms of James Hayes and Byron strategically fencing with the beast, striking it with their swords and backing swiftly away to avoid the slow, menacing blows of its mace.

Lost in her observations, she almost failed to notice the Khan soldier bringing his scimitar down toward her head.

She reflexively tucked and rolled away, springing to her feet and lobbing a fireball the size of a pumpkin into the Khan's face. As the orb struck him at the speed of a charging horse, his body slumped forward, sans head, a smoldering neck hole all that remained in its place.

The stench of his burnt flesh and fur lingered in the air, like expensive incense to her nostrils.

Her veins filled with fury, the old fallback mental state she lapsed into in the heat of battle. Rising to her feet, she channeled her magic into the very ground, gouts of flame and magma engulfing handfuls of the Khan soldiers at the rear of their formations. She would not risk such a spell with her allies close by—they would wind up victims of her onslaught as well.

For a moment, she was caught up entirely in her dance of death, hurling bolts of fire and cones of flames, summoning walls of heat and marching them through dozens of Khan.

But the expense of her magic wore on her quickly, and there appeared to be no end to the Khan.

As Selena glanced about, she saw that while the number of Khan soldiers, Illeck and Human mages barely dwindled, the number of men and women fighting for Byron, Viper and Morek was slowly being chipped at. Yet, there also appeared to be no change at all in the number of combatants on the field. As Selena Bradford visually scoured the battlefield, she saw, to her horror, why the odds were beginning to seem in Vandross's forces' favor. Standing amid a circle of Illeck Q Mages and Gaiamancers, protected by earthen and support magic, stood a gaunt, pale figure, a woman with raven-black hair and eyes the color of a swamp: a Necromancer!

As the combatants fell in combat, regardless of alliance, the Necromancer summoned their bodies back to life, using them to press the Renkas' forces forward.

She had to warn Byron.

As she darted through the onslaught, swords and pikes barely missing or grazing her arms and legs, a stray claw strike knocked her to the ground several feet from the source. She turned over, and saw a towering Khan who stood unarmed, his armor torn apart, but his eyes still livid with the bloodlust that can only be had by living, sentient creatures.

The beast approached her, fangs dripping terribly with the thought of another kill, a sorceress no less. But as the Khan reared up to bring its heavy claws down into her chest, a single, shimmering arrow pierced the soldier's face.

Shock registered for a moment on that quickly paling creature, and as the flash of light from the arrow blinked, a sound like a walnut cracking in two split the air, and the creature dropped backward, its head split evenly to the throat.

Blood sprayed across Selena's legs as she regained her feet, but she had no time to feel revulsion; she still had to warn Byron, warn the others, of the Necromancer's presence.

She saw as she got closer to the Dread Knight that he and James Hayes had already finished off one of the Renkas, and were quickly backing another one against a tree, which Ellen Daires had just brought to life with her Gaiamancy.

She had to risk shouting now, or the tide of the battle could be turned against them. "Byron," she shouted. Her lungs felt clogged and weighed down with soot and ash—yet another price to be paid for her brand of high power, high-speed magic.

She caught his attention just as James Hayes launched an assault of holy magic on the bear demon.

The Dread Knight turned his head for a moment, and James turned to face her as well.

"A Necromancer! There's a Necromancer in the middle of their—" she gasped for breath as she watched the Dread Knight and the Paladin smashed aside like rag dolls by an enormous Renka, this one easily twice the others' size.

It was the creature that had led the overall assault, she realized.

Vandross had sent a formidable forward offensive at them, and she watched in horror as Byron and James Hayes began their struggle with this larger, much more fearsome opponent.

Shoryu, she thought; his arrows were enchanted, and he was the best shot with an arrow she knew. But as she searched the trees for him, she could find no sign of the cuyotai. Orders were being shouted throughout Viper and Byron's army, orders to fall back, to concentrate on the undead first. They were going to lose ground, time, and more lives. And the more of their own that fell, the more undead the Necromancer would wield against them.

Selena realized, in a moment of clarity, that she only had one option left. That great final spell that all Pyromancers of great knowledge know of, but cannot use.

The spell was best known as Immolation.

* * * *

Byron had to choke down a hell of a lot of pride to issue the order to retreat. But he couldn't get a bead on the Necromancer that Selena Bradford had been trying to warn him about before Major Tamriel had knocked him and James Hayes further back into the woods. Byron hadn't suffered much in the way of injuries: he was still, for all intents and purposes, a Dread Knight, wearing the armor of a Paladin. Both his armor and his training easily negated such blunt force trauma.

James, however, could not count on undead status to protect him. The Human Paladin got up from the ground with much more effort than was required of the undead warrior, who gave him a hand at the last moments of grogginess. After that, they began to move the lines back, taking care to ensure that everyone knew to destroy the undead first.

The second order he issued was flat-out refused by Thaddeus Viper, which was to cut off the heads of nearby fallen comrades. Without the head attached, Byron had reasoned, it would be nearly impossible for the Necromancer to bring them back from the dead. But Viper had refused the suggestion, barking at the Dread Knight that it was "inhumane."

Byron would have argued the point that warfare in general wasn't humane, but he didn't have the benefit of time to do that. As he fell back with the troops, he fended off the constant attacks of the huge Renka who led these Khan, Illeck and Humans against them.

He had to duck and weave through the clustering lines of combatants when he noticed a single figure, clad in crimson robes, slowly and calmly approaching a small circle of mages. He knew immediately that it was Selena Bradford, and he feared the worst for her.

The Dread Knight sent a current of holy energy ripping through Major Tamriel. The energy held him still, his huge, furry body thrashing in pain.

It was the opening he needed, and Byron sprinted back in the direction of the rest of the waiting Khan and the circle of mages that Selena was approaching. She was going to get herself killed.

"Selena," he shouted, swinging the Morning Glory like an oar through a river, felling and cleaving men and women as he went like a wind tearing leaves from their branches.

The Human Pyromancer stopped, and looked back at him with a smirk, shaking her head. The look in her eyes told him to stop, and Byron felt his legs lock him in place. He could not hear her over the din of battle behind him, the screams of the maddened soldiers coming at him, but he could read her lips, and the words she spoke struck home so hard, he didn't even feel Shoryu and Morek Rockmight tear him out of harm's way.

The words she had spoken were, "It's my time."

* * * *

Finally, Shoryu thought as he leapt down out of the tree he and Ellen had been using as refuge, *a chance to let this out of my system.*

As Humans and Illeck followed the units' retreat, Shoryu let go of the hostility and aggression that had been gnawing uncontrollably at him during their marching days. The price of his gifts of blood to Byron had to be paid, and now he had the opportunity to do so.

Strapping his bow to his back, the Cuyotai Hunter unleashed his fury on the oncoming assailants, his claws tearing and rending everything and everyone he got close to. In his maddened frenzy, he even tore the throats of allies who got between himself and the few Khan giving pursuit. But he felt nothing for these losses. The world, for him, was a playground of destruction.

"What in the name of Karagesh," shouted one Khan in heavy chain armor as Shoryu bit into his shoulder and tore the arm free of his body.

Screaming in agony, the Khan fell, and Shoryu proceeded to beat the Khan about the head with his own severed limb. When the man went limp, Shoryu stomped down hard on his head, bursting skull inward upon gray matter.

In thrall to battle lust, he almost didn't survive that frenzy.

A pair of Illeck mages struck him with a handful of spells from his right flank, and the pain and damage done knocked Shoryu's senses back into order.

As they closed for the kill, he drew his bow and put arrows through their hands, wounding them and cutting off their magic. He sprinted away from the front to fall back.

He would have continued, but saw that Byron was rushing out to meet the attackers by himself.

Morek Rockmight approached Byron from his right, and Shoryu assisted him by hauling Byron back from the left. He appeared to be watching something far off, and when his struggles ceased, Shoryu looked at Selena Bradford, who approached certain doom.

* * * *

As she turned her back on the Dread Knight for the last time, Selena thought about what he had been trying to do. Perhaps he wasn't a monster after all. Had she really ever doubted him, though? *No,* she thought, shaking her head with a bemused expression. Not since Desanadron, when they had first met.

She looked around her, not focusing on much of anything but her own magic as she called it forth. The circle of mages had made no move against her, and the Necromancer woman in the middle of the circle simply smiled at her with the utmost contempt, as if to say, 'you think you can harm me?'

She intended to do more than harm the woman and her toadies: she intended to reduce them all to less than ash.

She waited patiently as the main struggle behind her fell just outside of the range of Immolation. The Khan soldiers being held in reserve were not going to be so lucky. They too would perish in the mightiest flames a Pyromancer could summon to their aid.

With a sigh of resignation, Selena weaved of the symbols of fire in the air, speaking the words that had to be spoken to conjure the spell.

She did not think on the one thing that most mages think of when they read about the spell of Immolation—that the spellcaster would perish in the flames as well.

As she neared the completion of Immolation, she looked up into the once smug face of the Necromancer.

The woman was losing focus on her own undead minions, and her smile was completely gone, replaced with a slight eyebrow raise of curiosity, perhaps even concern.

"Ka'ludruhn, Mefastus, Ifritinus, Meteordum, Ingulfum," Selena chanted, raising her hands and revealing all of the symbols she had drawn in flames in the air.

The symbols formed a wall of loosely connected flames before her, and only a single word remained. A single word, and her friends and allies would have their chance at completing their objective. A single word, and the road to Mount Toane would probably be cleared. A single word, and no more of her friends or selfless soldiers would have to die in vain.

But she waited, looking up at the Necromancer, who opened her mouth to speak to the Pyromancer.

"And just what has this accomplished, Pyromancer," the woman spat, smiling that smug smile of superiority once more.

"It has sealed your doom." Selena waved her hands to her sides and slamming her palms together. "Immolatus," she whispered.

The spell of Immolation commenced. A bloom of crimson fury pulsated around her chest, a single, tight ring of magical force. As she bowed her head, the ring gained heat, energy, drawing it directly from within Selena Bradford, and the ring pulsated and stretched.

The Necromancer woman stood, transfixed by what was occurring.

The Khan soldiers all sniffed the air, distrustful of any magic they themselves didn't possess or know of. They shuffled about uneasily, but held their ranks. In the end, their training and discipline killed them.

The ring pulsed once more, and then shot outward in a circumference around Selena Bradford, turning every living thing it touched, man, woman, animal and plant, into standing ash replicas of what they had once been. In the next instant, those piles began to crumble and blow away in the wind, and Selena Bradford fell dying to the ground.

* * * *

There had been a terrible burning sensation, not fifteen feet away from Byron and James Hayes, when the undead soldiers all dropped to the ground, reduced to their state of death. All that remained of Tamriel's forces were a few mages, some soldier Khan here, and the Khan that Lieutenant Amon stood with in reserve.

Of course, Tamriel hadn't yet realized that they were all dead, even the strategically ingenious Amon.

Viper, Byron and Morek all turned their units back to squarely meet the remains of this assault, but the clever Renka issued an immediate order of retreat. So their undead soldiers were no more; there still stood nearly two hundred Khan behind the Necromancer, waiting to be unleashed...

Or so there had been a few minutes ago. *Where are they?* the bear demon thought in a panic. *Has Lord Vandross taken them back? Did the mad warlock only intended to harm Byron's forces and leave Tamriel and his brethren to die at the Dread Knight's hand? Surely not,* he thought, as he turned his attention back to the undead warrior who was hacking and slashing away at him with that accursed holy weapon of his.

But as he looked back, his huge claws swiping just wide of the Dread Knight, his fear of having been abandoned turned into a different fear altogether—all who had remained behind had been reduced to ashes.

As he turned back to focus on the Dread Knight, he saw on Byron's skull what looked like a horrifying mockery of a smile.

As he reared up to swing his lethal claws, Tamriel felt the cold, hard blade of James Hayes's broadsword pierce through his belly, where his chain shirt didn't quite reach.

Major Tamriel was stunned for just long enough to allow Byron to leap up on his massive shoulders in a single bound, chanting odd words under his breath. The Morning Glory sheathed, palms pressed down toward the Renka's head, Byron unleashed the Paladin spell of Holy Cannon straight through the demon's body.

Blood and bile sprayed all over him and Hayes in a shower of gore. The remains of the major's body folding inward like a house made of wet paper.

With their officers dead, their Necromancer reduced to dust in the wind, and no aid coming, the remaining troops attempted to flee in all directions— and were cut down by Elven archers and Viper's mages.

No more than ten minutes after it started, the battle was over.

Byron, James, Morek, Shoryu and Ellen ran down the slopes of the woods to where Selena Bradford lay dead.

Byron was the first to notice that Alex, his first real friend since becoming a Dread Knight, lay burnt to death next to her head. He had been with her in the end. No one in the company spoke, nor groaned about their own injuries (which were thankfully few), standing silently to honor their friend and ally.

Finally, James Hayes rolled her over, folding her arms over her chest, and made the sign of Oun over her corpse.

Byron copied the gesture, then left the group to their grieving. He hated to be cold about it, but he had to get a report from the other officers regarding the casualties. He had to get an idea of what sort of resources they would have after resting the army.

Byron stalked through the long swaths of blood and corpses to Wilhelm

Von Rook, Lieutenant of the Second Grade. The Elven man had a large gash across his forehead, three diagonal claw marks, but they appeared fairly shallow, and so Byron wasn't too concerned with his health to allow him rest before a report was taken.

Von Rook gave him a stiff salute and stood as straight as a board. "My lord," he said, his voice slightly weak and trembling.

"Casualty report, Lieutenant," Byron barked, rather more harshly than he had intended to. He was trying not to let his own feelings about Selena Bradford's death affect his judgment, but already his emotions overwhelmed him.

Two had fallen in his personal service.

"Well, my lord, we've had a rather bad time of it, I must say. We've lost one hundred and thirty-four men, nearly all of them infantry and unmounted cavalry. We suffered a few losses to our mages, and a handful of archers, but as a whole in terms of numbers, nothing crippling. However, sir, I knew many of those who fell in this battle. They have families, friends, who are going to miss them terribly sir."

Byron nodded. *Such is war*, he thought rather dismally.

"And, my lord, Sergeant Cassandra Payne fell to her wounds. A vicious spell of some sort was cast on her after she received a minor cut, and the wound spread from her stomach to her throat. She fell almost instantly, my lord."

Once again Byron shook his head, miserable at the thought that Vandross had once again gained the upper hand before him. As he thought of the young Sergeant-at-Arms, he was reminded of the uncompromising nature of war in Tamalaria. Young, old, middle aged, it didn't matter to the gods of war—once you joined the battle, you were as expendable as the next soldier.

So what of Selena, he wondered with a twinge in his heart. What of little Alex?

He had read the words on her lips: "it's my time," she had said. That much he had been afraid of. Voice, deep in the recesses of his mind, had told him that that one of his friends would not survive the coming battle.

He had assumed that Voice had been speaking of the battle they would face at Mount Toane, but it had been here, long before they could even reach the lair of the one-eyed warlock Richard Vandross.

"Thank you, Lieutenant," Byron said, absent-mindedly. "Let's get our dead buried this evening. We'll be staying right at the edge of these woods until morning. The troops need time to heal their wounds, physically and emotionally. That will be all. You may tell everyone to be at ease after the bodies are taken care of. And Lieutenant?"

"Yes, my lord," asked the Elf as he snapped off another salute.

"Don't bother burying our enemies. Let the scavengers have them." Without another word, Byron moved back toward the company he had brought with him into this mess. How many of them would survive the onslaught of Mount Toane? And if any survived, what would their lives be like afterwards?

Hard questions to ask himself, he thought, and no answers anywhere in sight.

Later that night, when everyone else in the army's camp was eating or tending to the injured and the company's supplies, Byron and James carried Selena Bradford away from the encampment, Shoryu, Ellen and Morek following closely behind. Alex had been tucked under Selena's hands, the Ki Fairy barely recognizable from the damage.

They carried the two companions almost to the northernmost edge of the woods, a full mile and a half away from the army. When they laid them down, the company stood about in silence. Morek had brought three shovels from the supplies tents, but no one made a move to pick them up.

"What should we do now?" Ellen's voice was timid, her eyes filling with tears that threatened to break her resolve.

Morek and Shoryu moved slowly toward the shovels, but James Hayes put his hand up to stop them.

"No," he said, softly. His own eyes were almost cold and steely, but he wasn't being unemotional: rather, he appeared to have an idea in mind. "I'll stay here with her. You two, Ellen, Byron, go gather up some wood. We'll give her a funeral pyre. I think that's what she would have wanted."

The Dread Knight nodded, seeming to understand James's request.

Selena had been the first member of the company James had known, had fought with. She had seen him at his worst, his most hopeless, that much Byron was certain.

The Human Paladin had been trapped with her in Desanadron as word of what had befallen his kinsmen reached him. He would want a few words with Selena alone, even now, when he had only one last chance.

Byron marching into the woods, ostensibly to find suitable firewood, although wood was all around them, branches and sticks of good enough size and brittleness to burn quickly and powerfully.

When James saw that Byron had understood his meaning, he knelt next to Selena Bradford's body, laying his head on the ground next to hers, and wept as softly as he could.

He let out everything, all of his aches and pains, tears running in thin rivers down the landscape of his face. After so much fighting and training, it was beginning to be a rough terrain for even those precious, salty streams to flow through, but they found their way.

"I couldn't, I couldn't do anything Selena," he whispered hoarsely, trying not to sob, getting the words out all in one rush. "I don't know what to do anymore. You have been the only person I could hope to keep safe, the only one who knows fully what I have felt. You know how close I have come to losing all faith, to disbelieving everything the Order has taught me." Sobs threatened to rack his body loose of its spirit.

"And even you, little Alex," he said, touching Alex's limp form with a single finger. "I could not protect even the littlest of us." James shook his head disconsolately. "And though I know you cannot hear me, know this: I am most sorry for my failure. I am not worthy of my title any longer." He reached for the lashings that held his breastplate on his upper body. The symbol of Oun, emblazoned across the metal, was worn and battered, covered with blood. He felt unclean, unfit to bear the mark of his great god any longer. He prepared to strip away his armor when he heard the faint sound of hoofbeats.

James Hayes looked around, but could see no one. Nothing stirred, nothing made a noise. It seemed the entire world around him had come to a halt.

What had happened to him, he wondered. Is this the delirium of regret? The hoofbeats came closer, closer, as though they were right on top of him, and still he could see no horse.

He whipped his head around, hearing the braying of a horse. Standing beside Selena and Alex's bodies was a huge, pale stallion. Astride it, holding a scythe in one skeletal hand, was a figure he instinctively knew all mortal beings must some day meet.

He dared not utter or think its name, for to do so would mean his own immediate departure with the entity.

The black cloak and robes billowed about the entity as it dismounted, all tattered cloth and shadows. Yet Hayes felt no menace from it, no malcontent—he could almost detect a sense of duty about the entity. It stood by Selena's corpse, the tiny Ki Fairy resting atop her chest, making no move, uttering no sound.

The wind that blew past James's ear carried the faintest hint of a whisper on it.

HAVE YOU SAID YOUR GOOD-BYES, it asked.

James was so startled by the raspy, thick feel of the words that he barely had the capacity to think of what they meant.

MY TIME IS PRECIOUS, AND I HAVE MUCH WORK TO DO.

James collected his composure, straightened himself up before this most revered, and mostly feared, being.

"She can hear me?" he asked, fully aware of how much his voice trembled.

FOR NOW SHE CAN, MORTAL. BUT YOUR TIME IS MY TIME, AND MY TIME GOES QUICKLY. THERE IS MUCH MORE WORK TO BE DONE THIS NIGHT, AND I HAVEN'T THE PATIENCE FOR LONG FAREWELLS. BESIDES, DO YOU HAVE ANY IDEA HOW DIFFICULT IT IS TO KEEP THE REST OF THE WORLD ON HOLD?

James looked up the hill to the west, and saw Byron and the others, each frozen in time, all carrying bundles of wood.

"My apologies." James knelt and kissed Selena Bradford as tenderly as he could on the forehead.

For a moment, she appeared to smile at him.

"Good bye, my friend. Perhaps we shall meet again, if mighty Oun allows it."

As James stepped back, the entity swung his scythe down with such speed that all the Paladin could see was a flash of silver light.

Two orbs of light fluttered up and into the darkness of its robes, shining there like the pinpoints in Byron's eye sockets.

As the being turned back toward his steed, James had a single question burning in his heart. If he didn't ask it now, he might never be granted another chance.

"Wait! I do not want any trouble, but I must ask you something!"

The dark rider mounted his horse, but turned to face his darkened cowl toward the Paladin.

SPEAK QUICKLY, MORTAL. I SHALL ANSWER AS BEST I CAN.

"Who has granted me this opportunity? Why me, and not another? Why have I been given this gift to seek forgiveness for my inadequacy?"

The rider circled his horse once, for the steed seemed more impatient than the rider who James would not name. There was a pause, and it seemed to stretch infinitely on, eons of moments passing around them.

I WAS AFRAID YOU MIGHT ASK THAT, FOR THE ONE WHO MADE THIS REQUEST OF ME REQUIRED THAT I ANSWER YOU. IT WAS INDEED OUN. NOW, JAMES HAYES, I MUST DEPART. AND KNOW YOU ONE THING MORE, the entity said as it began to ascend into the air, fading from existence. SHE SAYS, THERE IS NO NEED TO SEEK FORGIVENESS.

A small pain exploded behind James Hayes's eye, and he found himself sitting next to Selena Bradford's body once again, Byron and the others just now coming over the hill and out of the woods with the firewood.

It would appear to any outside observer that nothing had happened. But for James Hayes, the most important event of his life had taken place.

He had received forgiveness, and confirmation of his faith.

Chapter Seven
Anticipation

The following morning, loud pounding awakened Richard Vandross on his bedroom door.

He couldn't even remember having come back to his room to rest, and his body certainly didn't feel as though it had gotten a break. He felt instead as though he had been awake all evening, perhaps trying to tear the mountains from the very earth. But he knew that when someone came pounding that hard and that long at his chamber door, he should probably get up and answer it.

Perhaps he'd even be nice enough to let the messenger live this morning. He hadn't yet decided.

When he dragged himself to the door, Vilec Roak stood before him, a mixed expression of apprehension and triumph on his demon face.

Perhaps I should kill him, Vandross thought smugly for a moment. *After all, what good has he done me lately? I did away with Bael quickly enough when he had outlived his usefulness and fealty. Why not Roak?*

But every efficient plan needed a scapegoat for the very last minute, and Roak would certainly fill the role well. Vandross had no qualms with sacrificing the Shadowbeast Prime at the last. "Well, what is it General," he asked, his voice hoarse and scratchy.

"Word has just been received, my lord. The assault on Byron's army failed rather spectacularly, sir. We managed to kill fewer than two hundred of their men. But there is some good news, lord Vandross."

The one-eyed warlock shot Roak a quizzical look as he took a drink of water from the jug on his table.

"And that would be," he said, moving his cup in the 'let's get on with it' motion.

"Another of Byron's personal company has fallen," Vilec Roak said.

These few words tasted like the sweetest honey ale to Vandross as he let the feel of them wash over him. Another one dead? How could that be? How could one of Byron's companions fall in battle to anyone but Tamriel or Amon? This he had to hear.

"Give me the details," he rasped harshly, anxious to know what had befallen one of those enormous thorns in his side.

Vilec Roak proceeded to tell the tale of how the battle had gone as his spy had viewed it, with the aid of a spell of Farsight. It was a useful spell that most mages could learn very easily, if they bothered to take the time. But of course, most didn't.

The demon related how the Pyromancer, Selena Bradford, had used the most powerful and lethal spell known to Pyromancers, indeed, one of the most potent known to all magic users in the lands of Tamalaria. Immolation, the price for the spell's use being the very life force of the caster.

As soon as the battle neared its end, and Major Tamriel fell, the spy had used a Blink spell to return himself to his chambers in Mount Toane.

Richard Vandross grinned quite broadly, pleased that at least one more of Byron's friends had died. He too had suffered many losses in that battle—the three enormous Renkas, hundreds of Khan soldiers, and Amon. The Lieutenant had potential, but that would not come to fruition. And Tamriel would have fared much better at Mount Toane, but he had become more of a burden than was worthwhile.

Ah, well, Vandross thought. *That's two more strings I can cut to focus on the task at hand.*

Byron's army was only ten days away now, Vilec Roak informed him. Nine days to reach the top of the hills around Mount Toane, and another full day for them to descend the hills and make their way to the entrance. That would give Vandross's forces within the stronghold time to prepare for the approaching onslaught.

It had been much the same the first time he had dwelled here, Vandross thought. Tanarak of Sidius had known that the Final Push was at hand, and had been so well prepared for it that he had repelled the effort. However, even with the aid of the mighty Dread Knight Byron of Sidius, his hold over the lands began to slip afterwards. Tanarak had put too much of his energy into making Byron what he was, into fortifying the defenses of Mount Toane. Vandross, of course, had already avoided one of those pitfalls; he didn't intend to take any prisoners. And, he had avoided another pitfall by sending a forward offensive to gauge the full strength of the undead warrior's forces. He would not be caught unawares, as his master had been all that time ago. Where the Final Push marked the beginning of Tanarak's end, this conflict would mark the age of terror for Tamalaria, a terror and fear that Vandross would bask and feed in and upon. His deserved immortality was close at hand.

So why, he thought as Vilec Roak left the room, *am I trembling?*

* * * *

That same morning, Byron awoke to find Bael, the Lizardman who had formerly been Vandross's General, standing over him, with a wry reptilian smile plastered to his face.

"Rise and shine, my friend," he said, his tone full of laughter, but cautious laughter. Apparently, he had been apprised of the situation concerning Selena Bradford and Alex the Ki Fairy, for James Hayes stood next to the Lizardman warrior.

Byron got slowly, painfully to his feet. He ached in places he hadn't ached since his mortal life, and the renewed sense of pain and fatigue almost stole him back into the sleeping world.

He removed his still bloodied gauntlet, and shook Bael's hand. The rough, scaled palm felt strange, alien to the touch, but Byron welcomed any sensation other than the wear and tear his legs presently complained to his mind about.

"Good day, Bael," Byron said, clearing his 'throat'.

"I mourn the loss of your friends, lord Byron." Bael inclined his head ever so slightly. "Though I did not know them well, they stood truly as your friends and allies. And as you well know, a friend of yours is a friend of mine." Bael's forked tongue worked with great ease over the 's' sounds of his words.

He was, Byron realized, one of the only reptilian warriors who seemed to have no trouble with the common tongue of Tamalaria. He didn't hiss or spit at length, and unlike most of his kinsmen, his slatted eyes didn't rove when he focused on a conversation. Such a tiny detail to notice, Byron thought, yet so pivotal in defining this man.

"I mourn their loss as well, Bael. However, Selena's sacrifice was not in vain. Thanks to her efforts, we lost only a handful of men and women, where a heaping mound might have been the result without her spell."

Byron stretched his arms and legs, checked over his equipment, and made a brief scan of the encampment. Most of the tents and lean-tos had been torn down and packed away: the army would be ready to march within the hour.

Shoryu, his Cuyotai snout wet with the morning dew, came over to the Dread Knight with a water skin in hand, the sides of which appeared to be slightly stained a crimson hue. Despite his earlier decision, Byron took the skin and thanked the young Cuyotai Hunter with a nod of approval, then turned and unashamedly poured Shoryu's fresh blood over his skull.

An instant later, he felt renewed and full of vigor. He was even beginning to feel a little younger at heart, as though the youth of Shoryu's lifeblood were affecting his own personality. Perhaps that's a good thing he mused.

Byron gathered the remaining members of his personal party together with the ranking officers and Bael, who had brought a contingent of four hundred Lizardmen. They were not all, of course, from the same village. Some were not even from the same tribal backgrounds as Bael's people. But he had banded them all together with his commanding presence, and the promise of honor gained through combat for the greater good. Though some few didn't appear to care much about honor as much as they did about fighting, they appeared to be a rough and capable bunch. They bore no ranks or uniforms; their whole command structure seemed to be centered on the idea that they were all equals, and only Bael had the right, among all of them, to lead.

Byron didn't ask if Bael had been challenged for the position of command. Any Lizardman foolish enough to do so would surely be missing a limb or a vital organ. Say, an eye or an ear slit. Perhaps an arm, as one fellow was.

Byron stood in the center of the assembled officers, waiting until their private conversations had died down to speak. "We have only a few days' march ahead of us before we are in the region of Mount Toane. When we have reached the bottom of the hills surrounding the warlock's stronghold, we shall wait. There are inevitably going to be more forces joining in the fray, and we should wait until all are present before we begin an assault. Now I know what it's like to attack Mount Toane. I've done it once already. My body is proof of what occurred that day. We charged in too soon, without a structured plan of attack. We went in without the benefit of some form of intelligence from within the mountain.

"However, I am not the only one who has been there once already. Morek Rockmight served with me in the Final Push years ago, and he too knows the interior of that accursed place to some degree. We will not be going in blind, or unprepared. We will have experienced mages among the separate units to detect magical traps and locked spells as we go. The last time we rushed Mount Toane, we went in without anticipating traps, and it got a good number of our men and women slaughtered."

Byron fell silent for a moment, waiting to see if any of the officers had anything to offer. When no one spoke, he continued.

"The next three days will be harsh on us. We'll be passing directly south of the Allenian Hills, and that is historically one of the most Khan-populated regions in Tamalaria. Surely by now the wind has carried the smell of their many dead kinsmen to them. They will be looking for answers, no doubt, and we may need to contend with them on their own turf. They are not soldiers—they will attack without discipline, but with swiftness and cunning. Be on the lookout, gentlemen and ladies, and keep each other informed.

"Also, you may be wondering how a force of this size is going to travel such a large distance in the coming days. We have many mounted riders, and a good number of Q Mages to enhance the running and walking speeds of the footmen. It's going to be a hell of a strain on those mages, but we need you officers to make certain they focus on it as hard as they can. Each man and woman needs to be able to move as swiftly as a jogging horse if we're to make this trip in so little time. I may also be able to help in this matter in some way."

How exactly he would accomplish that, Byron didn't know, yet he felt confident enough in his powers to offer his aid.

"Lastly, before I hear suggestions or reports from any of you, I need you all to go to your units. Tell the men that if any of them want out of this business, this is their last chance to return to their homes and families and friends."

Though not many died overall, many were injured and maimed, and of those unharmed, several had just been in their first real combat. A bit of a shitstorm for a man's first battle, and he could understand if the younger men had experienced second thoughts about dealing with the one-eyed warlock.

The officers, some of them newly appointed to their posts, saluted and walked to their own individual units.

First Sergeant Alowar Fleetfoot had been promoted to Sergeant-at-Arms upon Cassandra Payne's death, and was trying to get accustomed to being a unit leader instead of the second-in-command who constantly busted balls. He was an older Elven soldier, having served in three wars for the Elven Kingdom, and had always been used as the sort of gruff middle-management man that every unit needed. In command, but never with the final say-so. Now, Lieutenant Rook had given him the at-Arms patch that had been taken from Cassandra's uniform when she was buried, and had told the old soldier that he was now in command of the unit.

"At least until we get back to Whitewood, old friend," Rook had tried to jest. "Then you can put in your papers to be demoted back to First Sergeant. Ha ha ha." Little did Rook realize that that was exactly what Fleetfoot intended to do.

James Hayes and Morek Rockmight moved away a short distance from the troops as they assembled their marching lines and files. James looked up and down the field and hill that the army had rested on near the edge of the woods. There had to be easily two or three thousand men and women, all willing to give their lives for a cause the whole land shared. Nobody wanted another Tanarak of Sidius, that much was clear from the ferocity with which they had fought during the previous afternoon. When the army did reach Mount Toane, it would be a much different battle than had occurred there twenty years previously.

The Dwarven Boxer looked up at the Human Paladin, his eyes searching. He had seen something there last night, something that had previously not existed since meeting the man in Whitewood. There was a quality of relief, even revelation, in Hayes's eyes, his tight-lipped grin, and even his movements. The man had apparently shaken off some huge burden on his soul.

Morek envied him that, though he wouldn't admit as much.

The taciturn Dwarf had been friends with Ellen Daires for years prior to that morning, and had never known her to be the adventurous sort. She seemed so frail, even when casting her magic about her. Though her power was great, and her new husband well skilled with a bow, Morek still feared that like Selena Bradford, Alex, and David Spore before them, she would not reach the end of this journey safely.

"Don't be troubled, Morek," Hayes said suddenly, his eyes still fixed on some far off point on the horizon. "We shall succeed in our given task. Of this, I am most certain." Without another word, the suddenly enigmatic Paladin walked away from the confused Dwarf.

Morek scratched his thick red beard a moment, shrugged his shoulders, and set about giving out orders to his men. The Q Mages had begun their work, positioned at points around the army in a large circle, focusing their power into a single enhancement, making the foot soldiers move as swiftly as horses. The work would be tiring, but they would endure. They had to.

Because more than anything, the members of Byron's new army wanted to get this dark business over with.

* * * *

Several hours later, as Lee Toren and a few of his associates scoured the battleground for what profitable goodies they might find in the wake of Byron and his army, the Gnome Pickpocket thought long and hard on his dealings with the Dread Knight. The man went, he left a trail of destruction behind him. His time as Tanarak's General didn't differ much more than the quest he was on right now. The only difference, Lee thought as he watched one of the Wererats near him pocket a nice looking shiny, was that he was on the 'good' side of the struggle.

Good and evil, as far as Lee was concerned, were relative terms, and only truly mattered in the minds of men who concerned themselves with ethical and spiritual matters. He didn't consider himself such a man.

Yet, there was a noble quality to the Dread Knight's mission. He was attempting to redeem himself for the sins he had committed as Byron of Sidius. Atone for his atrocities.

"Feh," Lee muttered as he rummaged through the pockets of a fallen Khan soldier. Most of Byron's men and women who had fallen had been buried, and Lee wasn't about to disturb their bodies. He may not have been a man of ethics, but superstitions? By the gods and hells, yes he was, and disturbing the eternal rest of a buried man wasn't going to be his fault.

"Hey boss," one of the Wererats hollered from off to his left.

Lee snapped his small, fat head around to look at the wiry creature, and saw that the Wererat was backing ever so slowly away from something downhill, in the burnt-out crater filled with ashes and bones that Lee had rather pointedly avoided.

"Come 'ere and get a look at this."

Lee obliged the Wererat, and came over to see what could have spooked such an otherwise merciless bandit. Flint usually didn't shy away from anything.

As Lee got to the edge of the crater, he looked down and saw what had taken Flint so off guard—from beneath the pile of rubble and ashes, a single arm clawed its way free.

Even from this distance, Lee saw that the arm was plainly burnt nearly to the bone, but the glint of claws and the muffled groans and half-dead roars of whatever was coming out of there told Lee to keep his distance.

After a few minutes of digging, the arm stopped, burying its claws into the earth outside of the pile. The soot and bones and armor shuttered, and a bloodied, blackened Khan half emerged from his living tomb.

The tiger man gasped for air in huge, violent gasps, his chest heaving up and down as he fell on the side of his face, squeezing his eyes shut against the sunlight.

Lee Toren had taken a couple of steps back, not realizing that he had done so. Flint, meanwhile, had begun to descend and circle around to where the Khan lay still half-buried by armor and bones. The muscular Wererat grappled the Khan under his good arm, and what Lee saw was half of an arm—the Khan had lost his left arm from the elbow down in whatever magical assault had clearly created the crater.

Flint, caring little for the state of his nice green and tan tunics, hauled on the Khan, pulling him fully out to reveal that the Khan was also missing his entire left leg and had a gaping wound on that side of his abdomen.

Lee could hear Flint grunting to haul the man out, but also heard the distinct, guttural cursing of the Khan tongue issuing from the tiger man.

Tough bastard, Lee thought. *Too bad he probably won't survive those wounds.*

Yet the Khan's wounds didn't bleed, as Lee was certain they must. They were purest black, cauterized by the magic. *Most likely Pyromancy,* Lee thought.

Flint brought him out of his thoughts and into action as he yelled at Lee, "For the gods' sakes, Lee. Bring one of your healing potions."

The Gnome Pickpocket rolled his eyes, and fetched a spare one from one of the other scavenging Wererats in his employ. They weren't the best thieves, but Flint was an all right sort. Of course, he came from a premium crop, a guild known as the Hoods in Desanadron.

The Wererat was currently available for employment, however, since the city was rebuilding.

Lee went over to Flint as the Wererat propped the Khan's head on his lap, handing him the potion, which Flint promptly poured down the Khan's throat.

A subtle blue light shimmered over the Khan as the potion worked its magic, and the Khan's eyes fluttered fully open.

The tiger man tried to stand, but Flint held him fast to the ground.

"Not yet, Khan." The Wererat had little love for their kind. He didn't, however, approve of suffering, and when he could keep someone from Death's door, he would. "In case you haven't noticed, you've been badly injured. You're naked, your fur is blackened, you're missing half an arm and a leg, and without that potion, you'd be missing a good portion of your abdominal region." "Now answer us some questions, and we may not let you figure out how to get somewhere where you can get help on your own."

The Khan said nothing, only nodded and grunted at Flint.

"Very good," said Lee Toren, sitting cross-legged next to the Khan, on his injured side. An injured Khan still had claws, and teeth, and the Gnome wasn't fond of the idea of being this Khan's meals for the next day or so.

"Now, first thing's first. What is your name?"

The Khan spat away from the Wererat and Gnome, clearing his throat in an attempt to gain use of his voice. He spoke, but his throat was too dry for words to come out.

Flint handed him a water skin, which the Khan took greedily and drained. Wiping his mouth and handing the skin back, the Khan answered them quite clearly. "My name, is Tiberious Amon. And what has happened here I must tell you, for one woman was strong enough of will and spirit to do what had to be done, despite the cost."

Lee and Flint looked at each other quizzically.

"The cost was her own life."

* * * *

By midday, Byron, Viper, Morek and Bael's forces had cleared the majority of the land leading to the stretch south of the Allenian Hills. The Q Mages had done wondrous work with their magic, but two men now carried each, holding one end of a medical litter on which the spell users laid.

The Dread Knight jogged along at a good clip, content to feel the wind blow past him as he ran the soft, springy soil of the Center Plains and the Allenian Hills region. With any luck, the army could avoid another large-scale encounter that day. However, despite the magic that had been used on the entire body of the army, several men and women had dropped. Some were Elven, some Lizardman, and a few were stout Minotaur warriors—those three Races tended to have a natural resistance to magic, whether the power was used for their benefit, or their detriment. As a result, the magic was wearing off on their kind quicker than on the others.

Byron called out to Shoryu, who had been running not more than twenty paces ahead, his own natural grace and readiness as a scout and sprinter serving him even better now that the Q magic was affecting him. The previous night, Byron had given Shoryu some maps of the lands they would be passing through and had instructed the young Cuyotai Hunter to memorize them as best he could. Hunters of almost every Race made certain they could read, decipher, and memorize even the minutest details from such maps and travel catalogues. Some of the soldiers had their own personal questing journals regarding the areas they were to pass through, and some of them proved to be quite recent. Shoryu had read over them all long into the night, and Byron had stayed up just long enough to watch him fall asleep next to Ellen Daires, his snout still buried in a journal.

"What can you tell me about this area, other than the danger of being so near the Allenians, my young friend," Byron asked between jogging strides. He sounded comical, even to himself, his words coming out bumped and distorted as he tried to jog and speak at the same time. He hadn't been much good at this in life, and certainly his undead nature wouldn't make it any easier.

Shoryu turned his head, snout plastered with a bemused grin.

"Well, friend, there isn't really much to tell. There are supposed to be several dozen men in an Order of Oun fort just an hour away to the east, and some small Gnome tradeposts have been established since times I cannot remember. Unfortunately, this is about raiding season time for the tradeposts, and the Gnomes barricade the buildings and hide. They do this so that when the Khan or Simpa come down from the Hills to plunder supplies, none of the Gnomes themselves are harmed. In addition, most of the weapons and armor that are left out are silver, so neither Race will take them."

"I thought Khan weren't lycanthropes." Byron was beginning to huff and puff. The Q magic was wearing off of him as well, and the army would soon be forced to stop so that the rested Q Mages could cast their collective enchantment on the army once more.

Shoryu cocked his head sideways for a moment, thinking about Byron's statement.

"No, they are not, but for some reason, they are allergic to silver in the same way as their Simpa rivals. The Werelions, however, cannot even get close to silver without getting sick, unlike the Khan. Also, a clever Khan will simply wrap the weapons or armor in cloths, so that they can pawn them off in another town or village. For the Simpa, the silver is useless, a good deterrent. The Khan, in their greed, are also often distracted with trying to smuggle the weapons someplace where no questions will be asked. As a result, over the years, the raiding season has ended in the same way as every season and generation before it; neither side makes any headway."

"Anything else," Byron said, actually having to make an effort to keep up with the swift Cuyotai now. "Anything to watch out for?"

Shoryu shook his head, trying not to seem too pessimistic.

"Not really, except for battles between the Khan and Simpa. Their struggle for claim over the region is older than most of us here in the army, and they see outside interference as an affront to both of their peoples. Were they not so pointedly interested in killing one another, the whole Allenian Hills region would be most dangerous to traverse. Thankfully, their definition outside interference doesn't include getting close to or observing the battles. We would have to have someone foolish enough to actually get involved before we had any trouble to deal with."

The two companions were silent for a while, Shoryu falling back a bit to carry his wife on his back as he ran along.

As the army crested of one of the last hills in the region, lord Viper and Bael called a halt to the army's advance. They would all take an hour and a half to eat and rest before the Q Mages performed their magic again.

Ellen slid down off of Shoryu's back, gave him a quick kiss, and whispered something in his canine ear that Byron couldn't quite make out.

Shoryu looked at her solemnly, then nodded, keeping his eyes shut. Byron stalked over, his legs cramping. They hadn't cramped since his time as a Human, his mortal life. He was beginning to realize that there really were advantages to being truly undead.

As the army went about the business of resting and preparing a sort of lunch-dinner hybrid meal, Byron decided to have a short conversation with Voice. He sat down near the eastern front of the forces, cross-legged, and closed his 'eyes', concentrating on nothing, letting his entire consciousness slide into a state of semi-trance.

He quickly found himself floating in the void, as happened when he spoke with Voice during his waking hours. Only during sleep did Byron come to the cemetery.

Byron called out in his mind, into the void. "Voice? I believe we have some things to discuss."

"I hear you, Byron Aixler," Voice said through the darkness. The sound reverberated off of the barriers in Byron's mind. "Indeed, there is much to talk about. I am truly sorry for the loss of your companion."

Byron bowed deeply in his soul-space.

"As am I. But you had warned me that she was going to do something like that. Her time was coming, and she chose when to make her stand. A good thing she did, too. We might have lost many dozens of times more soldiers had she not made her particular sacrifice. And James Hayes and I needed something to distract that bear thing. I didn't want to have to unleash my full potential on such a creature."

"Indeed, that may have destroyed everyone else around you."

Byron nodded.

"Something else plagues your thoughts, Byron Aixler. What is it?"

Byron had to think about how to word this next question; Voice often responded to him in riddles and half-truths, never revealing everything. He needed to know a few things before he arrived at Mount Toane, and he wanted to get as direct an answer as possible. His problem was not one of knowing what questions to ask, but rather, how to ask them.

"You have told me this much, Voice. You have told me that not all of my allies shall survive this particular voyage, that those who survive shall be forever changed. Pray, will anymore of them suffer the same fate as Selena Bradford?"

"None of them shall sacrifice themselves in a flare of magic," Voice responded.

Damnation, Byron thought. Too specific a question. Voice would take everything black-letter literal.

"All right, fair enough. Will those who joined me prior to this army perish before this undertaking is completed?"

"This undertaking shall never truly be over, per se, Byron Aixler," Voice responded after a moment's hesitation.

He was, Byron realized, trying to avoid the questions, which was rather unsettling. Voice may very well not want to upset him further than he was by letting him know that once again he would not be able to save one of his friends. Or perhaps, he thought, Voice didn't want to set anything in stone; everything the being had told him thus far had come to pass. Perhaps, if Voice didn't say anything concrete, fate could be changed.

Byron considered this possibility seriously for a moment, and decided to drop that line of questioning. It would lead him nowhere.

"Very well. I have other questions for you. Firstly, why did Richard Vandross send a forward assault force at us? Would it not have been wiser to hold them in reserve, for the defense of Mount Toane?"

"The warlock is mad, Byron Aixler, mad with the power of the Glorious Mother of Destruction. He also seeks to act in a different fashion from his former master, Tanarak. This much I have learned from Locke, who still keeps an eye on the warlock's activities."

Locke, Byron thought. The enormous, crimson-armored Keeper. How had Vandross managed to expel such a being from his very soul?

"Your time grows short, Byron Aixler. The army is preparing to march once again."

"Thank you." Byron brought himself back to full consciousness.

The soldiers under his command were already moving out, as Voice had said.

Byron stood and moved forward, flanked on both sides by James Hayes, Ellen Daires, Morek Rockmight and Shoryu Tearfang.

For a moment, he expected Selena to join them, Alex on shoulder, but they would not be joining them again. Still, the friends he had with him, he would keep from the same such fate. He would protect them as best he could.

* * * *

"So, none have returned? None at all," Richard Vandross asked, his twin harmony voice resounding through the throne room as he spoke with Vilec Roak.

"No sir, none. I believe Colonel Molis suspects you sent them to their graves."

151

Vandross smiled knowingly; he was certain that the half-breed would be furious with such a tactically unsound course of action, being the good soldier that he was. However, Molis wouldn't question him out-right, even if he had struck Roak. After all, Roak was just another demon: *he* had become a god.

"If the Colonel has an issue with my strategy, he can take it up with me directly, General." Vandross's eyes glimmered with crimson light, and he felt the powerful urge to test the power of the Mother of Destruction. "Aside from the Dread Knight's forces, does anyone else march against us?"

"One of our sources in Ja-Wen tells us that their private army secretly moves from the east to fight us. They appear to be traveling slowly, cautiously. I believe they intend to join the main force of Byron's army when they arrive, sire." The Shadowbeast General scanned a map of the land of Tamalaria. He pointed out a small token he had placed on the map, just west of Ja-Wen, between the sprawling city-state itself and nearby Mount Toane. It was only a two-day march from the city to their position, and Vandross had sent several raiding parties into the city. They had come back unscathed, reporting that they had met with little resistance. Could it be that their army had been lying in wait, seeking the opportunity to strike back when he wasn't looking?

Of course, he thought. *Roak is correct; they are waiting for Byron's forces, that they might have aid against us. Too bad they won't be around long enough to help the Dread Knight.*

"Vilec Roak, prepare a single battalion to march for that smaller set of units, the one from Ja-Wen." The warlock stalked directly toward the exit from the throne room that would lead to his chambers. "Have them ready in two hours. We shall take the fight to those fools, and crush them."

"Sire? What about Byron?"

Vandross turned on his heel to look threateningly back at the Shadowbeast, who cringed slightly away from him under that glare.

"We'll be done with Ja-Wen and back in plenty of time to deal with the Dread Knight, General. I want to go have some fun, first. I want to make certain that the Glorious Mother of Destruction holds up to reputation."

Vilec Roak shuddered inwardly as he nodded his black, shadowy head, shuffling off to go prepare a battalion.

Vandross himself stalked to his bedchamber, where Power stood, seemingly waiting for him. When had he released her into the physical world? Had she somehow escaped?

The one-eyed warlock approached her at a creeping gait, trying not to gain her attention. But as he reached her, the Orb of Eden's Serpent manifestation whipped its head to look him dead in the eyes.

She flashed him a wide, mirthless smile, her eyes flashing in the torchlight of the sleeping chamber. "You play a dangerous game, host." Her tone of voice and the cold, steely glare she gave him told Vandross that she was not at all pleased. "You should not play with the Glorious Mother of Destruction as though it were a child's toy. Remember, we have given you access to it: that does not mean that you have the ability to use it whenever you wish. You will be severely taxed, physically and mentally. You should not fool around with it."

Vandross grunted at her, stepping past the bed she sat on, sitting on his stone hewn chair.

"It is my choice how I wield my abilities, Power. You should tell me how you got out of my soul without my noticing."

The Orb manifestation smiled wider, the flesh around the corners of her mouth crinkling, threatening to split open and bleed.

"I never left, Richard Vandross, host and holder of the Orbs of Eden's Serpent. I am merely impressing myself upon your field of vision from within. None of us can now leave, for to do so would unleash the power of the Glorious Mother of Destruction on the very position we appear at. In short, Mount Toane would be brought down around your ears. The only way for us to be freed now, is for you to die."

Richard Vandross did not trust at all the smug look of satisfaction on the Orb manifestation's face, but he only had to see it for another moment. Power faded from his vision like a desert hallucination. A small chill ran up his spine; his own demise would lead to the Orbs of Eden's Serpent' release. Did they want that? Did they want him to use the Mother of Destruction on Byron of Sidius, and then die, so that they would be free to inhabit another warlock? *Surely not*, he thought.

Because he was Richard Vandross, and no one would defeat him.

* * * *

Evening approached, and the army of the Dread Knight, Thaddeus Viper, Morek Rockmight, and Bael settled down due southeast of the Allenian Hills region. They had managed to get through without encountering a single raiding party from either the Khan, or the Simpa. Patrols of soldiers were set to guard the perimeter of the army, however, as a precaution. They were to pay special attention to the supplies and healers, and most of those put on the duty were Minotaurs, Dwarves, and some of Bael's more skilled warriors.

Byron didn't want to take the chance that the men and women of the army might be too tired or hungry to fight once they reached Mount Toane. He sat around a campfire with his friends Shoryu, Ellen, Morek, Hayes, and Bael, each member eating their meal in respective silence.

The Dread Knight kept mulling over the situation, the familiarity of it all. When last he had marched from the west toward Mount Toane, he had not encountered any opposing forces—Tanarak had made the mistake of keeping all of his followers in and around Mount Toane. That had allowed the Dread Knight to arrive with all of his forces fully intact.

One of the officers in the Elven battalions approached the company and snapped a quick salute. His fingers stayed just away from his forehead, which was still wrapped in bandaging from the battle with Tamriel and the Khan.

Byron stood and returned the salute, Bael and Morek rising with him.

"My lord, one of the scouts just returned at a full run. A large group of Khan approaches from the Allenians, apparently intent on raiding our supplies. We are prepared for them, but the men want to know how hard they should resist."

Byron understood; already the stench of death hung on some of the soldiers' clothes. Elves didn't care much for warfare, or for death, and would avoid bloodshed if they could.

"Allow myself and my comrades to deal with the situation," Byron said gruffly, motioning for Morek, Shoryu, James and Ellen to accompany him.

The remains of the company from Whitewood, armed and looking for some way to take out their frustrations at the loss of Selena Bradford and Alex the Ki Fairy in the battle with Tamriel, stalked solemnly towards the back of the amassed army.

Many of the enlisted men and officers stood to salute the company, and both Morek and James Hayes returned the gesture to the brave men and women, who were largely there because of them and their quest against Richard Vandross. Many of them most likely belonged to other, smaller militias, ones that could approach Mount Toane unnoticed and better supplied. But they had chosen to make Byron, Morek and Thaddeus Viper their champions; they would follow those three men, and Byron's company, into the mouth of the Hells themselves if they had to.

Byron, unlike the Dwarven Boxer and Human Paladin, did not return the salutes of the men and women, but not for any reason against them: he felt unworthy of their admiration and trust, their commitment. He was, after all, still a Dread Knight, an abomination in the name of the gods. Despite what Voice told him, Byron felt himself to still be a monster; only the defeat of Richard Vandross at his own hands would change that.

The company moved through the large, city-like camp of the army, nodding here and giving words of consolation and encouragement there. Tales of the Final Push battle were being passed around the campfires like the words were a communal water bucket, and everyone drank deeply of that water. Though the body count had been high that day, it had led, inevitably, to the downfall of the house Sidius, and that warlock's control would never rise again.

After about a half an hour of milling through the camp, the company found themselves looking at a small collection of young soldiers of many Races, all looking scared beyond all wit and reason.

These young men hadn't seen real combat until the attack by the Renka and his Khan. Several were still bandaged and bleeding, others were jittering their teeth together nervously, but all of them had their eyes directed northwest. They clutched their weapons, prepared their spells, and the air hummed with the deep vibration of animalistic brutality, fury, and fear boiling through their blood. They were liable to make lots of mistakes. Byron knew, as did James and Morek that nervous young soldiers didn't live long without someone to lead them, or to fill in for them.

Byron grabbed the largest, loudest-speaking one of the groups, as they were all boasting about what they were going to do when the Khan arrived at the camp. The Dread Knight wrapped a large knot of hair around his gauntlet and pulled the corporal's head back, staring him in the face with his own undead countenance.

The young Human soldier was bent back over Byron's left leg, his face turned suddenly from a fiery-red, intense scowl, to a blank-white sheet of terror. The transformation didn't take long.

"It is only a handful of raiders," the Dread Knight said, letting the enlisted man go. "If their courage stays high and they do approach, they shouldn't be hard to scare off. There's no need to be going on about how you're going to slay them." But even as Byron said this, he could sense a subtle change to the air around him. There lay some hidden savagery, but it did not come from the men nearest to him.

He cast his eyes around his immediate vicinity, and for a moment, his heart quavered. Where, he thought, is Shoryu? But he thought he already knew the answer to that. So long as he lived and his Cuyotai charge continued to feed him his blood, young Shoryu Tearfang would be in need of opportunities such as this. Byron sighed wearily. "Give you joy of it," he whispered to nobody.

The Simpa, or were-lions, of Tamalaria have a saying, and it was used for time out of mind. 'Para nu nimo natch kama, te kama cumo wees'. The closest translation for this was, 'When one does harm for no reason, they too are wounded'. Of course, those Simpa had never been under the strange, spiritual contract that Shoryu Tearfang had with Byron of Sidius. All totaled, the Khan who had approached the encamped army numbered fifteen strong, a goodly number if only a handful of men were to stand against them. For only one scrawny Cuyotai to come at them would normally seem like madness itself, and so when the lead raider saw Shoryu coming at them with a full head of steam, he almost laughed.

His head had tipped back to do just that, when the Cuyotai, moving with the alarming speed that was the heritage of Cuyotai in lycanthrope rage, ran past, his claws flashing out. The lead raider's throat split apart in a spray of meat and blood. He hadn't even become aware of his own demise when, behind him, two of his fellows suffered much the same fate.

The twelve remaining raiders drew their weapons, their eyes wide, their nostrils a-flare. Shoryu had just finished a direct run through their ranks, and was circling around some forty yards away from the closest Khan. This fellow hurled his short spear at the Cuyotai, who performed a small twirl, snatching the projectile neatly in his left hand. "By great Coali," the spear-thrower rasped, invoking his goddess. Shoryu cocked his arm back and let fly. The spear's course from his end flew true, and split open the Khan's face with a sickening crunch.

Five of the raiders broke off and rushed Shoryu en masse, swords in the hands of three, axes in those of two. Shoryu leaped up and forward, landing squarely on the shoulders of the foremost fellow, whose companions didn't think quickly enough about his safety. An axe fell through his neck as Shoryu jumped down and away, laughing like a lunatic.

The other four took to their heels, back for their beloved Allenian Hills. Only six now remained, and they kept their distance from this strange young

Cuyotai, who snarled and grinned at them. The Khan who had been second-in-command, a brave and brash young tribesman, slowly approached, a spear in his hands. He wouldn't throw it; he'd seen about how effective that was, and didn't care to duplicate the experience.

When he had closed to striking distance, the Khan jabbed rapidly at the air, feinting several times, but the Cuyotai didn't bite. Shoryu stood very still, his claws matted with blood, his ears pointed to the moon. The Khan lunged this time, making for a killing blow. But there was suddenly nothing there to strike, and he knew he would soon be with Coali.

Shoryu was on his right side. The Cuyotai buried his entire right hand, claws first, into the meat of the unarmored Khan's side. Bright pain flared in the Khan warrior's body. A moment later, little more, and the pain had ripped around his entire body, accompanying a wet tearing sound that rang in his ears. He stumbled, and looked up from his kneeling position. There stood the Cuyotai, holding up a swatch of the Khan's flesh and muscle. He looked down, and saw that his entire midsection had been torn away, exposing his guts and ribs to the sky.

He was dead of shock before he bled out, and many would have considered that a kindness compared to what happened to the rest of his fellows that dark night.

* * * *

Molis couldn't make himself form a cohesive pattern of thought. Deep in the bowels of the mountain, something rumbled, came to life.

While the half-demon couldn't be certain of what it was, he knew where it was coming from: Richard Vandross. The warlock's presence was fluctuating in and out, as though he were in Mount Toane and yet not. Most likely, the warlock was preparing to teleport away from his lair.

How many would be going with him? Molis thought, gathering himself from the floor of his private chamber. His armor clanged and scraped harshly as he rose from the ground, wondering further how many victims there would be this time. The nearby villages had already been left barren and lifeless by the bloodlust of the warlock and his horde.

Only one target remained, and that was Ja-Wen.

Molis had utilized his limited capability to shape-shift, making himself appear as a battered Paladin, about a month before. He had warned the citizens of Ja-Wen after the first assault on their city that they should hold their forces in reserve, keep them hidden as other threats might yet come along. And now, he knew instinctively, that threat was about to go headlong into the city.

Molis looked over to the full-length mirror against the wall, taking notice of the way his eyes glowed yellow like a common demon. He was not some common, bloodsucking Shadowbeast for the gods' sake. He was not the sort of monster that Vilec Roak had the potential to be.

Thankfully, he thought with a wicked grin, he had probably put an end to a lot of the Shadowbeast General's plans. By putting the Prime in his place, Molis had struck a chord of emotions that Roak had been completely unfamiliar with:

fear, the depth of which seemed to know no bounds now.

Twice since severing the Shadowbeast's arm Molis had spied on him, felt the sheer panic and terror dwelling there. However, Molis sensed that he stood as only one basis of Roak's fear, and he had a pretty good idea what the other source was.

Colonel Molis checked himself over quickly, assuring himself that his weapons were strapped to his hips, his magic was readily available, and his armor showed no signs of its recent metamorphed form. He had, the day before, gone through the Shadowrealm to the city of Desanadron, far in the west, to check on the state of rebuilding efforts there. He had been pleasantly surprised. The people of Desanadron were hardy folk, all of who had a great appreciation for hard work, especially when it came to their homes. Not a single gold piece changed hands during the process, a friendly Elven woman had told him as he sat in the shade of a tavern patio.

"What do you mean," Molis had asked, taking a sip of lemon water as he concentrated on retaining his metamorphed appearance as a young Knight.

The Elven woman, sitting in her simple yellow sundress, smiled invitingly at him, almost imploring him with her eyes to stay and speak at length with her. The folk of Desanadron were also friendlier than most, it seemed.

"I mean, the Elves in the lumber yards don't ask for money for their labors in making the wood for reconstruction. The Dwarves aren't charging anyone for their hard labor in putting the buildings together. The Jafts do not charge any fee for their work in reworking the city walls. And lastly, all of the supplies for the shops that require rebuilding are being provided by the traveling merchants who were trapped here when Richard Vandross and his horde attacked the city."

The Elven woman took a sip of her fruit wine, delicately cupping the glass in her left hand, wiping the cherry colored lipstick from the rim of the glass. Molis had not seen anyone so calm, so centered, in a very long time.

Likewise, he had not found himself so attracted to a woman since his acceptance of the demon's offer of life. Her form could be described as simply aquiline, all grace and smooth skin, flowing curves in all the right places. Though her breasts did not appear large in her slim dress, Molis nevertheless found himself staring at them with a longing he had become unaccustomed to.

Shaking his head, his thoughts returned to what the woman had been saying. He could hardly believe her. Not a single coin had exchanged hands, in a metropolis that was known to run almost solely on cold, hard currency? That such kindness and trust existed in the mortal realm was almost unfathomable.

"So not a single person has been paid for their efforts," Molis asked in a pleasant, Human voice. "That's almost too good to be true." He took another long pull of his lemon water, smacking his lips in the fashion that he had seen young men do when they drank such sweet drinks. He felt awkward performing like this, but he had to do it if he wanted to remain unsuspected.

"That's what everyone else thinks, too," the Elven woman said with a sigh and a smile, finishing off her drink and setting the glass down gently. She got to her feet, laid two silver pieces on the table next to her, and adjusted her dress.

The wind swept down the cobblestone streets, whipping her hair from around her long, pointed ears and into her face.

She laughed like a cherub for a moment, putting her hair back behind her ears and holding the bottom of her dress down, smiling at Molis in that kind, serene way she had spoken with him. "Are you going to be in town long, good sir Knight?" As she stepped down off of the patio steps, she turned to face him, her hands behind her back.

Molis was almost overpowered by his mortal urges, his want for pleasures of the flesh. But the demon within spoke warned that very soon his disguise would wear off, and this young Elf woman would be as horrified then as she was attracted to him now. Molis wiped his brow, chuckled softly, and shook his head, tucking his chin into his chest.

"My apologies, my lady," he replied, looking her square in the eyes for the first time since he had sat down next to her on the tavern patio. "But I am only here today to check up on the status of the city's reconstruction. I am most pleased by what I see."

The Elven woman raised an eyebrow at him questioningly. She appeared to have come to a conclusion.

"Are you one of the new guys over at Fort Flag? I heard there were a number of you boys coming to fill in the holes after the assault."

Molis smiled, glad to have a cover for being here.

"Yes, I am. I am Colonel M-" he began, stopping himself just in time. Why was he telling this woman his name? Why should she care? Why was he attracted to her? A myriad of disturbing questions rose through his thoughts, and he quickly turned and sprinted away. "Colonel Maelstrom," he shouted over his shoulder, not pausing to look back, afraid now that the demon he shared his body with was going to become more hostile than imaginable if he stopped to look back one more time.

He had already become far too interested in the Elven woman than he should have been; after all, he was only here to see how Desanadron had recovered. That much he had told her in truth.

And now he stood in his secret chamber, looking at the truth of what he was. A half-demon, a freak of nature, an abhorrence that the mighty Oun would never forgive. He shook his head, aware now of what it must feel like for Byron of Sidius to get through his life.

At least the Dread Knight had friends, Molis thought sourly. *The sort of company I keep, I'll never have any friends.* Adjusting his weapons' belt, he stepped to the barrier of his chamber, held up his right palm to the blue, shimmering field of light barring entrance, and conjured up the force to deactivate the field.

With a thrumming vibration, the field rippled and disappeared, letting him out of the chamber.

As he stepped into the humid tunnel of Mount Toane, he turned around and brought up the field again, blocking anyone from entering.

His heavy metal boots rapping off of the stone tunnel floor, Colonel Molis stalked upwards toward the surface. He was going to check on the status of Vandross's forces. At least, those that were still present.

A moment later, he felt a huge influx of magic surge through the ground over his head. Richard Vandross had just left, with about two hundred of his men. They would be starting the assault on Ja-Wen shortly.

* * * *

Another day, Byron thought, fairly miserable after a poor night's sleep. He had spent much of the time he should have used resting trying and failing to connect with Voice. He had transported himself into the depths of the cemetery, the inner sanctuary of his soul. There, he had called out for a good ten, twenty minutes. After that he had simply taken a seat on a headstone, wondering when the Keeper would respond to his summons.

It didn't appear, after a while, that it would. Finally, however, just before Byron gave up and decided to get himself some sleep, Voice appeared to speak with him. But it didn't seem to be in a proper frame of mind to speak at length.

"Yes, Byron, I, speak."

Byron looked into the sky over the cemetery, but saw nothing amiss. Everything was in its proper place, and he could sense no malicious magics from any outside source. What could be the problem? Could something from outside of Byron's soul even affect a Keeper in this fashion?

"Voice! What's wrong," Byron had shouted to the abyss, jumping down from the headstone and scouring the cemetery for some visual sign of the Keeper. As usual, there were none. At least, none that would indicate that the Keeper was not the same. Voice had only appeared to Byron in a physical form once, but all other times had come as simply an audible creature. The tone the Keeper had used a moment ago had fluctuated, starting with the soft, masculine whisper, but then rapidly jumping into a banshee screech and almost immediately down to an earth-rumbling bass. Through that, Byron could tell that something worked against the Keeper and his best interests. "What has happened to you?"

"WHAT, yoU, are TALkiNg, ByRon, aBouT?" It conversely shouting and whispering the different syllables out of contextual order.

Byron jogged, then sprinted about the cemetery, looking into every tree, trying to decipher the script on the headstones.

None of them had even a single name etched on them. That much had also changed. Why, he wondered again futilely.

Before he could make another inquiry, he felt himself slide into the normal dreams of a sleeping man. Well, a sleeping whatever he could be called.

He had awoken unrested, discouraged, and in a fairly foul mood overall. For the first ten minutes he was awake, Shoryu was trying to speak to him, but the young Cuyotai Hunter's voice sounded more like a bothersome insect, the kind that waits until you're totally still and about to fall asleep before it buzzes right into your ear.

Byron waved his hand dismissively at Shoryu, who knew better than to persist. Despite Byron's not having any flesh or muscles on his skull, Shoryu had become well versed in the reading of the Dread Knight's mood and disposition. The young Cuyotai moved on to his wife and Morek Rockmight, who sounded as though they had struck up a conversation about the final outcome of their long and tiresome journey.

"Aye, lass, it shall indeed be a battle to remember," Morek said to Ellen Daires as Shoryu joined them around a morning cooking fire. The sun had not yet finished coming over the horizon, and Shoryu looked east into its brilliant yellow and scarlet light as it chased away the darkness of night. "Ah, young man," the Dwarven Boxer said with a crooked smile and a twinkle in his eye. "Decided to try and wake the beast did ye?"

Shoryu flopped down cross-legged next to his wife, giving her an affectionate lick on the cheek.

"Indeed, though I'm not certain I should have." The Hunter sighed as the Elven girl giggled and wiped her cheek clean. The tan fur on his forearms ruffled as the morning breeze blew through the army's encampment. "He seems in a mood most dire. What were you and Ellen speaking of?"

The Dwarf chuckled slowly, almost thoughtfully. Ellen, a very soft spoken but expressive woman, folded her arms and turned slightly away from Morek, the creased lines of her long-uncleaned green dress folding to accentuate the dirt and grime on it.

"We, ah, were discussing the seemingly endless string of wars that the mortal Races of Tamalaria get themselves into. You know, Racial wars, tribal wars, wars over territory, wars over religions, that sort of thing." Morek poked at the contents of the frying pan that one of the soldiers had provided him with. He was presently preparing a good-looking meal of bacon, eggs, and wedges of cheese melted over dried bread.

Shoryu took a long sniff of the food, the fumes of sizzling foodstuffs filling his nostrils like an inviting hearth fire in a small cabin home. A home much like Ellen's. Or rather, like their home, as it now would be. He shook his head to clear his thoughts, and consider what Morek had said.

"And how do you feel about the subject, my dear?"

She scowled at Shoryu, a fierce look that the young Cuyotai Hunter had scarcely ever seen on her face outside of combat situations. He almost fled the circle for sudden fear of his manhood.

"I believe you know my feelings well enough, husband. War is not a natural part of mortal existence. It is simply the invention of a bunch of primitive…"

Oh boy, Shoryu thought. I hope I don't have to break up a fight here. I'm rather ill equipped to do so.

"Blood-thirsty," she continued, "or power-hungry hatemongers! War is not an essential part of existence, or of history. And that's that." She crossed her arms in front of her ample chest.

So beautiful, Shoryu thought, even when she's furious.

Morek sat there, not moving the pan an inch, and then bust out in a riot of gut-laughter that Shoryu feared might become suddenly contagious, like a plague. The burly Dwarven Boxer set the pan down and rolled on the ground, pounding his fists to try to contain his hilarity.

Has he gone mad, Shoryu wondered. But Morek sat up and became stone-faced almost as suddenly as he had gone into his little fit. He readjusted his tan tunic and his enchanted gloves, staring at the married couple across the fire, the flames reflected in his small, brown eyes.

"And I tell you this, both of you, so that you may know a practical man's point of view on the matter," he said, his voice low and focused. His eyes wavered only slightly, going back and forth to meet both Shoryu's eyes and his wife's.

The effect unsettled the Cuyotai, giving Morek the facial appearance of a murderer.

"War is an essential, ingrained part of our mortal existence. Without war, there is no clear-cut way to prove who is the superior man or woman. There is no peace without violence to win it, protect it, ensure it. There is no kindness in the world without a cruelty to make kindness necessary and beautiful. Without war, without violence, we would not know kingdoms, city-states, nations, or empires. That is fact, pure and simple."

Morek stopped his speech part way through in order to put the amalgamation of food into a large bowl to cool, throwing more ingredients in to make a second batch. He set the pan down on the spit over the fire, and waited for one of the others to speak.

At this point, Byron and James Hayes had wandered over to hear the conversation. Neither Morek nor Ellen had spoken at great length of such matters, and the rest of the company that remained wanted to hear how things would turn out, and perhaps put in their own two cents.

Byron had, since Shoryu had left him, felt a little guilty about growling at the boy to leave him alone. He wasn't some pup he could dismiss: he was a married man, and an accomplished archer, essential to the group's survival.

He had been listening to the conversation since the middle of Ellen's speech, and had kept his distance until now. At the moment, however, Morek had paused, almost seeming to invite the Dread Knight to join.

James Hayes had been slumbering peacefully nearby, but the Elf girl's shouting had roused him from his slumber. He had managed to catch something about bloodthirsty beasts, and had taken a quick swig of water from his canteen before ambling over. However, the harsh, stones-slamming-into-the-ground tone of the Dwarven Boxer had brought him fully to, and Morek's words had shaken him to the core.

Was this just how Morek thought? Or was this the attitude of all Dwarves, or Boxers? He decided to sit in during the pause as well, seeing that the hulking Dread Knight had apparently opted to do the same.

"Let us take, for example," Morek began again, stirring the food with a poker. "The Elven-Dwarven War. Took place from the year three twenty-seven A.F. to the year four thirty-seven A.F. In case you didn't know, my friend, that whole conflict started when the Elven Kingdom's patriarch, King Sedmon III, decided that he wanted his kingdom to stretch north to south across the entire western coast." Morek's tone was deadpan. But there, in the dark corners of that statement, lurked an accusation.

The Elves were among the longest-living creatures of Tamalaria, sometimes living as long as nine or ten centuries before age even began to touch upon them. "Mind you, now, that King Sedmon III was nearly four hundred years old when he became king. He had seen the Fall of Mecha, lived through it. He knew what the expansion could do to a country that had already become fat and bloated,"

Morek spat, stirring the food in the pan rather more brusquely than was necessary. "But he decided on a course of action anyway, one that history tells us leads to bad things. He sent platoons into the northern plains, into the area where Desanadron was slowly regaining a population and some semblance of order. He ordered his troops to seize the city, by force if necessary. Now, what sort of Elf does that?" Morek waited a moment, but was met by only the sound of the rest of the army preparing their morning meal before packing up camp to move on.

"So," the Dwarven Boxer continued, finishing off the meal preparations and divvying out the food to his companions. Despite his obvious state of mind, he handed Ellen her plate across the fire, nearly putting his arm right in the flames. Shoryu, Byron and James all sighed a silent sigh of relief; this was nothing personal for the Dwarf. He was just venting, just trying to explain his view on the subject.

But man, thought the Cuyotai Hunter as he began to eat his meal, *is he scary when he gets on a tangent.*

"The King's troops meet a little resistance, but they quickly and quietly take care of that little problem. The city is occupied, the entire territory claimed as land of the Elven Kingdom, and the troops set up base. More platoons are deployed almost immediately, and go further north into Dwarven and Minotaur country. Now, this is important," he said, diving into his own meal for a few brief moments, eating like a savage, his cutlery and silverware be damned. "When the first of the platoons reached the southernmost Dwarven settlement, they didn't even wait for orders. They sent in mage-warriors to destroy everything, kill every Dwarven man and woman of adult age, and loot the stores. The children were orphaned, and told to go with a detachment back to Desanadron, where they'd have to live in an orphanage until someone took pity on them."

This was a grim but accurate account of that part of Tamalaria's history, Byron recalled. He had pored over hundreds of historical texts as a young Knight in training, and even more so when he attained the title and magics of a Paladin. The Elves, while one of Tamalaria's most beautiful and noble of Races, had suffered a dark period of history, one which most of their Race was deeply ashamed of. That Major from Whitewood, Svelk, probably wasn't among those humble enough to admit the Elves' collective wrong in that era, the Dread Knight thought.

"Well, word spreads quick among my folk. Our language, while it sounds gruff and horrid to most, is actually rather terse, allowing us to relay broad ideas and amounts of information in a short span of time or paper. One of the survivors of the assault made it to Korgingal, the first large settlement in the southern ranges of the Dwarven Territories. He told the elders and priests about the attack, and word was immediately sent by messenger bird to all of our kinsmen.

When the bulk of the Elven army reached the first of the mountain ranges, near Korgingal, they were met by eleven thousand angry, bitter Dwarves. So confident in themselves were they that the Elves had only sent a force of two thousand. Their mages and mage-warriors surely could handle simple mountain folk, right?" Morek smiled and raised an eyebrow as he wolfed down the rest of his meal.

The other members of the company handed their dishes to a nearby soldier to be cleaned. The young Human saluted Byron, who returned it in kind, before sprinting away.

Morek must have appeared to be a raving lunatic to someone so green.

"Well, that's what one would think. But we Dwarves, though not terribly inclined to be mages, make great clerics. We had magic of our own, magic to heal the wounded, protect the fighting, and frighten our enemies." Morek got to his feet, clenched a single fist in front of him, and pounding his chest with it. "Our Knights, our Soldiers, our Boxers and our Berserkers went out into the fields, swords, axes, picks and gloves in hand, and slaughtered them as they attempted to cast their spells. We lost five hundred fighting men and women, some of the cloth, most of the blade. But all two thousand of those Elven troops were dead or left to die where they lay. Ha ha! What a victory!"

Morek's fierce and fiery smile slowly faded into a look of dismay, then to stone once more. He sat down heavily on the tree stump he had used as a bench, both to sleep on and to sit on as he had cooked. "We had hoped that King Sedman would learn his lesson, leave the Dwarves alone. But no, he didn't."

"That's right," Byron said, and all of the company turned their heads to look from Morek to the Dread Knight. He stared into the fire as Morek had, losing himself in the flames. The sun had fully risen, and the sounds of the rest of the army packing up camp told him that he would have to hurry the tale along. "He spent the next one hundred and ten years of his reign sending waves of troops at the mountains of the Dwarves.

The Dwarves suffered some casualties, and one particular battle saw them lose Korgingal. But after that, they had enlisted the aid of the Minotaurs, and both Races joined together to beat the Elves all the way back to the Great Forest that is now their kingdom. The Dwarves did not occupy Desanadron, did not set up outposts. They simply beat the Elves back into their original territory, and harried them from their own borders from there. King Sedman III went himself to the front lines in the last major battle of that terrible war, claiming that his might and magic could strike enough fear into the hearts of the Dwarves and Minotaurs to send them packing, even make them subject themselves to his rule."

Silence enveloped the company.

"Then what happened?" Shoryu's whisper was expectant, anxious. He had never heard of these tales, never known much outside of his home village about customs and history.

"When he gave the order to attack, he charged in with his men. He misjudged the amount of time one of his spells would take to cast, and a Dwarven General split his head in half with a stone pick-axe."

Morek smiled half-heartedly at that, but quickly lost his smile. "The entire battle stopped then, before it had even began. Only one man died, and it was King Sedman. That is why that battle was known as the greatest battle in the war. Only one man had to die, and it was all over. The battle, the war, everything.

The Elves were devastated, demoralized, and awakened to the terrible wrongness of the things they had done because their king had decreed that it must be so. The soldiers of the Elven Kingdom dropped their weapons, and the Dwarves and Minotaurs turned and began the long march home."

Byron tossed one last twig on the morning fire, watching as lower-ranking enlisted men packed up his company's tents and belongings for them. "The war was over. The next morning, Sedman's eldest son, Alarus, was named king, and he declared that as penance for starting a war they couldn't win, the Elves would never rule anything more than the Great Forest. Since that time, they have kept their word."

The company stared at the Dread Knight with a soft awe, keeping their eyes on him as he rose and collected the remainder of his things.

It was going to be a long day.

* * * *

The sun had risen over the horizon, spreading waves of orange and crimson, blood-tinted light.

Blood, thought Richard Vandross. *Now there's something I need to see.* He stood atop a hill overlooking the city of Ja-Wen below him. Behind him, hundreds of Shadowbeasts and assorted Races of mages hunkered down, preparing to attack.

The one-eyed warlock drew his sword, holding the cutting edge toward the sky. He plucked a single hair from his thick black beard, holding it high over the blade, staring down at the town with a fire in his eyes. He looked back at his waiting deployment, searching their faces and eyes for the anxiety, the bloodlust, that would surely be building in them. He would let them have their fun, very soon.

Vandross kinked his head to the left, looking at Vilec Roak, who approached as quietly as he could. Any loud, sudden noise, and the city of Ja-Wen might be alerted to their presence. It was taking enough of an effort on Vandross's part to keep a barrier around the forces assembled in order to keep themselves from being detected. Any loud noise would ruin everything.

As the Shadowbeast General got within a few feet, Vandross leaned in close. "Spread the word, that when I give the forward signal, they may strike.

But the moment I send a bolt of lightning into the sky, they are to retreat to this position."

Vilec Roak knew why Vandross would issue an order of retreat; he intended to use the Glorious Mother of Destruction on the city of Ja-Wen. And nobody would want to be in front of that sort of power. Nothing would survive, of that the Shadowbeast Prime was certain.

Vilec Roak nodded silently, sending the message to his kinsmen mentally, and to the rest of the deployment through whispered word of mouth.

The entire body of the forces shivered with anticipation once again. Vandross looked down at the city below him, removed the barrier, and dropped the beard hair. As it slipped down to the blade's edge, it split cleanly in half, and Vandross thrust his weapon forward. Without a single word spoken, he sent his troops rampaging down the hill and into the city of Ja-Wen, battle-ready roars of fury rending the air.

The townspeople panicked, running this way and that, the few city guards present barely able to raise their weapons before the slaughter had begun. Vandross himself sauntered down the hill slope, easing his way into the city streets to witness his forces' handiwork.

What he found was somewhat disturbing. The bodies of civilians and guards lay about, but not in the high concentration that a city like Ja-Wen should yield. He had expected a much greater force of resistance as well. Something was terribly amiss.

The main force of Ja-Wen's standing army was probably already holed up underneath the city surface.

Rather than waiting for one of his men to stumble upon a way to the forces of Ja-Wen, he thought with a widening grin, he would tear the ground itself asunder. He thrust his right palm toward the sky, pulling energy from the center of his being, drawing on some of the reserves available within Power, Vengeance, Spite and Deceit. He shot a single, steady stream of brilliant, yellow lightning into the skies over his head.

Vilec Roak, understanding the signal and what it meant, screamed the command to pull back, and thankfully, the troops listened. Nobody was eager to see the power of the Glorious Mother of Destruction.

Turning and sprinting up the slope of the hill skirting the edge of Ja-Wen, Vandross felt dozens of his minions brush against them in their bid to stay out of the line of fire. As soon as he gained the summit of the hill, Richard Vandross turned and faced the city. Hundreds of the surviving citizens and guards had begun to assemble in the middle of the city, still too few, in Vandross's view. He didn't care to see their faces, know their exact numbers; all he wanted to see was their blood fly across the landscape.

Slowly, like a symphony conductor preparing to stand to full height and begin his orchestration, Vandross rose. His hands rested against his sides, palms open, flat against his chain mail greaves. He had not been shown the movements for this ceremony, but he knew it, felt it within his soul. A deep, malicious burning sensation, buried in his chest, scouring away every last trace of mercy, of sympathy, of weakness. The dust and stones, rocks and scrub grass began to wave and sway back and forth, as a light wind began to blow in a huge circle around the city of Ja-Wen, its origin rooted in Vandross himself.

The scent of sulfur filled the air, and all of the warlock's men shuffled further away from him than they had before. The sound of stone grinding on stone slowly, gently rose into a deafening crescendo as the wind whipped through the area faster than before, blowing the one-eyed warlock's flat-topped hair about his head. His black cloak flapped madly about him, a bat struggling to free itself from its perch.

Not lifting his feet even an inch, Richard Vandross slid his feet apart, inch by inch, scraping the dirt with his heavy metal boots. His knees bent, and he thrust his hands out before him, the palms open, facing the sky. His mouth opened, and crimson and violet light poured from his throat, his head bent down to look at the tearing, shaking ground under his feet. His elbows locked at his sides, pressed against his ribs, translucent cords of aquamarine force flowing around his arms, his hands, his every fingertip.

Sulfur burned in every living creature's nostrils within a ten-mile radius, blending seamlessly with the stench of burning flesh. A hoarse, demonic roar escaped along with the streaming light that poured from Vandross's mouth now, a thick, raspy call of rage and ecstasy.

Several of the Illeck mages behind the warlock dropped dead where they stood, their life force flowing from their chests and into Vandross's back.

Vilec Roak, in a state of panic fused with rationality, ordered his Shadowbeasts to shadow-walk back to Mount Toane. He followed after them a moment later, taking one last look back at Richard Vandross. *I hope this kills you*, the Shadowbeast Prime thought bitterly.

The power, Vandross thought in crazed wonder. He clamped his teeth together as the light ceased to flow from his mouth, rising from his half-crouched position, clenching his hands into shaking fists. As he approached a complete standing position, he hefted his glowing, throbbing fists over his head; the odor of burning flesh permeated the air further, choking and gagging many of the remaining inhabitants of the city of Ja-Wen.

For a moment, Vandross's eyes flared with burning fury; in that one, perfect moment, he could see every one of them, taste their fear, smell the sweat and urine on their clothes, on their skin. He could feel the sands of their life emptying into the bottoms of their individual vials. The Reaper would have his work cut out for him this morning, Vandross thought with glee.

Richard Vandross howled, the demon within released, the Glorious Mother of Destruction writhing within his soul in a quasi-orgasmic fit. The warlock slammed his clenched fists into the ground, and watched as a wave of translucent violet and blue energy wrapped around his body, thickening like a wall of magical protection, laced here and there with streaks of yellow power, shaped like screaming, flaming skulls. His entire body shook with convulsions, his body nearly tearing itself apart. The pain shot through him like quicksilver, flowing over his every nerve, his every bone, muscle and organ. Finally, unable to contain it anymore, he shrieked in agony, and saw the wave of energy blast forth from his personal ring in a circumference, tearing apart everything it came in contact with. The buildings of the city of Ja-Wen started instantly ablaze, exploding and flying apart moments after catching fire.

A fragment of a skull struck Vandross across the back of his left leg, and he turned and picked it up. He recognized the slain servant as soon as he sought out the body. A high-ranking Human mage he had employed for his Q Magic skills. *Oh well,* he thought, salivating at the sights and smells of the carnage around him.

The energy ripped the body of the Q Mage apart further still, spraying bits and pieces here and there over the area. The ground trembled, crumbling apart around him, sending boulders flying through the air from the sudden tension applied by the ground's destruction. The warlock heard the agony-riddled shrieks of the dead and dying in the city of Ja-Wen, and felt the soft whimper of children crying their last mortal breathes into the bosoms of their soon to be decapitated mothers and fathers. Blood ran through the streets like tributary streams into a river, draining into the sewer access grates laid throughout the city.

Vandross clenched his right fist against his chest, and raised it to the sky. He looked back for his own men and women, but found that only a small handful had avoided the lethal effects of the Glorious Mother of Destruction. Those few were already heading for Mount Toane on foot. He should let them go, he knew, but something inside of his soul urged him to kill them as well, and mount their heads on pikes and spears, as an example to the others of what happened to deserters.

Without control over himself, Richard Vandross flicked his fingers in their direction, snaring them with entrapment spells. He sauntered up to their struggling forms, and disemboweled every one of them, letting their innards spill on the dust and dirt. *Let them die slowly,* he thought. *Yes, that seems fitting.*

Richard Vandross had no true idea how much damage he had caused, and at the time, it didn't matter. He felt suddenly very weary and weak. He used his last available magic to teleport himself back into his bed inside of Mount Toane. He had slain over eight hundred people, in a matter of six, perhaps seven minutes. As for the farmland that had been struck by the energy wave, well, no one would be able to grow anything there for at least thirty years or so.

Vandross lay on his bed, reveling in the vast amounts of fear and pain still coming his way. Finally, he fell asleep, comforted like a child.

He never saw the glowing yellow eyes in the shadows, or whom they belonged to.

* * * *

The sky overhead swelled with clouds as gray as wolf's fur, and a single shaft of crimson and midnight power shot into them. Byron knew immediately what that power was: the Glorious Mother of Destruction. He had witnessed Tanarak of Sidius use but a small portion of that power once, and it had been terrible. It was an awesome and terrible power, to be certain, and whomever

Vandross had just used it on was sure to be dead. If there had been men and women nearby...

Ja-Wen, he thought, almost coming to a complete stop as the others of his company surged ahead of him. If Vandross had managed to ensnare their army before they could arrive at Mount Toane, then he would have no allies in the upcoming siege. That would make things more difficult. The Dread Knight put the spurs to himself, sprinting forward to catch up to his company, casting his gaze back and forth among them.

All had witnessed the same power in the distance, and it still reflected in their eyes. They all knew it was the final power of the one-eyed warlock.

The army halted around noon, in order to rest up and get something to eat. The provisions were running low, so Shoryu took a small handful of Elven Hunters into the nearby flats and woodland to hunt for edible game and fruits.

Morek Rockmight set about trying to rally his Dwarven and Minotaur troops, telling long, Dwarvish jokes and a few well-known Minotaur favorites.

Ellen Daires sat on a flat patch of grass and meditated, mentally gearing herself up for the confrontation she would be involved in at Mount Toane. Hers was a magic not often used for straight combat or killing; she had to adjust her mental attitude.

As Byron stalked like a wraith at hunt through the ranks of the army, he saw James Hayes standing in a circle of the few clergymen that accompanied the militia, talking over matters of faith and belief.

How many have died, Byron thought as he approached his officers, who had joined together in a small camp circle to discuss battle strategies and formations. How many, since Richard Vandross had begun this conquest, his collection of the Orbs of Eden's Serpent and consolidation of power? How many had died, suffered, lost family and friends? How many sons and daughters, brothers and sisters, fathers and mothers, would the warlock kill before he was satisfied? How much terror did he need to instill in the lands of Tamalaria before he would be done?

It didn't matter, he decided. These were just questions he felt he needed an answer to in place of a corpse. He stepped right up to the circle of officers, who all stood straight and saluted as he entered their group. He returned the salute with a snap, an authority and sincerity he hadn't fully felt before.

"Report," he said, looking to his senior man.

The Major looked around at the surrounding troops, made a grimace through his half-faced helmet, and turned back to the Dread Knight.

"My lord, several of the men have reported seeing strange creatures tracking us. Shadowbeasts, from the way they are described. Also, my lord, I believe some of us have seen an outsider in our ranks." Byron tried to raise an eyebrow, failed, and waved his hand in a circular motion in order to indicate he wanted to hear more.

"My lord, I have seen this creature as well. He is tall, dark-spirited, and has an all silver, shimmering suit of armor. His face, however, is indistinguishable. None of us have seen it."

Byron knew they were referring to the half-breed, Molis. He had been the only member of Vandross's army that Byron intended to spare once he had spoken at length with him. *Edgar Cesar,* he almost said, thinking back on those last few moments before he and the Human Knight had parted ways.

"If you see him again," Byron said, standing straighter than before. "Do him no harm. Approach with your hands open and at your sides. His name is Molis, and he is in a strange position. Tell him that he should seek me out, if he would speak with me." Byron swept the ranks of the officers with his pinpoint lights.

The half-demon, silver full-plate armor and all, stood only about twenty yards away, somehow totally unnoticed by the regulars around him. If he had been seen, Byron thought with a wry smile, he most likely had himself disguised from them all. Yet, the Dread Knight could make out almost every detail from his current distance, from the slightly off-angled tip of his helmet's faceguard, down to the scuffmarks on his huge silver boots. A lucky thing that Shoryu isn't here, he mused. The Cuyotai would have gone berserk in the presence of so much silver, lethal as it was to him. But the Cuyotai Hunter hadn't protested to the half-demon's proximity in the mountains, so Byron signaled with his left hand for Molis to come over and join them.

When the half-demon approached the back-most ranks of the officers, a chill shot through the air, as serpentine as venom through the bloodstream of a bite victim.

"By Oun's grace," one of the officers muttered shaking with cold and her teeth chattering.

Molis stalked forward, and all of the mortals, Elves, Humans, and the smattering of Dwarven and lycanthrope officers present, cleared a path for him. He exuded the same sort of presence that the Dread Knight did, one of leadership, strength, and something otherworldly.

However, his aura was different from Byron's in one, very noticeable and essential way. While Byron's presence instilled courage and respect in the hearts of those around him, Molis's inspired aggression and fear. Everyone around him suddenly turned on edge, hands on weapons, not quite ready to draw. Byron had told them to withhold, and so they did, for the moment. One false move on the half-demon's part, however, and the Dread Knight knew that his officers would turn on him. In the end, Molis would probably kill them all, or at least maim them beyond reasonable healing. Regardless of what would happen, he had to be in the moment, focus on the now.

Nobody moved except for Molis, who had stalked forward, closer to Byron with every passing moment.

But Byron felt no malice in those strides, saw no hatred in the gimlet, yellow eyes deep in the shadows of the creature's helmet. Instead, he felt a calm coming from the half-breed, a centering much like his own.

Molis halted several yards away from Byron, knelt, and drew his sword, which blazed with yellow power. Molis held the weapon from the underside, his palms flat and open, as if offering the sword to the Dread Knight.

The Dread Knight's Redemption

Byron gave a low chuckle; this was how he and Edgar Cesar had first met, when he accepted the Knight's request to join the Order of Oun. Byron reached down, plucking the sword from Molis's hands. He watched as Molis lowered his head, keeping his hands up. Byron swung the sword of the half-demon through the air a couple of times, then placed it back on Molis's hands.

The half-demon sheathed his weapon and stood to full height, coming only an inch or two short of meeting Byron eye-to-eye. *I always was a little taller*, Byron mused internally.

"Lord Byron Aixler, you know that my position is perilous," Molis began, speaking in a strange twin harmony, his old, mortal voice chiming partially through the rough, raspy growl of the demonic. "I come to offer what little aid I may. Richard Vandross has used the Glorious Mother of Destruction on Ja-Wen. Their militia was just far enough away to avoid damage, but the city itself was nearly turned to nothing but rubble. A mystic barrier helped alleviate some of the destruction, and the city's leaders were prepared for an attack. I warned them not long ago to leave, as did their city elders. But the civilians and many of the guard refused to budge. 'Better to die bravely, in our own home, than to scurry away and let it fall undefended,' they said. I am sorry, my lordship." Molis hung his head. "I failed in even the small task of saving them."

Byron placed a huge, heavy hand on the half-demon's epaulet, and felt the regret and pity of Edgar Cesar surfacing. The Knight had never been one for bloodshed. Every soldier expected to be harmed in combat, but civilians and simple constables should not suffer so, he had said once. Byron patted his shoulder a couple of times, holding him in place.

"You did everything you could, old friend," he whispered, pulling the half-breed close to speak privately with him. "Sometimes, it is the valor and courage of simple townsfolk that makes the biggest difference in war. They feared no evil, feared no pain or death. They gave their lives for their beliefs, for their homes, for their families. Their sacrifices were not in vain. Now," he said, pushing Molis slightly away, speaking louder, indicating he had a question to ask that was on everyone's mind.

Molis stood board-straight and stiff, easing rather quickly back into the role of the right-hand man. "We need to know everything you're willing to tell us about the warlock before we arrive at Mount Toane. Any small detail could prove very useful, and vital to our efforts."

"Well, my lord," Molis said, clearing his throat.

James Hayes, Morek Rockmight, and a handful of Paladins were approaching the officers' circle, Byron saw, and their presence was likely making the half-demon uncomfortable.

Byron waved his hands over his head, gaining Hayes's attention. The Human Paladin sprinted over to the Dread Knight, who asked him to waylay the other Paladins if he could for a bit.

Hayes saluted, gave Byron a wink of understanding when he recognized the half-demon from the mountains, and headed off with his kinsmen and the confused Dwarven Boxer.

"My thanks. First of all, and most importantly, were any of you aware that there is more than one way into Mount Toane?"

Byron nearly broke his neck whipping his head around to stare in shock at what Colonel Molis had just said. All of those years in Tanarak's service, and he had never learned of a second way in or out. Yet this half-demon, who had once been his dearest friend, had discovered a way? It didn't matter, he thought, shoving his pride and concern away.

"How certain are you of this entrance," he asked, slowly, calmly. "How many others know of it?"

"None know of it, except for me."

Byron heard the grin forming in Molis's tone. There, in the shadows, for just a moment, the Dread Knight could see the face of his old comrade and right hand man. Edgar Cesar, tactician extraordinaire.

"Simply," the half-demon said, "because, well, I just made it. Let me tell you how it works." Molis went on to explain the workings of his own, secret passage.

This war had just taken a turn, Byron thought, listening with a giddy anticipation. *And for once, it's in our favor.*

Chapter Eight
Elsewhere...

Lee Toren, master Pickpocket and Gnome gentleman as he liked to proclaim himself to be, rode just ahead of the large black stallion that cantered along with Flint, a Wererat member of the Hoods, and the bandaged, mangled form of a once-brutish looking Khan Lieutenant, whose name was Amon. The Gnome couldn't help looking back over his shoulder at the Khan, who gripped the support straps that they had fastened him to the horse with an iron will. Amon had explained that he only survived the Pyromancer Selena Bradford's Immolation spell by the will of the gods. He hadn't been far enough away to avoid the spell, and it had been well documented that anyone struck by the spell who didn't possess some form of higher magic, like a Phoenix's Feather, or a locked Resurrection spell, died.

Since the time they had fastened the Khan to the stallion that Flint had 'borrowed' from the guards' stables in Desanadron, the proud tiger-man hadn't spoken a single word. He grunted and growled here and there, most likely out of necessity than out of an attempt at communication, Lee thought, but at least it meant the man was still alive. He didn't feel like helping Flint pry a Khan in rigor off of a mustang today.

The small thieves' company traveled south by southeast, heading for a region of Tamalaria known either as the Fiefdom of Lemago or the Golden Lands, a small fiefdom controlled and governed almost solely by Monks, Samurai, Boxers and a few elemental mages. The region was a moderate size, consisting of five villages that surrounded a large, central temple. Each village sent a representative to the temple once a week, so that the headmen could discuss the state of their own village. In this way, order was kept, supplies shared, and mouths fed. And all the while, not a single gold piece changed hands. It was sort of a joke, the area's title—the people who lived within the Golden Lands called the region Lemago, which in their own self-made tongue meant 'land of equals.' Outsiders could not understand how any government could survive without the use of a monetary unit, and so they called it the Golden Lands.

Lee had fielded several questions from other members of the pack regarding their destination, the first among them being that it was pointless for them all to go to a country where the citizens had little or no money. There would be no profitable business for them there. "Now, now," Lee said, waving a hand back at them atop his pony. "Remember, you fellahs can always *try* looting valuables. I wouldn't recommend it."

"Why not boss?" one of the Wererats in the pack of hire-ons asked.

Lee smiled smugly to himself, reveling in the fact that even though he wasn't physically the equal of anyone present, he was more than their intellectual superior.

"Because, dear, ah," he said, trying to remember the Wererat's name. They had six of them in their party aside from Flint, who only had two of his own men from the Hoods among the pack. *Bogart*, Lee thought, raising his pointer finger to the sky, a bad habit he had tried to curb. Whenever he got an idea, or remembered something, his finger shot straight up—it had nearly gotten him arrested several times. "Because, dear Bogart, in the Golden Lands, the punishment for theft is life imprisonment."

A shocked gasp sounded from all of the others, save for Flint and Amon, who didn't seem fazed by anything. "That's roit, boyos, life in prison. I don't imagine any of you is lookin' forward to the idea, is yah?"

The mounted Wererats all shook their heads, and kept them tucked low, pulling up their travel cloak hoods. A storm wind had kicked up from the north, and it blew against their backs with building fury. They would have to take shelter before long, Lee knew, but they were out in flatlands. The nearest patch of woodland was still about an hour off at their canter, and the Gnome Pickpocket would not risk the Khan falling off of Flint's horse if they began to sprint. The Wererat would have his head: after all, it had been Flint's idea to save the man and keep him safe until they could get him somewhere.

Amon had, before being secured to the horse, promised to tell the Gnome and Wererat pack about the events taking place in the land, and what had led up to his eventual maiming. However, since that promise had been made, not a peep could be coaxed from the great cat.

Lee wanted to get into cover from the weather, and at the same time, get Amon to talk. *Oh, what to do*, he thought desperately. He looked over his shoulder to the north, and watched as storm heads collided about twenty minutes away. They would all be soaked to the bone before they could reach the woodland. But, it didn't have to be that way, now did it?

Lee circled his pony and came to a halt, calling in the others to form a circle around him. He reached into his tan and yellow tunic, pulling out a spyglass, sweeping the object south, so he could find the exact location of those woods. He hadn't been here in almost a year, and couldn't get his bearings quite right. *There*, he thought elatedly, finding the copse of trees he had holed up in once after stealing a priceless gem from one of the headmen's homes.

"All right, gentlemen. There's a bad bit of weather coming up on us quickly, and I'd like to be in out of it before too long. You gents are going to take yourselves full speed to that wooded area to the south and a little west of our path. There's a natural shelter in the trees there. Find it, and set torches on either side of the shelter. Flint and I have to take a slower pace, him because of our guest, and me, well, because I'm riding a fuckin' pony, roit?"

The Wererats chuckled among themselves, still unable to get over how ridiculous Lee Toren looked atop a pony. "Flint and Mister Amon can't go too fast eifer, seein' as our guest is mostly 'eld on wif leather straps, okay?"

They all nodded, but didn't quite leave just yet.

"Bogart, Simon, give us yer cloaks."

"Aw, boss," whined Simon, a small, pudgy Wererat. He was an Initiate in the Hoods, Flint's thieves' guild, and Flint had brought him along on this particular series of jobs to hopefully build the boy's character.

173

It wasn't going so well, Flint thought with an inward growl.

"Do we 'ave to?"

"Yes, you do maggot," Flint spat at him, barring his teeth at the youth.

Both hirelings tossed their cloaks at Lee, who had forgotten to specify that he wanted Flint to take them, so as to cover and protect Amon from the rain they were bound to ride through.

The diminutive Pickpocket was hit full-on by the heavy leather coats, and, unable to maintain balance, flailed about as he fell off of the pony's back and onto the blissfully soft grass with a thud.

Covered in cloaks, his harumph of wind being knocked out of his lungs barely registered in Flint's ears, but he had to chuckle a little anyway. As he dismounted to help Lee up, Flint looked back over his own cloaked shoulder and saw the first genuine smile from Amon that he had seen since meeting the man. There were very, very sharp teeth in that grin, and he suddenly remembered that in the animal kingdom, cats ate rodents.

Shuddering a little at the prospect, Flint hauled Lee to his feet, throwing the leather cloaks over his own shoulder and placing Lee Toren back in his saddle. The Gnome brushed himself off, scowling and cursing in Gnomish the whole while.

"Bet you fink that's funny, huh?" Lee grumbled at the two lackeys. "That's comin' out of yer pay." He started his pony forward at a canter.

Whining about yet another hit to their pay, the pack of Wererat underlings sprinted ahead on their mounts, quickly becoming indistinguishable dots in the distance.

Lee rode on, silently, next to Flint, who had helped Amon put the two cloaks on over Flint's extra, which he had given to Amon before securing him to the horse.

"Hard to find good help these days, eh," Amon managed to croak before he grasped for his water skin. Flint looked sidelong at Lee, who could only look at the Khan and shrug his shoulders to Flint. "I completely understand that problem. It's difficult to be in charge of so many fools, I know. I could hardly keep up with it all," he growled, spitting some of the water to the ground after washing his mouth out. "Well, let's be going then."

"Wait a minute, you 'aven't talked for hours now," said Lee, looking back up at the thunderstorm approaching at speed. "Wot gives?"

Amon smiled a small, creeping smile, sending shivers down the Gnome Pickpocket's spine.

"I'm not big on talking to people who would rather have let me die back there. You two took a risk on me, you know. A half-dead Khan is still a Khan. And we are dangerous, my stout friend." Amon sighed heavily, relaxing his body in the straps that held him fast to the horse. "At least, most of us are. I'm not feeling particularly capable at the moment."

Flint patted Amon on the shoulder, trying to give what comfort he could to the once-proud tribe leader. The first pellets of rain splattered against the Wererat's facial fur, and he turned to look into the sky. They were going to get pounded. He didn't mind in the least; for the gods' sakes, he lived in a sewer system. He was used to it. But Lee Toren was picky about this sort of thing, which was out of place for a Pickpocket. If he could avoid it, Lee wouldn't even go out to pick pockets in the marketplace of Desanadron on a rainy day, saying that it would ruin his good leathers.

And Amon, well, he was a great big cat if one thought about it long enough, Flint mused. Poor kitty, heh heh heh.

"Well, you've still got your pride," Flint whispered to Amon through the reverberating thunder that hummed through the air around them. "That should count for something."

"Among my people, it means everything," Amon grumbled as he ducked his head under his borrowed cloaks.

"And what about honor," Flint inquired, squinting his eyes as the rain began to pound down on and around them with increasing ferocity.

"To my particular tribe, honor is gained by destroying our foes, and doing what is best for the people of the tribe. Many tribes of Khan care not for honor in the field of battle. I, however, led my people with the ideals of straight-forwardness, strength amid impossible odds, and the protection of those weaker than oneself. Service to the tribe before service to oneself is the ultimate honor. I—" he choked on the words.

Flint could almost hear the hint of a single sob as the large Khan shifted his weight forward, away from him.

"I cannot serve anyone as I am."

Flint put his hand out, then pulled it back. He wasn't sure how the tiger-man would react to more sympathy. This most likely was the most kindness or help that Tiberious Amon had received in his entire life. Best not push the envelope.

And so for an hour and a half the three of them trotted along through the pounding rain, until at last they entered the shelter of the trees. The other Wererats had posted signals on the trunks of trees, pointing them toward the cave-like shelter of a hollowed out tree, taller and broader than the other arbors around it.

Lee immediately dismounted and sprinted into the shelter with the other Wererats, while Flint swung his legs off and started working on the belts and straps he had used to secure Amon to the horse.

As he worked, he heard a soft, low growling coming from the Khan.

Oh boy, Flint thought, *I must have really pissed him off back there, patting him on the shoulder.* But when the Khan didn't move, Flint moved himself through the thick, springy moss of the wooded area around to the front of the steed: Amon was fast asleep.

"Gods I wish Stockholm were here," he said softly aloud. The soaked Wererat finished taking the belts off, and eased Amon down off the mount, trying not to wake him. The man needed rest, food and shelter. Flint would not be held responsible for keeping any of the three from him.

With the tender movements of a father carrying a slumbering child to bed,

Flint brought Amon into the shelter of the tree, and moved him over to a single pile of hay that lay against the innermost wall of the tree. One of the Wererats made a snorting noise in his throat at the sight, and Flint, after having laid Amon down, came back and slapped the younger Wererat in the mouth.

"The hells was that for?" complained the younger lycanthrope, rubbing his snout.

"This man has seen and been through more in his life than you ever will, whelp," Flint growled. He barred his yellowed teeth at the younger man. "And with the right help, he'll probably go on to do even more with his life. I'll not have you scoffing at him, or my treatment of him. Remember, I am your superior in the guild."

Flint took a trembling step forward; he was older than this upstart, which gave him the advantage of experience. However, Tony was slightly shorter than he, and was a profoundly accomplished grappler. Close quarters combat was not his specialty, and if the underling decided to grab him, he would most likely be pounded. But his age and the set of his eyes, cold, unmoving, unafraid, set the young Tony to shaking visibly in his spot.

Then Flint remembered his other advantage: unlike most other members of his Race, he wasn't allergic to copper. His copper short sword hung on his hip, ready to be drawn at any time.

"Remember your place. And if Tiberious asks for something, you get it for him, understood?"

Tony nodded, if barely, and as Flint looked to the others of his brethren, they too agreed.

"Very good. Now, we could all use some rest, but someone has to go get food. You all wait here, and I'll go bag us something."

The scent of burnt ozone scoured his nostrils as Flint stepped out of the shelter and into the woods. He could scarcely smell anything else, so powerful were the bolts of lightning tearing through the skies overhead. The sound of animal life could just be discerned on the edge of his hearing, and he used his Race's innate ability to amplify this sense.

Suddenly, he could hear everything around him, from the slow, rhythmic filling and emptying of Amon's lungs to the skittering of a spider on a nearby tree. Squirrels and rabbits chitchatted from boltholes, trying to make sense of the great fury in the sky. *Stupid animals,* Flint thought with a chuckle. *It's called a storm.*

He moved stealthily through the shadowed woodland, bolting from cover to cover for a good fifteen minutes, tracking the sounds of deer in the woods. The feel of the moss underfoot did wonders for his disposition; it was soft, springy, and slightly moist, providing good footing for the hunt, as well as some relief for his city-spawned calluses and foot-sores.

Running on cement for most of his adult life had made his bare feet tough as nails, though few understood his reasoning for not wearing anything on his feet most of the time. He believed that one could feel the heartbeat of the city under one's feet, and that footwear just hampered that. Here, it let him feel the essence of the woodland. And it was a lovely essence to absorb oneself in.

There. He spotted a deer drinking from a nearby stream.

Flint slowly, carefully drew his bow from his back, taking note of every creak of his clothes, every twitch in the animal's muscles.

He focused his hearing further, to its limit, listening to the deer's heartbeat. Normal, steady beating, he noted, making sure to keep his own movements slow and silent. *No room for error, no mistakes,* he chanted his silent mantra. The bow was now out in front of him, and he drew and notched an arrow, again, slowly and silently. Another noise, close by, caught his attention. A snapping twig. *Oh gods no!*

The deer looked up, its heartbeat suddenly rapid, pounding like a piston in one of those confounded Gnome devices. But as Flint watched, stuck in place, another deer, a large buck, approached.

The female's heartbeat slowed and steadied once more, and Flint took aim at this new specimen.

Half an hour later, as the Wererat dragged the huge buck back through the woods to the shelter, he wondered at the wisdom of taking down the larger beast. He could barely haul the thing, and his aging bones screamed at him in protest. Fire burned through his legs as he made his way the last twenty yards to get the thing next to the shelter tree.

He dropped his burden and shuffled inside, heaving for breath.

Everyone except for Lee and Tony was asleep, and he ordered Tony to carve out the meat on the deer, and to think of some way to use the organs and bones, so as not to dishonor the large beast.

Tony sprinted outside, glad to do something other than rest.

"Get enough for everyone?" Lee looked up from his whittling.

Flint nodded, looking at Amon for a long minute. *How much do Khan eat?* He sat against the wall next to Lee and taking out his water skin.

Lee put his hand on the water skin, and pulled out a silver flask.

Flint grabbed it out of Lee's hand before the Gnome could even offer it, and drank deeply. *Ah,* he thought, *Elven wine. Good vintage too.*

"Stole that in Eringwood a few months back. The liquor, not the flask." Lee didn't look away from the little piece of wood he was carving into the image of himself.

The two companions sat for a while, neither bothering to say anything.

"E's a tough ol' sod, he is," Lee finally whispered, nodding his head toward the sleeping Khan warrior.

"Indeed. It's a miracle he survived. I think I know the spell that he was hit with. No one else in recorded history has survived it without being a Pyromancer themselves."

"You think maybe he's one, but doesn't know it yet?" Lee blew away the last shavings before setting the wooden piece on the floor next to him. Lee kept four or five of the little idols with him at all times, leaving them behind after a big score on a well-to-do house or mansion. If he sacked a castle, he left two or three of them. Or if he hit a thieves' guild, he left all four or five behind, his own little trademark. But, there was always one guild he would never hit, that being Flint's guild, the Hoods. And one residence he'd never strike; the old Aixler estate. Even though the Aixler line would die with Byron, he would honor the Dread Knight in this way. The old boy had done him a great number of favors in life.

"Don't know, though I highly doubt it. Just smiled upon by the gods." Flint took out a wedge of cheddar from his rucksack. He swallowed the whole thing down in three bites, chewing thoroughly, savoring the taste of it.

"I'll never understand your obsession with that stuff," Lee noted, shaking his head and smiling. Flint swallowed the last of it, and turned to the Gnome as he stood up.

"Well, I'm essentially a big, talking, bipedal mouse, my friend," he said with a chuckle. "It's sort of instinct."

Tony came back in with a huge armful of deer meat, and the two Wererats sifted through it for the best bits, taking them outside to cook while Lee salted the little bit they left behind for later use. An hour later, they came in and roused everyone to eat. As Flint leaned down close to Amon, the huge Khan hefted himself into a sitting position with his one arm.

"We've got food ready, Tiberious. Come on, I'll help you out," Flint said, but stopped just short.

Amon stared out of the hole in the tree at the cooking fire, the flames reflecting in his huge, green eyes. For a moment, the Khan warrior shook, almost a convulsion, but then steadied himself.

"Yes, of course." He allowed Flint to be his second leg as he hopped over to the entrance. He indicated where he wanted to be seated to the Wererat, well back from the fire. When he was handed a strip of venison, he glowered at the fire for another moment before devouring his food.

Lee had seated himself directly across the flames from the former Lieutenant, and Amon looked him over as he sat in silence. He had noticed that the Gnome had been carving a little statue of himself before he passed out for a quick two-hour sleep. "Mister Toren, could I have a word with you?"

Everyone looked expectantly at their employer, who shrugged his shoulders and set his meal aside. Lee waltzing around the fire, and took a heavy seat on Amon's left side, Flint on the right. They appeared to be the only two in the group brave enough to get close to him, and Amon admired them both for their courage.

"Wot's on yer mind there, fellah?" Lee smiled broadly at the Khan.

"Please, don't spoil your fake smiles and pleasantries on me, Mister Toren. I hardly deserve them." Amon heard the mixed snickers of the others assembled around the fire.

Lee Toren's eyes went wide a moment, and he let the smile drop.

"You don't trust me, and that's just fine. It proves you have good judgment."

At this comment, Lee grinned a little, quite genuinely to Amon's perceptions.

"You're quite good at shaping wood I noticed."

"Not as good as an Elf or a Cuyotai, but yeah, it's a little hobby of mine. Why?"

Amon took a long draw on his water skin before he continued. "I'd like you to take a thick branch from one of these trees, and shape me a leg."

Flint and Lee's eyes both went wide with astonishment.

"D'you 'ave any idea how long that'd take," Lee nearly screamed, hopping to his feet. "First off, I'd have to find a branch thick as your real leg, and mind you my friend, that's a pretty monumental task in and of itself!"

"No it's not," Amon said, keeping his voice level and cool. He pointed up at one of the lower limbs of a large spruce. "That one there will do nicely."

Lee turned and looked at the indicated branch, stunned into silence for a moment. The bastard's thought this one out, he thought.

"And it shall have to be made of three separate parts, mind you, as to be jointed. I'm sure one of these gentlemen can teach you how to do that. If they can't, I can," he added. "I've seen this done before, Mister Toren. The former Chieftain of my tribe had a leg made of wood. Lost his real one in battle with the Simpa in the Allenians. We're not true lycanthropes, you see. We're just tiger-men, Mister Toren. Our regenerative powers do not include the re-growth of lost limbs."

Lee looked at him with a shocked and appalled glare for a minute before slowly breaking into a smile.

"Can't regenerate, so you improvise, eh? Must say, I'm impressed. But are you sure about this? I mean, I know some great Alchemists could whip you up a real leg no problem."

Flint was grinning from ear to ear: the Wererat bastard was going to help him get this done, he knew it. There would be no getting around it.

"No, I prefer to go with the wood. True strength comes from taking the bad with the good, my friend."

Lee was flustered for a moment, and had to stall for time.

"Well, that is, erm, well, it'd still take a damned long time to carve it out."

Amon finished what little was left of his meat in a few pulls.

"No matter. I'm sure you have a couple of days to spare." Lee got to his feet and stomped back around the fire, taking up his plate and shoveling food in as fast as he could. Flint could see the frustration and anger building in the Gnome. He could understand. After all, two more days' pay for he and his men would be an additional two hundred gold pieces, and Lee's budget was already running low. Flint couldn't ensure that his men would want to stick around for that long in any case. And the trip back to Desanadron would be another eleven days, even on horseback. That would be time unpaid for. But he couldn't let Amon not get his request. Something about the Khan's survival seemed essential. And after all, he couldn't just come this far and be left for dead.

"As a matter of fact, we d-," Lee began in protest, before Flint stood up to interject.

"Do," the Wererat said abruptly. "You boys can head home," he said, addressing the members of his crew. "Mister Toren can't afford to keep you around any longer. Take the mounts and head out at sunset."

The Wererats stared in astonishment at their leader. "And Lee, you are still going to pay me."

"But, sir," stammered Tony. "Are you going to be okay?"

Flint cast a disdainful glare at the younger Wererat, who slinked toward his other companions.

"Sunset is only a couple of hours away. Start getting your things together, gentlemen, and prepare to head back to Desanadron. Give Stockholm the word that I'll be a week or two behind you, due to the extra travel time. That, and there's someplace I have to go on my own before returning home. Understood?"

The pack nodded as a whole, and started to put their camping gear in the proper containers and packs. The horses were brought over shortly, and the sun lowered towards the horizon. Flint, Lee Toren, and Tiberious Amon sat in studied silence, each taking in the situation and their surroundings.

Shortly before the sun set, Flint stood and stalked over to the branch that Amon had indicated. The tall Wererat hacked at its base with his short sword, chips of wood flying, the echo of wood splitting vibrating through the air.

"Right then, sir," Tony said, mounting his steed. The others weren't looking too happy about the situation, and Flint knew exactly why: they didn't trust the Khan in the slightest. As far as they were concerned, fashioning him a leg would only make him more dangerous. But they knew that their leader was capable and competent. Flint had been an effective second-in-command of the Hoods since the Guild's restructuring, and many of the men considered him to be the real leader of the Hoods.

But he knew his place, knew that Jim Cline was the man in charge. And he wouldn't do anything to upset that order, like they did in other guilds.

"We're all ready to go, sir. Mister Toren." The young Wererat turned his horse to look at Lee Toren, the master of Pickpockets. "It's been a pleasure working with and learning from you."

Lee simply smiled a fake smile at the youth before turning his head away and grumbling unhappily to himself.

Flint approached at speed, dropping the thick, heavy branch on the ground before the diminutive Pickpocket, then walked up to Tony's side, and patted his horse on the flank.

"Ride hard and quick, my boy. And remember, tell Stockholm I'll be along shortly. He'll get the message to Master Cline."

"Um, why don't I tell Master Cline myself?"

"Because, Master Cline is not going to be pleased that I'm not returning with you. You would most likely be spending a good deal of time in the infirmary if you were the messenger of such news. Stockholm, as you well know, cannot be harmed or injured so easily."

Tony nodded, agreeing with the elder Wererat's advice. The Red Tribe Werewolf, Stockholm, was the Guild's third-in-command, and their resident ass-kicker. He had been a Soldier, a Knight, a Boxer, and a Wrestler. The huge, war-hardened Werewolf was currently spending time with the Hoods as a combat advisor and a discipline instructor. Why he had chosen to stick with the Guild after his first contract was a mystery. After all, he was a man who spoke constantly of honor. Why would he work with a thieves' guild?

No matter, Flint thought. Other things to worry about for now.

Tony and the rest of the hirelings took off into the sunset, riding northwest as hard as their stallions could be driven. Flint waved good-bye to them one more time, and then turned his attention to Lee and Amon. "How's that leg coming, Lee," he asked as he approached the grumbling Pickpocket Gnome.

"I've only just started, ya filthy mouse," Lee spat, holding his whittling knife up over his head and stabbing the branch, hard. "I nay ken why we don't just find oorselves an Alchemist ta whip 'im up a real leg. This is a big pain in my ass, carvin' this thing. And you," he shouted, pointing at the seated Khan.

Amon looked up from his silent musing, his eyes locking onto those of the Gnome Pickpocket. He was surprised to find true anger and resentment in the Gnome: perhaps he would be better off letting the Wererat help him. After all, Flint seemed to know something that neither Lee, nor Amon himself knew about the tiger-man's fate.

"You are by far the worst guest I've ever had the displeasure of keeping company with. You're costing me money, time, effort, and an awful lot of headache. Give me one reason I should finish this leg of yours. Give me one good reason I should make it jointed."

"Well," Amon said, without so much as moving a muscle. "For starters, I don't think the gods would look very favorably on a man who saves someone, just to let them live in helplessness. Secondly, I'll be of much more use to you in the future if I'm mobile. And lastly, it is not like you have to, Mister Toren. It is simply a request from a nearly crippled Khan, to a very capable and handy Gnome fellow." Amon smiled, surprised that he could still be such a deceiving individual. He hadn't meant to lie, or cheat Lee Toren out of his own services. He simply had to convince the conniving little Pickpocket through sugarcoated words, and that was the end of the matter. But the guilt held on only a moment longer, and Amon didn't feel the need to defend his own actions for the time being.

"Well, I am pretty good with me hands, all roit." Lee looked at the tree branch. He had already removed the outer layer of bark, and the fine white wood underneath shone through the deepening darkness as the moon rose above the woods in the night sky. "And maybe doing the joints won't be so bad, so long as I make the measurements and cuts roit now. Okay, mister—" the spry Gnome shuffled over towards Amon with a length of some sort of cord. Out of training or instinct, Amon grabbed a nearby rock, keeping it hidden in his palm. He made absolutely certain to keep the movement slight, like a muscle spasm or other involuntary movement.

As Lee pulled the cord out, however, Amon barely made out little sets of numbers on the cloth: *a tailor's tape*, he realized, letting the rock roll away. "

S'a good thing you leggo' of that rock, chum," Lee said, not looking away from Amon's eyes, which had gone wide with amazement. "I'm pretty observant of such things as that. 'Ave to be, seein's I'm so small and everything. Now, make yer leg as straight as you can get it." The Gnome took down notes on a piece of parchment, compensating the measurements for what remained of the stump on the Khan's hip.

As soon as he had the numbers, Lee set to work on the leg, and Flint kept a watchful eye on the surrounding area. Somewhere far in the distance, in which direction he didn't know, the fate of the lands of Tamalaria was about to be decided. Would it matter if Amon got his new leg in a day, maybe two or three? Would there be a world left for him to re-learn how to walk in after another week had passed? And if there was, then what role would he play in that world? Furthermore, what would become of this amazing Khan, who had survived the impossible? He supposed that if he was to ever find out, he'd have to get back to living in the present, so that the future could come on time.

Chapter Nine
Mass Destruction

The army of the Dread Knight Byron, Thaddeus Viper, Morek Rockmight, and the free lands and peoples of Tamalaria, had advanced to within seven miles from the entrance of Mount Toane.

Richard Vandross had sent several platoons out into the fields between the Dread Knight's army and the mouth of the mountain planning an ambush but the army of Ja-Wen, which had managed to be just outside of the shock wave from Vandross's Glorious Mother of Destruction, had revealed themselves on the southern front of Mount Toane, making a pre-emptive strike in the night when they arrived.

The ruckus had roused most of Byron's forces from their slumber, the surprised shrieks of Illeck mages and Shadowbeasts as they came under assault by angry, now-homeless soldiers and former constables of Ja-Wen.

Byron had let out a furious battle cry, and had launched himself, along with a small handful of Knights and Paladins, to include the members of his own company, into a skirmish with the guardian forces of the mountain's main entrance.

They had slaughtered the one-eyed warlock's forces without much effort. High on sudden courage and the realization that they could use this assault as a ploy to further their plans, the ranking officers and their men who had gone with Byron the night before had gone into the fray with few or no worries. Thus, they had fought without regard to their own well-being.

"Such a lack of self-preservation sometimes leads to our greatest victories," Morek Rockmight had said to the Dread Knight as Byron cleaned the Morning Glory off after the fracas.

Morek had sustained the most severe of the company's members that evening. An Illeck mage had run an ice lance through his left side. He had lost a lot of blood, and the best of the Clerics in the army had been required to mend his wounds.

"There will be some pain and discomfort for a few days yet," one of the healers had informed him. "You will have to be very careful, for even healing magic can be undone by carelessness."

Now, standing on a ridge some seven miles distant once again, Byron thought on the wisdom of Morek's statement. *It also leads to unnecessary deaths on both sides*, Byron concluded grimly.

Colonel Molis had provided Byron and his company a back way into the mountain's catacombs, a secret tunnel through which to gain access to the warlock's inner forces. Though the passageway would not allow more than a single platoon in with Byron and his company, that should be enough of a counter-balancing measure to send Vandross and his cronies reeling for cover. The shock factor would do most of the initial damage. Byron swore on his late wife's soul that he and his Morning Glory would do the majority of the secondary damage. He originally thought to ask for volunteers among the army's ranks, but James Hayes had cautioned against that.

"Every man and woman would try to tag along, mighty Byron. It would be best to hand-select those needed for our unit." The Human Paladin was looking over those who stood closest, his eyes squinting as he thought long and hard about whom to select. "And may I make a suggestion, my friend?" Hayes asked with a near whisper.

Byron leaned toward him without looking away from the face of Mount Toane.

"Certainly, James, what is it?"

"Well, sir, it's about your selections for the unit. Look at a man, speak with a man, spend time with a man, and soon enough you'll know if he's got someone back home or not. Same goes for women, though they are usually more forthcoming about their emotional connections, sir." Hayes walked in front of Byron, blocking his view of Mount Toane. "Sir, soldiers with nobody to fight for don't generally do well in these situations. They need to stay in groups. The best warriors are the ones with family, the ones who have people and homes to defend, to go back to when everything's said and done. Sir," he said, adding the title as an afterthought.

Byron clapped Hayes on the shoulder, thanking him silently for his advice on the matter.

"Very well then, James. Take Morek and interview the candidates. You have a couple of hours, but try to be quick about it. We need a platoon of two hundred men and women, warriors and mages both. Be as swift as you can be. As soon as the platoon is assembled, gather the forces for one final address. I shall speak to them, rally them to our purpose one last time. Because after the assault on the warlock, my friend," Byron said, walking away from James and whispering. "I shall not be able to speak to anyone, ever again. When I fell Richard Vandross, I too shall die."

Hayes looked at his undead companion for a long, silent moment, then saluted and moved away to find Morek Rockmight and begin the selection process.

As the Paladin and Boxer made their way through the ranks, Byron thought on what he would say to the men. How would he tell them that no matter how valiantly they fought, the world would not be as it was before Richard Vandross's rise to power? How would he tell them that of the nearly twenty thousand of them, more than half would most likely perish? He couldn't be certain, because he had never, in his mortal life, been that straightforward with his troops. As a proud, noble Paladin in the Order of Oun, he had never thought about the defeats suffered on the battlefield. Overall victory, that was the message the Order cared about the most.

But what about the dozens, maybe even hundreds of lives forever altered by the death of a single soldier? Friends, family, loved ones, all deprived of that one common link. In retrospect, Byron supposed that the end of one man's life rippled throughout the entire world, regardless of his Race, his Class, or even the kind of person he was.

Looking out over the thousands assembled, he groaned inwardly: not the best time to be having such revelations. Especially when he personally held himself responsible for every death.

Shoryu Tearfang sprinted toward Byron from the south, having been dispatched to check on the status of Ja-Wen's standing army. He stopped a few feet short of the Dread Knight, flashing him a keen, toothy grin, his eyes aglow with anxiety and good news. "Good Byron. Ja-Wen's forces are bolstered with men and women from the Port of Arcade, the village of Holenwik, and Monks and Samurai from training grounds in the northeast and southeast. They number nearly twelve thousand strong, and suffered only twenty or so casualties last night. They are standing in full readiness, prepared to march when we make our move."

Byron smiled, a deep rictus that caused his lower jaw to stretch and distort out of real proportions, the twisted nature of his existence once again rearing its ugly head. Yet there was no malice in that expression, as once there most certainly would have been. It held only joy, and an extreme satisfaction. Richard Vandross had lost all of his advantages. Or so it seemed.

* * * *

"Two armies, Vilec Roak, two. And you mean to tell me that they outnumber us? " Richard Vandross hurled bolts of lightning through the dark space of his throne room at the Shadowbeast General, his fury barely contained. "If they are only two armies, how can they possibly outnumber us? I have summoned nearly every available Shadowbeast and lesser demon from the Pit. I have collected together thousands of Illeck mages, each more than capable. I still have many hundreds of Khan at my disposal. How did we take that beating last night?"

Another bolt of lightning, this one wrapped in the swirling, purple energy that reeked of decay, power from the Orbs of Eden's Serpent siphoned into Vandross's own mundane magic.

Vilec Roak, having kept to the shadows of the throne room, removed himself from one, exiting the Shadowplane for long enough to explain the situation to his leader and summoner.

"My lord, we took such a heavy pounding due to the fact that, as per your orders, we have kept the majority of our forces in check, here, inside the mountain itself. If any platoon from without dares to march inside, they shall surely suffer as your many minions fall upon them, sire," Vilec Roak explained, finally having regained a sense of calm, a sense of control.

Colonel Molis's aura had disappeared in the midst of the previous evening's assault, and Roak presumed him dead. Probably the best news in a while.

"And besides, you can always use the Glorious Mother of Destruction on them, my lord," he added, knowing full well that the one-eyed warlock could not, as yet, call upon that force again. At least not for now.

"No, I can't Roak," Vandross said with a heavy heave and a sigh, slouching into his throne of rock and bones. His hands smoked with spent power, his boots scorching the floor as he dragged his feet.

Roak realized, rather suddenly, that Richard Vandross was exhausted, and still had not properly rested since utilizing the Glorious Mother of Destruction. "I need to rest before I can call upon that again. I'm going to my quarters in a minute," he droned lazily, his one good eye already quickly closing. "I trust you can defend Mount Toane for a day or so," he asked, already nodding off.

"Yes, of course, my lord." Roak slunk away. He had plans, and they didn't involve sitting back and waiting to be attacked. With Molis gone, and Vandross recovering, the Shadowbeast would go on the offensive, send wave after wave of demon and tainted man out into the fray. But he would have to distribute the forces in a fashion that would utilize the strengths and weaknesses of his own ranks, and those of the armies set against the mountain and its masters. Vilec Roak passed out of the throne room and down through sets of tunnels, passages blurring by him as he swiftly traveled through the mountain. The old, familiar scent of fear clung to all of the mortal creatures within the confines of the mountain fortress, the salty stench of sweat and tears mixing together like airborne nectar to his senses. The sounds of grunting, growling, praying and conjuring echoed through the halls, and Roak could identify the purpose of each.

The growling of the Khan Soldiers, Knights, Berserkers and battle Clerics, all enraged that Lieutenant Tiberious Amon had been sent away, unable to lead them in this final confrontation. Here and there, as Vilec Roak slid through the shadows of their barracks and meeting halls, he heard words of dissent and defection. One Soldier Class Khan even mustered the gumption to say rather loudly that, "Lord Vandross is a mad dog, and we should not be taking cues from him any further. I am leaving this mountain at the first opportunity."

The grunting that Roak had heard throughout the mountain turned out to be nothing more than several scores of Orc, Troll, Goblin and other assorted humanoid soldiers of varying Classes training themselves, getting ready for the onslaught ahead of them. The praying, for the most part, happened to be the Necromancers, all assembled into the lowest livable reaches of Mount Toane, raising the bodies of the long since dead, and jumbling them together into strange grotesqueries that could surely curdle the blood of most mortals. As for the conjuring, literally thousands of Illeck, Human, Khan, Greenskin and demon mages and shaman inside the mountain were busying themselves with the setting of magical traps and caltrops, defensive barrier spells and the memorization of offensive, combat spells.

Outside, as Vilec Roak poked his head out into the noon daylight, the armies of the Dread Knight and Ja-Wen were stirring. It would appear that they intended to send skirmishers once again, as they had the night before. The key difference, of course, was that this time the outer perimeter of the mountain had been fortified with ranks of Vandross's own troops. Shadowbeasts lazed about in the draining sunlight, weakened by the golden rays of heat and illumination, but they were, for the most part, the throw-aways of Roak's kind. Most had been hand selected by the Shadowbeast Prime to shore up defenses during the daylight hours. He didn't care much if they died; after all, death for a demon in the mortal realm merely sent them back to the Hells. Provided, of course, that they weren't destroyed in very particular fashions.

Roak shuddered slightly as he thought of the various methods of sending a demon back to the Pit to be a tortured victim, instead of a gleeful and malicious servant. One of those very ways was to simply be cut down by a Paladin of true faith.

Another of those methods popped up rather unwanted in the back of Roak's mind: destruction of a demon's soul. Unbeknownst to most mortals, the majority of the demons that dwelled in the seven realms of the Pit had once been the souls of mortals themselves. Some became demons through contracts made with the Timeless Ones, also known as the True Demons. Filled with malice and darkness so pungent and pure as to make angels writhe and cringe at their presence, those demons alone could say that they had always been in the Hells. Some other demons had been spawned from the mating of two True Demons, and they too held sway and power in the Pit, unlike the lessers.

Most, however, were the tortured souls of sinners who had grown numb to their eternal torment, or even those who began to enjoy their constant agony. Yet at their core, through the demon soul imbued upon them, beneath the ethereal flesh that covered their now misshapen bodies, dwelled the soul of a mortal.

A mortal that could be sent back to all that agony. Vilec Roak himself came from that category.

But the likelihood of Roak himself being felled in any of those methods felt slim to the Shadowbeast Prime. After all, when the battle began, Lord Vandross's armies would be more than enough to stand against the rush of the mortals without. Many of the warlock's own troops came from the mortal Races of Tamalaria, and so the deaths of those troops meant little or nothing to the General. However, he didn't like the idea of having so many of his own kinsmen slain in the name of the madman's cause. Perhaps there had been some wisdom in the Khans' grumblings and musings.

As darkness wrapped lovingly around the demon, caressing his black, oily flesh like a long waiting lover, he smiled, pearly white razors gleaming through the shadows. He didn't intend to be among the casualties of the massive battle that loomed ahead. He intended to leave the mountain the moment the tide of battle swung against him. And then Richard Vandross, rested or not, would have to do the commanding on his own. Roak had already decided how he would leave. Shadowbeasts could walk through shadows whenever, wherever they chose.

Even if the rest of the mountain came down around the warlock's ears, Vilec Roak would live to see another nightfall.

* * * *

"What exactly are we doing, m'lord," one of Byron's officers inquired as the Dread Knight barked orders at the top of his lungs to the platoons within earshot, trusting the officers further down to continue the message.

Byron gazed at the swelling ranks of Shadowbeasts, Illecks, assorted

Greenskins and Khan shuffle and adjust around the outside of the mountain, apparently not willing to be caught off guard again.

"We are forming a wall, Major," the Dread Knight responded coolly, his voice calm and sure, but his pinpoint eyes roving back and forth over the opposing forces. "A wall of men and women, five people deep and as long as the stretch of our forces, so that we may appear to be in constant readiness. Behind the wall, down the slope of the hills and the plain behind us, the remainder of the armies shall rest and take food, train a little for what's ahead. One doesn't lay successful siege to a base or domain by simply charging in at the onset, Major," he said, adding a hint of scolding to his tone for the Human Knight.

The man had served, apparently, with James Hayes at Fort Flag, one of the only half a dozen survivors from Hayes's unit. After the Dread Knight's company had left the city, young Steven Blaine had been asked to join Desanadron's new standing army, which still had very few members, due to the city's destruction. He had accepted immediately, and quickly been assigned the rank of Major for his hard work in helping the city rebuild. Now, here he stood, long blond mane of hair flowing back over the backing of his plate armor.

Pretty boy, Byron thought with an internal growl. Some Knights are just like that.

"Of course, sir. You are still quite the tactician, aren't you, sir?" The question came out awkwardly from the Major's lips, and the Human immediately cast his eyes downward, embarrassed or ashamed of something he might have implied in the question.

"How do you mean, Major?" The Dread Knight folded his arms across his barrel chest.

The Major floundered for a brief moment before standing at full attention and saluting. "Permission to speak freely, sir?"

Byron said nothing, simply waving his hand as if to say, get on with it.

The Knight relaxed visibly, and Byron could make out the faint, relieved sigh that huffed from the man's lungs. "I've read all about your use of tactics in service to the Order, m'lord." Blaine's hands balled up as he posed rather exaggeratedly towards the undead warrior. "And I know this one. Byron Aixler's 'Wall of Unseen Readiness'. It's just like I read in the Order's latest tactics guide. You know, you've got about six or seven entire entries in the book." The young Knight edged just a little too much for the Dread Knight's comfort.

He quickly scanned the area for James Hayes, his mind working feverishly to think of a reason to get rid of this suddenly insufferable youth. He understood awe and respect, but Blaine was giving him the willies.

As Blaine's eyes sparkled near to Byron's breastplate, Byron found the Paladin he had been traveling with. He flapped his left arm up and down in a flurry of attention-gathering sweeps, his hand flung open and barely visible due to his rush to get someone to take this man away from him.

The white mustache and goatee of James Hayes whipped around. As his eyes met Byron's, he grinned widely, knowingly. *Spare me this please, my friend,*

Byron's pinpoint lights seemed to beseech Hayes.

Sure, you've suffered enough, Hayes's replied. The stalwart Paladin sauntered over to Byron and the impressionable young Knight, a smile pasted across his face. "Steven, my good man, we have some patrol duties to assign, rations to disperse, the usual officer sort of things. Come along then."

Blaine saluted Byron quickly, then sprinted off to follow James Hayes.

Byron sagged with relief, free from the unexpected adoration of a young man.

Shoryu approached from the plains beneath the hillcrest, coming from among the men and women already preparing to get some precious rest. The Cuyotai Hunter had ranged around Mount Toane since sunrise, and had gone off to get some food before making more reconnaissance checks. He smiled broadly at the Dread Knight, the fur of his canine snout pulling back with his lips to reveal a mouth full of dagger-like teeth. Any farm boy or inexperienced adventurer would have gone chilled to the bone at the sight of such a smile, thought the young Cuyotai's eyes flashed wide and bright. The potential for murder lay deep in those green eyes, tucked away behind the kinder, jesting and joking attitude of Shoryu Tearfang.

But Byron had become intimately aware of that component of Shoryu's being; the boy was deadly accurate with that enchanted bow, and would have no qualms with proving it to anyone or anything that got in his way or threatened the well-being of his wife and himself.

"Anything to report thus far, my furry friend?"

"Yes, good Byron. Military food really is terrible."

Caught off guard, Byron laughed a little bit as well before shaking his head, and trying to regain his composure. The ordeal of handling Richard Vandross had become overall rather taxing on Byron's rotten nerves. The peoples of the lands of Tamalaria had gone seemingly overnight from wanting to cut the Dread Knight down, to declaring him the only hope they had against a formidable warlock. Well, not the *only* hope, or nobody would have bothered sending an army, but everyone seemed to be in agreement; when the final blow was to be struck for victory, the undead warrior would deal it.

"Other than that, I haven't observed anything too out of the ordinary. However," Shoryu said, holding up a finger pointedly. "I can tell that there are some very experienced Necromancers in the back rows of the guarding ranks out there, my friend. Already they prepare spells of conjuration to bring their ungodly minions to bear against us."

"How many?" Byron moved toward the wall of men and women set up as a ruse atop the hill slopes. As he approached, the armored troops of mortals in his service parted, allowing him to look down at the perimeter forces of Mount Toane.

Shoryu loped along with him, and as Byron scanned the area, Shoryu pointed a long, narrow finger at the Necromancer group he had spoken of.

Byron concentrated, and focused all of his visual attention on them. Utilizing magic of a neutral nature, as he had once before to search for demons, he brought his field of vision bearing right down on them, while keeping his sense of hearing back with the young Hunter. "Hrmm."

"Seven, by my count," Shoryu reported.

Byron has seen only six; he moved his vision slightly west, and found yet another. The one female Necromancer stood apart from the men, all of them Illecks.

Stupid, he thought, to separate the one woman from their midst, simply because she happened to possess a different set of reproductive organs. Then again, almost all of Illeck society was like that—the men ruled and made the decisions, while the women were made to simply comply. Of course, this only served as the surface of their dark society. Truth be told, Byron thought as he recalled his many conversations with the dark Elves he had worked with in service to Tanarak of Sidius, the women were simply more capable of carrying out orders and plots than the men. Sure, the males were the great schemers, but the females of the Illeck Race held the physical and magical potency of their people.

Perhaps, he thought, this Necromancer woman had separated herself from the men. Perhaps her talent stood much higher than theirs.

He sincerely hoped not. That many Necromancers working together chilled him to the core. If she held more power than those six men, that would prove fatal for many scores of the men under his command.

"Shoryu, be completely honest with me." Byron brought his vision back to its normal range. "Can you get a clean shot on one of them? Go for a kill right now?"

Shoryu stepped shoulder-to-shoulder with the hulking Dread Knight. He covered his eyes to adjust for the glare of the sun, which had begun its long march to setting. After a long moment, he grinned at Byron and nodded.

"I assume you'll want me to aim for the woman," Shoryu said, not a question, but rather a statement of fact.

Byron nodded. A wind howled through the hills, tearing at the air with an eerie wailing reminiscent of the banshees of the night world. The air held no magic in it; this was a natural breeze, one that whispered of the death that soon would visit these hills, the fields, and the interior of Mount Toane.

Byron shuddered, his confidence slipping for a fraction of an instant. What was being asked of him was more than he could have done in mortal life. He had tried once to stop a tyrannical warlock who resided in Mount Toane, and this accursed, wretched body and un-life had been his reward. What if he failed again, against the one-eyed madman within the earthen fortress?

He gripped the handle of the Morning Glory hard with his left hand, feeling the holy power therein. *No*, he said to himself. *There will be no failure this time.*

"That's right, young one. Aim for the head, in case she's already performed the Rite of Rotting."

Shoryu raised an inquiring eyebrow at Byron, and motioned his hands in a circle, asking him without a word what the Rite of Rotting was.

Byron heaved a thoughtful sigh. "It is a Necromancer's ritual, the ultimate spell of their teachings, in its own way. The Rite is a ceremony that each Necromancer of high power and status performs when they realize that their own time on the mortal coil is limited. Most don't recognize their inevitable fate for dozens of years, but when they do, they decide that they would rather become one of their own beloved creations than pass on to the seven Hells. Some few reach the heavens of some darker gods, but most burn for eternity in the Pit." Byron had abhorred the undead in life, and here he was, standing as one of them. "Anyway," he continued with a shrug of his shoulders. " Necromancers pray to the dark gods, mostly to Necros or Necrophite, lords and overseers of the activities and un-life of the undead. They beseech these dark gods for a new body, a chance at un-life, when they are felled. Most return as Lordly Zombies, a variety of Zombie that is both physically and mentally their own equal in life. They're also called Uberzombies. Like all zombies, they crave for the flesh of the living.

"Some, however, have been chronicled to return as Wraiths, some as Mummies, and even a very select few as Liches. They are the most powerful and fearsome of the lot," Byron said. "Though Liches are not the most powerful undead creatures overall, these particular ones return with all of the powers of the Necromancer in life, and the unholy powers of a Lich. This woman could very well be one of those."

"So why the head shot? If she's just going to come back, I don't see any reason not to shoot her through the heart like an animal."

"Because, Shoryu, if a Necromancer is slain by having their brain destroyed, they cannot be brought back through the Rite of Rotting. The damage cancels the whole spell out."

Shoryu smiled and drew his bow and arrow.

Notched and readied, Shoryu knelt to take careful aim at the Illeck woman. Who knew what sort of creatures she could summon if she indeed had that sort of power? Shoryu thought. Best not to take any chances.

As soon as he had the Necromancer's forehead trained with the arrow, he let fly his mystic weapon.

All of the ranks of the wall gasped in shock as a single projectile fired from their midst, each man silently praying that the attack would go unnoticed by the perimeter forces of Mount Toane.

Only seconds later, a shimmering light and an explosion of blood and brain matter came from the Necromancer woman's forehead.

Byron tightened his fist and almost shouted *buyah*! He resisted the urge, and focused his sight down on the collected male Necromancers. As he had hoped, they all had broken their little circle to rush away from their fallen comrade. Chaos soon erupted along the back lines of the perimeter forces of Mount Toane, and that chaos slithered along on its belly through the entirety of those troops, an invisible serpent that struck each man and woman in a mental vein. The cries of alarm rang through the afternoon air, a sweet symphony to Byron's *ears*, as they were.

"Good shot, my boy." He put a heavy, armored hand on Shoryu's shoulder.

The Dread Knight's Redemption

The boy didn't look up from the teeming swarm of Vandross's men. His face had a dour and serious cast, and Byron looked out once again to see what it was the Cuyotai Hunter had spotted.

Immediately Shoryu notched another arrow, and Byron spotted the creature that the Hunter had trained his next shot upon: a Dreadnaught.

Among the Necromancers' most fearsome conjuring was the Dreadnaught, a creature assembled from the remains of several powerful men or beasts, lashed together with magic and stitching. Most came with a large variety of weapons attached to their bodies or buried in their rotted flesh, held there by the dead muscle tissue that the Necromancer to summon it had reanimated. The circle of Necromancers had clearly pooled together their resources long before coming to the perimeter of Mount Toane. There had not been enough time for them to conjure and assemble a Dreadnaught during their stay outside of the mountain fortress. And the female must have been placing some sort of charms and protections on the beast, for now it made its way through the rambling lines of confused defenders of the mountain, a single, deadly silhouette against the afternoon light.

Byron tried to hone his vision on the creature, but his attempts failed. Some magic repelled his magical sight from the Dreadnaught, and he was forced to rally together several officers and the members of his own traveling party. All stood at full readiness, as the three-man deep wall of the Dread Knight's army tensed to do battle with the fearsome Dreadnaught. Among the officers assembled stood Colonel Molis, disguised as an Elven Soldier. The outline of his aura gave him away to Byron, as well as to Ellen Daires, but neither the Dread Knight nor the Elven Gaiamancer mentioned him to the others, or indicated to the half-breed that they could see through his ruse.

"There is a Dreadnaught approaching the lines, perhaps five minutes away from them. Have any of you ever dealt with such an abomination," Byron asked the soldiers.

They simply muttered among themselves before shaking their heads collectively.

Only Morek Rockmight nodded his head in acknowledgement.

"A few years back, we 'ad a drifter come through Traithrock, a Rakah," he said. "Raven-men, if any of you've never 'eard of 'em. Anyhow, their kind tend ta be a bit too curious for my liking, and this one 'ad some of the most disturbing books and artifacts in 'is arms and rucksack when he was checked at the gates. Still, even after I was apprised of the situation, I gave the go-ahead to let 'im in. Big mistake. Apparently, he'd been gathering bits and pieces of things to assemble one of those things." He pointed in the direction of the Dreadnaught's approach. "Wanted a Dwarven spine or two to put in it. We Dwarves are fairly well known fer the strenth of our skeletal structure. Well, a couple of guards went missing that noit, an' the next mornin', we 'ad one of those things attacking the city. They're damned tough, especially when someone wif half a brain makes 'em. The Rakah, he only meant to do it as a study, but things got out of hand. He'd forgotten to put a limiter on the thing before he woke it up, and he had to come into our town and destroy it wif 'is own magic."

"So, what happened to the Rakah," one of the officers asked.

"Oh, I dusted 'is brain wif a couple well-placed punches after that," Morek said matter-of-factly. "Not 'afore I asked him how to stop those things on our own, though," he added after several officers cringed from him. "See, they can take a hundred axes to the body, swords to the face, if'n they've got one, an' they 'aven't got any concept of pain fer the most part. Most magic won't work on them either, seein's they most times have skins from different magic users implemented on their body," Morek added, looking hard at one of the Cuyotai officers in Elven Kingdom uniform. A Lieutenant, and an Aquamancer as his primary Class. "However, blunt force works real good on 'em. Their bones never fuse quite roit during the construction, or so the Rakah told me. Break the limbs, then just tear it apart he'd told me. And fer some reason, lightning spells work just foin on 'em."

"I have a couple of those on hand," said the only Minotaur officer at the meeting, a tall, brutish looking figure by the name of Big John. His half-plate armor gleamed with patches of gold that the beast-man had banged into the armor himself. Captain Jonathan Reeves of the Port of Arcade Constabulary, or police force had come with Thaddeus Viper from the port city in the northeast, hand selected by the old bandit himself.

Byron had not heard the man speak once in the whole time he had marched with the armies, but now he wanted the man to say more. After all, he had what they needed in this clinch situation.

However, more time could not be spared to plan a defense against the constructed monstrosity, as it had already reached the front line of the wall and was roaring as it tore into the foremost soldiers.

Blood sprayed the ground and dozens of troops, and the thick, metallic scent of it clung immediately to the air. The officers all spun around to face the creature, splitting up and barking orders of retreat and cautious attack, and Byron's company readied themselves in combat formation.

Byron let Morek take the front position, since his enchanted gloves, along with James Hayes's mace, were the only blunt weapons the company had.

Morek wanted a piece of this freak.

Finally, the creature came into full view of them, an Elven man impaled on the sword that had been attached to its left arm to serve as its main weapon. The sword bled with a wicked, purple aura, enchanted by the sorceress that Shoryu had shot in the face.

No face graced the dreadnaught's contorted form. Instead, two large nostrils had been attached to its blackened chest, flanked on both sides by sheets of metal grafted onto the outer flesh of its mangled form. The reek of death and blasted muscles and flesh filled the air as it hurled the lifeless body of the Elven Hunter from its sword arm.

It reminded Byron vaguely of the Shadowbeast in Whitewood that had pierced its own body with weapons, so that it could career through the Elven capital like a whirlwind of weapons and death.

Maggots fell from small seams in the stitching of its flesh, crawling over its body with practiced ease. After all, much of this abomination had previously been their meals, and it made sense to see them writhing about on what they considered their property.

The mere sight of the bugs made several dozen of the troops vomit uncontrollably as they recognized the disgusting nature of the Dreadnaught.

Slipping in their comrades' blood and pools of their own excretions, several of the troops fell as they tried to follow their officers' orders to pull back—and were stomped to death by the massive bulk of the Dreadnaught. Its torso was easily five feet around, and its legs appeared to have belonged to a horse or Centaur, making effective stamping and kicking weapons. Dagger blades had been attached to the sides of its feet, and a whole new dimension of danger presented itself as the beast lashed out with spinning kicks and thrusting stabs with its sword arm.

It was tearing his men apart, and Byron felt helpless to stop it.

"Move," Morek shouted as he charged toward the behemoth construct, weaving and dodging between men and women as they fled this way and that. The whole area appeared to be a mass of chaos now, on both sides of the conflict. A single arrow had started this all, Byron thought in horror. An arrow that I ordered Shoryu to fire. Damnation and hellfire, Hell and blood.

As he and the company surged forward, Ellen Daires could be seen summoning magical force into her clasped hands, green light swirling around her chest.

As the company closed to within melee range of the Dreadnaught, Ellen unleashed her spell, creating an outer skin of stone around Morek Rockmight's body, save for his fists, that he might still strike with them.

"Much appreciated deary," he shouted as he rolled to his left to avoid the downward strike of the Dreadnaught's sword arm.

Before the Dread Knight could move to assist the diminutive Boxer, he peered to his right, down the hill, and saw that two waves of troops had been sent from the perimeter defense of Mount Toane. "All assemble for battle," he screamed down the slopes to the resting and preparing members of the army.

Much to his satisfaction, he saw that they had already started forming ranks to come to the aid of their stricken comrades. Already more than two score troops had fallen to the deadly construct, and by Byron's calculations, only three or four minutes had passed. The creature had to be stopped before the slowly marching ranks of Vandross's men reached the top of the hill.

Morek Rockmight danced this way and that, unable to find an opening in which to strike out at the beast, its movements impossibly quick for dead flesh and nerves.

The moment he thought he had an opening, he lashed out with a powerful cross at the creature's hip, which was at his eye level. However, the Dreadnaught had purposely left the opening there, and lashed out with a third, hidden arm from its back, bashing Morek in his right side, tossing him dozens of yards away.

The Dwarven Boxer landed with a heavy thud and a "Hoomph," mere feet from Shoryu, who had taken up a position behind a rock barrier that his wife had constructed for him with her magic.

Byron hung back, Morning Glory in hands, observing this mighty foe. Surely the creature had some other weakness aside from the blunt weapons and lightning, but what was it? Where should he strike? His training had taken over, and he skirted the perimeter of the skirmish with the construct, which had turned its full attention on his party. *Good,* he thought. *Come at us, we're more than capable of handling you, you fucking freak.*

Morek managed to get up, but his right arm hung low, the hand covered in the enchanted glove dipping lower as the seconds ticked past. He knew his arm had been damaged, but now that he was in the fray once again, he discovered the true extent of the injuries, and felt the slow venom of doubt creeping through his blood. He couldn't fight at full tilt, and probably the effect was permanent. If he survived this quest, he might never properly fight again.

The creature reared back, spreading its forward arms wide to expose its nostril-holding chest. A patch of its flesh just below those large nostrils peeled back to reveal a thin, feminine forearm stretching out, magical force flaring from its fingertips.

"Everybody down," James Hayes cried, diving for cover to the ground.

Ripples of air in the shape of large, crescent-shaped blades flew out from the hand, striking Byron hard in the breastplate and legs, throwing him back and tearing open the greaves that covered his upper thighs. He slid back several yards, his heavy iron boots dragging through the dirt and tearing the topsoil apart as he stood his ground.

"Astrominus Raxium," Ellen Daires screamed, launching her own magical counter-attack on the outstretched arm coming from the construct's belly. The ground shook with fury from her goddess's power, and the ground split a few feet in front of the Dreadnaught.

Caught, perhaps, by a bit of surprise that was left over from a previous body part's owner, the creature looked down to witness a large, stone and metal ore-riddled arm protrude from the earth itself.

The arm came up to chest height on the monstrosity, cocked back, and pounded the creature with a mighty, close-fisted blow that sent the construct flying perhaps a hundred yards back toward Mount Toane.

The surrounding troops let out a rally cry of triumph, and set themselves for a charge at the approaching minions of Richard Vandross.

Byron sprinted over to where Morek Rockmight was slowly stepping from foot to foot, wobbling back and forth. Still dazed and a little edgy, the Dwarven Boxer took a swing at the Dread Knight, who had been wholly unprepared. As the Dwarf slammed his fist into Byron's leg, the Dread Knight let out a howl of pain that was more genuine than he would have liked: the blow landed right where the Dreadnaught's Aeromancy spell had torn his armor.

Morek's vision cleared, and he saw Byron knelt down, holding his leg as plumes of fury-induced smoke billowed from his eye sockets.

"Oh moi goodness, look, hey man, it was a total misunderstanding," the Boxer stammered, perhaps truly afraid for the first time in his long life.

Byron did something unexpected, though: he started to chuckle, a low, demonic laughter that began to rise in pitch and volume as he raised his head and straightened his back.

As Morek tried to inch away, the Dread Knight reached out and grabbed him fast by the tunic, which was no longer covered by the stone skin Ellen had cast on him.

"Do you have a middle name, Morek," Byron whispered in the Dwarf's face as he pulled him slowly close.

Morek simply nodded, his eyes locked onto those red, swirling pinpoints of light. "What is it?"

"Ralin," Morek stammered. "Morek Ralin Rockmight. Why, friend?" He plastered a shit-eating grin on his face, hoping for mercy.

"I just wanted to know, so that if I come back as a specter to haunt your fat ass, I know what to moan in the middle of the night." Byron pushed the Dwarf back and laughed in a more mortal fashion. "No worries, master Morek. Simply caught me by surprise is all. We have other things to attend to presently."

He sheathed the Morning Glory as he rose to his feet. Having gotten a good sense of the creature's aura and power, he now knew what to look for in terms of weaknesses. The metal plating laced to the Dreadnaught's body served as conductors for lightning-based magic spells and thunder spells. That much could be rationalized. And the insides of Dreadnaughts often remained hollow so that weapons like the Aeromancer hand and other similar nasty surprises could be concealed beneath the patchwork flesh and muscle.

That hollow space could also serve as a means of destroying the creature, Byron thought with a wry smile. If someone could get close enough to strike with a bladed weapon, one with a spell locked on it, it could be set to go off inside of the behemoth. The creature would surely do little more than remove the weapon from its outer shell and wield it in battle, unaware of the damage being done to it from inside its own macabre body of assembled corpses. And if the spell were lightning-based, it would continue to conduct through the metal attachments, rebounding through the hidden weapons inside and the metallic components inserted into its main body.

"Captain Reeves," Byron shouted over the roars of combat that had ripped the afternoon air asunder, like so much wet parchment. "To me."

The Minotaur officer, having heard his name called out amid the battle between the Dread Knight's army and the outer defenses of Mount Toane, smashed a Khan in the skull with his war hammer and sprinted over.

The Minotaur deflected incoming blows from Shadowbeasts and Khan, leaping this way and that to avoid Pyromancy spells that flared to life mere feet away.

Byron's own company had come under attack as well, and unbeknownst to the Dread Knight, an Orc of considerable weight and strength was about to attack him with a cleaver.

Byron noticed the rush of splitting air as the world around him came to a near stand-still, his vision blurred shades of gray, the color going out of reality.

The smell of long-dried animal blood, the kind one might smell in a butcher's shop. The faint grunt of a Greenskin heaving its weapon at him.

Taking all of these signs in, Byron detected the slight splatter of energy sent through the ground into the back of his feet from something heavy rushing toward him from behind. The ever-present strands of energy rippled through the ground itself vibrating in tune to his attacker.

To the common naked eye and set of perceptions, the Orc was swinging his cleaver full bore when Byron executed a back flip at nearly the speed of sound, landing in a crouch behind the offender.

The Orc finished its swing, looking around in a daze for his target.

It should be noted, at this point, that before a mortal being in the realm of Tamalaria dies, if it is bound for the Pit, it is given awareness of the fact mere moments before death. This short span of time is given by the gods, so that the creature has a few brief moments to apologize for his sinful ways, and beg forgiveness from the gods he had offended, including whatever god the creature is supposed to be worshipping by Class or Racial preference. The Orc had just begun to turn towards Byron when it was informed of its awaiting, eternal torment.

For most combatants, this is the fatal moment when they slip up, make an error of judgment, or otherwise fail to do whatever task they are about. For the Orc, it proved no different. As it laid its hateful, baleful eyes upon the Dread Knight, Byron swept his palm up and pressed it against the Orc's forehead, white-hot light flaring from his open hand.

The Dread Knight's eyes flashed golden light as he bellowed, "Holy Cannon."

A blast of holy power, and all that remained of the Orc was a quickly draining torso. Byron had cut the fiend's legs off at the knees when it was finishing its turn, sweeping his Morning Glory from a quickdraw and casting the spell at the same movement.

The Dread Knight gazed over at the Minotaur, who had finally arrived, only to join a melee with James Hayes, the two veterans standing back to back as they circled, besieged by Shadowbeast underlings. They appeared to be having a fun time, though, as both men wore savage grins of battle on their war-weathered faces.

Much as he would have liked to let the two of them have their fun, Byron noted that the Dreadnaught was coming back towards his company, sweeping aside Byron's and Vandross's men alike to get at the creatures that had fought it back. And though the Cuyotai Hunter was an excellent marksman, nothing he shot seemed to cause the creature to slow. The mystical projectiles weren't exploding in time—the Dreadnaught pulled them free and tossed them aside, the arrows exploding moments later.

"He's got a Necromancer's defensive spell on him," Shoryu cried from atop a pile of Khan corpses.

Minutes earlier, the mound hadn't been there, and those Khan Knights had been fiercely attacking a group of Soldier Class troops from the Elven Kingdom.

Byron shook his head in surprise and a grim satisfaction: the young man could kill, that much was certain. In a macabre display of in-field improvisation, Shoryu had stacked the bodies and crouched atop them, using the additional height as a sniper point, since the battlefield was devoid of trees in good enough locations to be used by an archer. The fact that the Khan appeared to have been shredded by claws and teeth instead of downed by arrows didn't escape Byron's attention.

"Understood," the undead warrior called back. He turned back to the squad of lowly Shadowbeast servants, sprinting around them with the speed of a tornado, his weapon held at waist height as he cut them all cleanly in half. The Morning Glory flashed with each fallen foe, blinking more rapidly than most could see. As he skidded to a halt before James Hayes and John Reeves, stones and soil sprayed the air from his heels dragging through the soft soil.

"Aw, you've ruined our little game," the big Minotaur breathed as he sucked in breath. A constable through and through, the big Soldier-Thunder mage Reeves was not accustomed to such frantic fighting conditions. However, push having come to shove, the towering officer had proven to himself and everyone around that he could indeed endure the harsh conditions of grand-scale warfare. "We were just starting to play."

"I appreciate your newfound love of the sport. But we have a bigger problem. The Dreadnaught is coming back this way, and we have only a minute or so before he arrives again, this time with the slightly better understanding of what we are capable of. Do not misunderstand, the construct is a thing of the undead, but they always have a smattering of sentience left behind by their creators. It shall not fall for the same tactics again, so I need you to lock a spell of lightning of some sort on the tip of my blade."

John Reeves asked no questions and made no arguments, putting two fingers on the flat underside of the Morning Glory and lifting it to his chest height.

"Agurium Strovus, Pounding of Power," the Minotaur chanted thrice as he spent his reserves of manna on locking the spell's casting onto the tip of the sword.

Immediately, Reeves stumbled back, seating himself heavily on the blood-soaked ground. Hayes knelt beside him, a look of worry on his face. "I'm fine," the big man muttered, coughing heavily. "Just winded from the effort is all. Keep me guarded for a minute?"

Hayes nodded his acceptance of the charge given.

Everywhere the pair looked, Human Paladin and Dread Knight, blood choked the scrub grass of the hilly region. Swaths of corpses lay congealing in the baking afternoon sun, the reek of blood, vomit and death-induced bowel movements filling the air. For as far as they could see from their position in front of them, down towards the face of Mount Toane, mortal men and women rampaged against each other, seeking to spill their foes' blood. How Vandross had managed to sway the Greenskins became apparent after a few minutes of thinking on the nature of Orcs, Goblins and Trolls. Might is right, that was their collective view of the world. Those with power should seize control.

The Shadowbeasts and other assorted lesser demons also seemed clear to him. Vandross had summoned them from the Pit for his own purposes, which the Dread Knight knew to be heinous and mad. Coveting power and control was the instinct of such villains as the one-eyed warlock.

Vandross's goal, engulfing the world in fear just to slip back into the darkness for centuries, seemed that of a delusional sociopath.

But the Khan and Illecks' reasons for joining Vandross's side of this continent-wide struggle eluded the Dread Knight, even now, as he watched the sorcerers and warriors of both Races collide with his own army.

Before he could give any more heed to such thoughts, the malevolent undead construct burst into view over the crest of the hill, sweeping its sword arm in wide arcs to cleave those in its path in twain.

The metallic shine of the blade had gone dull with blood, droplets of crimson life falling like spatters of rain to the ground. But the Dreadnaught did not come for Byron, or for the young Hunter who continued to volley arrows at it from nearly point-blank range. Instead, it bore down to the ground, squatting low and holding itself forward on its right hand. Firmly planted as it was, the top of its torso was targeted straight at Ellen Daires, who currently stood engaged with an Illeck Aquamancer, their spells lancing at each other with the ferocity of their nature-related schools of magic.

Heedless of the danger that might come from getting the mystical crossfire, the Dreadnaught lunged forward, throwing itself like a bull at full tilt toward the two dueling spell wielders.

Such speed, Byron thought, trying to get himself to move.

He found that a pair of dying Khan had latched onto his legs, and were trying desperately to drag him to the ground to do battle with the last breaths of their lives.

Bothersome creatures, the Dread Knight thought, his thoughts nearly in a panic. He had to get to Ellen, or she would be crushed by the Dreadnaught.

As Byron tore the dying Khan from his ankles and looked toward the Elven girl, he saw a streak of brown fur and fangs flash past, slamming full force into the Dreadnaught's left flank.

Shoryu tackled it to the ground with a heavy crash of metal and the wet, meaty smack of dead flesh hitting the blood-softened soil.

When the tumult of motion had come to a full stop, Shoryu Tearfang stood atop the construct. His claws flashed back and forth as he rent large sections of flesh from the creature's outer husk. Finally he jammed three fingers from each claw into the gaping nostrils on the Dreadnaught's chest. Tearing them open, he somersaulted backwards through the air, away from the lethal being.

The Dreadnaught was instantly on its massive feet again, throwing up its left sword arm to block an incoming blow from James Hayes's mace.

The Dread Knight's Redemption

Big John Reeves had apparently gotten to his feet and joined the fray once again with the defenders of Mount Toane, and from all indications that Byron could see, his army was starting to take heavy advantage of the daylight and their numbers, as well as skill. Order had been restored by the calm and tactical minds of the officers under his command, and units moved in groups of ten or twenty men, making surgical strikes to the disorganized and failing minions of the warlock.

Why has Vandross decided to go on the offensive? Byron wondered. It made little sense, as it was a move that Vandross's predecessor would have made. *Perhaps the outer perimeter is under someone else's command at the moment*, he thought, weaving his way through the throngs of combatants with ease as he closed into melee range with the abomination.

The Dreadnaught took several swift and hard swings and stabs at the Dread Knight, Byron parrying and blocking each blow with a practiced ease.

His feet remained planted for only a few seconds each time, his training keeping him in a position to strike the moment the opportunity came. A moment later, after he blocked a roundhouse kick from one of the creature's bladed feet, his opportunity came.

As the construct brought its heavy leg down, it cocked its sword arm back for an overhead blow. Byron thrust the tip of the Morning Glory into the left side of the torn nasal cavities on its massive chest, his eyes flashing as the discharge of thunder magic on the end of the sword riveted his body.

Then Byron withdrew the blade, and took several shuffling strides back, watching as the Dreadnaught began to spark and smoke. Its weakness to the nature of lightning magic became abundantly clear. The protective charms that had kept Shoryu's arrows from exploding on contact did not work on magic coming from inside of its body, and the metal plating all over its arms and in its legs and back smoked and smoldered, streaks of blue and yellow power coursing through its undead flesh.

After a full minute, the Dreadnaught began to fall apart at the seams, stitches flying everywhere as patches of flesh and chunks of muscle and bone came apart, dropping to the ground and leaving the stench of burned, spoiled meat hanging to the air as it ceased to function.

Seeing their leader's victory over the Dreadnaught, several of the officers and all of the members of Byron's personal troupe gave out a vicious, ear-splitting roar of triumph. The minions of Richard Vandross, pierced to their hearts by that sound, turned tail and took flight back towards the safety of Mount Toane.

"Shall we follow them," Thaddeus Viper shouted across the battlefield to Byron.

The Dread Knight looked up at the old reformed bandit, and saw that the aging Human had not fared well in the skirmish, though being alive still was better than many. A hole the size of a gold coin had been punched through his right forearm, his hair and face held soot and singe marks from Pyromancy, and a black, ashen mark of the Pit lay across his bare chest.

It was a demonic power that Byron was very familiar with: the Black Mark, an inversion of the Holy Blast Paladin spell, had destroyed his armor. Had Viper gone into battle without his standard mirthral chain armor, he surely would be among the casualties. Frail and old as he was, he shouldn't even be on the field of battle.

"No," Byron called out, sheathing the Morning Glory across his back and visually doing a brief status check on his companions. Morek Rockmight appeared to have unleashed a great deal of aggravation at his failure to take down the Dreadnaught on a collection of Illeck, and he sat amid a circle of their broken bodies, smoking a pipe of tobacco. His right arm looked somewhat crooked.

Shoryu and Ellen were holding one another for comfort and joy at having survived yet another assault. And the stalwart Paladin James Hayes was applying his healing magics to several wounded men not twenty yards away.

"For now we wait. We execute our original plan, tonight."

Byron lowered his voice. "Viper, I don't think you should join in the assault. You are already laid bare." Byron put one heavy hand on Viper's shoulder.

The old man winced a little, and Byron eased the weight of his armored hand off. Viper opened his eyes and grinned wryly, patting the undead warrior's hand and nodding, acquiescing to Byron's request.

"Perhaps you are right, young man." He sat with his legs crossed, stretching out his arms behind him for support. A loud pop came from his hip, and once again he winced with pain, much more obviously this time. "Damnation! Popped my hip out of place. I'm getting too old for this shit," he said with a chuckle, and waved off Byron's offered hand of help. "No, I think I'll sit here a while. Good master Morek," he called over to the Dwarven Boxer, who exhaled a plume of smoke and looked over at the old man with a cocked eyebrow. "Mind sharing some of that with an old timer?"

Morek walked over to share a smoke with Thaddeus Viper.

"Mi'lord," a young Lizardman shouted as he charged over to Byron, saluting him as soon as he stopped. Byron returned the motion, and turned to face the young reptile. "Lord Bael gives his congratulations on your victory over the Dreadnaught. He wishes to take council with you sssstraight away, my lord." The young warrior bowed deeply.

Byron motioned for the youth to go ahead of him, and he turned to address his company.

"I'll be right back, so don't go anywhere. I need you four," he said quietly, lowering his eyes from them. A pang of guilt raced up from his stomach to his heart. He had formed a bond with his traveling companions, one that had sustained him throughout the long ordeal of battling against Richard Vandross and his intentions. The Dread Knight wanted to spend some time with them all before they rushed Mount Toane for the assault.

After all, if things went according to plan, he had less than a day to live.

* * * *

Vilec Roak sent a blast of vitriol from the end of his outstretched fingers into the wall of the mages' hall. Mountain gut rock exploded in a shower of stones and pebbles. The Shadowbeast Prime's fury unchecked as he sent it out once again, this time striking a Human Q Mage in the face, melting his head into a bleeding neck stump.

"Hellfire! Mighty fuck and damnation," he screamed. He had personally aided in the construction of the Dreadnaught for the last week, and had kept it carefully concealed near the entrance of Mount Toane, hoping to spring it on the unsuspecting Dread Knight and his forces and have it deal a heavy blow to their numbers. He had watched from a Mage's Eye spell from above the battlefield, and had witnessed his offensive turn to dust as the Dread Knight destroyed the construct. He had almost made it seem easy, though he had suffered an injury to his legs.

And where had Colonel Molis been all this while? The half-breed had slipped back into the mountain fortress after the defenders of Mount Toane had retreated, regrouping and taking themselves for the most part back inside the mountain tunnels and caverns. The army of Ja-Wen had not done quite so well as Byron's forces, but they too had turned their attackers aside, leaving things a total mess for Vilec Roak to clean up. So here he stood, his demonic rage unchecked as he scolded the mages who had served as officers on the front lines, letting them know that anymore foul-ups meant their inevitable doom. He had just demonstrated that point rather well, though he hadn't intended to. Still, it had proved an effective way of getting the message across, regardless of his purpose.

Now, however, he had to go up several flights of earthen stairs to the section of the mountain where the remaining Khan warriors and shaman had taken up residence. All had gone out to serve in the assault, and only about half had returned. But none had chosen to stay outside.

As Roak hurried up the stairs, taking them two and three at a time where he could, he could hear the anger in the tiger-men's voices. While he could easily intimidate the Human and Illeck mages, he would not have so easy a time with these beasts.

Khan were nothing if not tenacious and ruthless. Those very qualities had made them among the best choices for foot soldiers in Vandross's cause, and their thirst for power had brought them easily under the warlock's influence. However, Roak suspected that they had become more and more aware of the sorcery that had tricked them into staying with the cause when so many of their comrades had fallen in combat. The power of the Orbs of Eden's Serpent had let Vandross see into their heart as a whole, and manipulate them with promises of territory and authority.

Continued failure and countless deaths had made that manipulation a whole other matter.

The feel of the mountain rock softened the higher up Roak ascended. The chambers began to take on a more hill region feel underfoot, something the Khan had taken to rather well, considering their ages-long residence in the

Allenian Hills region. Some of the chambers up this high even had holes in the outside of the mountain, allowing sunlight through the mountain face. The taste of the air held a metallic, blood-filled quality, and as Vilec Roak strode through the hallways into the enormous cavern where the Khan resided, he saw that they were stripping off their crimson-stained uniform tunics and casting them aside.

"And what do you think you're all doing?" he growled. He manipulated the shadows of the room, pooled them to his own body to give himself the appearance of greater mass and strength. A mere parlor trick, he knew, but this was a demon's parlor trick, not easily recognized by such lowly intellects as these.

The Khan seemed slightly put off for a moment; the optical illusion had done the trick, for now.

"We are leaving," one of the older Khan said, his fur matted with blood and patches of gray showing through the typically vibrant orange and black. His left arm was resting in a makeshift sling, bone protruding through the bandaging at the elbow.

A serious injury, Roak thought, yet still this elder has the strength of will to move and be rebellious. *I shall have to make an example of him.*

"A group detached during the battle on the front, and they have likely begun their trip back to our glorious hills," he groaned, his injured arm moved gingerly to pull off his uniform tunic. "We intend to join them, dark one," he roared as Vilec Roak took a step forward.

The Shadowbeast was stunned still for a moment; the fire in those dark eyes of the elder Khan, the sheer willpower it must have taken for the old man to draw his battle axe in his left hand as he shouted. It had been unwise to try to fool these creatures into helping them, he suddenly realized. Vandross at the very least should have kept Lieutenant Amon at Mount Toane. That proud Chieftain had at least possessed a sense of duty, and hadn't questioned orders. Now, he was staring at a chamber with nearly one hundred of these beasts, all of them glaring murderously at him.

Yet, that served as a double-edged sword, he thought with a wide and razor-filled grin. Without the proudest of their numbers among them, would they have the spine to stand against him? Was not this stare-down and banter a sign of their inability to actually do anything?

He decided to test the Khan, and whipped his left arm out toward the old man, stretching the fabric of his body and forming a spear with it. With blinding speed he struck at the old Khan, was sure that he would pierce the tiger-man's heart.

But as the appendage raced faster than the mortal eye could see toward the elder, a figure dropped from somewhere above and knocked the offending weapon aside, sending it hurling back into Roak's body harmlessly.

The figure stretched as it stood, sword in hand, staying in front of the Khan. It was Colonel Molis.

"How dare you, Colonel," Roak spat with manic rage. His eyes flared with yellow, demonic light. He decided to undo the restraints that Vandross had placed on him when he had been summoned: after all, he had no more need of a power checking system.

Vilec Roak stretched and grew his body to twice its normal size, towering now over the assembled Khan and the strange, cold visage of the half-breed. Purple and red swirls of power raced along Roak's arms, his talons extending into fine scythes, their edges gleaming in the little bit of sunlight that came into the chamber. "You do not know your place," Roak's voice boomed, echoing off the walls of the cavern, grating on the nerves of every mortal being in the room.

He had thought over his earlier wound, and had managed to finally put it aside. After all, he had basically been ambushed by the half-breed. Such a defeat would not be suffered again, surely. Fear is not a part of a demon's natural makeup.

No longer did he care about the nature of Molis's demonic heritage. He had stepped far beyond his station yet again. "You have forgotten the chain of command, both in service to lord Vandross, and in the Pit. You are only a half-demon."

"Let them go." Molis's voice was level and calm, devoid of emotion. The half-demon removed his helmet for the first time in Roak's presence, and all assembled saw the coils of black, snake-like flesh that squirmed over his head. Only demons of status could retain those coils on the mortal plane, as they were an indication of rank in the seven Hells. Six of them wriggled in the air around Molis's head.

Vilec Roak stutter-stepped back, mortally afraid of this half-fiend once more.

"They have no desire to serve the purposes of the warlock any further. I do not intend to let there be any unnecessary bloodshed," Molis droned, his tone still cold and devoid of inflection. His voice barely carried to Roak's ears, but the shocked Shadowbeast could very well have been mouth-to-ear with the half-demon. "So you shall let them leave, now."

The Khan assembled behind Molis had stopped moving, entranced by the powerful aura radiating from Molis. He half turned away from Roak, catching the eyes of a strong, middle-aged warrior with his own crimson eyes. "You there. What is your name, good man?"

The Khan stammered for a moment.

"Larkun, sir. Larkun Fleshsunderer," the Khan pronounced proudly, puffing out his already barrel-like chest.

"Larkun," Molis said, seeming to test the word on his tongue. "Respect your elders. Help this veteran pack his things. Understood?"

Without another word, the younger tiger-man swept over and helped the injured elder assemble his things.

"These lowly dogs aren't going anywhere," Roak bellowed, having regained his sense of control. It was odd, he thought. As soon as those eyes had ceased to meet his own, he felt liberated, as though invisible shackles had been undone from his wrists and throat. "Barrac Minak Mooden," he shrieked, sweeping his huge left hand in front of him and unleashing a wave of pitch-black energy toward Molis and the Khan warriors.

Molis had only a split-second to react, and he hadn't in truth expected such a powerful demon spell to be cast at him. Unable to do much of anything else without a counter-spell readied, the half-demon lunged forward, arms crossed in front of his face.

As the spell made contact with his armor, an explosion of purple light erupted on Molis's forearms, and he was sent flying into the wall behind the Khan warriors. He slid slowly down the wall, grunting with agony as he hit the floor.

The Khan nearest to him helped prop him on his feet, asking feverishly if he wanted their help. The younger ones seemed the most eager to fight, but Molis smiled and wiped his mouth, blood coming away on his hand.

"No, I shall dispatch this devil on my own. Continue to make your preparations for departure." *One-on-one combat*, he thought. *That was what I had lived for as a mortal man.* His vorpal blade in hand, Molis dashed across the chamber to Roak, who had begun to follow his enemy as he swept a handful of Khan Knights and Soldiers aside.

As Molis approached his target, he spared those men and women a cursory glance.

No fatalities—good.

As Vilec Roak swung a massive set of claws down at him, Molis took to the air, and brought his blade sweeping across Roak's swollen chest.

Roak's cry of pain shook the very mountain itself, but he resumed the attack.

With his left hand, Molis blocked the kick that the Shadowbeast leveled at him, pushing the offending foot with all of his considerable strength.

Sending Roak into a spin, Molis once again leapt up, landing squarely on the Shadowbeast General's shoulders. "Die," he muttered, his tone once again cold and devoid of feeling.

He gripped his sword in both hands and plunged it into the base of Roak's skull, sending tremors down through the giant demon.

"Musodeken Mihai Enyacko," Molis conjured as he twisted the blade.

Two spiders of green energy spilled from Molis's mouth and crawled lightning-quick into the open wound.

Molis jumped again, leaving the sword in the stricken Shadowbeast's head as Roak spun on him. "Fool," Roak groaned as he cackled with demonic humor. "Did you think a stab to the head could finish m-" he started, but stopped as he faced Molis. Roak's enormous, gimlet eyes went wide, and his body quivered and shook as it reduced back down to the size of a man. His arms exploded in a shower of meat and blue blood, the oxygen having been taken from his entire body by the Wraith Spiders that Molis had summoned and sent into his body. As they severed the tendons and muscles from the bones, the ungodly magical arachnids drained the oxygen and demonic power holding Roak together from him, leaving him a wasted, limbless corpse when they were finished.

Without another word, Vilec Roak's demonic soul was sent hurtling back into the Pit.

Molis casually removed his vorpal blade from the smoking husk of Vilec Roak's body. He turned back to the stunned Khan, who had nearly finished packing. Sheathing the blade, Molis approached the injured elder. "Will you be all right until your return to the Allenians?" he asked, his voice suddenly Human in nature, and filled with genuine concern.

The Khan were once again left almost speechless.

"I'll be just fine," the elder said, catching his voice again. "I may be old, and I may not be the purest soul, but I owe you a great deal, Colonel. I only wish my boy was here," he said, hefting up his rucksack with his good arm.

The rest of the Khan all lowered their heads for a moment in respect to Molis, as well as in response with the old Khan's statement.

"And who is your son," Molis asked, helping the old man put his battle axe back in its holding loop.

"Tiberious Amon," the old man said, his voice a sorrowed whisper. "I am Rexus Amon, his father. But my son was sent into a foolish battle by the warlock, and now, he is dead."

"Was his body ever recovered?" He had seen the tiger-man only the day before, when he had decided to see how the rest of the realm was dealing with the war raging here at Mount Toane. Amon had been riding on a horse with a tall, noble-looking Wererat, if their kind could ever be described as such.

The old man seemed to understand the implied question, the underlying statement that Molis kept cleverly concealed. He shook his head, and gave the half-demon a heart-felt smile of his own.

"If ever you are in the Allenians," said Larkun from the front of his pack. "We shall offer you what we can. It is the least we can do. I know that sounds like the words of a Simpa, but I mean it." The middle-aged warrior spit the word *Simpa*.

The werelions were the Khan's most hated enemies, and their rivals for control of the Allenian region. Most Khan tribes were not seen as having honor, or a sense of duty. And in truth, Larkun's tribe had been one such pack. However, seeing Tiberious Amon in command, and the way this half-demon had defended them and treated them with respect and honor, Larkun was beginning to question the ways of his particular tribe of Khan. There would be changes when he and his kinsmen returned to the Allenians. Big changes.

"I shall consider that an honor," Molis said, bowing deeply to the group. "Now, you should make good your escape. I shall accompany you outside, so that there can be no misunderstandings. We shall be stopped, I am certain, by Byron Aixler's forces," he said, turning about and leading the way.

"Who is Byron Aixler," one of the young warriors asked from the back of the moving platoon. "We know only of a Dread Knight by the name Byron, and he is Byron of Sidius."

"He is of Sidius no longer," Molis whispered, his voice carrying softly to the back rows of the Khan. "Or haven't you noticed which side of this conflict he stands on?" Without another word spoken among them, Colonel Molis led the Khan down the twisting tunnels and stairwells, and out into the light of day.

* * * *

Byron marched like the embodiment of death through the wounded and dead bodies lying about the fields and hills. The young Lizardman had waited for the Dread Knight to catch up with him, and together they walked toward the west, where Bael and his troops surrounded a rather large pack of Khan, and a single man in silver armor.

As Byron approached within earshot of the familiar half-demon, he laughed aloud and greeted him.

"Colonel Molis, you never cease to amaze me," he said, embracing the half-demon as soon as he was within arms' reach.

Bael took a step back, clearly surprised that this creature with the serpentine head attachments was the turncoat Colonel.

Molis returned the embrace, much to Byron's pleasant surprise, and the two men stood like that for a long minute, patting each other on the backs of their armors.

Pulling away from the half-demon who had once been his best ally, Byron surveyed the Khan behind him. "Heading home, are you?" he asked the Khan pack, who all nodded in unison. "Very good. Bael," he turned to face the Lizardman warrior. "Let them pass. These gentlemen and warrior women would like to go home, I believe. Back to their beloved hills."

Shouts of agreement rose up from the Khan ranks, and Bael smiled ruefully.

"Well, I suppose there isn't much I can do to change your mind about that," Bael said. "Break the chain," he hollered

The reptilian troops parted, breaking their circle around the marching Khan.

They moved as one group, heading away and off into the distance.

Within minutes, they had almost marched double-time out of sight. Byron made note of the sun's progress toward the horizon. It would be nightfall in a couple of hours.

"What are your orders now, mighty Byron," Bael asked, coming to attention.

"Hold the line, and be ready to take command when I head in through the tunnel, as planned," Byron said, speaking rapidly now as he turned away. "Molis, are you going to stay with us until then? Or have you decided to leave as well?"

"I must return inside the mountain for an hour or so," Molis said. "I have a resignation to formally submit, and some news to give Richard Vandross about his great General."

Byron turned and looked at Molis's wicked smile, an eerie green light gleaming from within his throat.

"You mean the one named Vilec Roak? What happened to him? Did he flee for fear of his accursed life?"

Molis laughed the cackle of the damned, a piercing chuckle that left Byron feeling slightly uneasy. True, half of the soul of this man belonged once to his friend, but the other half was still that of a demon from the Pit.

"No, good Byron. I had to slay him in order to secure the Khan's defection. A minor setback of time, of course, but satisfying nevertheless. Ha ha ha ha haa!" Colonel Molis donned his helmet again, drawing it from the air itself, and placing it on his deformed head. "I shall see you when the sun is about to set. Tonight shall be the end of it all, Byron Aixler."

As Byron turned to reply, the half-demon was nowhere to be found.

* * * *

Richard Vandross had been sleeping the sleep of the dead, a dreamless, empty void of darkness serving to let him rest properly. Without the meetings with the Orbs of Eden's Serpent' manifestations, he awoke well rested and feeling refreshed, slinging his legs over the edge of his bed. He couldn't remember having made it all the way to his resting chamber, but apparently he had, and his back seemed to silently thank him for that.

The one-eyed warlock stretched his arms and legs, and stood tall in the middle of his chamber. What sort of feeling would he have hundreds of years from now, when he awoke from the Eternal Rest? He felt sure it would be damned good, and require a whole day's worth of stretches.

Something tingled in his chest, and the warlock immediately sensed a great foreboding, as though while he had slept, his entire world had come crashing down around his ears. Panic flooded his psyche, the dam of confidence and assuredness in his own power and control bursting in a violent cacophony of internal explosions.

Muttering almost too fast to properly execute the spell, he cast a Mage's Eye over the outside of Mount Toane, and saw to his dismay that Roak had gone on the offensive with the armies of Byron and Ja-Wen. His perimeter forces had been laid waste. Only a handful of Greenskins and Shadowbeasts remained to guard the outer walls of the earthen fortress. The Dreadnaught that his General had prided himself so much in making lay in a heap atop the hillcrest where a wall of Byron's men and women stood guard.

Hundreds of the Dread Knight's troops lay in heaps of death, but makeshift mass burial trenches were already being filled. Foolish, mortal sentimentality, he thought, smiling despite the appearance of the situation. It mattered not, in the long run, that his outer defenses had been dealt a hefty blow. The interior of Mount Toane crawled with demons, Orcs and Ogres, mages of several Races, and the strange but definitely deadly half-breed Colonel Molis. Magical traps had been laid throughout the tunnels and corridors, set in the chambers and caverns to target only those forces that had not pledged allegiance to Vandross.

He threw open the door of his chamber and stalked out into the tunnels of the fortress.

Demons and Greenskins saluted him as he passed by them, all of his troops having taken up positions after the assault on the hilltop outside. Yet he sensed that there were was a large number of men missing, and he suddenly realized that as he had passed through several tunnels and poked his head into a handful of caverns, that he hadn't spotted a single Khan. Then again, he thought with a shrug of his shoulders, they liked to stay in the upper reaches of the mountain. He had to admit to himself that aside from the demons, they proved to be the most stalwart of his soldiers. They all possessed a will to fight and kill that let them battle until all but their arms and head had been removed from their bodies. Only magic seemed to be an effective way of doing away with one, and even then, the tenacious tiger-men could survive long enough to do in their killers.

Odd, he thought as he stopped suddenly in a tunnel along the western side of the mountain. Why am I thinking so much about them? Once again that sense of impending doom settled on his heart heavily, a boulder that weighed more than he could judge by strength of muscle alone.

Feeling rushed and dreadful, he sprinted down the corridors to the rock stairwell that would lead him up to the cavern that the Khan had chosen to stay in. Finally, he ran headlong into a bumbling Ogre, who had himself been running down the stairs to find him.

As Vandross picked himself up off the stone floor, he grabbed the huge Greenskin by the shirt, pulling him down to meet Vandross eye to eye. Crimson light swelled behind his eye patch as he growled at the Ogre. "What's wrong?"

The mighty Greenskin warrior thrashed a moment, his eyes flooded with mortal fear.

"You're not gonna want to go up there," the Ogre, a Sergeant by the number of his stripes, moaned fearfully.

"And why, not?" Black power surging through his arms as he levitated the Ogre over the steps and away from him.

"You don't wanna see it, lord," the Ogre moaned like a wounded child.

Vandross hurled him down the stairs, crashing him into the wall without killing him. He had a little self-control, but he knew that if his fears were confirmed by the Greenskin, he would have slain him without a second's thought. Taking the steps three at a time now, Vandross mentally said to Hells with it, and levitated his way up, finally arriving in the Khan chamber.

He stood in stunned silence, looking at the mostly empty room, and the single, silver clad creature standing there with what appeared to be a bundle of black cloth in his hand.

Colonel Molis, thought Vandross with a visible shudder. He had never known much about the half-demon, and had thought him only a potential nuisance at best. Now, however, the creature radiated an aura that nearly equaled that of his hated enemy, Byron of Sidius.

"What are you doing here, Colonel?" Vandross asked in a harsh whisper, keeping the black power from the stairwell at the ready. "I demand an explanation. I own you, and you will give answer to my questions. Where are the Khan? And what is that that you're holding," he said, pointing a single finger, wrapped in magic, at the cloth in Molis's hand.

"The Khan have left," Molis said, his tone level. "And I believe this belongs to you." The half-breed hefted the cloth-like material at Vandross.

As it landed in a heap at his feet, the warlock realized with a sudden and violent shock to his heart that it had been the body of Vilec Roak.

"What have you done?" He looked up at Molis with murder in his eye. Crimson fury blazed from behind his eye patch, nearly destroying the cloth. "What have you done?" he screamed, shaking the entire mountain as Vilec Roak had done merely an hour before.

"The Khan wished to leave. Your General sought to stop them by force. I intervened," the half-demon stated coolly, taking a few slow steps forward.

Vandross raised a barrier of hellfire between the two of them with a flicker of his wrist, his rage threatening to explode from his just-rested body. He had to keep it in check, he knew; he had to conserve his power for his meeting with Byron of Sidius. Despite all of his traps and minions, the warlock knew instinctively that the Dread Knight would find his way to him. And when that time came, he wanted to have all of his power available to bear down on the undead warrior and utterly crush him. He could not afford a confrontation with this traitor.

"You intervened by slaying my General? You are a fool, turncoat," Vandross said coyly, gaining confidence from the fact that Molis had ceased his approach. Demons from the pit had no fear of hellfire, for it was part of their natural environment, but this freak was only half-blooded. The wall of flames would burn him asunder. "What is your intention now? Do you plan to attack me? You know you cannot. I brought your demon soul to earth. I likely provided you with the mortal body you inhabit." He brought more magic to his available arsenal. He was tensed, readied. Surely a small release of power would be enough to do away with this meddlesome beast.

"I have no intention of fighting you. As you have said before, the binding laws of the magic you used to bring me to the mortal coil forbid such a direct assault." The half-demon's voice remained emotionless and cold. It was the voice of one who was trying to keep himself in check, Vandross noticed. But there was also the heft of truth in those words—though a traitor, Molis did not intend to fight against the warlock. He obviously had other plans that had nothing to do with the conflict here between the warlock and the Dread Knight. There was the soft clink of metal touching metal from the other side of the wall of hellfire.

Two eagle-shaped pins came over the wall and landed to the warlock's left. "Those also belong to you. I have no need for them anymore."

"Mark my words, freak," Vandross shouted in fury. "When I am through with the Dread Knight, I am coming for you. There are no words in the mortal tongues that can describe the agony I shall visit upon your head and your soul." Vandross let his power subside. This conversation, he could sense, was nearing its end.

"It shall not come to that," Molis proclaimed, a hint of pride in his tone now. "Byron Aixler is going to cut you down."

Vandross sensed Molis move outside of the mountain, through the earthen walls, and out of his life.

* * * *

Sunset cast a shade of orange and purple flames across the evening sky. As Byron admired the image, he wondered if he would ever be graced with such a vision again. The heavy winds that had kicked up carried on their drifts the scent of wildflowers, and he breathed deeply of the sweet fragrance, remembering the orchards and flower gardens that his wife had cared for and plucked from.

"I'll be coming home soon, dear," he whispered to the wind, unsure if those words held any semblance of truth. Was not his soul damned for the atrocities he had committed as Byron of Sidius? Shoryu had argued against that thought not many days ago, as they had finished their march to Mount Toane.

"Your soul had been imprisoned in your very body," Shoryu had reasoned. "You had no control of your actions. And when you did gain control, once, did you not tell me that you refused the warlock's orders?"

That much had been true, Byron thought. But to have a soul of such weakness told him that he was doomed for the Pit. Best to just do what good he could before his inevitable demise, and pray that his eternal torment would be lessened by what he had tried to accomplish here.

Byron and his company now stood with a platoon of one hundred and ten men, the best that the armies of the Dread Knight and the army of Ja-Wen had to offer. Most were enlisted men, those that had not wanted to take command, though they had been offered officers' posts.

Their position was on the northern side of the mountain, where no obvious entrance could be found. Bael had remained on the hilltop on the southern front of the mountain, ready to lead the remaining forces of the Dread Knight and Ja-Wen into the mountain proper. Byron knew as well as the Lizardman that many thousands would perish inside the mountain. Traps would be tripped, ambushes launched, and units would be separated.

Despite being informed of such facts, all the soldiers had remained, determined to rid their lands of the threat of the warlock. Four words echoed in Byron's mind as he thought of their devotion to his cause: *No matter the cost.*

Before Morek Rockmight could open his mouth to inquire as to the whereabouts of their half-demon ally and guide, Molis appeared before them all, his magical bubble ruptured by will.

Morek took a hasty step back. "Crikey, couldn't just walk up to us loik normal folk, eh?"

The half-demon smiled in response. "We have only a short time before somebody notices something amiss," Molis said, his voice rushed and filled with the emotions he had been suppressing. "We can wait no longer. "

Byron wordlessly motioned the platoon to form ranks, and the men and women, warriors and sorcerers, assembled themselves in five rows, twenty deep save one column of thirty.

Moving as swiftly and silently as their equipment allowed, the raiding party moved forward, Byron and his companions in a loose, scattered formation, as Molis guided them towards a single maple tree that grew some fifty yards from the mountain face.

As they approached, Molis spoke several words of power, and the tree uprooted and moved aside, a panel of rock sliding with it to reveal a single stone stairwell. Molis stopped and stood to one side of the entrance. Byron stopped, and the whole unit came to a halt with him.

"You're not coming, are you?" he asked Molis, more a statement of fact than a question. He did not look at the half-demon as he spoke, for fear that his memories of the man Molis had once been would take control, and he would begin to beg the man to join him.

"No, I'm afraid I have business elsewhere. You alone are fated to do battle with the warlock Richard Vandross." Molis's voice was once again flat and cold.

"Well then, I guess I'll see you on the other side," Byron said softly.

"No, you won't." A hint of sadness lingered in Molis's almost emotionless tone. "We are headed in opposite directions. I shall ne'er see you again. It has been good knowing and serving with you, mighty Byron Aixler."

"Likewise, Edgar Cesar." Byron held his head up and looking Molis in the eyes one final time. He saw there, in the darkness of the helmet, a pair of Human eyes. A moment later, they were gone, turned back into the harsh and feral orbs of a demon.

Shoryu rubbed the back of his head awkwardly, and James Hayes smiled grimly as he peered down into the darkness of the stairwell.

Silent as the shadow of Death, Byron cast a ward of silent movement on the entire platoon, ensuring their safe journey through the lower levels of Mount Toane. Without glancing back, he led the noble men and women of Tamalaria down into darkness. The sun had just set on his back for the final time.

A single tear ran down his skull. Another down Molis's cheek.

* * * *

Bael waited for the signal from Molis to make good the attack on the mountain fortress. The sun had just gone down past the horizon in the west, and the spring-loaded nerves in his body tensed. In the beginning of the mad warlock's quest for power, Bael had been his ally, unwittingly under his charismatic spell.

Having been freed from the shackles of that odd magic, the Lizardman took some time to think over why exactly he had agreed to join Vandross in the first place. Although he still believed in the need for a homeland that would accept lizardmen and greenskins, he couldn't think why he had believed Vandross's claims. Come to think of it, he mused as he awaited the half-demon's signal, he couldn't ever remember that first encounter with the warlock.

That mattered little now in light of the situation, though. The last streaks of vibrant, flaming orange winked out of the sky as the pale crescent moon loomed out from its hiding place. The eternal, futile hunt, he thought. "Fliego chasing Lunatis, and Lunatis chasing Fliego," he whispered, using his people's names for the sacred sun god and moon goddess. He didn't believe in their divinity, of course. They were just there, he reasoned, probably so far up in the sky that no bird or beast could ever hope to touch them.

At that moment, he looked down towards the direction that the Dread Knight and his company had gone, and saw the stark figure in silver armor raise a clenched fist from astride his mount. Molis, it appeared, would not be joining in the fun. Oh well, Bael mused. Perhaps I shall meet him again some day.

"Form, legions," he shouted.

Every man and woman in the assembled armies of the Elven Kingdom, Desanadron, the northwestern mountains, the Port of Arcade and Ja-Wen began their slow and steady march, formed into platoons of one hundred men apiece. Each platoon was one of seven or eight in a legion, each legion commanded by the highest ranked or most experienced member of the platoons that comprised it. Some positions had been shifted at Bael's request, and nobody had any complaints. Nobody disobeyed the orders they were given; everybody present, all twenty-three thousand, were on the same page.

To Bael, who had served for most of his life as a soldier in some capacity, it was a glorious, breath-taking sight.

Each legion waited its turn, falling behind the one that came before. The entrance to Mount Toane would only allow a maximum of fifteen or sixteen men into the bottlenecked entrance. Scores of traps and ambushes surely awaited them, and Bael knew about Vandross's ability to teleport mortal men en masse to different, far away locations. Many of the legions would most likely begin their battle inside of Mount Toane, only to find themselves doing battle with the warlock's forces in the dangerous terrain of someplace like the Desperation, the great desert of the southeast. All of the officers had been informed of such perils, and given advice by the Lizardman warrior concerning what to do should such a thing occur. They were to engage their enemies, regardless of where they were placed. If they emerged victorious, he said, the legion or platoon was to disband and head for their homelands. There would be no long marches back, Bael had advised. The battle would already be decided by then.

The repugnant odor of magic filled his lungs as he strode along at the front of the army, flanked on both sides by his own platoon of Lizardmen, Elves and Minotaurs. Only one hundred yards away, the mouth of Mount Toane seemed to yawn widely to accept its victims as food for its wicked inhabitants to break down and digest. The earthen fortress had a reputation that would outlive anybody present, Bael thought. There were good reasons for that.

"Sssir," one of his kinsmen said aloud as they found themselves within fifty yards of the entrance. There were no lights in that gaping void, and without any sunlight to repel them, Shadowbeasts could already be coming at them.

Bael had spent enough time among their kind, however, to know how to spot their barely discernable movements. He would not be tricked by the demons.

"What is it Renard," he asked, not looking away from that monolithic entrance to the fortress.

"Ssssir, the reek of much magic issss here, my tongue can ssssssmell it," the other officer said, his bonemeld armor reflecting a little of the moonlight present. Ogre bones had been used to make the armor, Bael knew, because he had had a thousand of the torso armors commissioned when he decided to aid Byron at Mount Toane. Few Ogres actually had to die for this to be accomplished—Lizardmen were known as some of the best bonemelders of all the Races. Only the Draconus, the dragon-men, could hold a candle to their skill.

Lizardman villages kept the bones of all of their enemies when they could strip the corpses without having to worry about being attacked. Ogre bones made some of the toughest armor they could fashion, and so every Lizardman village in the southwest and south-central plains and forests had taken their stores of the bones and went to work. Though usually not very chummy with one another, the various tribes of the Lizardman Race had come together for a common cause—a lowly Human had wreaked havoc on their lands, and they weren't about to have any of that.

"I am aware of the magical traps, Renard, thank you."

"Do you think one of our shaman can deal with them," the younger, less experienced warrior asked with heart-felt interest.

"I am not entirely certain," Bael confided to Renard quietly, so as not to demoralize any of the troops. "That is why our platoon is not completely comprised of our proud species, Renard. The Elves are quite handy as pertains to the arcane arts of sorcery. Our nature magics might not be enough to handle the dismantling of complex magical pitfalls. And you never know." He kept his eyes on the entrance that now loomed only a dozen or so yards forward.

Still no light could be seen within the demesne of the fortress. "Disabling one of the spell traps might trigger another, more powerful one. When the scent is at its strongest, we shall be at our closest to it, if not already triggering it. I shall take suggestions at that juncture insofar as what we should do about it."

He stopped the progress of the army once more, looking up into the darkness of the mountain's gaping maw. "For now, we shall have to trust our fates to the gods."

Drawing his war axe and holding it high, he gave out a courageous war cry, the sound echoed by every single warrior and mage that opposed Richard Vandross.

Forcing his way ahead, Bael felt as if he had walked headlong into a wall of slick, wet cloth.

Hundreds of yellow, gimlet eyes blinked in the entryway to the mountain fortress, fifty feet high. Hundreds of Shadowbeasts had linked their black, horrid bodies together, strands of dark vitriol lashed around wrists to stretch their blasphemous forms and hold them together. All in a split second's time, Bael felt the creature in front of him, jumped back, and shouted a warning to those closest to him.

The warning came out too late, as the demons had already descended and split apart, charging into the midst of the free mortal forces.

Blood sprayed in all directions as Shadowbeasts tore through armor plating and chain mail with claws as black as night.

Nothing could have prepared Bael for such a surprise attack. The stench of magic had been a ruse, and nothing more. As soon as the Shadowbeasts had parted to attack the first platoon under his direct command, the scent had dissipated.

Wielding his axe like a shield, Bael deflected blow after blow from all sides, keeping his head level and his manner calm and defensive. With so many of the creatures swirling around him, if he took the opportunity to strike he would be cut down without fail.

For the moment, he had to pull back and close the gap between himself and his platoon.

Risking a quick glance to his left, he saw that Renard had already been slain, his eyes smoldering holes where some form of black demon magic had burrowed into his head. "Fall back," Bael shouted, and his orders immediately took hold.

The front lines of his platoon cautiously withdrew, and the entire army's progress came to a halt.

"Severus maneuver, now," he shouted, throwing caution to the wind as he turned his back on his attackers and sprinted away for cover. As soon as the command echoed back through the ranks of the first platoon, the thirty archers in the second platoon loosed a wall of arrows down on the approaching Shadowbeasts. Taking careful and precise aim, they let their arrows fall as close as three feet from Bael's back leg as he tucked and rolled into the midst of his first row of men.

Even without the benefit of magic to enhance the destructive potential of the wooden and metal shafts, the missiles that flew into the oncoming Shadowbeasts struck their targets dead. Five separate volleys of thirty arrows rained down on them, turning the smarter and more cautious demons back into the relative safety of the mountain's tunnels and catacombs. Bael had fallen for the trap, but luckily, he had taken the time for several days of the march to Mount Toane to go over combat tactics and maneuvers with the head officers of the army. He hadn't had time to go over such things with Ja-Wen's forces, and had relegated the duty of tactical striking to their head officer, a Commander Argent of the Ja-Wen People's Army. Argent was a stout but capable Sidalis, or mutant as they were commonly called. With the power to bend space around and within his own body, the orange-skinned humanoid had used his strange gift for the betterment of the people of his fair city. And the man was a technical and tactical whiz, so Bael didn't feel the need to worry about Ja-Wen's troops, be they warrior or mage Class.

Ja-Wen's forces, however, also had another advantage in their favor; the Ninjas. Classified as thief-types, the Ninja clan Ryoken had signed on with the Ja-Wen army as the city's estates had served as their training grounds for generations.

Although highly perturbed by the arrangement, Argent had to go along with the city's Governor when the woman had declared that she would contract their services. Ninjas lived in the darkness and struck with surgical precision, so having them present in Mount Toane could serve as a sort of 'secret weapon' for Bael. He had let Commander Argent know full well, however, that the Sidalis himself had total control of the Ninja unit. Numbering only six men and five women, they didn't appear to be much more than a group of shadows trailing behind the army. However, once inside, the orange-fleshed Commander fully intended to tell them to "Do what you do best," as he put it.

After the arrows had thinned the shadowbeasts, Bael led the first and second platoon down the long, bottlenecked corridor that served as the main entrance hall to the fortress proper, keeping his eyes peeled for anything out of the ordinary. Flicking his tongue, he smelled the air of the passageway.

Goblins, but how many, he couldn't be certain, waited high up on the eaves and overhangs of the tunnel. Bringing up his fist, he halted the advance of his platoons. Three fingers up: archers, he silently advised in military signal code.

One of the Gaiamancers in his platoon, a burly Human decked out in a dragon scale cloak, began a slow and quiet mantra as the rest of the platoon readied their shields and protective magics.

"Barrag Monesta," the Gaiamancer finally cried, slamming one heavy fist into the ground at his feet. The mountain trembled around them, chunks of earthen stone falling all around the troops. The eaves and overhangs that held the Goblin Hunters gave way, and with shrieks of panic and doom more than two score of the green fleshed little savages came crashing down, hundreds of feet to their demise. As soon as the spell's duration gave way, Bael led the last of the first legion inside.

One step forward, Bael thought. Many more to go.

* * * *

Despite his advantage of being able to see in the darkest of places, it had been Shoryu, not Byron, who had spotted the single trap laid before them. The Cuyotai Hunter had leapt from his place several yards behind the Dread Knight, landing directly in front of him and kicking his legs out from under him. As the Dread Knight landed with a heavy thud and a "Hoomph," Shoryu crawled forward on all fours, standing on the other side of a trip wire set at head height.

Using the most delicate and furtive of movements, he hung a strip of leather over the wire, to show those behind him where the wire was.

Byron crawled forward, joining Shoryu and rubbing his lower back. "You could have just told me."

Shoryu smiled devilishly at him as the others of the platoon crossed on hands and knees beneath the trip wire.

"That wouldn't have been as much fun, though."

Cuyotai, Byron thought silently. *Ever the tricksters and merry-makers of the Races.*

The platoon pressed on, but this time Byron let Shoryu lead the way, his darling wife striding along easily beside the Dread Knight. For nearly an hour they marched forward, silence enveloping them. The aura that Byron had put up around them while they had waited outside allowed their movements and speech to be heard by the members of the platoon, no one else, but still they moved in studied quiet.

Near the end of the hour, before the tunnel came to an intersection, Ellen spoke softly to the Dread Knight.

"I must thank you once again, my friend," she said to him as she gazed into his small, white pinprick lights.

He tried to mimic a smile, but once more felt it came off as a grimace.

"Without your appearance in my life, I never would have met my beloved. We Elves hold marriage to be among the most sacred of bonds, second only to our connection with Mother Nature and our various gods. I believe fate brought you and Shoryu to me." She stunned Byron into silence by wrapping her arms around his massive left arm. "I am saddened, however."

"Why," he asked in a hushed whisper, his voice echoing back over the platoon and down the tunnel.

Shoryu looked back and gave him a smile, his livid green eyes mirroring the sorrow in Ellen's tone.

"Because I know that you have told us the truth. When you fell Richard Vandross, you too shall leave the mortal coil. It is your destiny." Her words trailed into the darkness around them.

Byron stood straighter, his heart racing in his chest.

In studied silence, the platoon came to a halt as Shoryu looked down the hallway that they had intersected, sniffing the air with his hypersensitive snout. After a minute, Shoryu continued straight ahead, ignoring the cross section. As they crossed the intersection, Byron returned a small squeeze of Ellen's arms.

"Indeed, it is. But it is something that has been delayed for too long. I must stand before mighty Oun, and receive his judgment. It is something I cannot escape. No mortal can." He released Ellen's arms.

Now wholly silent, the platoon marched on, following the reliable nose of Shoryu Tearfang. Byron thanked Ellen in his mind for her kindness. He would miss them all.

* * * *

The battle of Mount Toane had begun in earnest a few moments later, inside the caverns and catacombs that Bael had led the legions. Already several thousand men had been separated from the main force, having taken a series of turns apart from the course that Bael led them on. There were no traps here, in the set of halls and chambers that his legion and the one behind it had entered. There were only hundreds of Shadowbeasts, other demons, and Greenskins to be dealt with. Steel and magic coursed through the air, and a bloodbath of extreme proportions had begun. Bael himself was thick in the melee, his steel war axe cleaving foe after foe, his plate armor taking blows from blunt, Greenskin maces and cudgels as he dealt with the more deadly Shadowbeasts and apparitions from the Pit.

A heavy blow to the chest knocked him sprawling across the mountain floor, skidding and rolling along the hard, craggy surface.

His axe fallen where he had been struck, the Lizardman Soldier ducked and dodged claw swipes and weapon swings as he made his way back to his weapon and the Troll that had smashed him with its hammer.

Rolling away from an overhead strike, he balled up his left hand and took to the air, delivering an uppercut that would have made Morek Rockmight proud.

Dazed and injured by the mighty blow, the Troll staggered backward, falling on top of a handful of fleeing Goblins and crushing them to death.

Axe in hand again, Bael sprinted to the Troll's massive head, hacking at its exposed throat, once, twice, three times, crimson life spraying his face and chest, running down his front. Hefting the axe high over his head, he gave a mighty roar as he brought the weapon down a fourth and final time, cleaving the spinal cord in the monstrous Troll's neck, severing its head.

No time to revel in such small victories he thought, spinning about to block the incoming claws of a demon that had the appearance of a man bred with a turtle.

As he counter-attacked, the demon spun around, tucking its head and arms into its misshapen shell.

Easy enough to deal with, the Lizardman thought, kicking the legs out from beneath the demon and bringing his axe down through its exposed belly. On and on he fought, leading the legion deeper into the mountain fortress. Leaving thousands of bodies sprawled lifeless on the floor of those chambers and halls, he pressed on. Little did he know that the vengeful, watchful eye of the warlock in command of these creatures saw his every action. Vandross grinned with deepening malice.

"So, you've returned to me, I see," he muttered from high up in the mountain, in his throne room. "Fool," he spat, waving the Mage's Eye aside to peek in at another one. One legion had already triggered the teleportation trick, and Vandross watched as they fought against his minions deep in the Elven Kingdom's forests. All was going rather well for his side of things, the warlock mused.

Though he had suffered nearly three thousand losses within the hour of battle, he didn't mind. There were many, many more where they had come from, and already almost four thousand of Byron's troops had been removed from the mountain by the teleporting magic and by fatalities.

"But where are you, dead one," he muttered aloud, bringing the considerable power at his disposal to bear. He was prepared for the final confrontation, and wasn't going to waste his energy on anyone but the Dread Knight himself. "Why do you not show yourself," he asked, his good eye squinting as it scanned the nearly twenty Mage's Eyes spread throughout the room.

Not a single one of them had captured an image of Byron of Sidius, or the four members that remained of his original party. Were they waiting outside the mountain, biding their time until the main forces of the army had cleared out what they could of the warlock's minions? *No, that wouldn't be appropriate for his style*, Vandross thought with a growl. They were here, somewhere in his mountain retreat.

"My lord," Sergeant Torim said from the entrance to the throne room. The Illeck had been made Vandross's personal respondent after the death of Vilec Roak and the defection of the half-breed Molis. "The second and third Dreadnaughts have been activated, sire. We await your instructions." He smiled broadly with unhidden bloodlust.

Vandross stepped down from his throne, stalking over to the waiting Illeck. Gods he's a pale one, he thought, looking Torim in the face. Paler than most of his kind.

"Teleport one of them to the primary hall," he ordered swiftly. "Units are still pouring in from outside, though few of them are not within the mountain as yet. That shall cut the last of their forces off rather effectively. As for the second one," he said, looking back on the Mage's Eye that showed Bael, his former General. "Have it loosed upon the first battalion. I shall watch that Lizardman's slow and agonizing demise with glee. Have it targeted to his presence as a priority." The warlock looked back at the Illeck. "Did you put that arm on it like you suggested?" He referred to the arm that Tiberious Amon had lost when he had been struck by Selena Bradford's Immolation spell. The limb had been mostly intact, severed by the spell and tossed nearly a hundred miles away, back toward Mount Toane. One of Vandross's scouts had retrieved it, recognizing almost right away the tattoo near the elbow. The mark of a Khan Chieftain. Though Vandross had become fed up with the Khan Lieutenant, he had always admired the man's skill. Attaching it to the third Dreadnaught had been Torim's idea, and Vandross had rewarded him then with the promise of advancement. Once Robin had been dealt with, Torim had been given that advancement.

The Illeck sorcerer nodded. "Of course, my lord. The moment you approved, in point of fact, sire. Are you certain you want it targeted specifically on that man," he asked, pointing to the tiny image of Bael as the Lizardman destroyed yet another demon.

"Yes. Make certain that it is aware of the other threats, but it should only respond to others defensively. It should be made aware that it is only to be offensive with him," Vandross said, moving back to his seat on his throne. "You are dismissed, Torim," he said, once more pouring over the Mage's Eye bubbles.

Where are you? he thought again, gripping the armrests with considerable effort. *Where are you?*

* * * *

Up ahead, finally, a little bit of light. Byron's personal platoon approached the lower levels of the mountain fortress proper. But Byron sensed swaths of magic up ahead, a familiar group of spells. Mage's Eyes, from the feel of them.

"Wait," he called ahead to Shoryu.

The Cuyotai, his wife and companion James Hayes on either side of him, came to a stop.

The Dread Knight's Redemption

A set of roughly shaped steps led up out of the long tunnel to an incomplete barrier at its end. A secret escape route, Byron thought. Most likely made during Tanarak's stay here. Why then hadn't Vandross known to place guards here? Probably because the one-eyed devil had forgotten about it. Or at least its precise location. Some memory of another entrance must have remained to the warlock, because otherwise he wouldn't have bothered to place Mage's Eye spells around the area. Or perhaps, Byron thought with a malicious grin, he's just being paranoid. That showed a smidgen of wisdom on Vandross's part.

The Dread Knight crept up stealthily to the faux stone wall section, peering out as best he could from his limited perspective. "Damn it," he muttered softly, spotting one of the shimmering spots of light up the tunnel a ways from the exit to the left. The tunnel curved gradually upward that way, and he had to ascend the mountain interior to get to Vandross. Already he could sense the warlock's presence a long way up, and he knew that the warlock would spot them the moment they exited the tunnel.

"Are there any Q Mages among the platoon," he asked Hayes as the Paladin came up to take a look for himself.

"I'll go check." Hayes darted through the darkness to the assembled warriors and mages.

The best of the best are here, Byron thought, but we didn't make any sort of list to make sure we had a good variety of Classes. Most of them, he knew, were Soldiers and Knights, with a few Clerics for healing and protective spells. He hadn't been specific about mage Classes he wanted to accompany them.

He looked back and saw Hayes returning with a single middle-aged Half-Elf, his robes already torn and bloodied from the blitz attack on the mountain the night before. That a pure mage like this had survived the onslaught of the Dreadnaught and Vandross's defending forces said volumes of his competency with magic. "Just him, Byron," Hayes said.

"Good. I trust you have knowledge of a counter-spell to a Mage's Eye," he asked the man, who nodded immediately.

"The Mage's Eye can be learned by any sorcerer or sorceress, my lord," the Half-Elf reported in an unusually deep voice for an Elven man. His father must have been the Human of the coupling, Byron thought. Half-Elves tended to be much more like their fathers than their mothers. "It's a very basic spell. I can likely dispose of four or five of them at a crack, sire."

"Excellent." Byron put an arm around the man's shoulder and drew him to the faux barrier. The man immediately looked up to the Mage's Eye that Byron had barely spotted with heavy observation. The man was good.

"I assume you see that one."

"Yes, my lord, but it's very weak. Cast in a hurry, too. The whole structure is sloppier than Hell," he muttered, almost to himself. "I shall neutralize it." He wove arcane symbols of light in front of his face. "Mikon Soo," he whispered, sending out a single stream of white light.

It connected with the Mage's Eye, and both spells were suddenly gone.

Byron tapped a single piece of rock in the fake wall, and it slid silently open. His barrier of silence would soon wear off, he knew, so they had to move swiftly if they were to make any unnoticed progress.

"Stay up front with me and mine," Byron ordered the Half-Elf, who said nothing but prepared another counter-spell as the platoon spilled out into the hallway.

Byron led the ascent, counting the minutes left to them before they were attacked. He knew he wouldn't get to Vandross without a fight, and he drew the Morning Glory in preparation. Free of the darkness and into the fires, he thought.

* * * *

Vandross watched with a detached interest as the Dreadnaught wiped out more legions at the entrance of the mountain. But strength of numbers and the handful of skilled mages in the very last legion to enter the mountain fortress finally proved too much for the deadly construct to deal with.

No matter, he thought, watching another Mage's Eye bubble as half of a legion was swept away from Mount Toane by a teleportation trap. Dozens of men burst into flames as a hellfire trap went off in another part of the mountain, engulfing them completely as demons overran their panicked allies. But then, something curious happened.

Vandross's attention snapped to a Mage's Eye bubble that burst apart and vanished. His gaze locked onto where it had been. Someone had noticed it despite the combat around them, someone with a good sense of magic.

For a moment, Vandross might have dismissed it as a fluke, but when another one went out, he knew for certain that someone was targeting them specifically.

Strange, he thought. None of his troops had been sent to the areas near those ones.

Lining a separate set of tunnels and stairwells, as well as a handful of caverns, those Mage's Eyes had been set in the areas he least expected attack. Before his demise, Vilec Roak had suggested setting them in those areas, in case of a secret attack force.

His heart stopped for a moment; Byron! Of course the Dread Knight would find another way into his mountain abode. No one else among the armies would have the skill or knowledge to stage such an attack. While Vandross had deployed his forces to the most traveled passages and pathways, the Dread Knight was storming toward him through the back.

Thankfully, he admitted begrudgingly, *Vilec Roak left me some defenders on those routes*. To say nothing of the 'special' guard that had been placed in the enormous meeting hall that was connected to the throne room by a single passage. And then there was the matter of the entryway to that meeting hall. The undead could not breach it, and would be held fast in the doorway until the hall's defender was destroyed. And Vandross highly doubted that Byron's company could fell the beast if they had an entire platoon to help them.

Almost as if on cue, the beast stalked into the throne room, dragging its enormous sword along the ground. It made nary a sound itself, the noise of metal scraping along rock the only audible sign that it was even there.

Vandross looked directly at the creature, filled with both an appreciation of it, and a deep disgust. "They are coming, my lordship," the beast said through its thin, slit-like mouth.

The creature was only about five and a half feet in height, with horse-like legs and the upper body of a muscular brute, a mouth filled with ragged teeth gnashing and chomping the air around it. This second mouth lay across the creature's belly, and when struck with magic, the beast would open it and spew out a lump of what appeared to be flesh. This lump would instantly grow to the same size as the beast, identical to it in every way except individual actions and thoughts. And along with it, the freakish blade would be reproduced as well.

A magnificent demon, to be sure, Vandross thought. It could not be harmed by magic, and Vandross himself had tested the demon's skill with a blade. The beast wielded its enormous weapon with skill and savage strength, the sort of might that only demons were capable of. And without Byron of Sidius available to fight the beast, who among his company could, thought Vandross with a sigh of satisfaction.

Returning his thoughts to the beast's statement, Vandross smiled wickedly. "I am fully aware of that. Make ready for their arrival. Have you any idea how many there are, Drake?" Vandross took a swig from his water skin. "My Mage's Eyes are being counter-spelled out of the air, and I have no idea how many are coming up the back way."

"One hundred and fifteen altogether, lordship," the creature breathed heavily.

Its voice was much like Vengeance's, Vandross thought, pleased that this beast didn't stall and stop every couple words to shlurp in air like the Orb of Eden's Serpent manifestation. Without that, the sound was tolerable.

The one-eyed warlock could feel the Orbs inside of him trying to gain his attention, presumably to speak more to him of warnings and tell him what he should do. He had decided hours before, when the assault on his mountain had begun, that he had tired of them. He would heed them no more. After all, they belonged to him, not the other way around, he thought with a concentrated effort.

They were trying to pull him down into the depths of his own soul, but he could not afford to lose consciousness now, not when the end of his troubles was so near. The beast would slay the Dread Knight's companions, and he would go out and destroy Byron where he stood.

If the beast attacked the Dread Knight, the bonds that held Byron would break, freeing him into the chamber. The warlock knew without a trace of doubt that Byron would destroy the beast without effort, and then he would actually have to concentrate and defend himself while he prepared to use the Glorious Mother of Destruction on Byron, focusing it right on his skull.

"One hundred and fifteen, right," he muttered, keeping himself awake. "I don't need to hear your council," he whispered, tucking his mouth toward his chest. "I am your master, now and forever. Don't forget it."

The sensation of being pulled toward sleep lifted, freeing his senses. The beast was looking at him with a curious expression on its alien countenance.

"Prepare to deal with them, Drake. And remember, when the Dread Knight is stopped by the barrier, leave him be."

"I remember, lordship," the creature said, turning away and stalking out of the throne room. "Byron of Sidius is yours to destroy," it called back. Vandross smiled the smile of the damned. *Yes*, he thought.

"Mine to destroy."

* * * *

Bael looked back over to the stock-still troops under his direct command. They had come far, and fought hard for their lives and the lands they loved for nearly two and a half hours, without rest and without a stop. However, after disposing of a set of rooms filled with Shadowbeasts and Orcs, they all came to a halt. Less than five hundred of them remained from the entire thousand in the first two legions. Casualties had been high, and those that survived had been forced, thanks to Illeck Necromancers, to slay again their fallen comrades. The mages needed to meditate, eat, or otherwise recover their stocks of manna energy, for without some break in the fracas, they would be left defenseless, and without spells at their command.

Bael sat heavily on the corpse of an Orc, pulling out his pipe and tapping some tobacco into it from a small pouch at his hip. Lighting it with the small Gnome contraption he'd bought some years ago in Ja-Wen, he inhaled deeply of the burning tobacco, spewing out puffs of gray, ashen smoke a moment later. His heartbeat slowed as the effect of the plant took hold, calming his nerves. *Gods*, he thought. *Look at us*. The remaining combatants under his command were worn, beaten, and injured. To be truthful, he was amazed that they hadn't turned around and left, heading back to safer pastures and activities. But when asked, all had refused to leave. They had a purpose, and they would all be damned if they were going to run.

Bael smiled, despite the seemingly hopeless situation. Taking a long drag of the burning pipe, he puffed out another thick, opaque cloud of smog.

"Fifteen hundred men and women," he said to no one in particular. "That's how many we've lost. And that's just two legions," he said, uttering the words with a half-hearted smile. "And I know we've killed way more than that since we got in here."

"Sir," one of the Minotaurs in battered chain mail armor said as he came over, axe in hand. "Who are you talking to?"

Bael looked into the age-worn face of a Minotaur Soldier, a man whose eyes spoke of the dozens of battles he had participated in. The word 'battle', for most Minotaurs, meant 'war' to the rest of the Races. Streaks of gray hair had crept their way into the Minotaur's proud mien, but he fought and spoke with a youthful fire.

Bael admired him; he was himself perhaps half the man's age, and yet emotionally and physically, he felt about twice it.

"Nobody, my good man, nobody at all." Bael tapped out his pipe, emptying it on the stone floor of the grand chamber. "What do you need from me?"

"Well, sir, I sent a scout ahead, as ordered. He has returned, and tells us that we can make no further progress. From here, all paths lead toward the bottom of the mountain. He was almost spotted by another pack of Orcs, but managed to flee before they could see him. He saw that they were about to be engaged by another legion, sir. I believe if we are to make anymore progress towards getting near to the warlock himself, we shall have to go back down through the mountain and find another way."

Bael shook his head, knowing now what he had known all along.

"The warlock is not ours to take, my friend," he said, climbing to his feet. "Everybody, listen up," he hollered, letting the natural shape of the chamber echo his voice to every last man. "Our jobs are done here. We're leaving, right now." He wasn't surprised to hear much protest. "This was Lord Byron's intention all along. We did what we had to, we vanquished many a demon and ill-begotten Greenskin. We destroyed monstrosities that would have left here today to go on to commit other atrocities in our lands." He put his hands on his hips.

There were words of acceptance and agreement now rippling through the remaining five hundred combatants. They were beginning to understand, as Bael had only a few minutes before them, that Byron had never intended for them to destroy every last creature that opposed them in Mount Toane. Such a task was utterly foolish, and nearly impossible.

"Remember well," Bael continued, "that when we leave here today, we leave all that happened here behind. We shall honor our fallen comrades, but we must not begrudge the Illecks, the Humans, the Khan who fought for Richard Vandross. We must not hate the Greenskins for their alliance to him, for theirs is already hard enough lot. Our relations with them, along with their general ignorance and savage ways of life, makes them easy prey for predators like Richard Vandross to enslave.

"So raise up your heads and your hands, for though we may have more to slay on the way out of this stark and horrid place, our victory is earned already."

A cry of triumph escaped the lips of every mortal creature in the chamber, and congratulations and celebratory 'hoo-rah's went up from many a soldier. But as they began to move away from their spots in the chamber, a low, fierce groan escaped from somewhere nearby.

Bael looked to the far end of the cavern, where a hidden panel in the wall slid open. Looming in the shadows, he smelled the fetid odor of dead flesh and muscle.

Holding the head of a wide-eyed Illeck in its hand, another Dreadnaught, one even more horrible and enormous than the first they had encountered earlier in the day, stood watching him.

The bleeding corpse of Sergeant Torim lay in a heap at the creature's feet, though Bael hadn't known whom the man was. One of Vandross's own, the Lizardman knew. Still, he felt pity for the man. The corpse lay twisted and bent in ways that the gods of mortal man had never intended for Humans, or most any other living thing. It must have been a horrendously painful demise.

Unlike the construct that he had first seen outside of Mount Toane, this blasphemous resident of the mountain was structured and shaped in a very humanoid fashion, with two arms (that he could see), two legs, and a head, complete with a face. Also unlike the construct outside of the mountain, this one had the gleam of some limited, animal-level intelligence in its three eyes. Two blood soaked wings spread from its back as it stepped out of its niche in the wall, and it hurled the head right at Bael.

It seemed to ignore all of the other troops, who were all preparing to do combat with the abomination. Bael thrust out a single hand in their direction, catching their collective attention. Still the creature paid them no heed.

"Don't," he called to them, not looking away from the construct. "It wants me, that much is clear. Take yourselves and get clear of this foul place, immediately."

Even as he shouted at them, the men seemed hesitant to leave their commanding officer behind. The Minotaur who had spoken with him as he smoked, an Elven woman of middle-aged appearance, and six others came rushing to flank their commander. The rest of the troops stood rooted in place, looking to him.

"This many is too much still, but I think we can take things from here. Now go home, all of you. That's an order." He pointed to the exit with a waggling finger.

His nerves stood on end; never had he faced an opponent more dreadful than this creature. Even when he had squared off with Byron, he hadn't been so terrified. Then again, he had even then sensed an aura of mercy around the undead warrior. Here, there was only a sensation of cruelty and malice spreading from the evil construct. As Bael drew his war axe, he looked to his left and right, at the grim smiles set on the faces of these noble warriors and mages.

"Gentlemen, and ladies," he amended, remembering that two of his eight companions were female. "If the gods allow, I shall treat you to the grandest feast and festival of all times when this is over."

The Dreadnaught had cleared half the distance to him, smiling impishly and revealing several rows of actual blades that had been inserted into its mouth. Sergeant Robin had spent the better part of a year creating the Dreadnaught, his labors finally coming to fruition shortly after having it moved to Mount Toane. The arm of Tiberious Amon had been the final component, and now the creation had slain its new master, Torim. Though these facts were unknown to Bael, he had the distinct feeling that the headless man had had a hand in the Dreadnaught's construction. Gripping his war axe in both hands, Bael strode out to meet this awesome and mighty foe.

* * * *

As the last of the Mage's Eyes in the tunnel winked out of existence, the Q Mage stumbled. He had expended almost all of his reserves of manna, and required rest, or food, or both. Byron rummaged through his rucksack, finally handing the whole thing to the worn Half-Elf.

"My lord," he asked, raising an eyebrow. Byron smiled at him.

"I shan't be needing that much longer," the Dread Knight said in a light-hearted voice.

At the end of the tunnel they stood in was a single large doorway. There was some sort of magic laid over the portal, but from this distance, Byron could not tell what it was.

As the platoon advanced toward it, James Hayes sprinted ahead, a look of shock on his face. He pressed his hand against a shimmering wall of energy. Shaking his head, he came back to Byron, who had halted the march twenty yards shy of the Paladin. "What is it? What's wrong?"

"It's a ward, Byron. A Seal of Fate. You know what that means."

Indeed, he did, Byron thought with a growl. It meant that no undead creature could pass through the doorway. While the rest of the battalion could advance without a problem, he was screwed. No counter-spell could destroy a Seal of Fate. Only an attack directed at the undead creature from the other side could get rid of it, and the attack had to have malice in it, or the Seal would remain. Having Shoryu or Morek strike at him while he stood on this side would not work.

"Hellfire, hell and blood," he cursed, trying to think through his options. A Seal of Fate could entirely block his senses, as well as those of anyone on the guarded side of it. Nobody in the platoon would know for absolute certain what lay on the other side unless they stepped through. For all they knew, the other side of this Seal could be the face of the mountain, and they might very well march through and plummet to their deaths hundreds of feet below. But Byron thought not; these halls, or rather this particular hallway, was very familiar.

His vision blurred, and a loud ringing blared in his head. As he squinted his eye lights blank, he saw in his mind's eye the throne room that Tanarak had commanded him from, not far ahead. Only this tunnel and a massive, hollowed-out chamber separated the Dread Knight from the warlock. A seal of some sort would surely be up on the throne room's entryway as soon as the Seal of Fate was crossed, and the platoon would be cut off from the warlock.

Good, he thought with a heart filled with spite. *Vandross is mine anyway.*

"Oi, you all roit bone 'ead," Morek asked the Dread Knight, smiling up at him.

"Just fine, shrimpy," Byron replied with golden light gleaming from his eye sockets. "I can't pass through there, but rest assured, something awaits you all." Byron addressed the entire platoon. "Many of you will die here, you know," he said, his voice turning quiet. "I only brought you along to get us this far. Going any further may very well spell doom for you. You are excused, if you wish to leave."

But none of the warriors and mages moved.

Byron turned his back on them once more. "Well enough." He moved forward, toward the Seal of Fate.

"Byron, wait! You'll be stuck to the Seal," Hayes cautioned. "You're walking right into a trap."

"I know," Byron said with a grin. "And when I am, you'll all flood in and let the mages blast whatever's on the other side to kingdom come, correct?"

Derisive laughter filled the corridor as the mages of the platoon moved to the front of the ranks, preparing their spells of destruction. Ellen Daires strode right alongside Byron, while Shoryu flanked him on the opposite shoulder, a mystic arrow already notched. Morek Rockmight cracked his knuckles in anticipation, and James Hayes stayed only two paces behind the Dread Knight.

"We're with you," Shoryu and Ellen said in harmony as they stalked forward, matching their leader's pace.

"I know. I know it in my heart that you all are," Byron said to his traveling companions.

Chapter Ten
Showdown

Bael's struggle with the Dreadnaught had been mercifully short for the Lizardman. The construct's right arm appeared to belong to a Khan, and it held a giant broadsword in its hand. Bael dashed forward, spells released from his right and left sides by his compatriots. The rampaging Minotaur had lowered its horns and hit the construct at full speed, knocking it back as a ball of fire struck its face and a spear of ice had shoved through the waist.

Bael had launched himself through the air after those attacks and sunk his axe into its chest, burying it so deep that he had to leap away from its left hand as it grasped for him. Then, an incredible stroke of luck, or a favor from the gods themselves, occurred. Apparently, the right arm, that of the Khan, had decided to object to its current owner, and had turned the sword in on itself, stabbing deep into the chest and twisting.

With an animal howl, the creature had shivered and fallen, the right arm drawing out the sword and hacking away at its master's head, splitting it down the middle and cutting it clean off. After that, the Dreadnaught had fallen silent.

"What in the Heavens just happened," one of the Elves asked from behind Bael.

The Lizardman laughed aloud, a long, tired peal of laughter. "I don't know, but those very Heavens just smiled upon us." He pulled free his war axe and severed the Khan arm from the construct's body. "I'm not sure why, but I believe I am going to take this home with me. Clearly, it belongs to someone. Perhaps the fates shall conspire to have me meet the whole of the man this belonged to."

That said, Bael led the long, tiresome trek out of the mountain.

When he saw the entrance an hour and a half later, he could have sworn it was his eyes playing tricks on him, but it wasn't. Much more time had passed since entering than he had believed; the sun was rising over the eastern horizon.

As he passed out of the mountain's bottleneck entrance, he stopped to bask in the silent, warm glow of the sun's rays, letting the light wash over his bloodstained armor and clothes. "Well folks," he said, turning to face his valiant companions. "It looks like I owe you a feast."

* * * *

As soon as he came in contact with the Seal of Fate, Byron saw the chamber quite clearly. Something stirred in the shadows, behind a pillar of stone that stretched the entire height of the room. The faint rustle of clawed feet scraping softly against stone was just audible.

Byron tried to bring the Morning Glory up in front of him, but found that he was stuck stock still, just as James Hayes had said he would be.

There was nothing that could be done about it, he mused, watching the pillar out of the corner of his eye.

Something moved again, and he could hear the sniffling of flared nostrils. The scent of the chamber reminded him of the slaughterhouses he had gone to as a man, where he would pick up large slabs of meat to bring home for his wife to prepare. The metallic odor of blood, but with the hint of animal hides.

A flash of movement darted across his field of vision as a man-sized creature darted from behind the column to the cover of another such column on the right hand side of the chamber. Another movement, this one accompanied by the slow, clear 'snikt' of a blade clearing a sheath. Byron had kept his left arm back behind the Seal, free of its magic, and felt his hand move slowly as he beckoned the rest of the battalion forward. A single pair of smoky, crimson eyes appeared from around the pillar, accompanied by a set of teeth so slick with saliva that they appeared as though water had been poured on them. A cackle of maddened glee escaped its throat.

"The vaunted and feared Byron of Sidius," the creature rasped in a voice akin to the sound of glass shards scraping on brick. It slinked forth into the dim light of the room, and the opening at the other side of the chamber slid shut, stone grinding on stone as the doorway was sealed shut. The Dread Knight knew that Richard Vandross was in that chamber: he had seen a hint of the warlock's cloak as the door sealed.

"That's right, demon," he said in response, feeling the air with his limited senses and noting the demonic aura that positively radiated from the creature. Even the most mutated of the Sidalis Race didn't look that horrid.

Once again he moved his free left hand, putting it out to stop the advance of his allies. He knew from the feeling of the air out in that tunnel that Ellen and Shoryu were mere inches from coming in contact with the Seal of Fate. Wait, he told them with a hand motion. Not, just, yet.

"And had this sorcery not been placed, I would tear you limb from limb," he said. "Of course, if you came in reach, I could strike you with a Paladin spell or three and have the same effect."

"No thank you, Dread Knight," the creature said, taking a few steps away. Deceitful as demons were, Byron could not detect any traces of a lie. Then again, he was being affected by the Seal of Fate and its strange magic.

"I don't like such attacks." The creature brought its huge sword into the light. The blade was easily as long as the creature's height.

Now, he motioned with his left hand, and Ellen Daires and Shoryu Tearfang charged through. The creature's eyes went wide as they broke through the barrier, and Byron shouted at them immediately.

"Magic. Strike it with your spells," he hollered as James Hayes burst through with nearly a dozen Elven and Human mages in tow. A mystic arrow flew through the air, a stone of magic from Ellen's outstretched hand, a ball of flame, a stream of light from Hayes, and nearly a dozen other spells hit home against the demon's chest. It stretched and howled with laughter and Byron realized his error. The creature had tricked him.

As he watched in fury, the creature's belly split open and spat out fifteen lumps of flesh. Each flashed with a yellow light and in the place of those lumps stood fifteen exact copies of the demon, weapon and all. Damnation, Byron thought with a flurry of other curses under his breath. He was jostled and bumped as the warriors of the platoon broke through, engaging the copies straight away. Weapons clashing together, the chamber quickly filled with combat and its responding sounds. The clang of steel on steel, the rip and howl of men being torn apart and copies being slain tearing through the enclosed space.

Shoryu darted back and forth, only a few yards away from Byron's face as he dodged swings from the massive sword of a demon copy. Or was it the original? Byron couldn't tell any longer, and suddenly had doubts about the creature he had seen when he had become entangled by the Seal of Fate. Could it be that it, too, had been a copy? He couldn't be certain of anything regarding the demon until he watched it some more. But if he watched it too long, at the rate of damage it was dealing, even his own friends might be dead before he knew what to do about it. Utter elimination of all of the copies might be possible, but the mages could only defend themselves with spells, and when the magic struck the demon copies, they reproduced more copies.

Frustrated beyond belief at the demon's tactics, Byron struggled against the Seal's magic, unable to break free. He was incapable of lashing out to help the young Cuyotai Hunter against the considerable strength and raw demonic power of the beast that hacked at him.

Fifty dead, by Byron's silent count. Half of the men and women he had personally led here lay dead and in tatters across the chamber floor. The remaining fifty fighters were being driven back to their heels, pressed by the fresh assault of even more foes.

Assaulted on various sides by multiple foes, even James Hayes was being forced backward. Ellen Daires hid behind stone barriers and golems that she had summoned, using the natural environment of the chamber around her to aid in her swift casting and enforcing of the Gaiamancy she used to defend herself. Looking to his left, Byron could see Shoryu roll forward, evading yet another sword blow from the demon copy assaulting him. The Cuyotai Hunter leapt forward, digging his claws into the demon's throat and setting his feet against its chest. As he kicked off, he let his claws tear the demon copy's throat apart, blood spraying the air where the nimble Cuyotai had been.

Byron saw that the Cuyotai had put his bow back in its place across his back. What was the pup thinking? As Shoryu turned toward Byron, the Dread Knight saw the gleam of mischief in the Cuyotai's eyes.

Sprinting toward the Dread Knight, Shoryu zigzagged back and forth, weaving through a hailstorm of blades as a half a dozen copies sped toward him.

Shoryu collided into Byron, but the Dread Knight couldn't be budged.

"The demons—" But Byron saw that there was no need for worry; the copies had broken off their pursuit. Or rather, they had been attacked by other battalion members. Shoryu spat, his face livid with fury. "What is it, what were you trying to do?"

"Byron, you have been prone here the whole time, yet the demon has not struck at you," the Cuyotai whispered into Byron's skull. "I think I know why. It is the nature of such sorcery." With another of those dangerous smiles of his, the Cuyotai bound away, clawing at the back of another copy. Having caught its attention, he drew it towards Byron, ducking and weaving back and forth to avoid being cleaved in half. When he was only a foot away from Byron, Shoryu rolled away.

As the giant sword came down toward Byron's head, a look of blackest terror spread across the faces of every copy in the chamber. The Morning Glory was up over his head, and Byron felt the Seal of Fate shatter around him. With a heave and a lunge forward, Byron lopped off the copy's head that stood before him.

Thrown into confusion by the Dread Knight's sudden freedom and ferocious battle roar, the demonic copies lost sight of their much more numerous opponents, and several were hacked apart before they regained their senses.

"Remain on the defensive! Strike low and hard when you can," Byron shouted to his allies. He had caught at least one sign of weakness in the assaults of the demon.

Without any audible or visual sign that they heard him, the warriors of the platoon carried out the command, concentrating on defense until they found an opening. Their legs then cleaved off, the copies quickly suffered large casualties, and even the mages with their daggers and staffs managed to hold their ground, relying only on defensive magic to continue in the melee.

Byron charged about the chamber, finding those copies that had hidden themselves and splitting them in half with the skill and rage only he possessed. After only five minutes of this combat, all of the demons lay dead or dying. Thirty-one men and women remained from the platoon, excluding Byron's personal company, who had suffered a few wounds but all of whom survived.

Morek Rockmight (who, despite being told to stay behind, came along anyway, bullheaded as always) had been severely overpowered by the demons, and had several stab wounds and gashes in his chest, arms and legs. Bloodied but smiling, the Dwarven Boxer took a heavy seat on the floor as James Hayes went to work on him with healing magic. The Paladin was running low on manna, however, and couldn't offer much in the way of medical assistance.

"You know, you've done more damage to that arm of yours," Hayes informed the Dwarf.

Morek didn't seem surprised in the least. His time as an efficient fighter was most likely at a permanent end, but he had his political career still.

Thankfully, one of the Human Clerics had survived the ordeal fairly unscathed. This older man prepared a mass-healing spell, unleashing it on the chamber at large. Somewhat refreshed, the injured Shoryu, whose collarbone had been broken by an overhead hammer blow with the butt of a sword, forced a smile as he approached the Dread Knight. "Well, our job here is done, isn't it," he asked quietly.

Byron could not bring himself to look back into those huge, wet eyes of brilliant green.

"Yes, yes it is, my friends." Byron's voice echoing off of the walls of the chamber. "You are all dismissed," he said.

Even when the survivors of the platoon helped one another limp away from the chamber, Shoryu, Ellen, Morek and James Hayes remained behind, taking positions just outside of the entryway where the Seal of Fate had been placed. They all wore the brightest smiles they could as they planted themselves there, Morek leaning against one side of the entryway, Shoryu and Ellen sitting together like a pair of cups that fit one inside the other, and James Hayes leaning on the opposite side from Morek.

Without saying as much, they let Byron know that his fate was their fate. They would stick by him until the very end, whatever the outcome. And from their relaxed postures, their bodies told him that they felt confident in his ability to triumph over the warlock.

Richard Vandross stood opposite them all, his eyes filled with crimson malice, a wicked, curved scimitar in his right hand. "Byron of Sidius," he growled, his voice that of himself, and that of a demon speaking in harmony with him as he levitated off the floor.

Byron swung around to face the one-eyed warlock. This was not their first encounter, but it was certainly to be their last.

"Welcome to your final resting place, Dread Knight. I have been very patient, Byron. I have awaited your arrival since first your armies set foot in my mountain."

The gut rock of the mountain trembled beneath his armored feet, and the Morning Glory blazed brighter than before. Such power, Byron thought, with a tinge of fear in his heart. And such evil. "

You cannot imagine the powers I possess. The ancient knowledge granted me by the Orbs of Eden's Serpent is magnificent and splendorous," Vandross shouted, throwing his head back in mad glee.

Stretching out his arms to his sides, he held himself in the air for a long moment before looking back down at Byron. The eye patch had been burned off, and coils of yellow and purple energy swirled around his arms and chest.

The power of the Orbs of Eden's Serpent was being brought to bear, Byron knew, and he would need every bit of skill and power at his disposal to be victorious.

"I shall be knelt and cowered before, dead man," Vandross said. "I shall be the man named in legends and tales that parents tell their children in order to scare them into staying in line. I shall be the eternal, dreadful thing that brings the world to its knees in abject horror, Byron of Sidius. What say you to that?"

With a madman's smile, Vandross's face split slightly at the corners of his mouth, exposing a set of arachnid fangs, the influence of Vengeance coming to the forefront as Vandross drew on the full power of the Orbs of Eden's Serpent.

"What say I," Byron muttered, almost without being heard. The trembling of the mountain around him, and the blazing hellfire that a moment later spewed forth in patches throughout the cavern, made soft speech inaudible. "I say, Vandross, that you have my name wrong, yet again." He raised his voice, shouting, "I am Byron Aixler." Then he dashed forward with the Morning Glory at the ready. "And I shall send you to the Pit."

Several feet before he reached the warlock, a wall of hellfire sprang forth from the floor, the heat and force generated by the wall's sudden appearance throwing Byron back, black scorch marks dotting his armor. His field of vision went blank and white as the northwestern mountain tips in midwinter, and he shook his head to clear it.

As Byron stumbled backward, Vandross leapt over the fiery wall and lashed out at him with a vicious kick that seemed to come not from him, but from his shadow.

Letting out a heavy hoomph, Byron took the shot to the stomach, folding in half as he flew through the air and into a pillar of stone. *Damnation*, he thought. *He's powerful, and fast. I can't keep up with him.*

Letting his body slide down the pillar, Byron landed in a prone, seated posture, his right hand still grasping the Morning Glory, his left palm facing up and slightly forward.

Richard Vandross stalked forward through the smoke and heat haze of the chamber, a wicked grin plastered to his face. "Is that all you have to offer me, Byron? How very disappointing." He brought his scimitar into the air over his head. "I had hoped for greater things," he said with a heavy sigh.

Byron's eyes flashed as he whipped his head up to look Vandross squarely in the face.

"Holy Cannon!" The left palm, upturned as it was, flared with Paladin magic for a moment before unleashing a pillar of blazing white light into Vandross's chest.

The warlord's face registered surprise for a moment before he was flung, smoking and screaming, nearly one hundred yards away, into the opposite cavern wall. Crashing into the wall, jutting rocks breaking apart across his broad, armored back, Vandross landed with a steely crash of metal armor and groans of agony. But both men were swiftly on their feet once again, swords in hand.

"Very good." Vandross wiped blood from his lip.

Good, Byron thought. *Some internal damage has been done.*

Where the spell had hit him, Vandross's armor had been bleached purest white, but it remained intact. A demon or normal mortal would have a hole the size of a small barrel in their chest, but the Orbs of Eden's Serpent granted Vandross an unseemly amount of power and defense.

"I had hoped that this wouldn't be settled so easily. Now, Byron, know the power of Richard Vandross."

Streaks of lightning sped across the chamber, one of them catching the Dread Knight as he tried to duck and roll away from the magical blast. His muscled writhed and twitched, burning from the inside from the power of the spell that Vandross kept locked on him.

A moment later, Byron fell to the ground, his body smoking, his armor flaring with traces of the spell's effects. As soon as he got to his feet, another gust of force knocked him clear against another pillar of stone, breaking the earthen rock across his stomach and landing him in a heap. The pain he was in could not be described in simple words, so immeasurable was his agony. *Still*, he said to himself as he once again regained his feet, planting them in a defensive stance with the Morning Glory. *Still, I must vanquish him.*

"You do not hold all of the cards, dark one," Byron said as Vandross seemed to melt into the shadows of the cavern. No trace of his movements could be detected. "And I have had enough of your tactics. You no longer dictate the pace and nature of this battle."

Byron took one hand off of the hilt of his weapon, holding skyward with the other. "Mighty Oun, grant me light, that I may see my deceiver."

A small orb of golden light fluttered down from the ceiling, and Byron threw it hard against the floor. A sound like shattering glass filled the room, and a moment later a wave of white energy spread throughout the cavern. Vandross, creeping forward, had been exposed, his shadow magic countered. He was only three or four yards away, scimitar raised in both hands.

The sudden light nearly blinded him, and he positioned his arms to shield his face from the light.

Byron shouted, and thrust the Morning Glory to the hilt into Vandross's chest.

The stricken warlock's face fell as he dropped his sword, falling backward. But as he fell, he smiled once more the smile of the damned.

"You have not won, Byron. I still have one card up my sleeve. In the name of the unholy, of the great chaos, of the destruction I seek," he proclaimed, rising to his feet and levitating once more.

Oh gods, Byron thought. *The Glorious Mother of Destruction.*

With a black barrier of energy going out and wrapping around Vandross, he knew no way to counter this massive wave of destruction that was about to be unleashed on him, his friends, and every living thing in the mountain.

Didn't Vandross realize that he, too, might perish in the aftermath of the dark ritual? Or did he simply not care anymore? In either case, Byron suddenly knew what he had to do. He put his arms in front of his face and charged into the barrier wrapping around Vandross.

Wraiths and demonic souls raged at him from the barrier, the essence of the Pit all around him as the barrier slammed through him on all sides. *Join us*, they seemed to hiss at the Dread Knight, but he held his arms up, and prayed to mighty Oun for the strength to finish this final task he had given himself.

The barrier then seemed to stream around him, leaving him unfettered, untouched. The Dread Knight brought his hands back down to his sides, and stood proudly before the stunned warlock, who had ceased his incantation to stare wide-eyed at him.

"How," was the only word Vandross could manage to utter before Byron gripped the Morning Glory, drew it out of the warlord's chest, and brought it in the same motion fluidly through Vandross's waist, cleaving him cleanly in half.

The barrier disappeared, and the mountain ceased to quake around them.

Vandross landed in a pile of his own gore, wailing like a child having a tantrum, beating his fists against the ground under his back accordingly. He was bleeding heavily, and the demonic aura that had been radiating around him fell apart.

Byron's heart sank as he looked at the carnage he had committed on this man, who was nothing more than a victim of his own greed and power hunger. For a moment, he forgot all about the atrocities that the warlock had committed, forgot his own seething hatred of this mortal man. And though his anger resurfaced, he forgave him. After all, Vandross was only mortal.

"Please," Vandross begged, his voice wracked with sobs and suffering beyond compare. "Please, save me." One bloodied hand reaching up from the organs he desperately tried to hold in his body. However, he could not seem to keep them all together, or in the right order from Byron's perspective.

The liver didn't go there, did it, he wondered with a morbid fascination. Byron felt weak, though, and stumbled a step back.

"You know what will happen if I die, don't you?" Vandross spat through blood-soaked lips. "You'll cease to have any tie to the mortal coil."

The Orbs of Eden's Serpent pulsed inside of his upper torso, and one by one, the four began to leave his body.

The one-eyed warlock pushed them back into his body, clinging to them, as only they kept him from Death's door.

The Orbs, Byron realized, were trying to save themselves. If he finished the job now, the Orbs of Eden's Serpent would die along with their host, and no longer be a threat to the mortal Races of Tamalaria. They must have abandoned Tanarak of Sidius in his final hour, in order to preserve their malign power.

"You will die, Byron," Vandross shouted, tears running down from his formerly good eye, and that ruptured, mangled eye slid slowly out of its socket.

He's falling apart, Byron thought. Literally.

"I know this, wicked man," Byron proclaimed. "But it is my fate. It is the fate of all mortal men, a fate that you and your former master cheated me out of. And now I must die along with you, and face the judgment of my god, the great Oun. I must accept whatever punishment he doles out to me for my wrongdoings. I have accepted that fate, Richard Vandross. It has always been my way of life. We, who stand against the darkness, shall see it banished by our holy light. No matter the cost."

With his words echoing throughout the chamber, Byron drove the Morning Glory down through Richard Vandross's heart.

There was an explosion of light and darkness, melded together for one brilliant moment of blinding energy, and as Byron held the Morning Glory in place, he heard the shrieks of death of the Orbs of Eden's Serpent and their manifestations.

After the light died, he looked over at his friends, who had all risen to their feet and hung in the doorway, their bodies tense. "I believe, we are done here," Byron said, toppling over and falling prone to his back.

* * * *

Bael and his companions from the battle with the Dreadnaught sat up on the hillcrest overlooking Mount Toane. They had taken a solemn vow to go in and seek out the warlock himself if nightfall came again with no sign of Byron. But as they ate their meal of freshly hunted deer meat, the Lizardman made out four figures striding out of Mount Toane's rock face. They carried something, or rather someone, on a litter between them.

"By the gods." Bael threw aside his meal and raced down the hill toward the small company who carried Byron Aixler, now dying on a litter.

The Dread Knight's bones had begun to turn an ashen color, and the lights in his empty eye sockets were flickering.

Bael walked beside the group, seeing that Shoryu Tearfang, the Cuyotai Hunter who had spent more time with the Dread Knight than any others among the surviving company, held one of Byron's bare, Human hands. The effort of carrying his share of the heavy load and holding Byron's hand must have been enormous, Bael thought, but well deserved and heartfelt.

Atop the hill, as the company arrived at the Lizardman's camp, the other warriors and mages had their hands over their hearts in respect for the fallen undead warrior.

"Please," Byron croaked from his dry throat. "That, is not, necessary."

James Hayes now wore The Morning Glory strapped across his back, but its white fire had extinguished the moment Byron had dropped it.

"Over, over there," Byron said, trying to lift his free right hand, pointing to a single oak tree that grew despite the craggy soil of the area.

The company, Shoryu, Morek, Ellen and James walked with him between them, Bael and his own compatriots following closely behind. The company laid down the makeshift litter, made from two lengths of stone fashioned by Ellen's magic and the warlock's cloak, ripped from his mangled corpse by Morek Rockmight. The Dwarf tried to hide it, but slow tears ran silently down his cheeks and into his gruff beard.

"Is this where you meant," Ellen Daires asked softly, unashamed of the streaks running down her own face.

"Yeeeees." Byron sat up.

Shoryu tried to ease him back down with one hand, but Byron had strength enough to shove the hand away and get to his tottering feet.

He wobbled and swayed like a macabre marionette, but no one tried to help him. His eyes shone brilliantly once more, and he lurched forward to embrace the Cuyotai, who could no longer hold in his body-wracking sobs.

Bael lowered his head out of respect for the moment. Byron clapped Shoryu roughly on the back twice, then released him, and moved to James Hayes.

The Paladin opened his arms and accepted Byron gently, smiling all the while. He alone did not shed a tear among the four who had been so close to the Dread Knight. He alone held a genuine smile.

Byron then moved to Ellen Daires, who could barely hold the Dread Knight upright as he leaned into her with the last ebbing strength he possessed. Kneeling then, Byron gave Morek a mighty hug.

The Dwarven Boxer quickly shrugged him off. "Go on wi' ye, now. I'm not up ta this sort a thing." He kept his tone steely and rough.

With a final turn to the Lizardman, Byron extended his right hand. Bael shook it gently, then released it. Byron then lowered himself to the ground, his hands crossed over his chest in a dead man's position.

"I, must thank you all," he said in a harsh, raspy whisper. "You have truly been, my, friends. I, have been blessed, this time around."

As he gave a weary sigh, the lights in his eye sockets went blank.

The warlock Richard Vandross was slain, his armies defeated, and the lands would soon begin rebuilding.

Before parting ways, the company agreed, they would do their fallen friend and leader one last service. They began working on a proper grave, and in the twilight of evening, Byron Aixler was finally laid to rest.

Epilogue

Five weeks passed, and the land and its peoples slowly made progress towards normal life. Shoryu Tearfang and Ellen Daires had returned to their cottage home in Whitewood after a long day of bringing in crops from the fields near the city. Ellen was overjoyed to find an envelope on her kitchen table, and a familiar guest sitting at the head of the table with his feet propped up on a second chair. The master Pickpocket and Gentleman, as he liked to call himself, Lee Toren. "Oi, 'ope you don't mind, I showed meself in," the diminutive thief said as he whittled a small figurine.

Shoryu eyeballed him suspiciously, going into Ellen's and his bedroom to check and see that nothing had been taken. "Hey, I take offense to what yer doin'. I didn't take noffin."

"Guilty conscience?" Ellen asked as she took a seat on Lee's right hand side.

"No." Lee pulled his feet down and looked hurt. It wasn't genuine, of course, his expression. "I happens ta be a foin, upstandin, law-abidin citizen. Now, all jokes aside," he said in a rush, leaning forward as he pocketed his whittling knife and carving. "I did loik you asked, so if'n you don't mind, I'll be taking my payment, in full."

Ellen smiled and nodded to her husband, who stood in the doorway casually. Shoryu sauntered over to the icebox and removed a bowl that still steamed with heat from its contents.

"Here you are, Lee. One bowl of my wife's finest ontukara." Shoryu horribly mispronounced the title of the Elven dish.

The Gnome opened it and immediately pulled out his own wooden fork, digging into the savory meal.

"Don't get good home cooked meals often, do you?" Shoryu asked as he took a seat opposite his spouse.

"Nope. Comes wif the profession, lad," Lee said around a mouthful of stewed potatoes and deer meat. *Gods*, he thought, *this stuff is good*. "Too many warrants, too many cities lookin fer me. This place is one of the only kingdoms that I don't risk it. Too many honest folks. Anyways," he said, devouring the last bit of his meal. "That's the letter. He seemed to be doing just fine when 'e handed it to me, but he was in quite a hurry. Lots of work to be done, he says. Anyways," Lee said, standing up to take his leave. "You know how Morek is. Hell, you both spent a good deal of time wif 'im, seen a lot of rough stuff. Was, uh, there anything else you needed me ta do for you?"

The married couple looked at each other, shrugged, and said no in unison.

"Roit then, I'm off. You two be good, okay?"

As the Gnome thief walked outside, he took in the fresh evening air, the smell of pine trees and maples filling his lungs to bursting. Well fed and feeling a little better about his karma, Lee looked over at his new traveling companion. The tall, muscular figure strode over to the little Gnome, his wooden leg clacking against the ground awkwardly. Tiberious Amon was still getting adjusted to his new leg.

"You sure your arm is in this kingdom," Lee asked the black garbed Khan, whose eyes sparkled with newfound strength and determination.

"Quite sure, my little friend. I could almost feel it that day, as though it were still trying to take orders from the rest of my body. We'll find it among the Elven cities or Cuyotai settlements. We may even find it among the Lizardmen."

Lee nodded in agreement, and together they left the city of Whitewood.

* * * *

"You're entirely certain about this," the Cleric in charge of the Order's artifacts said to James Hayes as the Human Paladin handed him the Morning Glory.

"Yes, I am, Father Epps. It was never mine to begin with. It should be taken care of properly, placed in the cathedral. No arguments," he said, holding up a hand to silence the gaunt Elven Cleric. He had enjoyed his five days thus far in Fort Berring, and on the recommendation of the Order's highest priests and Paladins, had been given command of the entire Fort. He was now High Commander James Hayes, of the Order of Oun. And his work had begun with the assignment of exorcists to the Mount Toane region, to finish dealing with the demons that had taken residence in that foul mountain fortress.

If it had been within his authority, he would have hired Alchemists and Engineers to devise a way of blowing the whole thing to high heaven, but the Order wouldn't have approved of utilizing Scientists in their holy works. With time, James Hayes intended to change the general attitudes of the Order. It was a long road, and sure to be full of pitfalls and resistance, but it was the road he chose to walk down. "The easy path isn't always the right one," he muttered as he left the fort's cathedral.

"Commander," a young Knight in silver armor said as he rushed up to meet the Paladin.

"Yes, what is it young man," he inquired of the flush-faced Knight.

"Sir, there's someone rather odd at the gates. He's asking for you, very specifically. He didn't say he wanted the Commander, or our leader, or anything like that. He said he wanted to see James Hayes, the man who served in the Battle of Vandross with Byron Aixler. He was very clear that he wanted to see only you, and not inside the fort. What are your orders?"

James thought. Who would address him thus? His suspicion was that Bael had taken a rather lengthy and unnecessary journey, as Hayes had already written the Lizardman that he would be coming through the region to visit with Shoryu and Ellen in a couple of weeks.

"Stay here, and don't mind me. I'll go speak with him." Hayes smiled to reassure the young Knight. Sauntering confidently to the main gates, James came to a sudden halt as he peered at his visitor. The traveler was a man of average height, wearing the most brilliant silver plate armor one could see, sitting atop a great black stallion. Though the face of the visitor was decidedly

Human, Hayes knew that to be a charade.

Molis dismounted his steed as Hayes signaled for the gate to be opened. He strode out to meet Molis, a firm hand extended and received, shaken hard. "What brings you here, Mister, ah," he stammered.

"Tarren," Molis replied, lying so swiftly that it almost caught James off guard. "James Tarren. I just wanted to know how things are going for you now, James. Wanted to see how you're holding up."

"It's been odd, being in charge instead of being led," Hayes said, looking to the sky. "But I'm doing just fine otherwise. What have you been up to these days, Mr. Tarren?"

Molis shrugged his shoulders vaguely. "Not much. Traveling, seeing how the lands are doing now that the threat of Richard Vandross has passed. I've come across some fascinating people in my travels, including an odd young Cuyotai by the name of Straig," Molis said. "I believe he is without family, so I'm heading back to escort him to a young couple, to live with them for a while." He pulled his riding gloves back on. "They're friends of the Tearfangs."

"Ah, yes, the Tearfangs." James looked at Molis out of the corner of his eye. "Anything else to tell me? Perhaps you'd like to come in and confess your sins at the cathedral?"

"No thank you, my good sir," Molis replied rather hastily. "I must be on my way. You take good care of yourself now. I'll be checking in on you from time to time. I used to serve here, you know," he added, his voice carrying a hint of fading memory. "It was good for me, at the time. Not so much so anymore. Well, stay well, James Hayes. I trust Byron Aixler is in your prayers."

James nodded. "Indeed he is. He always will be."

With mutual waves, the Human Paladin and the half-demon parted ways, but not for the last time.

* * * *

Judgment, Byron thought, still wrapped in darkness. He had died several weeks ago, and had wandered through a dark void since that time. When first his life snuffed out, he stood before a blinding light, and a voice had spoken through the wall of clouds to him. "YE SHALL BE JUDGED NOW, BYRON AIXLER. KNOW NOT DESPAIR, FOR I AM A VERY BUSY GOD, AND HAVE MUCH TO DO." It had been the booming voice of the god Oun.

Despite being dead, time passed very slowly for Byron in the void. He had no body, no substance. He floated freely through the void. This was standard, however. He had been taught as a mortal man that the gods required long periods of time to pass judgment on a soul. And he certainly didn't begrudge that time. When he could see and feel again, he felt certain it would be the flames of the Pit that he witnessed.

But even as he thought this once more, he woke to find himself lying in a green pasture.

The End

www.ingramcontent.com/pod-product-compliance
Lightning Source LLC
Chambersburg PA
CBHW071430260626

47170CB00008B/2666